## FOR THE Q

Stories of danger that reach into present lives... the righting of old wrongs... wars threatened and averted... a jewelry theft with an unusual solution... love requited—and unrequited... treachery and repentance... fifteen tales from the Prince of Storytellers!

## BLACKMAN'S WOOD

Cartnell is getting ready for the pheasant hunt, but is informed that the birds need to be kept away from Blackman's Wood. The beaters won't go in there. A body has been seen hanging from one of the trees, and there is a nasty rumor of murder about the place. Cartnell reluctantly agrees. But of course, this is exactly where the birds end up. And now the situation must be faced.

# FOR THE QUEEN
# BLACKMAN'S WOOD

## E. Phillips Oppenheim

Introduction by Curtis Evans

**Stark House Press • Eureka California**

FOR THE QUEEN / BLACKMAN'S WOOD

Published by Stark House Press
1315 H Street
Eureka, CA 95501, USA
griffinskye3@sbcglobal.net
www.starkhousepress.com

FOR THE QUEEN
Originally published in the UK by Ward, Lock & Co., London, February 1912; and in the U.S. by Little, Brown & Co., Boston, June 1913.

BLACKMAN'S WOOD
First appeared in *The Grand Magazine*, December 1927. Published in hardback by The Readers Library Publishing Co., London, 1929 as part of *Two New Crime Stories with The Under Dog* by Agatha Christie; and in *The Best English Detective Stories: First Series*, Horace Liveright, New York, 1929.

All rights reserved under International and Pan-American Copyright Conventions.

"Deathstyles of the Rich and Famous" copyright © 2025 by Curtis Evans

ISBN: 979-8-88601-139-5

Cover and text design by Mark Shepard, shepgraphics.com
Cover art by F. Vaux Wilson

PUBLISHER'S NOTE
This is a work of fiction. Names, characters, places and incidents are either the products of the author's imagination or used fictionally, and any resemblance to actual persons, living or dead, events or locales, is entirely coincidental.

Without limiting the rights under copyright reserved above, no part of this publication may be reproduced, stored, or introduced into a retrieval system or transmitted in any form or by any means (electronic, mechanical, photocopying, recording or otherwise) without the prior written permission of both the copyright owner and the above publisher of the book.

First Stark House Press Edition: June 2025

# TABLE OF CONTENTS

Introduction . . . . . . . . . . . . . . . . . . . . . . . . . . . . . 7

FOR THE QUEEN . . . . . . . . . . . . . . . . . . . . . . . 15
For the Queen . . . . . . . . . . . . . . . . . . . . . . . . . . . 16
The Ambassador's Dilemma . . . . . . . . . . . . . . . . . 58
The Man Whom Nobody Liked . . . . . . . . . . . . . . 67
The Man Who Save the President's Life . . . . . . 76
In an Oxfordshire Lane . . . . . . . . . . . . . . . . . . . . 88
The Hidden Army . . . . . . . . . . . . . . . . . . . . . . . . 115
Sir Geoffrey's Guest . . . . . . . . . . . . . . . . . . . . . . . 125
A Sprig of Heather . . . . . . . . . . . . . . . . . . . . . . . 150
Lady Price's Companion . . . . . . . . . . . . . . . . . . . 159
The Tragedy of a Night . . . . . . . . . . . . . . . . . . . . 167
Mr. Ashley's Failure . . . . . . . . . . . . . . . . . . . . . . 181
Two Gamblers . . . . . . . . . . . . . . . . . . . . . . . . . . . 190
Lenore . . . . . . . . . . . . . . . . . . . . . . . . . . . . . . . . . 201
My First Diplomatic Mission . . . . . . . . . . . . . . . 219
Something in a Name . . . . . . . . . . . . . . . . . . . . . 226

BLACKMAN'S WOOD . . . . . . . . . . . . . . . . . . . . .239

# Deathstyles of the Rich and Famous

## By Curtis Evans

"[E. Phillips Oppenheim's] people are all clever, and drawn from high class types. Though battle, murder and sudden death are imminent, there is nothing brutal to offend." —Review of *Mysterious Mr. Sabin* in *Chicago Inter-Ocean* (18 February 1905)

"If you're blue and you don't know where to go to
Why don't you go where fashion sits
Puttin' on the Ritz"
—"Puttin' on the Ritz" (1929), Irving Berlin

### I.

Eleven years after English thriller writer E. Phillips Oppenheim's death at the age of seventy-nine in 1946, English novelist Robert Standish (a pseudonym of Digby George Gerahty), published a biography, of sorts, of the late bestselling author, entitled *The Prince of Storytellers*. Over roughly the first half of the twentieth century E. Phillips Oppenheim had been arguably the most popular thriller writer in the entire world, surpassing even the scarifying likes of Edgar Wallace, Sapper and Sax Rohmer. In his biography of "Oppy," as Oppenheim was nicknamed, Standish, who draws on not a single piece of personal correspondence by the author or his wife Elsie, was preoccupied primarily with divining just how the Prince of Storytellers had secured his princely crown. In his view the essence of Oppy's glittering success was his instinctive appreciation that what his middle-class readership really wanted from their escape fiction was a few precious, carefree hours vicariously spent among Europe's gilded and, preferably, titled rich.

Oppenheim himself, who during the Roaring Twenties left England to live with Elsie in a villa on the *Cote D'Azur* in the South of France, was eminently qualified to write about such people, even if the "real thing" in the jagged cacophony of the Jazz Age lamentably had become rather a *rara avis*. "Oppy dearly loved a lord and loved a prince at least twice as much," Standish pithily notes. Yet more even than lords and princes, the man dearly loved the moolah:

"Oppy invented literally hundreds of peculiar princes and princesses, dubious marquises and highly questionable countesses, with a good leaven of suave and urbane baronets....knights were almost beneath his notice.... In his private capacity he liked being near rich, smooth, pampered people, well-poised people with the gift of unerring repartee....his principal characters were nearly always rolling in money from the outset...his suave statesmen, captains of industry, bankers and other tycoons used money as a solvent of difficulties....Whether they are statesmen... ambassadors, grand dukes, or just ordinary characters, they possess, by virtue of limitless money, the power to find anyone or anything, no matter how well hidden. They can cause revolutions, dictate the policies of banks, send awkward royal favourites and mistresses into exile, foment wars and, if it becomes strictly necessary, organize a trip to the moon. Put money into competent ruthless hands and...there is almost nothing it will not achieve... . With unlimited money...fiction takes on an entirely new aspect, for money becomes as potent as death rays, guns that shoot round corners, clairvoyancy and coincidences...." —from *The Prince of Storytellers: The Life of E. Phillips Oppenheim* by Robert Standish (London: Peter Davies, 1957)

Writing in the mid-1950s, a decade of jaded European enervation and impassioned global revolutionary ascendance, Robert Standish found Oppenheim's gilded plutocratic fairy tales quaintly amusing and more than faintly absurd, though he stressed that these tales emphatically had not been such for their devoted worldwide readership in the decades before the Cold War. Oppy's readership, Standish argues, consisted mostly of middle-class men and women "perpetually harassed and hag-ridden by money cares, reduced to all kinds of degrading shifts and economies to make both ends meet... .To people who suffered rudeness and tyranny from shabby little shopkeepers, it was a glimpse into a promised land to read of a tycoon who, because he did not like the way the chef at the *Magnifico* prepared his *Sole Waleska*, bought the hotel and fired the chef. What more simple solution of the difficulty? All it required was money."

As the pop group ABBA warbled in the Seventies: *"Money, Money, Money! It's a rich man's world."* Oppenheim understood his readers. Before he made his fortune from his posh criminal fairy tales of princesses and peashooters, Oppy, compelled until he reached middle age to manage his father's leather business, himself had personally known "the strange yearning in the human heart to enjoy vicariously what cannot be enjoyed in any other way." Instinctively he grasped that "his harmless fantasies lifted people out of the long, deep grooves of their drab lives and gave them a glimpse of his own dreamland where nobody counted the cost of anything." Concludes Standish: "It was this profound understanding…which earned Phillips Oppenheim the crown of the Prince of Storytellers."

Today, a century or more removed from Oppenheim's great heyday as a popular writer, we may perhaps be somewhat less inclined to scoff at this almost magical power of the tycoon capriciously to bend the world to his urgent if eccentric desires. We have seen how this supposed "fantasy" still holds many individuals in its thrall, not merely vicariously in fiction but on Twitter, Instagram, TikTok and other social media. Once dismissed as "fairy tales for adults," Oppy's many gilded opuses, it would seem, have more relevance than ever as we enter the second perilous quarter of the twenty-first century. "Eat the rich" is just an empty slogan, mere trifling bravado, when we, the modest little people, cannot nerve ourselves even to get past the frowning brow of the maître d.

## II.

"I am," she said, "a spy!"
[…]
"It is a profession," I continued, "which is yet only in its infancy. It demands ingenuity, invention and originality. To succeed in it one must be an artist. The lights and shadows of human nature must become a close and constant study."

—"For the Queen"

Robert Standish estimated that between 1887 and 1943 the hugely prolific E. Phillips Oppenheim published 115 novels and forty collections of short stories. Oppenheim's fourth short story collection, *For the Queen*, was published in 1912, on the eve of the Götterdämmerung of the old-world order now known as the First World War, in which many of the major remaining crowned heads of continental Europe, the author's favored subjects, lost their crowns and sometimes their lives. The most substantial tale in the collection is the lengthy title novelette, one of Oppy's signal tales of courtly yet deadly espionage in the waning Edwardian era.

Originally published in *Gunter's Magazine* in 1907, "For the Queen" concerns a royal scandal in the Ruritanian kingdom of Marianburg, the consequences of which extend into the hallowed confines of dear old England itself. At the stroke of midnight, appropriately, the beautiful and mysterious Marianburg spy Marie Lichenstein pays a call upon the London flat of wealthy Maurice Lessingham, Earl Cravon, whose younger brother Reginald is employed at the British embassy in Marianburg. It seems that, as young men simply will do in these tales, young Reggie (the silly ass) exchanged indiscreet amorous correspondence with the now-Queen of Marianburg which he sentimentally failed to destroy as she requested him to do when she ascended to the throne—and now these embarrassing letters have been stolen! The secret police of Marianburg are determined to retrieve these unduly passionate epistles. But who has them now? When a man is murdered on account of the affair and the desperate Queen of Marianburg herself personally implores his help, Milord Cravon himself becomes involved in this byzantine Balkan affair. Laments the beautiful queen of her pampered royal life, with perhaps more than a smidgen of exaggeration: "royalty is the nearest approach to slavery which this century permits." Happily, the Earl has ample social clout and is not timid about wielding it in a worthy cause for the queen.

Quaint indeed in the 21st century is the opinion the Earl expresses on the imperative of exercising delicacy and restraint in the infant art of espionage. "I think you will admit that such methods are a little in front of the times; that they are, to say the least of it, not defensible," he chides an English diplomat. "Our methods will be decried before the whole civilized world.... We do not live in the days of Richelieu, or Mazarin. Such methods as have been used in this matter will never be tolerated in this country, or by international opinion." Sadly, two World Wars and a Cold War, not to mention sundry other diversions which in fact are too numerous to mention, have blasted Earl Cravon's proud, pretty words to the minutest of atoms.

The fourteen additional tales in this collection are in like vein, though some of them prove non-criminous. Originally published in *The Windsor Magazine* in 1901, "Mr. Ashley's Failure" is notable as an early, archetypal example of the jewel theft story, welcomingly leavened with humor; but to my mind the most intriguing of the other works is "The Hidden Army." Originally published in *The Windsor Magazine* in 1906, "The Hidden Army" details a German plot to assassinate peace-loving Lord Brentmore, British Secretary of State for Foreign Affairs, during his golfing holiday at the Grand Hotel at Settlingham-by-the-Sea. (Germany wants to precipitate a war with the United Kingdom imminently, before the latter country can further augment its navy, and they see good Lord Brentmore as the primary obstacle to the attainment of their martial goal.) The agents in this wicked and lowly plot to do a gentleman down during his golf holiday? None other than two of the no fewer than forty-six German waiters among the Grand Hotel's heavily Teutonic staff.

What is especially interesting about this short story is that it reflects the real-life British concern, as relations between the UK and Germany steadily deteriorated in the years leading up to the fateful assassinations at Sarajevo, about the prevalence of German waiters employed in British hotels. On the eve of the First World War, there were in fact more than 27,000 Germans living and working in London alone. Adolf Hitler's own half-brother, Alois, lived in Liverpool, waiting on tables at the Lyons Café. Indeed, Germans were so ubiquitous in this capacity in prewar England's hospitality industry that British soldiers digging trenches on the Western Front used to taunt the Germans opposite them with sneering cries of *Waiter!* Many of the German soldiers who spoke English owed this facility to their years spent in England as waiters.

With the commencement of actual armed combat between the two countries, hostility against German waiters became so intense that patriotic Sherlock Holmes creator Arthur Conan Doyle was moved to pen a broadminded letter to the *Daily Mail* complaining of the native prejudice against them. "The agitation against the German waiter has surely gone to lengths which have done harm," he avowed. "In the hotel which I know best—the Metropole—men have been thrown out of employment who have been naturalised for many years and married English wives. In the case of one man his son is actually serving in the Army.... If the hotel companies...had...stood by their old servants, everyone would, I think, have understood and endorsed their attitude."

E. Phillips Oppenheim, with his obvious sounding German name (though in fact Oppenheims had lived in England for generations) had not the luxury of Doyle's Teuton-free heritage. Once he overheard a Frenchman dismiss him as a damned "naturalized Hun." According to Robert Standish "Oppy himself detested the Germans"; and during the Edwardian Era he wrote any number of tales, like "The Hidden Army," portraying the looming danger to Britain and France of the insidious German menace.

## III.

"For beaters they're as good a lot as ever I handled. But Blackman's Wood! There's a many as wouldn't go within a half a mile of that, day-time or night-time."
—Gamekeeper Heggs in "Blackman's Wood"

Although in the Twenties and Thirties E. Phillips Oppenheim and the French Riviera became inseparable in the public mind, Oppy in fact resided in England until the mid-1920s, when he was nearing his sixth decade; yet he always proved restless in his native country. Previously he had lived with Elsie and their daughter Geraldine at Martinhoe Manor in North Devon, but he gave up that place as "too far from London." After World War One the family lived at Crossways in Woking, Surrey, but Oppy soon decried that residence as "too suburban."

Finally, in 1923 Oppy, now positively rolling in dough—his most successful novel, *The Great Impersonation*, which he had published three years earlier, had sold over a million hardcover copies in the United States alone—bought The Ollands, a great crenellated, Jacobean-style mansion on nineteen acres of grounds with "formal gardens, a conservatory and a mass of mature trees" that was located in the small market town of Reepham, Norfolk. There for a brief time before his migration to France in 1925 the hugely successful author took up the life of an English country squire, which included the staging of bird hunts. Even after relocating his primary residence to the Villa Deveron on the Riviera, the Oppenheims maintained ownership of The Ollands into the 1930s. Geraldine and her first husband Ryder Smith, a son of the late wealthy, knighted women's foundation garment manufacturer Sir Henry Smith, lived there for a several years until their divorce in 1928.

In the twenty-first century surviving locals recalled that Oppenheim brought with him to The Ollands his own butler and chauffeur, installing the latter man in the house's imposing coachman's lodge and stables. Every year during his time at The Ollands, the author staged, under his butler's supervision, a great fireworks display on Guy Fawkes Night. One woman told how when she was a child, she had once glimpsed the great man as he stopped by the local ironmonger and seed shop, memorably decked out like a true Twenties toff in flannel trousers, blazer and a straw boater hat while smoking a cigar.

Oppenheim portrayed this English country squire life in "Blackman's Wood," a short crime novelette originally published in December 1927 in *The Grand Magazine*. In 1929 it was reprinted along with Agatha Christie's 1926 Hercule Poirot detective novelette "The Under-Dog" in a small volume entitled *Two New Crime Stories* as well as in the anthology *The Best Detective Stories of 1928*. Appropriately, the Oppenheim novelette is one of his more Christie-esque concoctions.

The events detailed in "Blackman's Wood" take place at Cawston Farms, the country mansion of handsome Richard Cartnell, where he resides with his lovely wife Ella and younger sister Sybil. At their home the Cartnells are entertaining a number of weekend guests, including barrister Hugh Morden; solicitor Sir John Cunningham; stockbroker Freddie Samson; Jack Mason, "a clubman who seemed to spend half his time in country houses"; local MP Sinclair Johnson, and Jack Holloway, "a nephew of the house." Inside there are bridge and billiards to while away the idle hours, but the big event is to be a shoot of partridges, pheasants and woodcocks in the ample woods on the estate. Richard Cartell's gamekeeper, Heggs, worries that the prevailing winds will drive the birds into Blackman's Wood, where, everyone round these parts knows, two years earlier beater Barney Middleton strangled to death his faithless wife after catching her with her lover and then destroyed himself, leaving behind his ghost to haunt the wood. What will happen if the hunters dare profane Blackman's Wood? And what should Richard make of Ella's constant dalliance with Hugh Morden? Is it just another one of her many harmless "flirtations," or is it something more this time?

"Blackman's Wood" is a highly suspenseful crime tale and a fine example of the master's consummate skill at portraying the "deathstyles," as it were, of his many posh and privileged characters.

—April 2025
Memphis, TN

........................................................................

Curtis Evans received a PhD in American history in 1998. He is the author of *Masters of the "Humdrum" Mystery: Cecil John Charles Street, Freeman Wills Crofts, Alfred Walter Stewart and British Detective Fiction, 1920-1961* (2012), *Clues and Corpses: The Detective Fiction and Mystery Criticism of Todd Downing* (2013), *The Spectrum of English Murder: The Detective Fiction of Henry Lancelot Aubrey-Fletcher and G. D. H. and Margaret Cole* (2015) and editor of the Edgar nominated *Murder in the Closet: Essays on Queer Clues in Crime Fiction Before Stonewall* (2017). He writes about vintage crime fiction at his blog The Passing Tramp and at Crimereads.

# FOR THE QUEEN
## E. Phillips Oppenheim

## FOR THE QUEEN

"You are—Milord Cravon?"

I admitted the fact meekly, but with a lamentable absence of dignity, being, indeed, too utterly amazed for coherency. Whereupon my visitor raised her veil, flashed a brilliant smile upon me and sat down.

"I was sure of it," she remarked, speaking with great fluency, but with a strong foreign accent. "Milord's likeness to his brother is remarkable. I am very fortunate to discover you so early. It is but half an hour since I reached London."

That she had discovered me was obvious, but how or why was more than I could imagine. She was a complete stranger to me, she had entered my rooms unannounced, and the little French clock upon my mantelpiece had just struck midnight. However, she had mentioned my brother! I spoke of him at once.

"You know Reggie, then?" I inquired.

"I have met Mr. Reginald Lessingham once or twice," she admitted.

"At Marianburg?"

"At Marianburg—and elsewhere!"

"You have come from there?" I asked.

She nodded, and loosened her travelling cloak.

"I left Marianburg," she said, "exactly forty hours ago. It is rapid travelling, is it not? I am very tired and very hungry. If your servants have not all gone to bed, may I have some supper, please, and a glass of wine? Anything will do!"

I secretly pinched myself and then rang the bell. I had not fallen to sleep over my pipe and final whisky and Apollinaris. This remarkable and mysterious invasion of my solitude was an undoubted fact. By the time Groves appeared my visitor had removed her hat and was contemplating the arrangement of her hair in the mirror. Groves, who was a model servant, gave a momentary start of surprise and then looked steadily into vacancy. He received my confused orders in eloquent but respectful silence.

"Some supper, Groves—for one. Anything cold, and some wine!"

He disappeared. My companion succeeded in the replacement of a refractory curl, and with a parting glance at the mirror resumed her seat. I rose to my feet and began to collect my scattered wits.

"Do I understand," I began, "that you bring me a message from my brother?"

She shook her head.

"I have met your brother," she said, "but I have never yet spoken with him. He certainly does not know me or who I am."

I opened my lips to ask her bluntly what had brought her to my rooms at such an hour, but the words remained unspoken. Now that her hat was removed I was suddenly conscious that she was an exceedingly pretty woman. She lounged in my most comfortable chair perfectly at her ease, a charming smile upon her lips, her dark eyes meeting mine frankly and lit with a distinct gleam of humour. She was becomingly dressed, and although the dust of travel was upon her shoes and clothes, the details and finish of her *toilette* were sufficiently piquant to indicate her nationality. She was distinctly a very attractive woman. I felt my annoyance at her unexpected appearance decrease as my curiosity concerning her grew.

"Did I understand," I began, after a few moments' silence, "that you had come from Marianburg to see me?"

She laughed outright, and showed a set of perfectly white teeth. It was a dazzling smile, and the teeth were magnificent.

"Not altogether, Milord Cravon. I have come on a matter of very great importance, though, and you are concerned in it."

I signified my interest and my desire to hear more. She seemed in no hurry, however, to complete her explanation.

"I am so hungry!" she remarked, with pathetic irrelevance.

I moved to the bell, but at that moment Groves re-entered, bearing a small table. He silently but deftly arranged some cold things upon the sideboard and produced wine and a corkscrew. "You need not wait, Groves," I said, avoiding his eyes. "Bring in some coffee when I ring." He left the room and I proceeded to the sideboard.

"What may I give you?" I asked. "There is some collared stuff, cold salmon, and galantine."

"I will see," she answered, rising and coming to my side, "which looks the nicest!"

She made a selection, and was kind enough to express her approval of the result.

"Champagne or claret?" I asked.

"Champagne, if you please—one glass! Thank you. Now sit down and go on smoking, and I will talk to you."

I obeyed her. She was obviously a young woman who was used to having her own way, and it seemed to be the easiest thing to do.

"In the first place," she remarked, with something which sounded like a sigh, "who am I? It is what you want to know, eh? I would very much rather not tell you, Milord Cravon; for when you know, perhaps you will be sorry that you have been kind to me! *Hélas!*"

I moved in my chair uncomfortably, and murmured an insane desire that she would not needlessly distress herself by unnecessary revelations. She brushed my words aside. She was forced to declare herself.

"I am," she said, "a spy!"

"A what?" I cried.

"A spy! You understand—a creature of the police. It is you English, is it not, who detest so much the detective, who do not recognize the art of espionage?"

"By no means," I answered. "On the contrary, undertaken for the right motives and by the right class of man or woman, it is a magnificent profession, or, rather, I should call it a science!"

"You are right," she cried fervently, "Milord Cravon! You are charming! You are the most intelligent Englishman I have ever met!"

I bowed and waved my hand.

"It is a profession," I continued, "which as yet is only in its infancy. It demands ingenuity, invention and originality. To succeed in it one must be an artist. The lights and shadows of human nature must become a close and constant study."

"Milord Cravon," she cried, lifting a glass of champagne in her hand, "you are adorable!"

"The prejudices you spoke of," I continued, "are natural! As yet it is a profession which has been adopted only by persons of inferior calibre! It should be lifted to a place amongst the fine arts. I drink, Mademoiselle, to your calling with all respect and much enthusiasm!"

She leaned over and clinked the edge of her glass against my tumbler. Her eyes were very bright and her smile was bewitching. She was, I decided, the prettiest woman I had ever seen in my life!

"Milord Cravon," she murmured softly, "you are the most delightful man in the world!"

"And now," I remarked, "suppose you tell me in what I am to have the honour of serving you."

She shrugged her shoulders.

"You have not heard," she asked, "from your brother Reginald?"

"Not for more than a week," I answered. "Is anything wrong with him?"

She glanced at the clock.

"In a few minutes," she said, "he will be here!"

I looked up, startled.

"What, here in England!" I exclaimed; "Reggie?"

She nodded.

"Yes. He is in trouble!"

"In trouble! Of what sort?"

"He will tell you himself. It will be better so."

I rose to my feet, worried and anxious.

"You say that Reggie is in trouble, is coming here!" I said. "You are in the service of the police of Marianburg. Does that mean that you have followed him?"

She shook her head.

"No. The police of Marianburg are on his side. I am here as an ally, I am here to help him. You too, Milord Cravon, must help, for it is great trouble into which Mr. Reginald has fallen!"

A smothered groan from behind her startled us both. The cigarette which I had just lit dropped from my fingers and lay smoking upon the floor. A minute before I could have sworn that we were alone in the room, but at some time or other during our conversation the man who stood before us must have made his noiseless entrance. No wonder that we were taken by surprise! Only two of the electric lights were burning, and the room was full of shadows. Standing amongst them, with his fiercely bright eyes fixed upon us, was a young man whose features, in those first few moments of half-alarmed surprise, were only vaguely familiar to me. His face was the face of a boy, smooth and beardless, but its intense pallor and the black lines underneath his bloodshot eyes had transfigured him. His evening clothes were all awry, his white tie had slipped up behind his ear, the flower in his coat was crushed into a shapeless pulp, his shirt was crumpled and his clothes were splashed with mud. He stood a grim, dramatic figure, only a few yards away from our touch, glaring at us like a wild animal face to face with its captors.

The clock on the mantelpiece ticked for thirty seconds or more, and still my lips were sealed. For years people had told that my brother, Reggie Lessingham, was one of the smartest and most debonair young men in Europe. Was it any wonder that recognition dawned but slowly upon me?

My companion was naturally the first to recover herself. Indeed, after her little exclamation of dismay at his sudden appearance, she seemed to treat Reggie's presence as a matter of course. But for my part it was a terrible shock to me.

"Reggie!" I cried. "What—what in the name of all that's horrible is the matter, boy? Are you ill?"

He tottered rather than walked towards us, and stood still, with shaking hands resting upon the little table where my mysterious guest had been supping. He looked first at her and then at me, but when he opened his mouth to speak no words came—only a harsh, dry rattle from the back of his throat. He was like a man whom torture had driven to the furthermost bounds of insanity.

I caught up a tumbler, and filling it with champagne, forced some between his lips. He drank it with a little gasp. I helped him into a chair, and drew it up to the fire. He was still shaking all over, but his appearance was more natural.

"Come! You look a different man now," I said quietly. "What's wrong? Tell me all about it. I thought that you were in Marianburg. Are you home on leave?"

He did not answer. He looked from the girl to me, and then into the fire. It seemed as though he had lost the power of speech. I gripped him by the shoulder.

"Have you been drinking, Reggie?" I cried. "Come, pull yourself together. Remember, I have heard nothing as yet."

Still there was no answer. The burning light faded out from his bloodshot eyes. He sank back wearily in his chair—he was utterly exhausted by excitement and intense nervous strain. My visitor came softly over to my side.

"Make him tell you," she whispered. "There is no time to be lost. He can tell you what has happened better than I can."

I rested my hand upon his shoulder and spoke firmly.

"Reggie, old chap, "I said, "make a clean breast of it. Let me know the worst. Is anything wrong at headquarters—a row with the chief, eh? I shall stand by you; you can rely upon that. Come! out with it!"

Reggie looked up at us with white face and trembling lips. He was in a terrible state.

"Close the door, Maurice," he faltered.

I obeyed him. He followed me with his eyes, and then looked searchingly round the room. I began to fear that the boy's brain had given way.

"You are Marie Lichenstein?" he said suddenly, addressing my guest.

She nodded.

"Yes. I know all about it. You can speak before me."

"You were at Cologne?"

She nodded.

"I am more used to rapid travelling than you," she remarked. "I came from Ostend, and saved two hours."

"You have heard nothing from Marianburg?"

"Nothing. I was to come here and wait for instructions."

Reggie was silent for a moment. When he spoke again, it was to me he turned.

"Maurice," he faltered, "something hideous has happened to me. You will help me! For God's sake don't say no!"

"Of course I will help you," I answered readily; "only I must know what it is all about. Tell me the whole story."

He shivered.

"The whole story! No, I can't do that now."

"Something has happened at headquarters?" I suggested.

"Yes. I have been robbed! There was a burglary at the Embassy, and I was robbed of some papers."

A light began to break in upon me. After all, nothing so terribly tragic had happened. Reggie had probably been indiscreet. A few words to the Foreign Secretary would set matters right.

"State papers, I suppose?"

He shook his head with a groan.

"Worse! Much worse!"

The light faded away. I was more puzzled than ever.

"Worse than State papers?" I repeated vaguely.

"Yes!"

He looked at the door again and all round the room. His voice sank to a whisper. He took hold of my hand, and drew me down so that my head nearly touched his. I could feel his finger-nails burning in my flesh.

"Swear, Maurice—ay, and you too, Marie Lichenstein—upon your honour, upon your sacred honour, that what I am going to tell you shall never pass your lips—that you will lock it deep down in your memories! Swear!"

"I swear, Reggie!"

Marie Lichenstein inclined her head.

"To me," she said, "these things are holy. It is my profession. Besides, I already know what you are going to say."

His voice sank to a husky whisper! His eyes were afire!

"They were the letters of a woman—whom I loved—who loved me!"

"A woman!" I exclaimed. "Letters! Why, Reggie!"

The relief in my tone seemed to irritate him. He held out his hand.

"You do not understand. Those letters were mine. They have been stolen from me. It is a plot of her enemies. They were written by a woman who loved me. They were written impetuously, without prudence, signed with her name. I told her—that they were destroyed! I lied, for I kept some of them. I could not bear to part with all. They were precious to me. If I do not get them back at once, I shall shoot myself. I have sworn it! But God help her! God help her!"

"Have you any clue, any idea where they are?" I asked. "You have come to England. Do you think that they have been brought here?"

"She has enemies," he muttered, "enemies everywhere, and powerful. My servant must have been in their pay. He has absconded, and he has come to England. He had only a few hours' start, but I cannot find him!"

"What, Shalders?" I asked. "Surely you cannot suspect him!"

"Suspect!" Reggie beat upon the floor with his heel. "It is no matter for suspicions. It is he who robbed the safe. He is in England somewhere. I must find him! We should have caught him on the boat."

"Are they very bad, these letters?" I asked, "or were they only indiscreet?"

"They are absolutely fatal," he gasped. "But it is not that they are so bad; it is—who she is!"

We were all silent. Reggie's face was ashen. The girl was watching him curiously.

"If I am to be of any use to you, Reggie," I said, "I must know her name, I must know all the circumstances."

He half rose from his chair, clutching at the arms. His voice was hysterical.

"It is a little packet!" he cried with a sob. "There are only four letters and a ring, but with them goes—the honour of a queen!"

At first I had but one thought—Reggie was mad! But when I looked from his white, anguish stricken face to my other visitor, I saw that she, at least, did not think so. Apparently she was not surprised. Reggie's bitter cry had only told her what she already knew. Then, whilst I stood there wondering, a sudden memory rose up before me. I thought of a long visit of my brother's years ago to the capital where he was now *attaché*, and of certain half-jesting allusions to the beauty of a certain princess, which Reggie had taken very ill indeed. There had been a paragraph in a so-called Society paper, scandalous but vague; somebody had shown it to him, and Reggie's language had been awful to listen to. These things came back to me in those few tragical moments, and dimly suggested others. For years we in England had seen very little of Reggie. His leave was mostly spent at the capital to which he had taken special care to be appointed at his entry into diplomatic life. With contemporary history I was sufficiently well acquainted to know that the princess had become a queen. Conviction came to me with a sudden, lightning like rush. He had spoken the truth! I felt the perspiration stand out in beads upon my forehead as I recognized his terrible dilemma.

"Reggie," I said, "I want the whole story, please. If I am to be of any use to you, I must hear it all. Out with it!"

He hesitated, with his eyes fixed upon the girl. She shrugged her shoulders.

"You do not mistrust me, Monsieur Lessingham?" she exclaimed. He hesitated.

"I do not mistrust you," he said, "but—"

She stopped him with a little gesture.

"Ah, well!" she exclaimed, "I do not wish that you should have any further anxiety. Look, if you will, upon my credentials."

She drew a folded sheet of paper from her bosom and laid it upon the table. The words were so few and written so boldly that I too could see them?

"Trust Marie Lichenstein.—Fedora."

With a sudden movement Reggie lifted the piece of paper to his lips. Then he laid it reverently down.

"You recognize the handwriting?" she asked.

"It is enough," he answered. "You shall hear in a few words all that there is to tell. It is the story of a simple robbery. A packet of letters and a ring have been stolen in a most wonderful way from my room in the Embassy. They were kept—"

I held up my hand.

"Reggie, forgive me, but I must know! Were they written before her marriage or after?"

"All—save one—before. I have had letters since—a few—on my promise that I would destroy them as they came. I kept that promise faithfully —until last week. Then I was horribly tempted! I could not see her for several days. A letter came! Oh, I was foolish, but the letter meant so much to me!" he groaned. "I kept it for an hour or two, meaning to destroy it at night. It was stolen with the others!"

"That letter—" I began, looking searchingly at Reggie.

"It was—at least—imprudent!" he moaned. "To those who do not know her, as I know her, it will seem worse!"

I turned towards the girl. Had she anything to say? For my part, the matter seemed already hopeless. I could see no ray of light anywhere.

"Will you tell us, please," she said, "all about the actual robbery?"

"You have had particulars," he said. "You know all that there is to be known."

"It is true," she admitted; "nevertheless, your brother does not, and I myself would like to hear the story from your own lips."

He rested his head wearily upon his hand; he had taken a chair now, and began with his eyes fixed upon the fire.

"I kept the packet in a safe let into the wall of my room, and fastened with a combination cipher and Bramah key, exactly the same as the chief has for the treaty safe. The letter I speak about I received by hand on Sunday morning. I had it with me all day. At eight o'clock I went out to dine. I left the letter with the other packet in my safe. The key never leaves my person. I have a hollow gold band around my arm, and the key fits into it. When I returned at night everything was as usual. I opened the safe, meaning to read the letter over and then destroy it. It was gone and with it the packet and a ring. I rang my bell. There was no answer. I rushed along the passage of the Embassy shouting for Shalders. He was my servant. No one knew anything about him. I behaved, I am afraid, like a maniac. I should have been cool, but I was not. I could not contain myself. At last I heard news. He had been seen to leave the house about an hour after me, carrying a bag. I traced him to the station; he had taken a ticket to London. I followed him."

"The key?" I asked.

He touched his arm.

"It is here still. It has not left my possession for a second."

"How do you suppose, then, that the safe was opened?"

Reggie groaned.

"God alone knows! All I can say is, that it was done with a key, and the only other one made has never been out of the chief's possession, or, at any rate, out of the secretary's room. Sir Henry assured me of that himself. How the cipher could have been adjusted, and the safe opened— Oh, Maurice!" he cried wearily, "it makes my brain whirl to think of it!"

He dropped his head wearily into his hands and leaned upon the table. At that moment there was a knock at the door. Groves came softly into the little circle of light with a telegram upon his salver. He brought it to me. It was addressed to "Miss Lichenstein, c/o the Earl of Cravon."

"I thought that it might be for the young lady," Groves murmured.

I handed it to her. She studied it for a few moments in silence. Then she took her gloves from the table.

"Will you allow your servant to call for me a hansom cab?" she asked. "I must go."

"Is there any news?" Reggie asked, suddenly looking up with white face.

She shook her head.

"Not yet. These are my instructions; I must obey them at once. Monsieur Reginald, do not despair! I shall do my best. Milord Cravon, *au revoir*! It has been a very leetle visit, but—oh! so pleasant!"

Her dark eyes flashed sweetly at me, and she took her leave with a bewitching smile and backward glance over her shoulder. I heard Groves whistle for a hansom, and she drove rapidly away. Then I went back to Reggie. He was leaning forward across the table, and was breathing heavily. I bent over him quietly. He had fallen asleep. In the morning I was even more shocked to see the alteration in my brother. His clothes hung loosely about him, as though he were just recovering from a long illness; his cheeks were haggard, and his eyes deep-set and unnaturally bright. He held a telegram in his hand when I entered the room.

"Any news?" I asked.

He shook his head.

"None," he answered mournfully. "My message simply says, 'Situation unchanged.'"

I rang the bell for breakfast. Until he had eaten something I would not let him speak. Afterwards I pushed two easy chairs to the fire, and passed him a pipe and some tobacco.

"I am going to ask you some questions, Reggie," I said.

"Yes. Go on," he answered feverishly.

"How long has Shalders been with you?"

"For six years. Ever since I had a man."

"Has he been a good servant?"

"I would have trusted him," Reggie said, "with my life."

"Where are your rooms in the Embassy?"

"On the third floor."

"Anybody else near you?"

"Sir Henry's private secretaries—Dick Colquhoun and a fellow named Harris."

Dick was an old school fellow. I passed him by without a thought.

"Harris, "I repeated thoughtfully. "Is he by any chance a connection of the Foreign Secretary's?"

Reggie nodded.

"Nephew."

"Are you on friendly terms with him?"

"Not particularly. He is not a sociable fellow. He was away on a week's leave, shooting somewhere."

"When was he expected back?" I asked.

"The day I left."

"There was no one else who had rooms upon the third floor?"

"No one."

"Had you any difficulty in hearing about Shalders at the Marianburg railway station?"

"No."

"He did not seem to take any particular pains about concealing his identity?"

"None at all. I traced him as far as Paris easily. He took a sleeping berth in his own name."

"He travelled first-class, then?"

"Yes."

"And at Paris?"

"I lost him. I was only one train behind, and I believe that I reached London first."

"You think that he stayed over in Paris?"

"Yes."

"He took his ticket for London?"

"Yes."

"You have had no recent unpleasantness with Shalders? Your behaviour has been such that he would presumably consider you a good master?"

"I am sure of it."

"Then what possible motive, Reggie, could he have had in stealing those letters?"

"You might as well ask me," Reggie cried in despair, "how he could possibly have opened the safe. All I know is that he has bolted and the letters are gone."

"Can you think of any one," I asked, "to whom those letters would have been specially valuable?"

"No one—except an enemy."

"And has she an enemy that you or she knows of?"

"Not one."

"Then we must conclude that they have been stolen for blackmail."

"I suppose so."

"And this is utterly unlike anything you would ever have expected from Shalders?"

"Utterly."

"Have you seen her since, Reggie?"

He covered his face with his hands.

"For one moment—one horrible moment!"

"You have warned her?"

"Yes."

"Is she taking any steps?"

"She has interest with the secret police. They are following Shalders. Marie Lichenstein is their agent."

"Can you communicate with her, or some one absolutely trustworthy in Marianburg?" I asked.

"Yes. I have had two or three telegrams already."

"Any news?"

"None."

"Sit down and write out a telegram."

He obeyed without a word. I placed pen and ink and forms before him.

"Say, 'Is Harris at Embassy?'"

"Harris," he repeated. "What has he to do with it?"

"Never mind, Reggie. You send the telegram. An affair like this is mostly guess-work. There is no harm in asking the question, anyhow."

Reggie thought for a moment, turned it into cipher and wrote it slowly out.

"Now go and despatch that yourself," I said. "The walk will do you good."

He rose wearily.

"I don't see any object in sending this," he said. "It is ridiculous to think of Harris in connection with the affair. He wasn't even there. Shalders took the letters! There is no doubt about that. What we want to do," he concluded, with a feverish little burst, "is to find Shalders."

"Send it any way," I answered. "Promise that you will send it."

He nodded listlessly.

"Oh yes, I'll send it," he said. "I've told you that it's no good, that's all."

"Do you know if Shalders has any friends in London?" I asked.

"He told me once that he had a brother, a hall-porter at the Geranium Club."

"Why not go on there and see if he has heard anything of him? You might find out his other relations, and they could be all watched."

"There is more sense in that," he muttered. "At least, it will be something to do!"

He left the room. I spent the morning reading a file of *The Times* for the last six months. Gradually I became more and more interested. I began to see the glimmerings of a clue. I was interrupted only a few minutes before luncheon-time by Groves announcing a visitor.

I looked up from my papers.

"Who is it?" I asked impatiently.

"A gentleman, my lord," Groves announced. "He declines to give his name, but he has a large box and a note which he says that he must give into your own hands."

"Show him in," I directed.

A man was ushered in, tall and by no means ill-looking, with a thin black moustache, steel-grey eyes and somewhat foreign appearance. He was carefully, in fact, irreproachably, dressed, with a single exception—he wore a brilliantly red tie, which seemed a little out of place with the rest of his toilet.

He bowed and regarded me keenly.

"The Earl of Cravon, I believe?"

I admitted the fact. He produced a note and handed it to me without further speech. It was addressed to me in a delicate, feminine handwriting, and a faint, familiar perfume assailed me directly I touched the seal. It was undated and the notepaper was quite plain.

"My dear Friend,—

"Necessity, or rather your brother's necessity, compels me to ask what will seem strange to you. Yet do as I send you word, and later I will explain. The bearer of this has a box. Let it be placed in an empty bedroom of your house, unknown, if it be possible, to any save your own confidential servant. Further, send me by him a latch-key of your house, and do not you yourself retire for the night until you see or hear from me. You will think that I am asking you strange things. No matter. All that I can I will explain to you very soon; and for the rest— well, it is for your brother, you know. Is it not?

"Do not hesitate to do exactly what I ask. Very much depends upon it. As yet I cannot send you any news, but very soon our effort will be made, and you will know with what success.

"Farewell, Milord Cravon. It is for a very short time.

                                                        "Marie."

I looked from the note to the messenger.

"Where is—Miss Lichenstein?" I asked.

He spread out his hands.

"I cannot tell you, sir," he said. "It is better for you not to know. Will you give me the key? The box of which she has made mention is in your hall."

I went out and looked at it. It was an ordinary lady's dress-basket. Groves was examining it from a little distance, with his hands behind his back and a curious expression upon his face.

"Have this box taken into the guest-chamber upon the first floor, Groves," I directed.

He bowed and hurried away. I returned to the library.

"Here is the key," I said to the man who awaited me, taking my own latch-key from my watch-chain

"I will do what Miss Lichenstein has asked."

He accepted it with a bow.

"You will not regret it," he answered quietly. "By this time tomorrow I trust that we may report ourselves successful."

"You are from Marianburg?" I asked.

He took up his hat.

"I see no reason for concealing the fact, Lord Cravon, that I am of the Marianburg secret police. This affair has been placed wholly in my hands. You will forgive me now if I hurry away."

I watched him step from the pavement into a small, handsome brougham and drive rapidly away. Then I hastened to change my own clothes and order a carriage.

I drove first to the house of Sir Charles Wimpole, a somewhat intimate friend of mine, who had a seat in the House of Commons and held a minor post in the Foreign Office. I found Wimpole Lodge, however, in the hands of the whitewashers and decorators. Sir Charles, I was told, was staying for a week or so at the Hotel Maurice. A few minutes later I drove into the splendid courtyard of the hotel and made inquiries at the bureau.

Sir Charles, I was told, had gone out only a few minutes before, but he was expected back in a quarter of an hour. I lit a cigarette and subsided into one of the luxurious lounges in the hall. I wanted particularly some information which Sir Charles would be able to give me, so I decided to wait.

I had been there scarcely a minute when the rustling of a dress across the marble floor induced me to raise my eyes from the paper which I had picked up. To my amazement, it was Marie Lichenstein. She was charmingly dressed in a Parisian *toilette* of red and black, and a poodle, shaved in the latest fashion and wearing a jewelled collar, trotted behind her. I rose to my feet, hat in hand, and stepped forward. To my blank astonishment, she met my eyes with a stony stare of non-recognition. I muttered her name—she turned coldly away.

"Monsieur has mistaken me," she said. "I have not the honour of his acquaintance."

She retreated to the further end of the hall and sat down in an easy chair, with the dog by her side. I resumed my seat, and looked sharply round to see if any one had witnessed my discomfiture. I fancied that the head-porter, who had suddenly averted his head, was indulging in a faint smile; I was sure that a man, whom I had not previously noticed, and who was sitting in a dark corner by the cigar stall, was laughing softly to himself. I looked at him more closely. Something about the man's mouth seemed familiar. I leaned forward and saw him distinctly. It was the messenger whom Marie Lichenstein had sent to me scarcely an hour ago.

I threw my cigarette away and walked down to the cigar stall. I made some trifling purchases, glancing every now and then at the man, who was barely a couple of yards away. He neither avoided my notice nor courted it, but there was not the faintest gleam of recognition in his face. I purposely tendered a banknote to the girl in charge of the cigar stall. She left to get change, and I spoke softly to the man.

"We meet again very soon," I remarked.

He looked up at me with a bland but unintelligent smile.

"Monsieur is, I think, mistaken," he said. "I have not the pleasure of his acquaintance."

I muttered something which was scarcely polite, and returned to my seat. I felt that I was being drawn into some sort of a conspiracy. The man and the woman sat at opposite corners of the hall, and not even a glance passed between them. They did not know one another— they did not know me. Both had assumed with perfect naturalness the listless attitude of people passing away an hour of boredom. All the same I began to realize that they were waiting for some one. Every time the swing-doors were opened by the hall-porter, who stood like a machine at his post, the man looked up. There was no anxiety or nervousness in that slight, sidelong glance. It was to all appearance nothing more than the ordinary curiosity of the casual hotel-lounger. Only I, who was watching very closely indeed, could see every now and then faint signs of impatience underneath his insouciance.

I lit a fresh cigarette and waited. They were watching for some one! Was that some one the man who had planned and carried out this strange robbery?

I too began to scrutinize the little stream of people who were passing in and out. So far as I could see, they were the usual cosmopolitan throng who patronize such hotels as the Maurice. The majority were Americans, plainly dressed and carrying satchels with an occasional *Baedeker*. Every now and then a Frenchwoman, like a brilliant butterfly, came flitting in, and the gay chatter of voices, introductions and leave-takings filled the air. It was just when the hall seemed fullest that the door swung back and a man entered with a rug upon his arm, followed by one of the outside porters carrying a portmanteau. I glanced over at the face of the watcher by the cigar stall, and felt a sudden thrill of excitement. A look had flashed across from the man to the woman, and I intercepted it. I knew at once what it meant— this was the man!

The new-comer passed within a few feet of me, and I was able to observe him closely. He appeared to be from thirty to thirty-five years old, he was of medium height, sallow and thin. He was dressed in a blue serge suit of foreign cut, and he wore a black bowler-hat, which would have been the better for a good brushing. As he passed from the door to the hotel office, he looked quickly and furtively around at the loungers in the hall, and seemed relieved to recognize no familiar face.

He disappeared into the bureau, and almost immediately afterwards Marie Lichenstein rose from her corner and came quietly down the hall until she reached the space between the bureau and the lifts. She paused here and exchanged a few words with one of the hotel pages. As she dismissed the boy, the new-comer issued from the hotel office, and raising her eyes, they fell, as if by accident, upon him.

I know what I should have felt if a woman as beautiful as Marie Lichenstein had looked at me in like manner. She must have been a consummate actress. At first her glance denoted nothing but curiosity, in a second or two it had softened into interest, then she passed on with a faint, but bewitching, smile at the corners of her lips. The newcomer hesitated awkwardly for a moment. Then he handed his rug to the porter who was carrying his bag.

"You can take them into my room," I heard him say. "I shall be there in a few minutes."

The servant withdrew; the new-comer glanced after Marie Lichenstein. She had swung down the hall with slow graceful movements, and was looking idly into the restaurant. The man followed her as far as the cigar stall, where he made some trifling purchase. As he stood there the woman passed slowly back again. He turned and looked at her more boldly. This time her eyes fell quickly before his, but that wonderful smile quivered once more upon her lips. She walked on towards the lift and entered—the man followed her. It seemed to me that as they swung up out of sight I saw him bend down towards her!

When they had gone I drew a little breath and glanced down towards my fellow-watcher. He was lighting a cigarette and smiling softly to himself. In a few moments he rose and, drawing on his gloves, passed out of the hotel. I heard the whistle which summoned a private carriage and the sound of wheels driving away. It had all happened so quickly that it was hard to realize anything. Only I looked at the two empty seats, and I think I understood that the curtain had rung up upon the first act of the little drama of which I had unwittingly become the sole audience.

In a moment or two I rose and entered the office. I had intended to take a room, in order to see for myself under what name this latest comer to the hotel had registered. But as it happened this was not necessary. The office was crowded, and the visitors' book lay open before me. The last name was written boldly enough—the ink, indeed, was not yet dry. I read it over slowly to myself. It was quite unfamiliar:—

MAXIME DE CARTERET,
Buda Pesth.
No. 357.

I turned away and came face to face with Wimpole. He greeted me with some surprise.

"What are you doing here, Cravon?" he asked. "I thought you hated these huge hotels."

"I came to see you," I answered. "Are you busy, or can you spare me half an hour?"

"I'm off to the House presently," he said. "We'll have a cigarette first, if you like; and then, if you've nothing better to do, you might give me a lift down. I saw your carriage outside."

We sat down on one of the lounges.

"I have come to beg for some political information, Wimpole," I said.

He looked at me with a smile.

"I'm very much flattered," he said. "Are you going to speak on the Zanzibar question, then?"

I shook my head.

"No. I'm not going to speak at all—at least, I do not want the information for political purposes. Nor has it anything to do with Zanzibar."

"China?"

"Much nearer home."

"Europe?"

I was silent for a moment.

"You remember Reggie—my younger brother?"

"Quite well," he answered. "He came to Eton the year I left, and he followed me to Magdalen. Nice boy, but I haven't seen him for years."

"He has been at Marianburg," I continued, "and I am sorry to say that he has got into a scrape there. It's a very mysterious and complicated business, but I'd give a good deal to help him out of it."

"At Marianburg!" Wimpole whistled softly to himself and began to look more interested.

"I daresay you know," he said, "that matters politically are looking very queer there just now?"

"I know nothing," I answered, "except what I have gathered from *The Times*. It seems to me that there is something in the background there, and I have a sort of theory that Reggie has got drawn into it."

Wimpole looked around him.

"Marianburg," he said, "is giving us just now a great deal of trouble. This is scarcely the place to talk of it, but if you will drive me down to the House we can talk as we go."

We both rose. At that moment the lift doors opposite to us were opened, and Marie Lichenstein stepped out, dressed for walking and followed by the man in the blue serge suit. She passed me with unseeing eyes and perfect unconsciousness, chatting all the while gaily to her companion. Wimpole looked after her admiringly.

"What a handsome woman, Cravon!"

I smiled. We all four stood on the steps together, and a porter, who had recognized me, called for my carriage. I saw Marie's companion turn round as though he were shot. Wimpole looked at him curiously.

"The fellow with her seemed to recognize your name," he remarked.

I nodded, but took care not to advance towards him. The hansom arrived first, and I heard their destination

"Charbonell's, Bond Street."

They drove off. I stepped into my brougham, which followed up. On the other side of the court-yard a man was strolling up and down. It was the messenger whom Marie had sent to me—the man with the red tie.

There followed for me an evening of inaction during which I thought a good deal and smoked too much. Reggie had not returned, nor was there any message from him. About eight o'clock a telegram arrived from Marianburg, but, although I opened it without hesitation and with considerable interest, it was in cipher and unintelligible to me. After that the hours passed away very slowly. At twelve o'clock I fell asleep; at one I awoke with a sudden start and a chill consciousness that I was not alone. I sat up in my chair. At first I thought that I must still be dreaming. The woman who stood before me with uplifted and warning finger was dressed in the fashion of another age. Her hair and cheeks were powdered, diamonds flashed from her shoe buckles, her corsage, from the velvet which bound her hair. Her dress of green satin was strangely cut and looped up on one side to display a gorgeous petticoat. She held a fan in her left hand, and her fingers were ablaze with rings.

"Milord Cravon!" she whispered.

I knew her then, as indeed I might have done from the first, for her eyes and mouth were eloquent enough and her face was not one to be easily disguised.

"Marie Lichenstein!" I cried. "Why—"

She interrupted me.

"I have been to your Covent Garden Ball," she said. "Give me some wine quickly."

I had some at hand and poured her out a glass. The hand which took it from me was shaking like an aspen leaf. I looked at her more closely, and I saw that she was a sorry masquerader. There was a pallor upon her cheeks more real than the delicate blanching of the powder, and a fear in her eyes which was like the fear of death. Behind her, across a chair, had fallen a black opera cloak and a domino. She stood there in her brilliant dress a strange, wan picture.

I gave her more wine. She drank it eagerly and sank down in my easy chair. I took her hand and held it in mine. It was as cold as ice.

"I am afraid," she murmured, "that I am losing my nerve. Yet I never thought that it would end like this."

"Something—has happened?"

"A great deal has happened," she declared, "much that I would were undone. Milord Cravon, we have failed!"

My heart sank. Yet from the moment when I had recognized her I had felt sure of it. She was like a woman wholly unnerved by a great shock, and with it all I knew that she was not a woman to be lightly brought into such a state.

"He was—not the man then?"

"Of that I am not sure," she answered; "but it is very certain that he has not the letters. If he is the man who stole them, and of that Meyer is certain, then he has already made his bargain and parted with them. We were too late. We have run a great risk for no purpose"

"I am sorry—for your sake as well as Reggie's," I murmured.

"My friend," she said, looking at me with eyes which seemed suddenly very dim and soft, "by this time to-morrow you will not be sorry for me any longer! At the sound of my name you will shudder, at the thought of me you will shrink as one shrinks from a poisonous thing! But after all—what matters?" she added, with a hysterical little laugh. "I have but one thing to think of now, and that is to get away. Milord Cravon, have you servants whom you can trust?"

"Implicitly," I assured her.

"I need a carriage," she said.

"My night cab is ready," I answered. "I have only to touch a bell. The horse is already harnessed."

"And my box?"

I motioned her to follow me, and showed her the room where it had been placed.

"The cab—in five minutes," she said, as I turned to go; "I shall not be longer."

She kept her word literally. I was prepared for some sort of transformation, but scarcely for anything so complete. She glided into my study before the five minutes were up, a slim, sad figure in the sorrowful garb of a sister of mercy. From the rough, black gown which fell upon her ill-shaped shoes to the gold chain about her neck, the metamorphosis was absolute and complete. I gasped for breath as I looked at her.

"I have left you but one thing to do, Milord Cravon," she said. "The opera cloak and domino there—will you put them in the box which I have left upstairs? Keep that box in a safe place until you have an opportunity of destroying it, and every trace of Marie Lichenstein has vanished."

"But—where are you going?" I cried.

"To a convent at Highgate. I have letters from a sister at Brussels. When your door closes behind me, I am as safe as though I were a thousand miles away. Everything has been perfectly arranged, and I am expected to-night. Is the carriage here?"

"It is waiting," I answered. "Do you mean, then, that we shall not meet again?"

She sighed.

"It is a small world," she said softly.

"And Highgate," I suggested, "is a small suburb."

She shook her head.

"Not there," she said decidedly. "Whatever you do, do not come there, or make any inquiries. You promise?"

"Faithfully."

She sighed once more. I found myself holding her hand. Her dark eyes looked sorrowfully into mine.

"After all," she said, "it is true what I have told you. By this time tomorrow you will loathe me. If my hand lay within yours—as now—you would cast it away."

"I can assure you," I said earnestly, and raising it a little towards my lips, "that I should do nothing of the sort. I should do precisely what I am going to do now."

The little white fingers were as cold as ice. She drew them gently away and I walked with her to the door. With my hand upon the latch I paused. There was something I wanted to say to her, but she gave me no opportunity. With a sudden impulsive movement, she threw the door open herself, ran down the steps and vanished into the carriage. She did not look round nor say a word of farewell, but as she crossed the pavement I heard something which sounded like a sob break from her lips.

It was on my plate when I came down to breakfast. I saw it there when I entered the room, neatly cut and folded, by the side of a little pile of letters. How I hated the sight of it, hated the thought of touching, of opening it! *The Morning Post* is not a paper given over to sensationalism. I knew that whatever had occurred would be temperately and truthfully chronicled; yet none the less I shrank with positive dread from opening those innocent pages. Nor were my apprehensions ill founded. When at last I summoned up courage to take the paper into my hands, my worst fears were instantly confirmed. At the head of a column, in thick black type, it stared me in the face:—

TERRIBLE MURDER AT THE HOTEL MAURICE!

For a moment I was incapable of reading. I was dizzy and everything swam before my eyes. Then I pulled myself together. I gripped the paper with both hands and read with fierce eagerness every line.

"Early this morning the body of a gentleman, a visitor at the Hotel Maurice, was discovered in his room under circumstances which leave little room for doubt as to the manner of his death. We are at present without full particulars of the tragedy, but such information as we have makes it perfectly clear that a brutal murder has been committed. The deceased was found stabbed to the heart with a long, thin dagger of foreign make. He had only arrived at the hotel during the afternoon, and had registered under the name of Maxime De Carteret.

"*Later*. Further particulars are to hand with reference to the murder early this morning at the Hotel Maurice. The deceased was seen talking during the afternoon to a lady visitor at the hotel, who had herself only just arrived, and who had registered under the name of Lichenstein. The two were apparently on the most cordial terms and dined together in the restaurant, and subsequently left the hotel together for the Covent Garden Ball. They returned quite early, and went up in the lift to their respective rooms, which were in the same wing and on the same floor of the hotel. They were accompanied by a third person, who had also arrived during the day, and registered under the name of Jules Van Drooden, of Brussels. The three were last seen together talking on the landing outside their rooms, but about half an hour later the lady, still in her fancy dress, rang for the lift and descended to the ground floor. She asked the hall-porter to call her carriage, remarking that the gentleman with whom she had been to the ball had been taken ill, and she had been compelled to return with him, but as she had friends there, she was going back for an hour or two. She drove off, and up to the hour of going to press had not returned to the hotel. We understand also that Mr. Van Drooden, who, together with the lady, was last seen with the murdered man, has disappeared.

"On inquiry early this morning our representative learned that, although the clothes and belongings of the deceased had apparently been searched through, his money, jewellery and papers were untouched. On reference to the latter, it has been ascertained that his real name is Shalders, and that he was a valet in the service of the Hon. Reginald Lessingham, who is attached to the Embassy at Marianburg."

The paper slipped from my fingers. It was as bad as—even worse than I had feared. It was a horrible and unpardonable deed; not only that, but it was an ineffective one. If he had ever had the letters, he must have parted with them. Whatever his motive for the robbery might have been, he had met with a terrible retribution.

The door opened and Reggie walked in, followed by a servant with the breakfast. In the clearer daylight I was shocked to see how great a change the anxiety of the last few days had wrought in him. His eyes were set in deep hollows, his cheeks were thin and haggard. However it all might end, he would carry the marks of agony with him to the grave.

"Reggie," I said, "there is something here which I want you to read." He held out his hand. I gave him the paper.

"Read it carefully," I said, "and tell me what you think of it."

He devoured it with a sort of fierce joy, mingled with amazement. His eyes glittered with an unnatural light. I saw that I must keep him going as much as possible. Action of some sort was absolutely necessary for him. He was on the verge of madness.

"Very good! very good!" he exclaimed. "It is the man who robbed me whom they have killed. Very good! It is magnificent! Dead, is he? I am glad!"

"You must remember, Reggie," I said, "that this may be a very just retribution, but it scarcely looks as though it were going to help you. Let me tell you this. I have seen Marie Lichenstein since. He had not the letters. It seems as though he had parted with them."

"Vengeance is something," Reggie muttered; but he was white once more to the lips and his voice faltered.

"There were two telegrams for you," I remarked with a sudden thought. "Have you had them?"

"No! Give them to me!" he cried.

I fetched them myself from the library. He tore them open. As he read his expression changed into one of blank bewilderment.

"Listen to this!" he cried.

"'Your servant, Shalders, discovered yesterday in the attic at Embassy, gagged and chloroformed. Was attacked in your room on Sunday evening. Cannot identify assailant. Very weak and exhausted, but will probably recover.'"

Reggie looked piteously at me, holding one hand to his forehead.

"What in God's name does it mean?" he cried.

"Open the other telegram," I answered.

He held it out.

"There is nothing in it," he declared. "It is only about Harris. He has been back, but applied for extension of leave, and left again. Damn Harris!"

"There have been wishes," I murmured softly, "whose accomplishment has been more distant."

I declined to discuss the matter further until after breakfast, although, so far as my brother was concerned, the meal was little better than a farce. He made a pretence of eating, but all the time his eyes were following me. It was pitiful to watch him.

"Reggie," I said at last, filling my pipe, "in the first place, are you completely satisfied that your telegrams from Marianburg are to be relied upon?"

"They are unimpeachable," he answered. "I would answer for their truthfulness with my life."

"In that case," I said, "this means work for you, Reggie. If Shalders is really in Marianburg, we must find out who it was who robbed you and has paid the penalty."

He sprang up at once.

"I am ready!" he cried. "What shall I do?"

"Go to the Hotel Maurice," I said, "give your card and ask to be allowed to identify your servant. If it is Shalders—well, some one from Marianburg must be sending you false information. If it is not Shalders, say nothing at all. Be very careful that you show no surprise."

Reggie went out, and I heard Groves whistle a hansom up for him. I lit a pipe and studied carefully for some time certain numbers of *The Times* which I had sorted out from the pile. Just as I began to see a glimmering of light, Groves drew back the curtains which divided my rooms and announced a visitor.

"It is a lady to see you, my lord," he announced. "She says that her business is urgent and important."

"Her name?" I asked.

"She says that you would not know it, but that she must see you at once. She inquired first of all if Mr. Reginald were here."

"You can show her in, Groves," I directed.

A woman swept into the room almost as I was speaking, waving my servant away with an imperious gesture. She was plainly dressed in black and closely veiled. I could only see that she was young, and that she carried herself with the ease and grace of a beautiful woman. I rose to my feet.

"You are Lord Cravon?" she said quietly. "Will you send your servant away? I wish for a few minutes' conversation with you."

I looked at Groves and he withdrew at once.

She waited until the door was closed, and then she raised her veil.

"You do not know me?" she asked.

I shook my head. She was certainly a very beautiful woman, and of a rare type. Her hair was red gold and her eyes and eyebrows dark. Her features were delicately cut, and of patrician type; she carried herself in such a manner that my rooms seemed the smaller for her presence. Suddenly a very brilliant smile parted her lips, and at the same time I realized that her face was perfectly familiar to me! Where had I seen it?

"You are not like your brother," she said.

A vague uneasiness crept over me.

"You came—to see him?"

She shook her head. Her face hardened a little.

"I do not wish to see your brother ever again in my life," she said. "He has broken a promise to me."

"You—you are not—"

She held out her hand.

"That will do," she said. "I come from Marianburg."

I bowed low, but I was overwhelmed with embarrassment and dismay.

"Your welcome is scarcely flattering," she remarked with a smile.

"Madam," I answered, "I fear that your presence is a token that the worst has happened."

"On the contrary," she answered me, "nothing has happened at all. It was the waiting for news which wearied me so. I had arranged for an *incognito* visit to Paris, and I came over here by the night boat. Tell me, what news have you?"

I showed her the telegrams, and I told her of Marie Lichenstein and the murder at the Hotel Maurice. She listened without emotion or interruption of any sort. When I had finished, she was silent for several minutes.

"If your brother's servant was not the thief," she said at length, "I shall be inclined to believe that this is a political plot."

"Your majesty," I answered, "should be the best judge of that. It is hard to believe that there are people who would do you a wanton injury."

"Oh, I have enemies enough, no doubt," she remarked lightly. "The pity of it is that a woman in my position is never conscious of them."

"Is there any reason," I asked respectfully, "why you should have political enemies?"

"Yes."

She seemed indisposed to say more. I glanced towards the pile of papers at my side.

"I have been trying," I said, "to understand the politics of your country."

She glanced at them with contempt.

"Tear them up," she said; "they will not help you."

"They have given me an idea," I ventured to say.

"When," she asked, with apparent irrelevance, "shall you know who this unfortunate man at the Hotel Maurice was?"

"In less than half an hour," I replied. "Reginald has gone there now."

"I shall wait to know," she said; "but I do not want to see your brother, or to have him know that I am in England."

"It would certainly be wiser," I agreed.

She shrugged her shoulders.

"It is not," she said, "a question of wisdom. Your brother is a foolish boy, and he has disobeyed me. I shall not forgive him."

"He is terribly distressed," I ventured to say.

"I am glad to hear it," she answered.

"Do not think," I continued, "that I wish to defend him; but his motive for keeping those letters was, at least, excusable."

She shrugged her shoulders, and looked at me with a smile; but there was no tenderness in her face.

"Such sentiment!" she exclaimed mockingly. "Yet, perhaps, if I cared for him still, it might mean something to me. But that is all over. He has grown too dismal, he does not amuse me. And, my friend," she continued, leaning her head upon her shapely fingers, "Marianburg is very dull. It is very respectable, but it is exceedingly dull."

"I have always understood," I murmured, "that your majesty's court was a brilliant one."

She yawned.

"If I return to Marianburg," she said, "you shall come and judge for yourself. I will introduce you to the most beautiful women in my country. To look at they are adorable, but for wit, for conversation—well, you will find them nothing but statues. My court reminds me of a wonderful automatic model I once saw. You drop a penny somewhere, behind, and little waxen figures come out and promenade, exchange stiff curtsies and wooden speeches, and bow one by one before their king and queen, whose hands go up and down with the regularity of clockwork. There are times," she continued, speaking in a lower key, "when I have prayed for something of this sort to happen. If it were not for the scandal—well, I should fear nothing."

"It is the scandal, madame," I said, "which we must prevent. My brother would break his heart if you should suffer through his weakness and indiscretion."

She raised her eyebrows and smiled at me.

"And you?"

"Madam," I answered, "I would ask for no greater happiness than to serve you."

I could not keep the admiration from my face and tone, for she was very beautiful and very gracious. She looked away with the smile still lingering upon her lips.

"I wonder," she said, "what news I am most anxious to hear? If those letters are in the hands of enemies, if they are to be given to my husband? well, I shall be a free woman."

"Your freedom," I said, "would be bought at a great price."

She looked at me earnestly.

"My friend," she said, "there is but one life; and if you believe that to be a queen is to be a happy woman, let me tell you that you are very ignorant. Let me tell you this—royalty is the nearest approach to slavery which this century permits. I have felt, oh, many and many a time, that for one hour of real life I would give the rest of my days!"

"Your majesty," I said respectfully, "the price is too great."

She bowed her head.

"What is—is," she murmured. "I shall be none the worse woman if Europe has this story thrown to her scandal-mongers. Really," she continued, with a soft laugh, "it would be amusing. There have been princesses before who have—well, become independent, but a queen—never! Imagine the sensation! The music-halls would bid record prices for me, and great managers would discover that I was a genius, and they would beg me to go on the stage. I—"

"Your majesty "I protested.

She threw me a swift, sweet glance.

"My friend," she said, "forgive me. You are right. Believe me, if I ever did gain my freedom, my feet would never tread any stage, nor should I ever occupy the throne of the *demi-monde*. Would you like me to tell you what I should do?"

"Very much," I answered truthfully.

"I should desire," she said softly, "to disguise myself in some way, so that no one who had known me as I am to-day would recognize me in my new life. I would be perfectly free, and I would have a studio in Paris, so that I might paint when I was in the humour for it; a yacht always ready, so that I might sail when I chose; a cottage in Devonshire, that I might enjoy Nature when I was in the mood; and friends who cared enough for me to come when I summoned them, and leave when I desired it. Ah! when I dream of this, half the dread of the present vanishes."

I rose suddenly to my feet. I had heard a hansom stop at the door.

"It is my brother, madam," I exclaimed. "If you still desire not to meet him, will you come this way?"

She followed me across the hall and into my drawing-room.

"My presence, I trust, does not inconvenience you, Lord Cravon?" she said. "You are, I believe, a bachelor?"

"Your majesty's presence would be an honour in any case," I answered, "and a pleasure. I have the happiness to be unmarried."

She smiled, and sank into an easy chair.

"You will bring me the news?" she said.

"In a very few moments," I answered. "Your majesty—"

She checked me.

"I am Valérie Nevenstein for to-day, if you please," she begged. "If to-morrow I become a queen again, you will call me what you will."

I bowed.

"I am not a courtier," I admitted, "and, with your gracious permission, Mademoiselle Nevenstein will come more easily to me."

"Valérie Nevenstein," she reminded me.

"It is a long name," I said thoughtfully.

She looked up at me and laughed. At that moment I realized that she was really only a girl.

"If you should find it too long," she said softly, "you may choose which half you will."

Reggie's voice was in the hall. I was forced to go.

"There is no name in the world I like so well as —Valérie," I said, with my hand upon the door.

"Very well," she said, smilingly dismissing me; "you have chosen."

I found Reggie, as I had expected, in a state of great excitement. He was walking up and down the room when I entered, muttering to himself. He stopped short at once, trembling all over.

"I believe you knew!" he cried. "You knew who it was!"

I nodded.

"It was Harris, I suppose?"

Reggie sank back into a chair.

"Yes, it was Harris," he declared with a little shudder. "They sent me to Charing Cross Hospital —he had been moved there."

"You did not tell them who he was?"

"No. I simply said that it was not Shalders. Do you suppose that it was Harris whom I followed to England—Harris who stole the letters?"

"I never had the least doubt about it," I answered. "The shooting party was a myth. He came back with or without an accomplice, opened the safe with the Embassy keys, or with a false one, which he could easily have had made. He gagged and chloroformed Shalders, and when he was helpless got him somehow up into the attic. Then he started for England, giving the name of Shalders to put you off the scent. He was followed, of course, by agents of the secret police of Marianburg, and the end of that you know. The all-important question to us is, What had he done with the letters? Now I am beginning to be afraid that he either disposed of them or sent them somewhere through the post from Paris."

"But for what purpose?" Reggie exclaimed. "Granted that he was blackguard enough to steal them, what was his object? What use could they have been to him?"

"As to that," I answered, "I have a theory which I am going to test before I explain it to you. It will take me the rest of the day. How can you occupy yourself?"

"I shall write—to her," he said.

I laid my hand upon his shoulder.

"If I were you, Reggie," I said, "I would employ my time more profitably. If you write to her, I do not think that she will read it."

"What do you mean?" he cried fiercely.

"It is no use being angry," I said. "You will have to face facts. I have had direct communication with her since I have seen you. She will never forgive you!"

He dropped into a chair and covered his face with his hands. He asked no questions. He was, I think, already convinced of her unchanging anger. I laid my hand upon his shoulder.

"Come," I said, a little impatiently, perhaps—almost roughly, "come. You did not seriously intend to drivel away your life, the *cavalière servante* even of a queen. You have offended, and she will not forgive you. In the end you will be glad of it, but for the sake of the past, you owe her something. Don't give way like a girl. See this matter through first. There is just a chance left."

He sat up, pale and red-eyed, and listened to what I had to say.

"I want you," I said, "to describe the packet to me as carefully as you can."

"It is about eight inches square," he said, "quite thin, and it is tied up with white ribbon. The packet itself is of Japanese white silk, stained a good deal with crushed violets. The loose letter was just folded up and slipped underneath the ribbon. There is a ring inside, up in the left hand corner."

I nodded slowly.

"I shall remember that," I said. "Now, Reggie, I shall be away, perhaps, for the rest of the day. I want you to go to the club, and wait there for me. I might want you at any moment, and I want to be sure of finding you."

"Cannot I stay here?" he asked. "I don't want to see a lot of fellows I know."

"No," I answered firmly. "I want you to be at the club, and to show yourself. I want you out of the house, Reggie, in ten minutes."

"You will send for me," he begged, "as soon as you can?"

"As soon as I can—I promise that," I answered. "It may be some time. The longer I am, the greater the chance of success. Remember that, and it will help to pass the time."

Reggie left the house in a few minutes. Then I went back into the drawing-room. My visitor was still there, but she was lying upon the couch, and did not look up at my entrance. I walked softly up to her. Her eyes were closed, her head was thrown back upon the cushions—she was asleep. I walked softly away towards the door, but before I reached it some instinct prompted me to return. I stood looking over her for several minutes. After all, was my brother's infatuation so wonderful a thing? Even here, asleep, and in her travelling clothes, she was a beautiful woman. I could very well believe that, as the central and all-important figure of a brilliant court, she would be almost irresistible.

She woke, and found me looking steadfastly at her. Without any trace of embarrassment she sat up and smiled at me.

"Well," she said, "is there news yet?"

"Of a kind," I answered, "there is news. The man who was murdered at the Hotel Maurice was Leonard Harris."

"What, Sir Henry's secretary?" she exclaimed.

"Yes."

"And the packet?"

"There were no signs of it."

"The young man, Harris," she said to herself softly. "Well, after all, it is the insects who are venomous."

"He had cause, perhaps?" I ventured.

"Oh, I was rude to him once," she interrupted. "He was a boorish young man, and he presumed. But if it was he who stole the packet, I do not see why it was not in his possession."

I sat down by her side. She had moved her skirts in a manner which indicated her desire that I should do so.

"Your majesty," I said, "I fear the natural presumption is that he had parted with them."

"In which case," she remarked, with a look which rebuked my inadvertence, "they are in the hands of my enemies."

"I have," I said hesitatingly, "a vague theory as to what may have become of them. It sounds so far-fetched, and it is in itself so improbable, that I would rather say nothing to you about it for the present. But, with your permission, I will spend the morning testing it."

"You will leave me again so soon?"

She certainly had wonderful eyes. I found it safer to look downwards at the carpet.

"In your service," I murmured, "and with the utmost regret."

"You will be—as quick as possible?"

"You may be sure of it," I answered.

"And am I to remain here until your return?"

"If you will. I shall give you into the charge of my own servant, and will see that you are undisturbed."

I rose from the sofa. She gave me both her hands.

"My friend," she said earnestly, "you are very good to me! Whether I remain a queen or become a woman, I shall not forget it!"

In less than half an hour I was riding slowly down the Row, exchanging the barest greetings with the people whom I knew and carefully avoiding every one likely to detain me. There were a great many on horseback and a crowd of promenaders, but for a long time my search was a fruitless one. I had almost arrived at the conclusion that I must try some other means when, at the corner, I came face to face with two girls riding slowly and followed by a groom. The elder one, dark and moderately handsome, but without any special distinction, bowed to me graciously, and, to her evident surprise, I reined in my horse beside her.

"Good morning, Miss Ogden," I exclaimed, "I was beginning to think that you had given up your morning rides. You were not here yesterday, were you?"

"Yesterday, and the day before, and the day before that," she laughed. "There are so many people, and you seem to know them all!"

"They are a great nuisance sometimes," I remarked. "Don't you think that it is a great mistake to have too many friends?"

She shook her head. "Perhaps. My sister and I are not troubled in that way, are we, Carrie?"

The younger girl agreed, a little dolefully. I leaned over in my saddle.

"Won't you introduce me to your sister?" I asked.

Miss Ogden did so at once.

"Yesterday," she remarked, "you were riding with the Countess of Appleton. I think that if I were a man and riding with the Countess of Appleton, I should not see any one else. She is very beautiful, is she not?"

"She is my cousin, so I am scarcely a fair judge," I remarked, turning my horse. "May I come with you a little way?"

She was surprised, but frankly acquiescent. I had the advantage of belonging to a set of which they were not members, and my offer, therefore, especially as my acquaintance with Miss Ogden was of the slightest, was obviously welcome. I had danced with her a few nights ago to oblige a worried hostess, and had found her a pleasant, sensible girl.

She did not hesitate, as we rode slowly down under the trees, to admit their somewhat doubtful social position.

"It is quite interesting for us to be with some one who knows everybody," she remarked. "You see, this is only our second season, and until this year we never had a house in town. I suppose that is one reason why we know so few people outside the political set. Politicians may be useful creatures, but they are not amusing."

I laughed softly. Sir James Ogden was a politician who had worked his way up from the ranks. He had been a provincial manufacturer, mayor of his city three times, and knighted for a liberal entertainment of royalty. He had gone into Parliament, and, with the aid of a fluent tongue and a large business capacity, had worked his way into office. His methods were not altogether to the liking of his party, and he was yet to a certain extent unproven. But, on the whole, his success had been remarkable.

Unfortunately, he had married early in life, and his social prospects were hampered by a good-natured but uneducated wife. As usual, it was the daughters who suffered. London was a fascinating but unknown world to them, and there was no one to be their sponsor.

I rode slowly down between the two girls, receiving a good many surprised salutations, and doing my best to make myself agreeable— a task which, under the circumstances, was not difficult. They fully expected, as I could see, that I should leave them in a minute or two; but I did nothing of the sort. I answered my cousin's imperious little movement of her whip with a bland smile and an indifferent wave of my hat, thereby offending her grievously, and remained with them until the people began to thin off. Then, as we were walking our horses and talking under the trees, a stout, red-faced old lady rose up from a chair and waved to us. Miss Ogden's cheek flushed, but she reined in her horse at once.

"It is my mother," she remarked. "I quite forgot that she was looking out for us. I am afraid that we must go to her."

"By all means," I answered cheerfully. "By the bye, I have not the pleasure of knowing Lady Ogden. Won't you present me?"

"With pleasure," she answered readily. "Come, Carrie."

We rode up to the railings, and I was formally introduced. Lady Ogden was flustered but good natured. As it happened, nothing could have been more fortunate for me than this meeting. Lady Ogden was nothing if not hospitable, and before we had exchanged half a dozen words I was asked to luncheon. The two girls exchanged glances of resigned dismay, which speedily changed to surprise when I at once accepted the invitation. In a few minutes we rode off together again with Lady Ogden's carriage close behind.

I am free to confess that my behaviour that morning was the behaviour of a snob. Regarded from a certain point of view, it was inexcusable; yet, under similar circumstances, I know that I should do precisely the same again. I traded upon my position with the object of ingratiating myself with Lady Ogden and her daughters. I promised them cards for certain forthcoming events (a promise, by the bye, which was faithfully kept), and I was able to give them a good many useful hints and information with regard to their new position, its possibilities and obligations. I am quite sure that my luncheon at their house that day was regarded, both by Lady Ogden and her daughters, as the most important event which had happened to them since their arrival in London; and if to a certain extent I allowed them to be deceived as to my motives, I have at least made a very full atonement. The present social position of Lady Ogden and her family is largely owing to my efforts; and if Miss Louise looks a little reproachfully at me in the Park, when for several mornings I fail to speak to her, she is at least frankly grateful for the services which I have rendered them. Further, Lady Ogden can always rely upon me for one of her dinners; and nothing would induce me to be absent from any social function at her house to which I am bidden. I have been to a certain extent their good angel, and there are now very few houses in London which are not open to Lady Ogden and her daughters. Still, I fancy that none of them—except Sir James, who will keep his own counsel—have ever quite understood that morning. And beyond the fact that I have striven so hard to atone for my abuse of their first act of hospitality, there was my motive—strong enough surely to make a man unscrupulous. There was always before me the remembrance of my brother's white face, and the image of the woman who waited for my final effort. A queen to-day, tomorrow, if I failed, an outcast. No! I behaved like a cad, but I am only thankful for the inspiration which suggested this forlorn hope.

Luncheon was prolonged to its utmost limits. I talked to interest Lady Ogden and her daughters, and I succeeded. Sir James listened with a somewhat forced air of attention, but on the whole I could see that my presence also gratified him. He professed to be too busy, to have no tastes for society; but it was easy to see that as an ambitious man he was annoyed and irritated to find himself so small a figure here, and his social pretensions ignored, after his provincial triumphs. Evidently he had been told to make himself specially agreeable to me; he did his best, but, during luncheon at least, he had but little opportunity. The girls were really bright and naturally well-bred. They talked by no means badly, and we found plenty to say.

After luncheon, which was protracted as long as possible, Sir James proposed a cigar and cup of coffee in his room. I took my leave of the ladies, and followed him into the library.

"I have just one hour which I can call my own," he remarked, wheeling out a chair for me. "As a rule it is the only idle one of my day. I am old fashioned enough to enjoy my luncheon more than my dinner."

A servant brought liqueurs and coffee, and Sir James produced some cigars and cigarettes. I helped myself, and, whilst I sipped my coffee, looked around the room curiously. On the table was a black dispatch-box. Sir James, with a word of apology to me, took a bunch of keys from his pocket, and opened it. The match with which I was lighting my cigarette went out in my fingers, and my heart gave a quick beat. I was right then! A strong odour of crushed violets floated out into the room.

Sir James looked steadily into the box for several moments, with a faint smile on his lips. Then he carefully pushed it a little further back upon the table, and, lighting a cigar, stretched himself out in an easy chair opposite to mine. He began to talk at once on different subjects. Without being in any sense of the word a politician, I had made several speeches in the House of Lords upon subjects interesting to me, one of which had provoked considerable discussion. Sir James and I, being of the same party, our conversation naturally drifted into political channels. A chance remark from Sir James very soon gave the opening I desired. As carefully as possible I led the conversation up to the subject of our relations with a certain foreign power.

"If I were a genuine politician," I remarked—"that is to say, if I possessed the requisite ability to become one—I should be interested more than anything in foreign affairs. Diplomacy has always been a very fascinating study to me, although, of course, I have had no experience, and am ignorant even of its rudimentary principles. By the way, I was interested in what I heard last week—you can guess where—about a treaty with the power in question. There are some peculiar complications, are there not?"

"There have been some very peculiar complications and some unusual difficulties," Sir James remarked, smoking his cigar with evident relish, and gazing, with the ghost of a smile still upon his lips, into the depths of the open dispatch-box by his side.

"Well, it is a pity," I remarked. "The advantages of the treaty to us are very obvious just now. Is it permitted to ask you—unofficially—whether the difficulties are insuperable?"

Sir James removed the cigar from his mouth. He leaned a little forward; I could see that he was about to become confidential.

"The whole history of our negotiations will never become known," he said. "The fact is, a certain royal personage, whom I need not name to you, was very much opposed indeed to the signing of the treaty. All along we have had to contend with a strong antagonism from—after all, I do not see why I should conceal it from you—from the queen."

"The queen," I repeated; "I did not know that her majesty was a politician! One hears of her chiefly as a European beauty, and a giver of magnificent entertainments."

"I can assure you that her majesty is underrated," Sir James replied grimly. "She has had her finger on the weak spot in the treaty from the first. If the matter rested with her, it would have been torn in two long ago. Her influence, as you may be aware, is great, and while it remains so our relations are liable at any moment be become strained. It is one of those things which we have always had to contend with, of which the public know nothing at all, and for which, of course, they make no allowance."

"The public are hard taskmasters," I remarked; "I often wonder that they are so zealously and faithfully served. By the bye, Sir James, I noticed that you used the past tense. Is there any chance, do you think, of getting the treaty signed in the face of such opposition?"

There was a distinctly triumphant smile upon Sir James' thin, hard lips, as he glanced into the depths of the dispatch-box. It was standing at his elbow, and he had been carelessly playing with the lid. The perfume of violets, faint and sweet, seemed to be filling the room.

"The treaty will be signed within a few days now," he said quietly. "I do not think that we shall ever again have any trouble in that quarter. Of course, you will understand that I do not wish this to go any further at present; but, speaking to you in confidence, I may say that means have come into our hands which will put a summary end now and for ever to the opposition I spoke of. I cannot say more, even to you, at present; but the whole affair will be public property before long."

I leaned back in my chair, and nerved myself for what was to come. I had learned all that I needed to know. This was the climax.

"I trust not," I said slowly.

Sir James let fall the lid of his dispatch-box with a bang, and looked up at me in amazement.

"I beg your pardon," he said; "I think that I do not quite understand."

"I repeat that I trust not," I said. "The means to which you allude"—I looked hard into the dispatch-box—"are means of which no use must be made."

Sir James drew a bunch of keys from his pocket, and calmly double-locked the dispatch-box. Then he rose to his feet, and turned a frowning face upon me.

"I am completely at a loss to understand you, Lord Cravon," he said coldly. "Be so good as to explain yourself."

"I am here to do so," 1 answered firmly. "I am here for no other purpose. The means to which you allude are these. You have obtained possession of compromising letters, written by a certain personage to my brother, Reginald Lessingham."

"To—your brother?"

"Yes. You have probably overlooked the fact, Sir James, that my family name is Lessingham; and it is my brother, Reginald Lessingham, who is the senior attaché at Marianburg."

"The fact," Sir James remarked, "was unknown to me. I may add that it is also a matter of indifference. If the young gentleman has been imprudent, as he certainly appears to have been, he must accept the consequences."

"He is perfectly willing to do so," I answered. "At present that is not the point. Those letters to which you have referred, made public, would be the ruin of any woman, even a queen. You propose to make them public, and to ruin her! It is very simple. You are a patriot and a politician, and you would rise one step higher in the estimation of your party upon the wreck of a woman's honour."

There was a bright light in Sir James' grey eyes, a flush upon his cheeks. The lines upon his face had contracted and hardened. He remained cool, but he was desperately angry.

"Continue, sir."

"Diplomacy might sanction your use of these letters in such a case, Sir James," I proceeded, "if they had come into your hands by other means."

"You seem to be remarkably well informed, Lord Cravon. Can you tell me then exactly how I did receive them?"

"I believe so," I replied. "They were either sent you from Paris, or brought to you by a young man, named Harris, a distant connexion of your own, and one of the Embassy secretaries at Marianburg. Now I know you be an honest as well as a shrewd politician, Sir James, and I am perfectly sure that you have been misled as to how these letters came into young Harris' possession."

"He found—never mind, I will hear what you have to say first, Lord Cravon."

"You are wise, Sir James. He probably assured you that he found them. He did not. His zeal in your service led him further than that. He, or an accomplice, chloroformed and gagged my brother's servant, and abstracted these letters from his private safe, opened with the

Embassy keys. In other words, he committed a gross and criminal burglary. It is in your interests that I bring this information, Sir James. I think you will admit that such methods are a little in front of the times; that they are, to say the least of it, not defensible."

Sir James resumed his seat. His hard, worn face was puckered up with thought. He was silent for several moments. I could see that I was correct in my supposition. What I had just revealed was news to him. Harris' story had been a different one!

"My nephew's conduct," he said, looking up at last, "was indiscreet and exceedingly ill-advised. If necessary, he must answer for it. I cannot shield him, nor should I attempt to do so. At the same time the violence that was offered was within the walls of our own Embassy. That is the crux of the matter. I admit that the means were deplorable, but the end which has been gained is great. I am sorry for your brother, Lord Cravon, on whose behalf I suppose you are here; but in the face of the great national gain, the welfare of individuals must go to the wall. I shall hold to my course."

"Think well, Sir James," I said. "I have many powerful friends, and, however much I may blame my brother for his folly, I am with him in this to the end. I shall not let the matter drop. The story will get about. Our methods will be decried throughout the whole civilized world. You must admit that the letters were stolen. With this knowledge, shall you dare to use them?"

"I am ignorant of the fact that they were stolen," Sir James answered coolly. "I have no cognizance of it. It is not necessary. The letters are here. As an officer of the State, I owe no one any explanation as to how they reached me. I have not investigated, or discovered any theft. Such work belongs to the Secret Service Department. I hold the letters for my purpose, and you will pardon my adding that I have no more to say to you, Lord Cravon."

He laid his hand upon the bell, but I checked him.

"Then prepare yourself for a further shock, Sir James," I said. "Last night your nephew paid the penalty for his over-zealousness. He was murdered by an agent of the Secret Police of Marianburg at the Hotel Maurice."

Sir James had sunk back into his chair, pale to the lips. It was I now who was standing. I took a newspaper from the library table and showed it to him.

"There is a full account of the affair, Sir James," I said. "I am very sorry to shock you, but you left me no alternative."

He took the paper from my hand with trembling fingers. Suddenly a little exclamation broke from his lips.

"The name is Shalders," he exclaimed. "My nephew's name is Harris. This has nothing to do with him."

"It has everything to do with him," I answered gravely. "Shalders is the name of my brother's valet, who was chloroformed and maltreated at the Embassy. Your nephew took his name, and even dressed to resemble him, when he left Marianburg. When I read that paragraph, I knew at once who the unfortunate man was. My brother went to the Charing Cross Hospital this morning and identified him. There is no room for any doubt in the matter."

"It was—?"

"It was your nephew, Leonard Harris, Sir James. He took the name of Shalders when he left for England, and he intended to keep his visit here a profound secret from every one in Marianburg. He had laid his plans well. He had a fortnight's leave of absence from his chief, and he was supposed to be in the country on a shooting expedition. Unfortunately for him, he was matched against a Secret Service which is perhaps the finest in the world. He had, after all, scarcely a chance. He was doomed from the moment he left Marianburg!"

Sir James rose to his feet. He had regained his composure, but he was evidently shaken. I made a final effort.

"You have those letters," I said. "Good! Now ask yourself what they have cost you! First of all a burglary with violence; then a life—the life of your own nephew. If they had been secretly stolen, and the thief was unknown, I admit that you might have used them safely. As it is, I warn you that to use them is to terminate, once and for ever, your career as a politician. We do not live in the days of Richelieu, or Mazarin. Such methods as have been used in this matter will never be tolerated in this country, or by international opinion."

"It is impossible to connect me in any way with my nephew's blundering," he answered. "I was not the instigator, or the abettor. All I know is, that these letters were placed in my hands, and it is my duty to use them for the benefit of my country. Of their history I am completely ignorant. I shall certainly not give them up."

"Very well, Sir James," I declared, "your refusal leaves me but one alternative. I have an audience with the premier at four o'clock. It is now within a few minutes of that hour. I shall go to him, tell him all I know, and get him to wire orders that the seals which I have already had placed on your nephew's belongings are not disturbed until a special envoy has been through his correspondence. You may not have been his instigator! That is to be proved. In any case, Sir James, your resignation will be demanded within the next twenty-four hours."

Sir James walked to the window, and came back again. Slowly he drew from his pocket a bunch of keys, and unlocked the dispatch-box. With the little packet in his hand he lingered even now, as though loth to part with it. Then with a slight bow he handed it to me across the table, and the perfume of crushed violets had never seemed to me so sweet before.

"You are quite right, Lord Cravon," he said drily. "My position is untenable. Present those letters to your brother, with my most profound apologies for the manner in which they came into my hands. You can understand the reluctance with which I part with them; but I would like to assure you of this, I simply advised my poor nephew from time to time that any means of weakening the Queen's influence would be grateful to me, and would tend to his own advancement. Such means as he adopted were utterly unsanctioned by me. The limit of my instigation I have told you. In justice to myself, I desire to make it clear. Permit me to ring for your carriage."

Our leave-takings were not cordial. Sir James remained standing upon his hearth-rug in grim silence, with the empty dispatch-box before him. I drove swiftly homewards, and hastened into the library. Reggie was sitting there waiting for me, and, when I held out the box to him, he gave a great cry, and tore it open with passionate haste.

"They are all there?" I asked.

"Every one," he sobbed. "Every one! Thank God."

I left him watching a smouldering mass of ashes, fearful lest even a single line which could ever be deciphered should remain. Then I went to her. She rose to meet me, and her face, too, was drawn with emotion.

"Your majesty," I said, bowing low. "You have but half an hour to catch the boat train."

She drew a long breath. There was a look in her face which I have never forgotten, but which I have never understood. Only it seemed to me rather the look of the woman who bows her head once more to step back into the stone cell of a nunnery, after a little wandering in the rose gardens of life.

"You have succeeded?" she asked in a low tone.

"Your majesty," I answered, "has no longer any cause for uneasiness. The letters by this time are ashes."

She took my hands in hers, and held them tightly.

"My Lord Cravon," she said sweetly," may every woman in distress find a cavalier so generous and so wise as yourself!"

I felt a burning spot upon my hands, the delicate perfume of a woman's hair brushed against my cheek, the rustling of a silken gown swept the floor. I heard the door close, and I knew that she was gone.

A week later Reggie tossed me an evening paper. I glanced at the paragraph to which he pointed.

"The Opera House at Marianburg was on Monday night one of the most magnificent spectacles of the season. The royal box was occupied by the king and queen and a brilliant suite. Her majesty, who wore black velvet and diamonds, has never appeared more beautiful, and was certainly the most distinguished-looking woman in the house. Amongst others who were present we noticed, etc., etc."

"I wonder," Reggie said, "if she knows how much she owes you?"

I lit a cigarette, and looked thoughtfully through the wreath of blue smoke.

"I wonder if she does," I answered thoughtfully.

## THE AMBASSADOR'S DILEMMA

The Ambassador looked at me and I looked at the Ambassador. It was not by any means the first pause in an exceedingly awkward conversation.

"You see," he remarked, suavely, "you also are concerned in this affair. I am glad to observe that you contrive to retain your cheerfulness, but I am bound to point out the fact that—diplomatically, at any rate—you are in a parlous state."

I assumed as lugubrious an expression as possible and ventured to contest his point of view.

"I don't exactly see—" I began, but he stopped me.

"Perhaps not. I will explain. If I am—what shall we say?—removed, my First Secretary will certainly go with me. He is supposed to be equally to blame when anything goes wrong; he shares the reward when a small triumph is gained. Now, you are my First Secretary, Hamblin, and we are in no end of a mess; in your own interests I should recommend you to bestir yourself."

I drew a little breath. If I had not been in a way attached to my chief, I should certainly have used it for a different purpose. As Sir George had remarked, we were certainly in no end of a mess, but it was he himself and alone who had landed us there.

"If you could suggest any way, sir, in which I could be of the slightest use," I remarked deprecatingly, "nothing would give me more pleasure. Unfortunately, we seem to be sitting down before a great wall; it's too high to climb, and there's no way round."

"A very charming simile," Sir George said dryly. "Nevertheless, if you don't get over, yourself, or help me to, you won't marry my daughter."

I came to the conclusion promptly that Sir George was an unreasonable and disagreeable old man; but I kept my conviction to myself.

"I hope you will reconsider that, sir," I said most respectfully. "I am very fond of Clara, and I think she cares a little for me."

"Work for her, then," was the prompt answer. "Here's your chance. Get us out of this wretched muddle, and you shall have her—as soon as she likes!"

I pondered. I was very fond of Clara. I began to wish that the situation were not so hopeless. Sir George took up his penholder and marked time with it.

"The affair," he said, "lies in a nutshell; it is as simple as A B C."

"Oh, it's simple enough," I assented—"painfully simple!"

"England," the Ambassador continued, ignoring my interruption, "is at war with the Transvaal Republic. Last week there appeared in an issue of a foreign newspaper what purports to be an interview between the monarch of this country and the European representative of the Transvaal Republic. The interview—or, let us say, purported interview—you have read yourself. It is sufficient to remark that, if it was authentic, it was tantamount to a declaration of war against England. Now, you know what an artful old beggar Highbury is! He sends me across by Queen's messenger two sealed dispatches for the Emperor, addressed to him privately. One is marked 'A,' the other 'B.' Now, if the interview had been genuine, I was to have dealt the first blow by presenting 'B,' which is tantamount to an ultimatum couched in most formal and war-like language. If, on the other hand, its authenticity is denied, I present 'A,' which is a friendly little note assuring his Majesty that no notice was taken in England of what was obviously a ridiculous *canard*. You know, of course, what has happened."

"The Emperor has denied the whole story contemptuously from beginning to end," I remarked. "The Transvaal representative was never accorded an interview."

Sir George flourished the penholder with new vigour.

"Precisely. I accordingly left at the Palace the letter marked 'A,' and, returning here, proceeded to open and destroy letter 'B.' I read it first, and to my horror found that its contents were as per specification of letter 'A,' and that consequently the lettering must have been wrong, and the ultimatum left at the Palace."

"I don't quite see where we are to blame, you know," I interposed.

"Perhaps not," my chief remarked dryly. "You see, you are very young. But there is an axiom in diplomacy which you will do well to lay to heart. If anything goes wrong at your charge, no matter who is to blame, you are responsible. Those letters have been changed by spies, most likely, and I think I know who is at the bottom of it. It was probably done while they were in the possession of the Queen's messenger—he admits that he took no extra precautions. That is of no consequence. It is upon us that the blame will fall. There awaits for the Emperor a letter which will either plunge us into a ruinous, unnecessary, and unpopular war, or else will mean Highbury's resignation, our retirement to a Colony, and a most awful climb-down."

"The Emperor," I remarked, "is still at Meritzburg—manoeuvering?"

"Yes. He returns to-morrow. To-morrow night that letter will be handed to him."

"You're sure it hasn't been sent on to him?"

"Certain. I happen to know that his commands were most absolute. Nothing was to be forwarded. Von Butz has the letter, and knows its contents."

"Sure of that?" I ventured.

Sir George tossed an evening paper over to me.

"You see what the beast is doing," he said. "Strange rumour at the barracks, all-night work at the arsenals, mysterious notices to railway companies. It all means one thing—mobilisation."

"Von Butz has read the letter by fair means or foul. The Emperor will receive it in person to-morrow night. The letter awaits him at Von Butz's house," I remarked thoughtfully.

"Marvellous!" Sir George remarked with sarcasm. "You have the insight of a Mazarin."

One must put up with sarcasm from one's prospective father-in-law, especially when he is in as tight a place as Sir George undoubtedly was. I had sufficient magnanimity to ignore it.

"Have you made any effort to regain possession of the letter?" I asked.

Sir George shook his head.

"I might as well try to fly," he said, "as attempt to regain possession of it by fair means. Von Butz is our enemy and the enemy of our country. All the ill-feeling and friction of the last few years has been his making and his alone. This letter is the summit of his desire. In the light of the Emperor's frank and downright statement, it is nothing more nor less than a brutal insult. I cannot imagine any apologies which could possibly be offered sufficient to atone for it. It will mean war for England and the Colonies for us."

"If the Emperor reads it," I remarked softly.

"If the Emperor reads it," Sir George repeated, looking over at me.

I buried my face in my hands and tried to think. There came a knock at the door and a telegraphic dispatch. Sir George fetched out the code-book with shaking fingers. He groaned as he read it out.

"Understand mobilization secretly commended. Panic on Stock Exchange owing to rumours from Badenberg. Presume you only delivered letter 'A.' What does it mean? Have you blundered? Reply.
"HIGHBURY"

"We haven't much time, have we?" I remarked. "Let us make the most of it."

"How?"

I took up my pen and the code-book, and wrote a telegram.

"To HIGHBURY, Downing St., London.
"Discredit all rumours. Mobilization ridiculous. All quiet here. Duly delivered letter 'A.' Probably Stock Exchange rig. Will request audience to-morrow. "

"We'll start boldly, at any rate," I said, rising. "Send this, and I will be back in an hour."

"Where are you going?" Sir George asked.

"To call on Fräulein von Butz," I answered.

Youth is dauntless and excitement is sweet. So I walked through the broad, sunlit streets of Badenberg with a smiling face, a cigarette of delicate flavour between my lips, and tried to persuade myself that it was not a forlorn hope upon which I had embarked. In my pocket was letter 'A,' which should have been marked 'B,' in my right hand a fragrant bunch of Neapolitan violets, whose faint, sweet perfume had stolen out to me from a florist's shop in the Avenue. As I passed up the broad steps of the mansion where Von Butz lived, the Fates did me a good turn. The door before me opened and Fräulein von Butz came out, dressed for driving.

I bowed low and held out the flowers.

"A farewell gift, Fräulein," I said sadly. "You will deign to accept them, I hope!"

She held out her hands, and her bright smile of welcome changed to a look of interrogation.

"I will accept them," she said, "with very much pleasure, and I thank you indeed for thinking of me. But why a farewell gift, Mr. Hamblin? Are you going away on leave again?"

I shook my head sorrowfully.

"It is no matter of leave, dear Fräulein," I said. "I am quitting the

Service. I should have left to-day, but I wanted to say good-bye to you."

She turned back into the hall.

"Come inside," she said. "I do not understand."

I heard her instruct the hall-porter to send back the carriage. She led me into her own tiny sitting-room, as neat and dainty as herself, and motioned me to an easy-chair. She sat down close to me and loosened the furs from her neck.

"You are giving up the Service," she said, "you are leaving Badenberg! Is it not very sudden, Mr. Hamblin?"

"It has come upon me," I said gloomily, "like a thunderclap."

"You shall tell me," she insisted, raising her bright eyes to mine, "all about it. Have you come into the title, is your heath bad, or are you promoted?"

I was silent for a moment. It was silence which told. Then I shook my head.

"Fräulein," I said, "when I have gone you will hear from others what I would rather tell you myself. I have longed for this opportunity, yet now it has come—it is not easy!"

Her piquant little face was full of sympathy. By accident my hand fell upon the arm of her chair and touched her fingers. She drew them away—slowly.

"Fräulein," I said, "there is one profession in the world in which a single mistake is fatal. That profession unfortunately is, or was, mine—and that mistake—I have made."

"Oh!" she cried.

It was enough. My humiliation now required no pretence. It came naturally to me. I felt that I was a cad.

"Won't you tell me a little more?" she begged. "I am so very sorry for you—and sorry that you are going away."

Her hand once more fell upon the arm of her chair. Never were fingers more soft and velvety to the touch.

"Fräulein," I said, "if I may tell you, I will. I should like you to know the truth. It is this. Two letters were entrusted to me, one of which was to be delivered to the Emperor, the other destroyed. I delivered—to your father, as it happens—the wrong one."

She was perplexed.

"Is that all?" she asked.

I nodded.

"The action," I said, "is a small one—but the result is terrible."

"Terrible?"

"It is too weak a word," I assented. "Do you know what war means, Fräulein?"

She shuddered.

"Do not speak of it!" she begged.

"You will hear it spoken of before long, Fräulein," I said; "and, alas! I shall be the unhappy cause. War between your country and mine! It is fearful!"

I am afraid my fingers tightened upon hers. I am sure that the pressure was returned.

"The letter you spoke of," she asked—"has the Emperor received it yet?"

"Not yet," I answered; "your father has it. The Emperor returns to-morrow night."

She leaned forward, suddenly pale.

"He returns to-night!" she exclaimed. "Only an hour ago my father had a telegram from him."

"To-night or to-morrow night," I muttered—"what matters? The letter has gone from my hands beyond recovery; he opens it, reads, and war is as certain as to-morrow's sun. Oh, it is enough to make a man mad to think of it! War between the two nations who have brought the science of killing to perfection! It will be the greatest massacre the world has ever known, and the everlasting shame of it will be upon my head."

"Don't," she cried—"please don't!"

I drew myself up.

"At least, Fräulein," I said gently and with real tenderness, "I have no right to come here and make you miserable. Only I could not go away without seeing you and asking you to sometimes remember—a most unfortunate man!"

I stretched out my hand for my hat. She stopped me.

"No, no," she cried; "sit still! Let me think."

I watched the colour come and go from her cheeks. She pushed back the pretty fringe from her forehead. Ah, Gertrud von Butz, you wrote the memory of your dainty little self into my heart for ever in those few minutes!

She turned toward me.

"What if the letter were destroyed?" she asked slowly.

"It is impossible," I answered, with thumping heart.

"But if it were?"

"There would be no war," I said. "There would be no disgrace for me; I should remain in Badenberg. But it is impossible!"

"Should you know it if you saw it?" she asked.

"Of course."

She rose up.

"Come with me," she said. "Do not speak. If we meet my father it will be a convent for me. You must do what seems best to you."

She was as pale as a sheet, but she walked firmly and without hesitation. As we crossed the hall where several servants were standing she turned to me.

"Your own conservatories," she said, "are so much more beautiful. But there, you shall judge."

We turned off down a long passage. At the end was a conservatory, but she paused and listened at the last door on the right. It was empty. She turned the handle. We passed inside. She took a bunch of keys from her pocket and unlocked a cabinet which stood in the centre of the room. A pile of letters were there. My head swam with joy.

"Quick," she whispered. "Ah! We are lost. It is my father."

I dashed at the letters, seized a handful, but dropped them again as the lid of the cabinet fell upon my wrist. She whirled me across the room, behind a curtain into a long *annexe* to the conservatory. I could have cried with the disappointment. But for her sake I would have rushed out and torn the letter to pieces before Von Butz's eyes. Gertrud came close to me. I passed my arm round her waist; she was trembling violently.

Voices approached, and footsteps. The door of the room opened. Through the crack in the curtain I saw Von Butz enter, and my heart stood still. For behind him came a tall, familiar figure in a brilliant uniform partially covered by a long military cloak.

"And now, Von Butz, the letter at once," he exclaimed brusquely.

"Your Majesty shall have it," was the quiet answer, as Von Butz produced his keys. "When you have read it, you will say that I have done well in starting the great engine which your Majesty has constructed with such marvellous and wonderful forethought."

There was a moment's pause. Then I saw the letter pass into the Emperor's hands.

"You yourself, Von Butz," I heard him say, "are well acquainted with the contents?"

"My secret agents," Von Butz answered, "ever keen in the service of the Fatherland, borrowed it from the Queen's messenger and brought me a copy. We have saved hours which are worth millions."

The Emperor broke the seal. He stood up and a fierce light burned in his eyes.

"Von Butz," he said, "you will be my witness that these things which are to come are of God's ordination, not mine. With the finest army in the world, trained and brought to perfection under my own care and governance, I, the certain master of this great continent from the firing of the first guns of battle, have ever refrained from violence or provocation. With the warlike spirit of my forefathers in my veins, I have yet held out to all nations the olive branch instead of the iron grip. History must acknowledge this. Though I am all-conquering and almighty, I have yet been slow to strike. You will remember this, Von Butz."

"Always, your Majesty."

The Emperor tore open the letter and bent over it with serene forehead and expectant eyes. He read, frowned, re-read, and flung it passionately upon the table. He turned upon Von Butz with a fury which was paralysing.

"Dolt! Fool!" he cried. "You have been tricked! You have made me a laughing-stock! You have betrayed the nation!"

"Your Majesty," Von Butz faltered, "the copy I sent you was a faithful one. My agent copied it himself in the express."

"Listen, then," cried the Emperor.

He read out letter 'A.'

I walked home, my nerves tingling with excitement, relieved, but very puzzled. Sir George called me into the study immediately I arrived.

"Hamblin," he said, in an airy manner, "I'm afraid you have been disturbing yourself about a mare's nest!"

"Oh, indeed!" I found breath to say.

Sir George, nodded and tapped an open letter with his finger.

"It seems," he continued, "that Bucknell, the messenger, is rather a smart fellow. He found out that his dispatches had been tampered with, so wired Highbury for instructions. Immediately he received them he destroyed letter 'B' and duplicated 'A.' The duplication was to catch the thief, if possible, and I should imagine that it did."

"I should think so, too," I answered, smiling.

"One word more," Sir George said, coughing and assuming his most dignified deportment. "With regard to Clara, I have talked to her seriously, and found her, as I expected, amenable to reason. You are both too young to think of marriage, and an engagement does not seem to us desirable. In short, we have other views for Clara."

I drew a long breath—not of despair, but of resignation. That night, at the Russian Embassy, I sat out four dances with Gertrud von Butz.

# THE MAN WHOM NOBODY LIKED

He came into their midst unexpectedly, apparently unconscious of the sudden silence which seemed designed to act as a barrier between him and them. He only smiled—a little malevolently, it is true, but still with some sense of humour. He dragged a chair across the lawn and seated himself in a cool place within a yard or so of his hostess.

"How very enterprising of you, Mr. Lyndham!" she murmured, lifting her parasol a little on one side, and inwardly rebelling against her husband's express instructions to be always civil to this man. "Have you walked all the way from Broom Hill in this sun?"

He assented, but without speech. His gesture was of the slightest. Really his manners were worse than brusque. Mrs. Poynton languidly ordered some fresh tea and turned her shoulder upon the newcomer. He had come without invitation upon an afternoon of some importance—he should entertain himself. There were limits to her tolerance, obedient wife though she was.

So the conversation ebbed and flowed around him. Everyone followed their hostess's lead and made no attempt to draw him into it. Yet never was a casual visitor so little upset by the subtle but unmistakable rudeness of being ignored. He drank his tea absently, and notwithstanding his isolation, he made no movement to depart.

"My dear Eleanor," Lady Martyn whispered to her hostess, "what an extraordinary man! Is he a specimen of your country neighbours? I thought the people were quite decent round here."

Mrs. Poynton gently elevated her shoulders.

"Heaven only knows who or what he is!" she murmured. "We none of us like him except my husband, and you know how anything unusual attracts him."

"But where does he come from? Is he a neighbour?"

"His name is Lyndham, and he has taken a cottage a few miles away. No one seems to have an idea who or what he is, and he is most uncommunicative. He seems to spend most of his time walking in the grounds here and staring up at the house."

"A gentleman—but how uncouth!" Lady Martyn declared under her breath.

Mrs. Poynton looked sideways at him through the lace which drooped from her parasol. There was disparagement, but a certain amount of curiosity in her stealthy gaze. Mr. Lyndham wore old clothes, his beard was ill-trimmed, his necktie a subterfuge. But, after all, perhaps Lady Martyn was right. There was a certain air of breeding about the man, and his voice had the unmistakable quality which attracts. She lowered her parasol again.

"Why he comes here," she said softly—"especially whilst my husband is away—I cannot imagine. No one is civil to him, and he very seldom speaks to anybody. He asked Arthur for permission to walk in the grounds, and since then he seems to haunt the place. I met him one evening striding along the avenue and muttering to himself. I must have passed within a yard of him, and he took not the slightest notice. I was almost frightened to death."

"Your husband was always so good-natured," Lady Martyn yawned. "By the by, how about the lease?"

"Arthur has gone up to see the solicitors," Mrs. Poynton answered. "They do not seem to be able to get any reply from Sir Gervase. I don't think they even know where he is, and they have no power of attorney."

Lady Martyn looked across the terraced lawn to the long, ivy-covered front of the house.

"I hope you do not lose it," she said.

"There isn't another place like it in the county. Isn't it almost time she came?"

Mrs. Poynton leaned forward in her chair.

"I believe," she said, "that I can hear the carriage."

From where they sat, the lower of three terraced lawns, cool with the quivering shade of dark cedar trees, one could see the long approach to the Abbey, a mile of straight white road leading through a parklike expanse of meadowland, yellow always at this time of the year with buttercups and clumps of marigolds. Mrs. Poynton rose to her feet, and there was as much excitement in her manner as a well-bred woman would permit herself to entertain.

"The Princess is coming," she announced.

Only her unwelcome visitor sat still. Everyone else stood up to catch a glimpse of the victoria, now plainly visible. Mrs. Poynton glanced at this man, whom nobody liked, almost with aversion. He represented the one alien note in the little party of immaculately flannelled men, and women in all the glory of muslin gowns and flower-garlanded hats. He ought to have the good sense to go before the arrival of the Princess. He must understand that his appearance and strange humours were in ill accord with a gathering such as this. But Mr. Lyndham did not move. His arms were folded, his eyes were fixed on vacancy. He seemed to have passed into a world of his own creation—obviously a very rude thing to do. Apparently he was not even contemplating an early departure.

He had manners enough to rise, however, when the Princess, seeing them all gathered under the cedar tree, stopped the carriage and came smiling across the lawn to them. A trifle grave-eyed, perhaps, and a little wary, she still justified easily the extravagant praises of a too personal Press. In her white lace dress and parasol, without a vestige of color, her pallor seemed to speak of a fatigue not wholly physical. Yet it was impossible to deny her beauty.

In the midst of a little buzz of introductions, she found herself suddenly face to face with Lyndham, whom Mrs. Poynton had no idea at all of mentioning. In those few seconds of breathless silence which intervened before she held out her hand, there flashed backwards and forwards between the two, nameless things. She, if possible, was a little paler, and her admirable self-possession faltered. He, too, seemed to be struggling for self-control.

"I may be permitted to recall myself to your memory, Princess," he said, looking at her steadily. "My name is Lyndham—Richard Lyndham. May I hope that I am not quite forgotten?"

She held out her hand.

"One does not forget one's oldest friends," she said softly. "I am very glad to see you again, Mr. Lyndham."

Her hostess led her away. The Princess of Berlitz was a personage, even if her husband's estates had lain far away in a corner of Austria; and the suite of rooms into which Mrs. Poynton herself conducted her had once been occupied by royalty. Tea and fruit were ready on a tiny table in the sitting-room. Beyond in the bedroom a couple of maids were already busy unpacking. Mrs. Poynton looked around, and the stream of idle words which had been passing between the two stopped.

"I wonder," she said, "if there is anything else I can do for you?"

The Princess hesitated.

"Yes," she said, "there is something else. I should be glad if I could speak for a few minutes with Mr. Lyndham up here."

Mrs. Poynton was taken aback. She stared blankly at her guest.

"With Mr. Lyndham?" she repeated vaguely.

The Princess bowed.

"Yes."

Mrs. Poynton recovered herself, though she was still steeped in amazement.

"By all means," she said slowly. "I will send him up to you."

Mrs. Poynton returned to the garden. Mr. Lyndham was still there, sitting a little apart from the others. She went up to him.

"Mr. Lyndham," she said, and unconsciously her voice took a new tone in addressing him, "the Princess desires to speak to you in her room. If you will come this way, I will show you where she is."

Mr. Lyndham rose slowly to his feet. He did not appear surprised, but he showed no signs of eagerness.

"I will follow you," he said.

The door was safely closed. They were face to face. The Princess was in unfamiliar guise. Her eyes were full of tears, her voice, as she stood there with outstretched hand, shook.

"Gervase!" she exclaimed, "at last I have found you, then! You cannot escape me now. Come!"

He took her hand and raised it to his lips. He was almost unrecognizable. All the hardness seemed to have passed from his strong, weather-tanned face. His eyes and voice were as soft as a child's.

"Dear Gabrielle!" he murmured. "You believe still? You have not lost your faith?"

"Never! Never for one moment!"

"Thank God! Even though it be you against the world."

They were silent for several moments. There was so much between them which seemed better expressed unspoken.

"You keep still—your borrowed name?"

"I have no other," he answered.

"Yet you are back in England—here, of all places in the world."

"And in this room," he added, with a dash of his old cynicism. "Nothing is stranger than that!"

She stared away and looked around. Her dark eyes were full of shadows of some reawakened fear.

"It is true!" she declared. "The whole place is altered and modernised out of recognition. I did not realize where I was."

He moved to the window.

"It was from here," he said, "that the shot was fired; and there were a dozen people ready to testify that no one save myself passed out from this room."

She held out her hand.

"Gervase!" she exclaimed suddenly, "you are here with an object!"

"And you?"

"Also with an object. Tell me, you received a letter?"

"I did! It brought me from Alaska."

"And me," she declared, "from Austria. Look!"

He glanced at it.

"The same as mine," he declared. "Heaven knows, it seems improbable enough! But dying men sometimes tell the truth."

He was busy already at the wall. With his knife he gashed recklessly at the new and expensive Lincrusta Walton. For several minutes he pushed and strained and knocked. At last with a little cry he succeeded. A hidden door swung back a few inches. With a poker for a lever he forced it open. The Princess looked over his shoulder eagerly. It was a mere closet of an apartment, dark and empty, save for a single shelf.

"After all," he said despondently, "there is nothing here to help us."

"But do you not see," she exclaimed, "one part of the mystery vanishes from this moment? This is where the man hid who fired the shot!"

He nodded.

"I was an idiot not to have thought of the place before," he said, "but I was told that it had been blocked up whilst I was at school. You are right. One part of the mystery vanishes. But the other remains."

She pointed to something upon the floor.

"What is that?" she asked. "A book?"

He stooped to pick it up—a dingy, faded volume, with the word "Diary" stamped upon it on the outer cover, the sort of thing which was the weakness of the last generation of schoolgirls. It was thick with dust and yellow with age. He opened it carelessly at the last page and bent forward to catch the light. Then he gave a little cry.

"What is it, Gervase?"

"Heaven only knows!" he muttered, and the hand which clutched the book shook as though an ague had seized him. "Read, Gabrielle! I cannot!"

She snatched it from him. Followed by him, she carried it out into the light.

The man whom nobody liked, the man who was Mrs. Poynton's *bête noire*, remained alone with the Princess in her sitting-room for nearly an hour. Meanwhile Mrs. Poynton and her guests talked. The more tolerant assumed an old friendship; others smiled. The Princess was of ancient family, but in the days before her fortunate marriage she had been poor. It was rumored that she had been a governess. Who could tell what entanglements she might not have formed at that time? The Prince, who had been dead for little more than a year, had left her a wealthy woman. Her place in Society seemed assured. It was supposed that she was ambitious. She was indeed a splendid victim for the intelligent blackmailer. Mrs. Poynton grew weary of explaining how little she knew of Mr. Lyndham. He had come from nobody knew where. Arthur had taken a fancy to him, it was true, but she herself had mistrusted him from the first. Then there was a sudden hush. The Princess and Mr. Lyndham were coming down the steps and across the lawn.

"Dear Mrs. Poynton," the Princess murmured, as she joined them, "my rooms are perfect. But one of them, I think, has a history. Is it true that Sir Knowles Philton was shot from the window of my sitting-room?"

Mrs. Poynton was a little perturbed.

"I am afraid that it is true," she admitted. "It is many years ago, however, and I thought that everyone would have forgotten. I hope you are not afraid of ghosts."

The Princess smiled brilliantly.

"Already," she confessed, "I have seen one."

There was a little murmur of amusement. Then everyone suddenly realized that she was in earnest. She had something to say to them.

"I want you to tell me something about that murder, Mrs. Poynton," the Princess said. "Sir Knowles was shot as he walked upon the terrace, was he not, by some unseen person? Was the mystery ever cleared up?"

Mrs. Poynton shook her head.

"Never positively," she answered. "Never in the courts, that is to say. Of course, all the evidence pointed to Gervase Philton, Knowles brother; and although they never arrested him, he had to leave the country."

"Was there any quarrel between them, then?" the Princess asked.

"No open quarrel," Mrs. Poynton answered, "but it came out afterwards that there had been a great deal of ill-feeling for some time. Very fortunately for Gervase, no word of this transpired at the inquest."

"Dear me," the Princess murmured. "And the cause of the ill-feeling—was that ever known?"

Mrs. Poynton shrugged her shoulders.

"The one eternal cause. She was a governess to Lady Morrey's children—Lady Morrey was their sister, you know, and she was living here while her husband completed his term in India. They say that both brothers were in love with her, and Gervase was supposed to be horribly jealous."

There flashed between the Princess and Mr. Lyndham an illuminative glance which was a source of wonder to Mrs. Poynton.

"Anyhow," Mrs. Poynton continued, "one night Sir Knowles was shot as he walked upon the terrace, and the shot was fired from his brother's window. Some workmen were taking down a picture on the landing just outside, and they saw no one but Gervase himself come out of or enter his room. So, you see, as far as the negative evidence went, it was fairly conclusive. Gervase remained in England for several months; then he went abroad, and no one has ever heard of him since. We took the place a few months afterwards, and for my own part I can't help saying that I hope Sir Gervase never comes back. We could not possibly find another place to suit us so well."

The Princess smiled. Mr. Lyndham, wonderful to relate, followed suit.

"I am afraid that there is a disappointment in store for you, Mrs. Poynton," the Princess said. "Sir Gervase is back in England now. He is sitting by my side."

"Mr. Lyndham!" Mrs. Poynton screamed.

Mr. Lyndham bowed.

"I must apologize for being here under false pretenses," he said, "but I had a very particular reason for desiring to pay a visit to this neighbourhood, and you can understand that I did not care to venture here under my own name. Eight years in the Colonies and a beard will do wonders for a man."

"Yet the Princess recognized you," Mrs. Poynton said.

"It is true," he admitted.

"I, too," the Princess remarked, "have an explanation to make. You have heard that I was a governess for two years before I married the

Prince of Berlitz; but you perhaps did not know that I was a governess at this house, that it was on my account even that poor Sir Gervase here was accused of shooting his brother, who never spoke more than a civil word to me in his life."

A sudden silence fell upon the little group. After all, the evidence had been very strong. Yet they neither of them looked in the least like guilty people.

"Sir Gervase would rather, perhaps, that I told you what has happened—what we have discovered," the Princess said. "It is very simple, and the mystery which has baffled everyone so long does not exist any longer. Adjoining my sitting-room, from which the shot was fired, is a small secret closet, which apparently has not been opened for years. Some months ago we both of us received anonymous letters, dated from a hospital in Paris, advising us to explore this place. Hence Sir Gervase, hence my broken vow—for I had sworn never to set foot in England again. The closet appealed to us, as a likely hiding-place for the person who had fired the shot, but we have been fortunate to discover far more important things."

"You found something there?" one of the guests exclaimed.

"This," the Princess declared, holding up a little volume. "It is a sort of diary, and it is very eloquent. Is it your pleasure that I read aloud the last two extracts only?"

"This is very extraordinary," Mrs. Poynton murmured. "Yes, please do read anything which will elucidate the matter."

The Princess opened the book.

"This," she said, "appears to be the diary of one Jules Letrange, valet of the late Sir Knowles Philton. The first few pages are merely a highly sentimental and romantic account of his affection for Mademoiselle de Caliste, which under the circumstances you will not expect me to read. He admits that he has not dared to betray himself in any way, he pleads guilty all the time to a most becoming doubt as to whether his suit would be in any way acceptable. He works his way through all the stages of frenzy, however, to madness, and he is evidently very near that state when this entry was written. You will observe that it was on the day of the murder.

"September 11th—I cannot bear it any longer! If she is not for me, she is for no one. She favors Monsieur Gervase—a union impossible for her. Me she passes always by. I do not count with her. I am as the dust on which she treads. If she only knew that I have sworn it, perhaps she would not go out then to meet her lover, so blithe, so gay. If she is not for me, she is not for any other man.... If I see her with Monsieur Gervase again, it is the end ...

"Heaven help me! I tremble all the time! I am afraid! I have shot the wrong man. I have shot Sir Knowles, my master. I heard him cry out! If only I could get away from here! I hid till it was dark—no one suspects. It is all finished. Tomorrow I may go. I leave this book. They speak of Monsieur Gervase. I will hide myself, and send word of this book if they arrest him. I ..."

The Princess closed the little volume.

"The anonymous letters we both received were in the same handwriting. On my way through Paris I inquired at the hospital. The man is dead. He left no other confession. He left only this to tell his story."

Mrs. Poynton shut down her parasol with a snap.

"Really, it has been a most exciting afternoon. Only I am very much afraid now that I shall not get my lease renewed."

Sir Gervase and the Princess exchanged smiles. "That depends," he said, "upon the Princess."

## THE MAN WHO SAVED THE PRESIDENT'S LIFE

It was the second day out, and people were beginning to settle down into their steamer clothes and manners. The girl had already established a little court, as was usual with her wherever she went. The man had not yet appeared.

He came just as the deck-steward appeared with the afternoon tea. He was tall and pale, with dark, deep-set eyes and a sensitive mouth, notwithstanding its straight, firm lines. His features were hard and cleanly cut, his clothes hung loosely about him, as though his gauntness were merely the temporary result of some recent illness. He stepped out from the gangway with some hesitation; but once there, he swept the deck with a keen, masterful glance. A lurch of the steamer threw him against the side of a chair. He calmly seated himself in it and commenced to look bored.

The chair was next to the girl's, but he did not appear to notice the fact. Several of the young men who were in attendance upon her had coveted the chair, but in vain. The girl, however, made no remark at this act of calm appropriation. It was left for his servant, who appeared a few minutes later with rugs and a small library of books, to point out to him that he was a trespasser.

"I beg your pardon, sir," he said, "but I don't think that this is your chair."

The man looked annoyed.

"It will do," he said shortly, "unless," he added, turning to the girl, "it belongs to one of your friends."

The girl smiled upon him pleasantly.

"It is my aunt's chair," she said; "but I think that you may safely occupy it for the present, at any rate. She will not be on deck this afternoon."

The young man raised his cap, but he seemed curiously bereft of words. His thanks were barely articulate, and if it were possible for him to have become paler, he certainly did so. His long, white hands clutched nervously at the rug which covered his knees. Every now and then he cautiously studied the girl's profile. Under his breath he groaned to himself.

"This is the beginning! What a fool I am! What a fool I have been!"

There was a change also in the girl. Her high spirits seemed to have deserted her. Her laughter was forced, the sallies of her cavaliers failed to amuse her. She, too, was apparently conscious of the sudden approach of tragedy. One by one her attendants deserted her. Soon she was alone with the man.

They did not begin to talk at once. They both seemed interested in the tumbled gray waste of waters through which the steamer was plowing her way. But presently her rug slipped, and she felt it replaced with firm, skillful hands. She thanked him—almost shyly for her—and they began to talk.

Their conversation took its tedious but necessary course through the desert of the commonplace, but long before the dinner bell rang the probationary period was past. He had learned that she was the Miss Ursula Bateman whom New York society papers loved to allude to as the prototype of the modern American young woman of fashion. She was tired of Newport and Lennox, and, although she did not tell him so, she was also tired of being ceaselessly importuned to marry one or another of a goodly number of eager young men. She was an orphan and her own mistress. In a moment of inspiration she had planned this flight, a Continental tour amongst the unvisited places of Europe with an elderly aunt of purely negative tendencies. She was very enthusiastic over her escape.

"You can't imagine how it feels," she told him, as they leaned over the rail together to watch a shoal of porpoises, "to be really free from it all for a month or two, at any rate. We're too much in earnest over our pleasure. We make a business of it, as we do of everything else."

He looked at her with a faint smile.

"I'm glad to see," he said gravely, "that you have emerged from the holocaust without any ineffaceable signs of the struggle."

She laughed good-humoredly.

"Oh! I know what you're thinking," she exclaimed; "but it isn't in the face alone one carries the marks of deterioration."

"I suppose not," he answered thoughtfully. "Yet the face is a wonderful index."

She turned and surveyed him coolly.

"You would trust your own impressions of a face, then? It would be sufficient for you?"

"I think so," he answered. "Corroborating evidence would, of course, be reassuring."

"But suppose the evidences—all appearances were against your impressions, which should you rely upon?" she persisted.

"I dare say I should find it hard to make up my mind," he admitted.

She nodded and brushed back the hair from her forehead.

"That is exactly how I feel," she said, turning and walking back to her chair.

At dinner-time she was in unusual spirits. She increased at every moment the circle of her admirers. She sat at the captain's table, and everyone seemed to catch a little of the reflected glory of her bright sayings and infectious laughter. But someone asked her a question, about half way through the meal, which for a moment checked her flow of spirits.

"Who was the man who turned us all out this afternoon, Miss Bateman? We can't put up with that sort of thing all the way over, you know. No one man has a right to two whole interrupted hours alone with you—not even the President of the United States!"

"His name is Geoffrey Paish," she answered. "I really don't know much more about him than that."

The name awakened plenty of interest.

"Why, he's the fellow," someone eagerly exclaimed, "who's come in for the whole of the Paish estate. The old man was a banker in New York, you know—his uncle, I think it was. Mighty queer family, too."

"The old man died worth seven millions," the boy who sat on her left hand remarked enviously. "Nice little pile for him to step into."

"Did anyone ever hear of this Geoffrey Paish at college or anywhere?" asked Andrew Bliss, the man who sat opposite her.

No one had. A man from little higher up the table leaned forward.

"There were some very queer stories going about New York concerning this young man only last week," he remarked.

The girl caught him up sharply.

"There are queer stories about everyone," she said, "if people care to listen to them. Let us talk about something else."

She was a little later than the others when she came up on deck after dinner. As usual, she wore no hat or wrap of any sort. The wind blew her fair hair about her face, and she was obliged to gather up and hold the skirts of her black dinner-gown. Several young men came hurrying toward her, but she waved them away. She crossed the deck to where the man was sitting. He had just finished a frugal dinner which had been brought out to him by his servant.

"Will you come for a little walk?" she said. "I should like to go out to the bows."

He rose at once and led the way. The journey to the fore-part of the ship was a little devious, and once, after a moment's hesitation, he offered her his hand.

She took it frankly, and a sudden rush of colour came into his cheeks. The willing touch of her fingers possessed a certain significance for him.

They leaned over the white railings, and the fresh breeze blew strong and salt in their faces. She stood quite close to him.

"I wanted to come here," she said, "because we are safe against interruption. There is something which I have to say to you."

He moistened his dry lips. His interjection was scarcely audible.

"I was telling you only this afternoon," she said, "how monotonous my life had been. I seem to have been moving along the plane all the time. But once, for a few minutes, things were different. I had what I suppose people would call an adventure. It was while I was staying in Virginia with an aunt—not this one. I do not think that I will tell you the name of the place."

"Don't!" he muttered.

"It was a large, old-fashioned house, very low, and my room was on the first floor, only a few feet from the ground. One night we had a dance there. I fell asleep in my chair afterwards, leaving my jewels scattered about the dressing-room. When I woke up, there was a man in the room calmly filling his pockets with them."

"Pardon me," he interrupted, "but I hope you are noticing the phosphorus."

"We will talk about the phosphorus afterwards," she continued equably. "I suppose the slight noise I made disturbed him, and he wheeled suddenly round. He was a tall man and he wore a mask."

"A mask! Yes!"

"Which afterwards slipped," she continued. "Just at that moment all I could think of was that I was looking into the muzzle of a revolver.

"Of course you were not frightened?" he remarked, with a queer little smile.

"Not in the least," she answered him.

"I looked upon the revolver as a sort of harmless but necessary toy. At that moment I had no fear. But afterward—"

She shivered.

"Let me fetch you a cloak," he begged. "The breeze is too strong here."

"I am not cold," she answered calmly. "It was a memory. But to go on with my story. Naturally I asked the man what he was doing in my room, and as naturally he pointed to what were left of my jewels. For a burglar he was a terrible bungler. The hand which held his revolver shook so that I could have knocked it out of his hand."

"Look here," he said, "I've got to have some of these. It's life or death to me. I'm very sorry."

"I told him that he was welcome to all of them, that I was quite tired of them, and dying to get some new ones. I warned him of the bloodhounds, and told him of the nearest way to the State Road. And all the time he stood looking at me in a queer sort of way. I was absolutely certain that the man would never harm me. Perhaps I took advantage of my conviction. I began to laugh at him for his clumsiness. The man got mad. The first part of the whole thing ended very much as I had imagined it would. He threw down the jewels and made for the window. He was clumsy with the fastening, and I got up and helped him. It was then that his mask slipped. It was then also, for the first time, that the burglar misbehaved himself."

Again that queer little smile. The man looked up from the tumbling mass of cloven waters into the face of his companion.

"What did he do?" he asked.

"I shall not tell you," she answered severely. "Only, I think that I would rather have lost my jewels."

"You are not sure about it?" he demanded eagerly.

"It is not a matter which concerns you, is it?" she asked innocently.

He did not reply, and when she spoke again, her tone was graver.

"The comedy ended there, the tragedy began a few seconds later. The man was met upon the lawn by a confederate. There was a quarrel between them, presumably because the burglar declared that he had no jewels to share. I heard the second man declare that he would give his companion up to the police and earn the reward offered for his apprehension. I shouted to them softly to go away. They did not hear. Then I think that the second man decided to break into my room himself. I am surprised that he did not think of it before. It was absurdly easy. They quarreled. I could see that the first man was determined to stop him. Then there was the shooting. I saw it all. I could not move. I was terrified to death. They carried the second man into the house. I saw him clutch at the air and fall. It was horrible. The other man—"

"Yes?"

"He escaped. It was wonderful, but he escaped."

The man by her side touched his forehead lightly. There were great drops of moisture there, though the wind was still blowing about them.

"Well?" he said.

"The mask slipped," she murmured. "I have never forgotten his face for a single second."

They stood side by side, and the young men on the promenade-deck grumbled. The strains of shuffling feet came to them from the steerage. Then the man began to laugh softly, but very bitterly, as he tore open his coat.

"You think that he did not rob you—at all," he said. "You were wrong! See!"

It was a cracked and bent little ring of very thin gold, holding a single moonstone. He drew it from an inner pocket and held it out to her.

"You took that?" she exclaimed.

He nodded.

"That—and a memory," he said, looking into her face, "were the sole proceeds of my little attempt."

Her cheeks flushed a fiery red.

"How dare you remind me of that!" she exclaimed. "And I have always wanted to tell you—you took me by surprise, or I should have called out. Of course I should have called out."

He bowed.

"Well," he said, "I believe it. I took you by storm. All my life, I think—bah! What folly is this! I am quite ready, Miss Bateman."

"Ready?"

"You will tell the captain, of course, I shall not make any resistance. I always fancied that this would come some day, although I never thought that you would be concerned in it. I shall not deny anything. I had broken out of prison with the man Willard, and I shot him."

"Did you think that I was going to give you up?" she asked, looking at him with wide-open eyes.

"Of course. Why not? It is your duty," he answered.

"My duty?" she repeated.

"Certainly," he answered. "It will be quite simple. I shall deny nothing."

She was silent for a moment, leaning over the rails with her head resting upon her hands.

"Please to go away," she said to him. "I want to be quite alone—to think!"

He left her without a word.

"Sure?"

"Dead sure. We've got him, Jake. It's a thousand dollars sure."

The girl turned her head cautiously. She saw the red tips of two cigars. She herself was out of sight behind a ventilator.

"Pity we had to take the trip," the first voice remarked. "We could have nabbed him in New York."

"I guess we're all right, anyway," was the answer. "An ocean trip won't do either of us any harm, and I wasn't taking any risks."

There was a moment's pause. The girl felt herself shaking from head to foot.

"What bothers me is how he has managed to escape detection all this time," one of the men remarked.

"Guess everybody thought he was a pauper," the other answered. "Nobody thought of looking for him amongst the millionaires."

"Sure! Old man Paish left him all his pile. I forgot that."

"Guess he'll try and square this thing. He's been clever enough at keeping out of the way. He won't fancy being dropped on just as he's off."

"Won't do," was the terse answer. "Besides, it won't pay us. This is a big thing!"

The men moved on, the girl lingered there. Her eyes were fixed upon vacancy. This was to be the end of it, then. A prison cell, perhaps worse. A sudden shriek of the foghorn broke in upon her thoughts. They had steamed right into the midst of a dense bank of white sea mist. Under cover of the gray floating shadows she stole away to her state-room and locked the door.

Almost before the decks were dry the next morning she was out, and, curiously enough, she found him the only other early riser. A fresh, strong wind was blowing salt and vigorous, and the white spray was leaping high into the dazzling sunshine. She held on to the rail, and he came at once to her side.

"You see, I am not yet in irons," he said, with an attempt at gaiety which went ill with his beringed eyes and white cheeks. "What have I to thank for this respite?"

She looked at him in the face, and the breath seemed to die away in his body.

"I think," she said quietly, "that you know very well—that—that—"

The wonder of it kept him speechless, motionless. There was something in her face which he had never seen in any other woman's. He felt like a man mocked by a mirage of impossible joys. It was surely a miracle, this. He could not find any words, but for a moment their hands were clasped together.

"I wanted to speak to you," she said hurriedly. "There are one or two things which I must ask you."

"You shall ask me whatever you will, and I will answer you truly," he assured her.

"Are you really Geoffrey Paish?"

"Yes."

"You are very rich, then?"

"Very."

"Why did you break into my room?"

"I had just escaped from prison. I needed money to get away."

"And you were in prison for—?"

"For nothing I ever did. Please believe that. It is my only excuse for many things."

"I want to believe it," she answered simply. "I certainly shall, if you tell me so. Tell me what your plans are now?"

He shrugged his shoulders.

"My fortune," he said, "was a tardy recompense for the act of injustice which sent me to prison. I know that I risked a great deal in coming forward to claim it, but I had had enough of poverty. I was never known in my younger days by the name of Paish, and I have had a fever lately, which has altered me. I decided to risk it. I thought that if I could once reach Europe safely, I could find a dozen hiding-places."

Her eyes filled with tears.

"I am afraid," she said, "that you will not reach Europe safely."

"You mean that you will give me up?" he asked quietly. "It is your duty."

"You know very well that I shall not," she answered. "But there are others here on board, following you."

She told him of the conversation which she had overheard. He listened intently.

"I know the two men," he remarked. "I have seen them watching me."

"You must try and make terms with them," she suggested, eagerly. "Those sort of men are to be bribed, are they not?"

"Generally," he answered; "and yet, after all, I am not sure that it is worth while. I shall be hunted from corner to corner of the earth all my life. I shall bring disrepute and scandal upon my friends. Nothing worth having in life will be possible for me. I think that I will not struggle any more against fate."

"You must not talk like that," she answered. "You are a young man, and you should have a long life before you."

He laughed bitterly.

"The life behind has been too long!" he exclaimed.

She dropped her voice.

"For my sake," she whispered.

Again he looked at her in amazement. He was still weak from his fever, for his hands were trembling.

"You cannot mean—that you really care?" he said, in a low tone.

She smiled encouragement upon him. The breakfast-gong had sounded, and they were no longer alone.

"Should I be here if I did not?" she whispered.

She played shuffleboard badly that morning, for only a few yards away Geoffrey Paish and two men were sitting together and talking earnestly. Their chairs were pulled almost to the rail; their heads were close together. It was not possible for her to hear a word of their conversation, yet she found her attention continually diverted toward them. At last the two men departed. Geoffrey Paish was left alone. He sat with unseeing eyes fixed upon the sky line. She came softly to him.

"Well?"

"The men are honest," he answered. "They are not to be bribed. I have offered them half my fortune."

She reeled for a moment and then sat down in one of the empty chairs.

"What are we to do?" she murmured. "Oh! what can we do?"

"For you," he answered, "there is only one thing. You must forget. Our acquaintance must end here. We may renew it, perhaps—in the police-court."

She looked at him reproachfully. He was instantly ashamed of himself.

"Forgive me," he whispered; "but indeed I scarcely know what I am saying. Either I am a little mad, or those two men were. They talked like lunatics."

"In what way?" she asked.

He laughed shortly.

"Well, they seemed to think that the notoriety I should gain would be a sort of recompense for any minor inconveniences such as imprisonment, for instance, which I might have to undergo. They talked of the whole affair as a capital joke, and they seemed amazed that I should have attempted to keep my secret at all."

She shuddered a little.

"That is the American of it," she exclaimed bitterly.

He looked cautiously around. Her chair was behind a boat. He took her fingers into his.

"I'm going to adopt your philosophy," he whispered. "Let us make the most of these few days."

Of course, all sorts of stories went around. The one most favoured by their fellow-passengers, and which she herself had certainly encouraged, was that they were old friends who had parted years ago under some misunderstanding. No one else ventured to claim even a share of her time. The colour came back to his cheeks; his step upon the deck became positively buoyant. No one would have guessed anything of the shadow which lurked behind their apparent gaiety. Now and then they came across the two detectives, whose greeting was always perfectly respectful. He laughed once with a momentary bitterness as he returned their bow.

"What a devil's comedy!" he murmured.

Her fingers touched his, and the bitterness fled away.

"You are a witch," he declared.

At Queenstown she found Hoyle, the senior of the two men, in the saloon writing cablegrams, with a messenger at his side. He had covered them with his hand at her approach.

"You are determined to send those, Mr. Hoyle?" she said.

"I have no alternative, Miss Bateman," he answered.

"I, too, am rich," she said hesitatingly, "and I am engaged to Mr. Paish."

"Delighted to hear it," Hoyle answered heartily. "You mustn't let him get downhearted. Most of the men in the world would enjoy a little affair like this." (he tapped the cablegrams). "I guess it won't do him any harm in the long run. You'll excuse me now, Miss Bateman."

He was busy with another cable. She made her way on deck again. Only once during the rest of the way to Liverpool did she address the detective again.

"I want you to tell me," she said, stopping suddenly in front of his chair, "is—will—have you sent word to Liverpool?"

"Well," he answered slowly, "I guess so. I hated to do it, Miss Bateman, with you both so set against it; but there wasn't any use in bottling it up. I shouldn't be surprised if something didn't happen to Mr. Paish in Liverpool."

"At the docks?" she asked.

"At the docks," he answered.

Early the next morning came their farewell. She drew him behind one of the boats and pressed her lips passionately to his. She dared not trust herself to words. Then he went overboard into the gray mists and was lost to sight in a moment.

Twelve hours later he was shown into a sitting-room at the small private hotel which they had selected as their rendezvous. He was properly dressed, but he had the appearance of a man grown suddenly younger. His smile, as she rushed into his arms, was a trifle apologetic.

"You have seen the papers?" she cried.

He nodded.

"I must have been the densest of idiots!" he exclaimed. "I couldn't see what Hoyle was driving at all the time; and I suppose my head was full of the other thing."

"And all the time," she cried, half laughing, half sobbing, "you were a hero, and I didn't know it. You were the man who saved the President's life at Metrofuzo, and for whose discovery he offered a thousand dollars reward."

"It came my way," he said. "You can imagine that I was a bit reckless just then, and odds didn't scare me much."

She wiped the tears from her eyes.

"You have made yourself the laughingstock of the country, sir," she declared. "Fancy jumping overboard, even though it was in the river, to escape being lionised and interviewed! Why, it will be worse than ever now, when they do find you out."

He sighed.

"They mustn't find me," he said. "You forget, Ursula, the other affair remains."

She shrugged her shoulders scornfully.

"Pooh!" she exclaimed. "I guess the President will have to settle that for you. It isn't as though the man had died, you know."

He turned toward her suddenly.

"What? Say that again."

His voice sounded strange and harsh. He was suddenly pale again.

"I thought you knew," she murmured. "We took care of the man, and he got well. They took him back to prison."

He sat down heavily.

"And I," he said, "I carried with me all the way to Cuba, all through the fighting, and through many sleepless nights, that dead man's face! Great Heavens! Not dead! I never saw a newspaper. I never doubted but that he was dead. Not dead!"

He was trembling. She came and sank down by his side.

"If you hadn't met me," she murmured, "you would have never known."

He took her into his arms.

"Ursula," he said, "I am a free man. I can prove myself innocent of the thing they sent me to prison for. It was Paish's son who stole the bonds. He found it out, and that is why he left me his money. His son died in Cuba. I have his confession."

She laughed softly.

"Aren't you glad," she murmured, "that the mask slipped?"

He slipped a battered little ring on to her finger.

"After all," he remarked, "I wasn't such a clumsy burglar."

# IN AN OXFORDSHIRE LANE

It is a very common saying that every man has his hobby. Certainly, I have mine. There is nothing which pleases me so well as suddenly to transfer the cares and responsibilities of business on to the broad and steady shoulders of my junior partner, to don a rough walking-suit, and, strapping a knapsack upon my back, to disappear for a while from the dingy offices in Lincoln's Inn and from the civilized world generally, leaving no address behind me, and, indeed, very undecided myself, at starting, into which part of the country to make my leisurely way.

It is seldom that I wander far, however; for, strange though it may seem, the quiet nooks and corners of England are far more to my taste than the overrun Continental haunts of millionaire stockbrokers and Chicago pig-stickers. Two months, at least out of every twelve for twenty-five years have I spent in gaining my knowledge of them, and there are still enough left to keep me in my native land; so many indeed, that, unless I live to a phenomenal age, I shall not live long enough to visit them all: and until then I shall not seek to enlarge my mind or recruit my health by foreign travel. Why should I? I am a man of simple taste, and I enjoy my evening meal at a wayside inn or farmhouse far more than I should the many-coursed dinner of a fashionable hotel. Not only that, but I am even insane enough to find as much beauty, if not equal magnificence, in a Devonshire lane or a Westmoreland farm as in the snow-capped mountains of the Alps or the silvery lakes of Italy. It is no doubt owing to the simplicity of my tastes and disposition that I feel so much more in touch with our own humbler scenery; but certain it is, and I am never ashamed to own it, that the pure air, the quiet, the familiarity with the phases of the landscape, and the being in perfect accord with my surroundings have a more soothing and pleasing effect upon me than any association with the more magnificent and luxuriously developed sights of other lands. I do not wish to scale the lofty peaks of the Himalayas or the Rocky Mountains, nor do I greatly desire to gaze upon the pristine beauties of New Zealand or the glories of the tropics. Their grandeur would, no doubt, arouse my wonder and impel my admiration; but they would have no such pleasing effect upon me as a day's ramble through a picturesque corner of England. I should feel awe at their majesty; but awe is not pleasure or peace, and these I find in the contemplation of humbler and more accessible beauties. In another respect, too, I am somewhat singular. I prefer to travel alone. "How dull you must be!" every one whom I meet remarks. Not a bit of it. In my solitary rambles I am never dull. It is in London, surrounded by all my friends, dining at my club amidst a host of acquaintances, elbowing my way to the stalls on the first night of a new play— it is then that I am often dull. Society makes me dull; my own society never. This sounds egotistical, but it is true. I am neither poet, student, nor dreamer, but I can extract such pleasure from the contemplation of and communion with nature as another's society would mar. I tried a companion once. He was the most silent man I had ever met, and the dullest and most sedate amongst my acquaintance; but he was a complete failure. As soon as we were well in the country his dullness vanished, as if by magic, and he became facetiously and extravagantly gay. He cracked jokes with the farmers, made fun of the simple country people, and in his leviathan frivolity I actually once caught him making love to a milk-maid. He talked unceasingly of all things under the sun. Legal gossip he retailed by the hour, and gave me his own views at considerable length on all the prominent cases, civil and criminal, then pending. On Skiddaw, at four o'clock in the morning, while we watched the sun slowly emerge from its gorgeous bank of clouds and scatter its glory all over the eastern skies, he persisted in explaining to me the flaw in the counsel's defence *re* Smith *v.* Banks; and when late one night I slipped out from our cottage resting-place to gaze upon Coniston Lake, glittering all over with the silvery sparkle of the full moon, and encircled by the dim, spectral-like hills, amongst which the "old man" towered in sullen majesty, I found him at my elbow explaining the true reason of the rejection of the Ambleside Railway Bill. As time went on he grew worse, and speedily developed into the most irrepressible chatterbox I ever had the misfortune to meet. I stood it for a week, and then arranged for a telegram requiring my immediate return to town. Since that time I have never sought for a companion.

October and November are not generally favourite months for a walking tour, but they are mine. I do not care for a glaring sun, for a sky uniform and monotonous in its blueness, for dusty roads, a fierce light, and oppressive air. Give me a fine November afternoon, when the air is soft, yet crisp; the turf soft and yielding, not dry and dusty; the sky grey, and not blue. No longer does the sun oppress and burn in its monotonous heat, and its warm rays are now grateful and welcome, and the universal greenness of hedges and trees have given way to a magnificent combination of tints and shadings—orange, lemon, blood-red, and purple—which the painter loves to attempt to reproduce, and well he may. On such an afternoon ten years ago, my knapsack on my back and grasping a stout holly stick, I trudged along an Oxfordshire lane, and watched the sun—a glowing ball of red fire—sink slowly behind the Gloucestershire hills. An autumn sunset on a clear day is a sight to arrest any one's footsteps, nor was I loth when I reached a convenient spot to pause for a while, for I had already exceeded my usual daily distance. With a sigh of relief I unslung my knapsack, and, lighting my pipe—the inseparable companion of my travels—I leaned over a gate and gazed across the landscape of dark-soiled, freshly-ploughed fields, bounded by moss-incrusted grey stone walls, of rich-hued meadow land, of wooded knolls, and of snug-looking red-tiled farmhouses, becoming more patchworky and obscure as the distance increased, and bounded right away to the west by that long dark line of hills, behind which the glowing disc of the sun was slowly disappearing. It sank down and vanished out of sight; but the afterglow, the deep orange sky, and the rarefied air, which showed me as clearly as though they had been in the next field, instead of many miles away, the shape, and, indeed, the very boughs, of the trees on the summit of the hills, kept me gazing for a while in unlessened admiration.

I am a middle-aged-man, a lawyer, whose life has been spent in the compilation and consideration of facts, and whose life has had in it nothing of the romantic or fanciful. No one amongst my city acquaintances would dream of calling me sentimental or impressionable; nor, indeed, am I. And yet whenever in my solitary rambles I witness this, one of Nature's grandest efforts, I feel almost drawn out of myself and my humdrum life. Forgetful of my fatigue and absorbed by the scene, I lingered at the gate until the deep orange hue faded into a dull grey, and the shades of an autumnal evening rapidly descending blotted out the view; and then, made conscious of the growing lateness of the hour by the increased stirring of the chilly evening breeze, I turned away, shook the stiffness from my knees, and, buckling on my knapsack, started off to conclude my day's journey, feeling at peace with all mankind, and, to tell the truth, desperately hungry.

I had scarcely proceeded a hundred yards before I overtook two other pedestrians, one of whom, as I was passing, accosted me.

"Can I trouble you for a light, sir?" he inquired.

I slackened my pace, and, while I felt in my pockets for the required article, glanced with some interest at the inquirer. The question was an ordinary one enough, but the voice, full deep and yet with just a suspicion of affectation, was decidedly out of the common, and so it seemed to me, after a brief examination, was the man who had proffered this simple request. He was short, but stout and thickset, holding himself well together—so well, indeed, that, notwithstanding his tired and travel stained appearance, there was still perceptible a slight jauntiness and tendency to swagger in his gait and bearing. His eyes, small, but keen and bright, were twinkling with a perpetual merriment, and the ever-twitching corners of his mouth betrayed a decided weakness of the risible muscles. He was dressed somewhat oddly, in a brown check suit, which appeared to have seen better days, and round his neck—collar he had none—was twisted a red silk kerchief, carefully tied. His hat, likewise brown, and rather battered, was a trifle on one side, and increased the rakishness of his general appearance; but I noticed with surprise that his hands (one was extended for the desired light, the other was pressing down the tobacco into the spacious bowl of a well-coloured meerschaum) were small and shapely. His companion, a tall dark young man, stood aloof, with a frown on his well-arched eyebrows, idly kicking the pebbles out of his way and glancing round more than once with an impatient yet weary gesture, as if fretting at the slight delay. I could see very little of him, but he stood with his back to me, and I was more interested in the man who had addressed me. The latter accepted my matchbox with a little bow of thanks, struck a light, and then, after puffing away at his pipe for a moment or two with an air of great satisfaction, returned me the box.

"I am exceedingly obliged to you, sir," he said, in the same not unpleasant voice; "I have been longing for a smoke, but unfortunately had no light, and never a soul have we passed on this road for three miles. A somewhat lonely part of the country, sir, think you not? How far might it be to Chipping Norton?"

The merry black eyes were twinkling and the corners of his mouth twitching, as if in the joint fact of there existing at all such a place as

Chipping Norton and his being bound for it lay the most capital joke in the world. The sort of man this to force you, *nolens volens*, into a good temper, whatever lack of comfort there might be in the surroundings.

I pointed to the twinkling lights which lay down in the valley before us. "There it lies—two miles by yonder milestone. Our ways are the same, then," I added, moving forward.

"I am exceedingly obliged, sir. Do you hear that, Phil?" he went on, addressing his companion cheerfully; "two more miles and our little tr-er-tour is ended, and I for one shall not be sorry."

"Nor I," returned the young man shortly; and, moving a little way into the road to give us more room, he marched on in gloomy silence.

The man at my side was evidently more inclined for conversation.

"A glorious day it has been for walking, sir," he commenced, addressing me, and rattling on without waiting for my assent; "just the day for a good tramp. I'm not at all sure that walking is my favourite exercise, though," he added confidentially. "My friend there and I have done close upon thirty five miles to-day. Looks pretty well knocked up, don't he? I'm not tired, not a bit. I'm never tired, but all the same I'm beginning to feel as though I'd had about enough exercise for one day, you know. We've had the pull of you in one way," he remarked, tapping my knapsack. "I never could stand those things. Our baggage went on by train this morning to Chipping Norton. How far have you come today, sir? if I might make so bold as to ask; and are you going any farther?"

I had come from Oxford, I told him, and I purposed spending the night at Chipping Norton. I had been here once before, I added, in response to a further question.

"Ah, h'm! Happen to know the theatre?"

Theatre! No, I had never heard of the Chipping Norton theatre. Was he sure that there was one? I inquired dubiously.

Certainly he was.

"It's very likely a barn, though," he added briskly. "Not that it's the worse for that, if it isn't a draughty one, eh? Now I daresay you're wondering who the deuce we are, aren't you?" he asked abruptly, intercepting a curious glance of mine at his silent companion.

I hesitated, and was framing an ambiguous reply, for which he did not wait, however.

"Well, I'll tell you. We're missionaries."

"Missionaries! I should scarcely have thought it," I told him, with perhaps a little incredulity in my tone, and a good deal in my mind.

"Ha! ha! ha!" and the little man broke out into peals of the merriest laughter I ever heard. "Missionaries of art, sir, that's what we are. The rivals of the Kyrle Society in the elevation of the masses, the pupils and disciples of a master artistically divine, the—"

"In plain words, sir, we are strolling players," broke in the young man abruptly.

His companion did not seem in the least annoyed at this sudden interruption.

"My dear Phil," he exclaimed deprecatingly, "why will you describe our noble profession in such brutally coarse terms? I was about to explain to this gentleman that—"

"That we act damnably in any little hole of a town where the people are fools enough to spend their spare coppers in coming to see us," broke in the younger man again.

His companion, not in the least annoyed, turned to me with a shrug of his shoulders and a confidential smile, as though he would have said, "Don't mind the poor fellow; he's mad."

"He's rather tired," he explained apologetically. "You see, we've had a longish tramp; all his own fault, too—he would walk. The ladies of our company we shall meet here; they have preceded us by train: also, as I before observed, our baggage."

The younger man's lip curled, but he made no further observation. Just then we came to the first lamp-post, and I caught a glimpse of his face. Once he must have been very handsome, I decided; but what a wreck he was now, poor fellow! One could understand the bitterness of his tone, for suffering and want were indelibly impressed upon his careworn countenance. His features were pinched and hardened, and a dull light shone in his eyes. I had a pretty shrewd suspicion as to the reason for this "walking tour," and it turned out to be correct. We had entered the main street of the little town, and had come to a halt outside the inn.

"You are not going to put up here, then?" I remarked, rather disappointed; for while my elder friend hesitated, his companion, with a brief good night, walked on a pace or two, and glanced round impatiently.

"Well-er, no. The fact is," he continued, beaming all over, as if he were about to recite some most excellent joke, "our chancellor of the exchequer intimated this morning that, after the tickets for the ladies had been taken and several other expenses defrayed, there remained the not inexhaustible sum of eighteen-pence in the treasury. Ninepence of that we had, and in a fit of unpardonable extravagance we spent it on the way. The remainder we left in the chancellor's possession, in case the ladies needed any refreshments. So you see that until after tomorrow's performance," he concluded, with keenly twinkling eyes, as though he thoroughly relished the situation, "we are just a trifle short."

I intimated as delicately as possible, and with considerable earnestness, that I should be delighted to entertain my new friends if they would dine with me, and without hesitation the elder one accepted.

"Don't apologize for the shortness of the invitation, sir, I beg of you," he burst out cheerily. "Come along, Phil my boy; I'm simply ravenous, and our fellow-traveller here, like a good Samaritan, invites us to dine with him. I don't mind accepting your hospitality, sir; not a bit of it! I'm not proud. Your turn to-day, mine to-morrow. I've done as much for others many a time, and no one can say that Dick Andrews isn't as free to give as to take when he's able. Come, Phil!" But the younger man hung back, muttering something about not feeling hungry.

"Pray come," I begged him earnestly. "I mean to get a *quid pro quo* from you, after all. If I find our friend here in a good temper after dinner, I shall try and get a pass out of him for your performance this evening. Come, I'll take no refusal." And between us he had to yield.

Ah! what a comfortable inn that was! and, doubtless, is now, if it is not spoilt by the inroads of bagmen and commercials. There were none came to Chipping Norton then, and we had the parlour—they were ignorant of the term coffee-room—to ourselves. Dinner, after all, we had none, for there was only an hour before my guests had to meet the "ladies of the company," and proceed to the scene of their performance; so we ordered tea, and a better tea we could not have had. There were dark brown new-laid eggs, broiled ham, clotted cream, clear marmalade, rich butter, and fine-flavoured tea. Could epicure desire a more satisfactory meal? Apparently my guests thought not. For the first time during our brief acquaintance, the elder one's tongue ceased to wag, and his companion, notwithstanding his plea of non-hunger, was clearly famished. After the first few minutes, however, the former managed to combine the two processes of talking and eating, and once started he chattered away incessantly. He was the manager, it seemed, of the little company, and his companion "first walking gentleman," whatever that means.

Tragedy he much preferred to comedy (how is it, I wonder, that a short, jolly-looking man always prefers tragedy?), but they were playing a miscellaneous lot of pieces, he told me. There was a drama, the name of which I have forgotten, down on the programme for that evening, to be followed by a farce. I had been lately at Stratford-on-Avon, and the very mention of the place set me off on a new tack. Shakespeare, he informed me, was the greatest poet that ever lived, but as a dramatist he was nowhere.

"I've tried 'em all," he assured me vigorously, "from *As You Like It* to *Hamlet*, and every time it's been a dead failure. Why, I've played *Hamlet* to pretty well empty benches more than once." I fancied that I could detect the ghost of a smile in the younger man's face, and I myself with difficulty refrained from joining in it. Mr. Andrews, however, was absolutely unconscious.

"The stage, sir," he continued—"thanks, I'll take a little more of that ham. Delicious, isn't it? —the stage, sir, as I was saying, requires an entire remodelling. There are those at the very top of the profession who haven't the least right there, and there are others nearer the bottom—I include myself in that category," he added modestly—"who want a leg up. Not that I despise the career of the nomad actor, mind; far from it. He has a mission in the world, sir, if any one has. He has a mission, most decidedly."

It occurred to me that the present mission of this particular "nomad actor" appeared to be to consume as much ham and as many eggs as he could in a given space of time. I could not help thinking, as I watched him, of certain animals whose digestive organs are such that they can at one time lay in stock for a week. What a mercy for the peace of mind of our landlady that the same idea did not occur to her!

"These amateurs do us no end of harm in some of the towns," he continued, pausing only to pour himself out another cup of tea. "You see, people will go to see their friends make fools of themselves, and enjoy that quite as much, or even more, than seeing us professionals act; and you should just see our audiences sometimes, eh, Phil? Not that I care a fig where I act or before whom. I'd just as soon act in this barn here this evening as at Drury Lane or the Lyceum, if only the audience like it and applaud. That's the thing that satisfies me—

appreciation. If I can see every one in front looking pleased and interested, I'm happy. I'm not ambitious; never was. As long as I've got plenty to eat and drink and money enough to buy me an ounce of honey-dew, I'm all right. Now, my young friend here—just pass the butter, will you, Phil? — he's never satisfied. To look at him any one would imagine that he was sick of his profession, wouldn't they?"

"As if I wasn't!" he remarked. He spoke in a low tone, full of bitterness. "I'm sick and tired of it. I detest it, and it detests me."

He pushed his plate away from him, and strolled to the window with a weary gesture. My *vis-à-vis* followed his movement with a pitying glance in his eyes, but he suffered none of it to creep into his tone.

"Never quarrel with your bread and cheese, young man," he remarked sententiously. "If you do it may quarrel with you some day. Take things as they come, if you can't alter them. That's the only philosophy worth remembering."

The young man turned abruptly away from the window and walked to the door.

"I'm going down to the station now, sir," he said, turning towards me. "Permit me to thank you heartily for your hospitality. If you really care to see our miserable performance, Mr. Andrews will only be too delighted to give you a ticket. Good evening, sir;" and he hurried off—not before I had pressed a cigar upon him, however.

"Poor fellow!" remarked my remaining guest, making himself comfortable in the easy chair; "misfortune seems almost to have turned his head. Miserable performance, indeed!"

I was interested in the young man. His haggard, miserable face and bearing, which, for all its misery, had yet something refined and distinguished in it, had touched me, and I felt curious to hear something of his history.

"He has been unfortunate, then?" I ventured.

"He has. If you care to hear his story—it is a very short one—stroll down to the station with me, and I will tell it you as we go."

I assented willingly, and, lighting our pipes, we sallied out, crossed the spacious market-place, and made our way along the queer little street towards the station.

"I'll tell you all about him in a very few words," began my companion briskly. "I hate sad stories, so I shan't linger over it, I can assure you. Five years ago I was very much in the same way as I am now, only perhaps a little better off. I had a very fair company then, and I was travelling down the West of England, playing at nearly all the decent sized towns. Sometimes we did well, sometimes badly; sometimes we had our pocket full of money, at others we had scarcely enough to carry us on. Ah, I've had some queer ups and downs in my life, I can tell you, and some curious adventures; but I mustn't stop to tell you about them now. I had a young lady in my company—a Miss Knowles—a thoroughly respectable and remarkably pretty young lady she was, and no mistake; far too good for my work. I picked her up quite by accident. Her father died quite suddenly—he was an actor—and as I happened to be in the town, she came to me and begged for a temporary engagement. She was almost penniless, it seemed.

"Where was this?" I asked. "Not in London?"

"Lord! no. It was at a little town in Berkshire, which I don't suppose you ever heard of—Faringdon. Well, as I was saying, she came to me for an engagement, and I was only too glad to get her, for she was a cut or two above the ordinary actresses, and she only asked a trifling salary. She had been with me about three months, and we were playing down at a little town in Gloucestershire, when in strolls a young gentleman, and falls straightaway in love with her. He found means to obtain an introduction, and I must say that from first to last he behaved like a gentleman throughout. I don't suppose he found it very difficult—a gay, handsome young fellow he was, with all the appearance of unlimited wealth—to win a lonely girl's heart. Anyhow, he succeeded, and hung about with us all that week and the next, and came down again, after a brief absence, the week afterwards. He looked very grave this last time, and came straight to me, whom he seemed somehow to regard as the girl's guardian. He had broken the news of his engagement to his father—a very stern, hard old gentleman he must be, I should think—and he had absolutely refused even to listen to anything so preposterous as his son's marriage with an obscure actress. He had no mother, and was an only child, and I suppose he relied a little too much on his father's leniency. Anyhow, he married Margaret Knowles—I gave her away—and then took her home to beg for forgiveness. In less than a week they came back again to me. The old shoot—meaning the father—had refused to see them, had turned them both out of the house, and had told his son never to come near him again. Even then they were so ridiculously fond of one another that they could think of nothing else, and seemed quite indifferent as to the future. At last their money was all gone, and that brought them to their senses. We had a long talk, and it was arranged that I should have Margaret back again for a week or two while he tried to get some employment; and, accordingly, sanguine and full of hope, he started off for London. I don't know how it was exactly, but, partly because he had never been brought up to any business and partly owing to his father's influence, he could get nothing, and all his friends seemed to have turned against him. After about a month's absence he came down again to where we were playing in Wiltshire, altogether broken down and dispirited and well-nigh desperate. As a last resource, I advised him to try the stage. There seemed nothing else for him to do, so he accepted a minor engagement with me. That was more than four years ago, and here he has been ever since. That's his history."

"And a very sad one it is," I remarked. "You didn't tell me his name?"

"Farradale—Philip Farradale. His father, Sir Edward Farradale, is a great man in the city, I believe."

I stopped in the middle of the path, and repeated the name in surprise. During the last few months I had often been brought into contact with the wealthy railway director and ex-banker, and, indeed, numbered him now amongst my clients. A stern, reticent old man he was—one of the old school, and not at all the sort of father a son would care to trifle with. Little hope, I feared, for the young actor!

"Has he ever appealed to him again?"

"Twice. First when the child was born, and again when his wife—poor Margaret—lay desperately ill, and we could not afford the money to have her properly nursed. In each case the letter was returned torn through the middle."

"Beast!" I muttered. We were at the station by this time, and, as the train was slowly steaming in along the single line, my companion, with a hastily muttered apology, left me. I lingered on the platform, standing back in the shadow of the bridge, and watched Philip Farradale pause in his restless perambulations, and glance eagerly in at the carriage doors as the train glided into the station. Suddenly his whole expression changed, and with a glad smile of welcome he halted outside one of the compartments. A tiny little child stretched out its arms with an infantile cry of welcome, and was tenderly lifted to the ground. Then he turned round eagerly and gave his hand to a tall, pale girl, who welcomed him with a wonderfully sweet smile for such a wan, thin face. For a moment or two they stood talking; then he lifted the child up into his arms, took a small bag from his wife, and they moved slowly away, he apparently making anxious though fond inquiries, and she endeavouring to satisfy him. Almost at my side little Mr. Andrews was talking cheerfully to a motley group, whom I conjectured to be the rest of the company, but I did not pause to scrutinize them. Philip Farradale's gaunt, unhappy face haunted me. What a sad little romance to stumble across in an Oxfordshire lane!

Imagine a long narrow barn, with whitewashed walls and bare floor, dimly lit with rude oil lamps, save the rear part, which their flickering, uncertain light failed to illuminate, and which was consequently in semi-darkness. A couple of faded red screens and a curtain which bore the marks of much ill-usage had been called into requisition to conceal the whole of the top part of the room; but the shabbiness of each was artfully toned down by the little row of flaring footlights, which cast a sort of artificial halo upon their age and dinginess. Immediately in front of these footlights were several long rows of rude wooden benches; behind these were several other benches, still ruder in construction and without any backs to them, and in the rear part were no seats at all. To this temple of the arts I groped my way along a dark footpath (it stood about fifty yards back from the road), and, having discovered the door and paid my shilling, I was ushered into one of the front benches. I was then, if you please, one of the patrons of the Chipping Norton Theatre. The time fixed for the performance was close at hand, and I was surprised on glancing around to find that the little building was almost full. At the back was a hustling crowd of men and boys, interspersed with a few women, whose eager faces, owing to the dim light, I could only indistinctly catch. As if aware of their obscurity, and desiring by some means to testify as to their presence, perhaps emboldened too by their knowledge that they could not be distinguished from each other in front, they were creating, if not exactly a hubbub, at any rate, some degree of noise. Every moment or two some mirthful sally or rude joke from their midst would produce a hearty roar of genuine laughter; and there was also a continual cracking of nuts and stamping of feet, which, varied by an occasional whistle, was evidence of their impatience at the non-rising of the curtain. The seats at the back were all full, and as far as there the uncertain light allowed me to distinguish faces. There was a fair sprinkling of the youthful agricultural labourer, with his red face shining with soap and expectation, great coarse hands, tough clothes, and short pipe—for smoking was not forbidden. Then there were the village girls, with large, good-humoured faces and ill-fitting clothes, chattering and giggling amongst themselves, and exchanging open badinage with the male part of the audience, who appeared to be mostly ranged behind. A little nearer the front sat those whom I judged to be the tradesmen of the town, in their black coats and best ties, and bearing all of them on their exteriors the evident signs of having "got themselves up" for such unheard-of dissipation as a night's "play-acting." Nor were their wives and daughters far behind them in the splendour of their apparel, for bonnets and gowns which had an unmistakable "Sunday" appearance had been brought out and donned for this rare and never-to-be-forgotten treat. In the front seat close to me masherdom was represented by three youths—I am prepared to pledge my word that they were farmers' sons—in light suits and very stick-up collars, who carried elaborate walking-sticks and kid-gloves, and gazed round at the expectant audience with a semi compassionate gaze, as if they themselves were regular *habitués* of the theatre, and pitied exceedingly those who looked upon this sort of thing as a treat.

At last the wished-for moment arrived: there was a hush, and from behind the red screen a vilely strung piano gave forth the opening chords of the overture to "Masaniello." There is an end to all things, and, to my intense relief, that overture came to an end at last. Then there was some more rumbling of feet and whistling, until amidst a sudden breathless silence a little bell rang out and the curtain rolled slowly up (all on one side). The scene displayed was understood to be the grounds of an English mansion, and a subdued buzz of admiration and wonder testified to the picturesque effect produced by a couple of side wings daubed all over with green paint to represent the perspective of some gardens, a real iron seat, a green canvas turf, an Italian vase (which later on in the performance collapsed, and was found to be made of cardboard), a few shrubs in pots, and a baby's tennis-racket leaning ostentatiously against the seat. I wonder how it was that I (who am somewhat a critical playgoer) took such keen interest in the development of that worn-out plot, and followed its threads so eagerly; how it was that I felt such a sympathy for my gloomy young friend, when as the squire's only son, he was ejected from his rightful position by the machinations of the inevitable villain (a gentleman, by the way, whom I remember to have seen at the station laden with many brown paper parcels, and carrying an enormous umbrella); and how it was that I conceived such hatred for this said villain, who continually rolled his "r's" and frowned until his heavy eyebrows (false) met, and gnawed the ends of his black moustache (also false) until he really looked quite diabolical, and caused a small child, who sat near the front, to howl bitterly on meeting the evil one's eye. I don't know how it was, but there wasn't a credulous, open-mouthed rustic there more absorbed in the progress of the piece than I, and no one more savagely hissed the evil soliloquies of the villain, or more loudly clapped the noble speeches of the heroic but misrepresented son, or showed more frantic delight when the young lady administered a snub to the designing villain who sought her hand, but whom she very properly refused to have anything to do with, than I did. The first act terminated in the ejection of the righteous son from the parental roof, whilst the villain, who, by the bye, was his cousin, stood looking on with folded arms and fixed, satirical smile, quite unmoved by the home-truths and threats which the ejected one showered upon him, to the delight of the audience and the approval of the young lady, who, by some strange chance, had wandered upon the scene, and who subsequently went into hysterics after the most approved fashion. Then came the interval, which, by the bye, was a somewhat prolonged one. The three representatives of masherdom sported cigarettes and strolled down the front, arm-in-arm, whilst the humbler portion of the audience amused themselves by cracking nuts and simple jokes until both were exhausted, and then they betrayed their interest in the piece, and their anxiety for the curtain again to rise, by a steady rumbling of hob-nailed boots, varied and sometimes accompanied by shrill whistles: a piece of rowdyism which seemed very much to disgust the three young gentlemen in the front row, who had finished their promenade, and were now occupying themselves by staring at two demure-looking young ladies on my left, who appeared to be very indignant at the scrutiny to which they were subjected. My private opinion is, however, that the indignation was just a trifle affected, and that really they were not a little flattered at having gained the notice of three such magnificent creatures. That opinion was considerably strengthened too by such fragments of their conversation as unavoidably reached my ears, and by the continual giggling, which did not appear to indicate a very disturbed state of mind.

"For shame, Aggie! I wonder at your looking at them. Rude things they are, especially that Harry Franks!" exclaimed the elder, tossing her head, and immediately afterwards casting a demure glance behind her sister's back at the youth nearest to me, whom I immediately concluded to be the said Harry Franks. Just as I was getting interested, however, in this by-play, its further development was interfered with by the ascent of the curtain.

I shall not easily forget that second act. Many years have come and gone since I sat in that rude barn and watched the performance of that little company of strolling players, but still that scene is vivid and fresh in my memory. The young hero of the piece is joined by his beloved, and marries her. They travel to London, and he, blithe and sanguine, commences the search undertaken every day by so many eager and hopeful hearts for "something to do." Failure seems to wait on failure. Editors will not accept his contributions, no one wants a secretary, no one wants a clerk, no one wants a porter, and, at last, no one will spare a copper to save his young wife and child from starvation. I could call to mind half a dozen plays now running which have included in their plot such a scene and such a development, but I am quite sure that the part has never been played as it was played that night in the barn at Chipping Norton. For the first time, in her stage get-up of faded dress and thin shawl, I could see how haggard and emaciated young Mrs. Farradale really was, how puny and delicate looking her child, and how gaunt and misery stricken was his appearance. They played the part of starving man and woman, this young husband and wife, and as I listened to the bitter pathos in her tones and watched the dull despair in his face, a horrible suspicion stole in upon me that they were themselves almost in this terrible strait. Real tears glistened in his eyes as he felt his wife's frail form, and a heart-rending sob escaped him as he passed his hand over her scanty garments. The wild anger in his voice when he spoke of his unforgiving father was real, and, as if by some electric spell, his quivering tones touched and held spellbound the village audience. They thought it fine acting, and wondered at his art; I shuddered and turned away, for from the first I had perceived that he was but an indifferent actor. It was the stern reality of the whole thing that caused his voice to quaver and his eyes to grow dim, and reality of suffering that brought that woe-begone look into his young wife's pallid face. The situation had brought them recollection and realization of their own hapless state, and they had no need to act. I am not ashamed to confess that I could not sit it out. I left the place, hurrying away into the cold night air, and scarcely had the door closed upon me when a deafening burst of applause announced the termination of the scene. I had stumbled across a veritable drama in this quiet little country town, and I had been brought face to face with a misery which one reads often in books, but seldom meets. Could Sir Edward Farradale really be aware of his son's desperate plight? I wondered, as I walked up and down the little pathway which led from the barn to the road. A severe and unforgiving old man I could readily imagine him to be, but surely not so unforgiving as to let his only son and his daughter-in-law slowly starve to death on the miserable pittance of strolling players. I am anything but a busybody, and like nothing less, as a rule, than interfering with other people's business (although I am a lawyer), but it did not take me long to decide that immediately on my return to town I would risk the loss of a wealthy client, and myself inform Sir Edward Farradale of the desperate straits in which his son was.

The performance was over, and the audience came trooping out, laughing and talking, exchanging salutations and passing comments upon the performance which they had witnessed. Little did they guess how real was the drama which had been played out before their eyes! The two young ladies who had sat on my left hand came out with the rest, laughing and evidently in high good-humour, and close behind them their three admirers, arm-in-arm, also in very good spirits. At the gate I believe they all joined company, and down the dark road I heard their merry, chattering voices as they sallied homewards. I waited until the outpouring crowd grew thinner and thinner, until all but myself had cleared away, and then I re-entered the barn. The old woman who had sold me my ticket, and who was about to extinguish the lights, paused and looked questioningly at me; but before she could frame a protest, I had pushed on one side the screen and stood behind the scenes. All the little company were talking together in a cluster save the two in whom I was interested, and they were a little apart from the rest by themselves. He, Philip Farradale, was wrapping an old shawl carefully around his wife's throat with all the attentive tenderness of the most *preux chevalier* of an opera-house cloak-room; and as he put the finishing touches to it and stepped back to note the effect, she shot up at him a glance of gratitude, and for a moment her wasted face was illumined by a wonderfully sweet smile, which showed me in what way and in what fashion she had once been beautiful. The little child who had figured in the play was asleep. Small wonder, for it was eleven o'clock, and such an infant should have been in bed hours ago. Mr. Andrews was the first to perceive me, and he at once left the group and hurried to my side.

"Aha! sir; come to offer your congratulations, eh? Glad to see you! Not such a bad house, was it?" he remarked, rubbing his hands and beaming up at me jocosely.

"The place seemed quite full," I answered. "I should not have intruded here, Mr. Andrews, but I want you to breakfast with me tomorrow morning, and Mr. Farradale, if he will be so good."

"I shall be delighted, sir," was the emphatic reply; but Philip Farradale shook his head.

"I shall take no refusal," I insisted eagerly. "Won't you introduce me to Mrs. Farradale? Perhaps she will favour me too."

He mentioned my name with no very good grace, and Mrs. Farradale returned my bow in a perfectly lady-like and self-possessed manner. There was nothing in the least loud or stagey about her. Notwithstanding her dingy dress and faded shawl, she bore herself like a lady; and my heart ached for the trio as she turned with a mute, questioning glance to her husband, her hand still resting on the child's shoulder.

"You must come, now, Mr. Farradale," I urged, laying my hand on his arm. "I want particularly to have a chat with you; and bring your wife and the youngster. I insist," and in the end he promised.

I left them then, and made my way from the barn into the road. I had scarcely passed through the gate before Mr. Andrews caught me up.

"I see you take an interest in young Farradale and his wife," he said, as we walked down the lane together. "I wish we could do something for them. I declare my heart aches sometimes—it does indeed," he went on seriously—"to see them going down, down, down. I do everything I can; but that isn't much. Every penny we earn I divide in a fair proportion amongst the company, and yet I know that the little they draw can only just keep them going."

"You wouldn't care to lose them from the company, I suppose, even if something better could be found for young Farradale?" I inquired.

"By Jove! wouldn't I, though!" declared the little manager emphatically. "Margaret Knowles was a very fair actress once, but she takes no manner of interest or pleasure in it now. How could she, poor thing? She walks through her parts like a stick; and as for him, he never could act a little bit. I wouldn't have mentioned it for the world," he went on, dropping his voice and drawing a little closer to me, "but I should be far better off without them. They are neither of them the least bit suited for the life we have to lead. I keep them simply because if I sent them away they must either go to the workhouse or starve. There, that's in confidence, sir, of course; and now, good-night. I shall be with you soon after nine to-morrow morning. Good-night"—and with a parting wave of the hand he left me and trotted off to his lodgings at the other end of the town.

The slight, yet kindly, curiosity which I had felt as to the antecedents and history of this young actor and his girl-wife had very rapidly developed into a warm interest, and I spent most of the night in revolving various schemes for their benefit. By breakfast-time in the morning I had come to a decision as to the first step to be taken. First of all I had to interview my landlady—a dear old lady she was, in a widow's cap and a black silk dress, which rustled like brown paper. I have seen her many times since; but never save attired in that black silk gown which emitted from its folds a faint perfume of dried lavender, and in her neat widow's cap. A motherly, kind-hearted old lady she is, and she entered at once into my scheme with interest and approval. I engaged the room in which I had slept (can't you guess that in it the four-poster was as large as a tent, the sheets spotless and the furniture old-fashioned?) for a week, and also paid her a sum for which, if my scheme prospered, she was to board Mr. and Mrs. Farradale and the child for the same period. She was not on any account to reveal this arrangement to them, but on their leaving was simply to say that Mr. Andrews had settled the bill.

At a few minutes after nine o'clock who should arrive but that benevolent little gentleman, in his shabby brown check suit, of which he was no whit ashamed, and beaming all over his face, as if coming out to breakfast was the very richest of jokes.

"Good morning, Mr. Armitage; good morning, sir!" he exclaimed vigorously, as he caught sight of me engaged in my confabulation with the landlady. "I'm in good time, you see; the very essence of politeness, you know, to be in good time when you are invited out to breakfast; but I'm as hungry as a hunter, I do assure you."

I beckoned him to join us, and explained my scheme, of which he approved heartily. Then the landlady bustled away to superintend the getting ready of the breakfast, and I further explained my intentions to Mr. Andrews.

"I don't know yet what I shall be able to do for our young friend and his wife," I said; "but at any rate, until I decide upon something definite, I want you to pay them treble their present salary, and I will hand you the difference each week. You can let them think— think anything you like, as long as you don't tell them the truth. And, Mr. Andrews, you will particularly oblige me by not finishing that little speech," I went on hurriedly. "You would do exactly the same if you were in my position; I'm sure you would. I am a bachelor, and well off; I may even call myself rich. I shall never miss the little it will cost me to assist these young people."

Mr. Andrews shook my hand heartily, and though every muscle in his face seemed struggling to force a smile, I fancied there was a slight glistening in the keen, kindly little eyes.

"You're a good Samaritan, Mr. Armitage, that's what you are; and I thank Providence that we fell in with you. If ever a young couple needed a friend, they do, and I can't be thankful enough that they've found one in you. I declare it's made a miserable man of me sometimes, although I've always done what I could. Sh! Here they are!" he broke off suddenly.

"Farradale, my boy, how dare you come so late? It's ten minutes past nine, and I'm just about famished. Mrs. Farradale, good morning. Allow me to help you with your shawl. There, that'll do. And now come and pour out the coffee for us, do. I'm a starving man. Halloa! here's the youngster. Blessed if I hadn't forgotten him! Now, Phil, my boy, here's a seat for you next your mother;" and he hoisted the youngster who had stared shyly at me, but had welcomed vociferously his older friend, into a high chair, and then, taking a seat himself, rubbed his hands together and beamed round upon us generally.

The breakfast party was a great success, thanks chiefly to the genial manager's kindly tact. What little awkwardness there might have been was dispelled at the outset by his voluble conversation, which he kept up with brief intervals during the whole of the meal. The little boy Philip seemed rather inclined to be shy at first; but he soon forgot his shyness in his appetite, and, seated between his mother and myself, became with Mr. Andrews the principal contributor to the conversation. A capital breakfast we had, and it was good to see how they all enjoyed it.

"Why can't we always have breakfasts like this, Mamma?" inquired Philip the younger, somewhat plaintively, towards the end of the meal, as he meditatively disposed of a spoonful of marmalade. "Such a nice room, too!" he added approvingly.

We all laughed, a little uneasily, and I seized the opportunity to introduce plot number one.

"That reminds me of a little matter which I had meant to mention to you," I said, addressing Mr. Farradale. "I took this room and a bedroom for a week, meaning to have a little quiet fishing down here, but an important business appointment which I had quite overlooked calls me back to town for a day or two. Of course, I must pay for the rooms; but why shouldn't they be occupied? Why shouldn't you and Mrs. Farradale," I continued, "pack up your traps and come and stop here for the week? You would find the charges ridiculously low, and, of course, there would be nothing for the rooms. Come, now, I think that it would be a very good arrangement."

Philip gave a whoop of delight, and his mother flushed with pleasure. Mr. Farradale, however, looked doubtful.

"It is very good of you to propose it, I'm sure," he said hesitatingly; "but I fear that the charges which you consider ridiculously low would still be beyond our means."

"We can soon ascertain that;" and I touched the bell and inquired for the landlady. As I had arranged, the terms quoted were ridiculous, and Mrs. Farradale looked delighted.

"How charming to be able to stop here, instead of those hateful pokey lodgings!" she exclaimed; and a real tinge of colour came into her thin pale cheeks, improving her appearance wonderfully. "Phil, won't it be nice?"

He looked at her fondly, and smiled acquiescence.

"We really are most indebted to Mr. Armitage," he said heartily. "The arrangement will be a very pleasant one for us."

"It's a jolly good idea," declared Mr. Andrews, with a beaming face; "and, hang it all! if we have many more nights like last night the exchequer'll get more elastic, too! You seem to have brought us good luck, Mr. Armitage. I drink your health, sir, in coffee, and trust that it will be continued."

That morning, after a very cordial leave-taking with my friends, I returned to town, with the firm intention of calling at once on Sir Edward Farradale, and saying a few plain words to him. Much to my disappointment, however, I learnt that he was out of town—on the Continent, in fact—and was not expected to return until the New Year. I could do nothing for the present, therefore, save continue to remit the amount agreed upon to Mr. Andrews each week, and I was glad to hear from him that it was sufficient to enable them to live in, at any rate, tolerable comfort.

Coincidences do happen sometimes. Here is an instance. Amongst my letters on the morning before Christmas Eve was one from Sir Edward Farradale, the young actor's father. It was short, but to me intensely interesting.

> "Dysart House Kensington
> "December 24th.
>
> "Dear Sirs,—
> "Will your Mr. Armitage be so good as to call upon me this evening at the above address? The matter is important.
> Yours truly,
> "Edward Farradale.
> "To Messrs. Armitage & Hales, Lincoln's Inn."

Punctually at nine o'clock that evening I stood on the steps of Sir Edward Farradale's town mansion, and on application was at once admitted. At various times the duties of my profession, and in one or two instances social duties, have caused me to visit the houses of merchants and noblemen famous for their wealth and prodigality; but in none had I seen such almost profligate luxury and magnificence of appointments as the entrance-hall and interior of Dysart House disclosed. Such things do not as a rule impress me, but I had heard much of the state in which the railway king lived, and I saw now that such reports were by no means exaggerated. The hall was more like that of some of the most princely of the West End Clubs than the entrance to the dwelling-house of a childless widower, thronged as it was with mirrors, lounges, and rare exotics, amongst which several footmen in handsome liveries were lounging noiselessly about on a thick velvet carpet. The dining-room door was open, and, though the table appeared to have been laid for one only, the damask cloth, the gold plate and epergne, the chastely cut glasses, and the profusion of hothouse flowers and fruits, all these things, together with the splendour by which I was surrounded, filled me with an intense and growing dislike to the man who could let his son—almost his only relative—starve to death on the miserable pittance of a strolling player, while he himself was revelling in such insensate, and to my quiet taste almost barbaric, luxury. In a small room leading off the library, carefully dressed in evening clothes, with *The Times* in his hand, and a cup of black coffee by his side, I found the railway millionaire. On a table before him was a huge pile of letters, which his secretary, a man almost as old as himself, was busily sorting. As the servant ushered me into the room, he looked up from his paper and nodded in a not unfriendly manner whilst he motioned me to a seat.

"Wright, you can leave us for half an hour," he said, turning to the man who was writing beside him. "You have plenty to go on with at present;" and the obedient secretary gathered up his papers and vanished.

Sir Edward Farradale seemed in no hurry to broach the business on which he had sent for me, for, after pushing the cigar-box across the table (I knew better than to refuse one of his cigars), he leaned back in his chair, and, closing his eyes, seemed deep in thought. I watched him with a new interest, studying his face as I had never studied it before, and wondering whether my appeal—for I had decided to make one—would have any chance of success. I felt dispirited and very little sanguine as I recognized in his hard-set countenance the signs of a disposition obstinate and unbending in the extreme. The bushy grey eyebrows and low forehead, the thin, firm lips, well-cut, decided chin, and keen, steel-coloured eyes, all denoted such characteristics; and while they accounted to me for much of this man's extraordinary success, they filled me with apprehensions and misgivings lest my mission should prove a failure.

Suddenly he opened his eyes and spoke in his usual abrupt manner.

"Mr. Armitage," he said, "I am going to die."

The words were a shock to me, and for a moment I hesitated, wondering whether he was serious. "You think that I don't look very ill, perhaps," he continued. "Nevertheless, Sir Andrew Clark has told me only this morning in this room that I cannot live a year. This being so I have sent for you to make my will."

His coolness was wonderful. For a man who had lived for the world, and had been essentially a worldly man, it was astounding.

"I have always understood that Mr. Kendrick was your family solicitor," I faltered.

"Mr. Kendrick has no longer the management of any of my affairs.

He has offended me by persistently harping upon a forbidden subject. I have been pleased with the way your firm has managed several little affairs for me, so I sent for you. There is no time like the present," he went on, taking a thin note-book from his inner pocket. "You will find some papers on the table."

I drew some foolscap towards me and filled in the preliminaries. Then he began.

"First of all, there are the executors," he said, in a quick, business-like tone. "Well, I appoint you and Mr. Edward Roberts. To each I leave a thousand pounds."

I bowed and wrote in silence.

"I also wish to leave to Henry Thomson Wright, my secretary, five hundred pounds; to Alice Pratt, my housekeeper, Midland Railway Stock to produce two hundred a year; and the same to Robert Ball, my butler."

I wrote, and, having written, looked up for further instructions.

"I leave the whole of my shares in the Great Western Railway," he continued, "amounting at present to £57,900 10s, to be divided between St. Thomas's and Guy's Hospitals; and to my cousin, Mabel Padmore, the sum of £50,000, the estate and manor of Portland Towers, in Yorkshire, Dysart House, Kensington, with the whole of my furniture, jewellery, horses and carriages, plate, etc. The rest of my Midland Railway Stock and other investments, which I calculate to amount to a little under £290,000, I leave to my esteemed friend, Sir Charles Tomkins. You will find in this book and in documents which I will instruct Mr. Kendrick to hand over to you a complete list of all my investments, personal property, and estates."

I laid down my pen and prepared for the struggle.

"Am I to understand then, Sir Edward Farradale, that there is no one else whom you wish to benefit under your will?"

He looked at me keenly from underneath his bushy grey eyebrows.

"I have left you a thousand pounds," he said curtly.

"Money which I should never touch," I answered firmly, "for I should not even dream of accepting the executorship of such a will as this. You have a son, Sir Edward."

He turned pale with a sudden fury, and his steel blue eyes flashed with an angry light.

"Mr. Armitage, you are trespassing upon forbidden ground," he said, in a low intense tone. "I had a son, it is true, but I have cast him off, and never wish to hear his name again. I shall not leave him a shilling. You will oblige me by pressing that gong, and we will have two of the servants in to witness the will."

"One moment," I exclaimed, stretching out my hand to secure the gong. "It may interest you, Sir Edward Farradale, to know where and in what condition your son at present is. Only a few weeks back I lent him a helping hand to save him from starvation. Yes, starvation," I repeated impressively. "For while you are living here like a millionaire, your only son is earning a miserable pittance with a strolling company of players; tramping from town to town in the desperate attempt to earn enough to support his wife, your daughter, and his little son, your grandchild. He did wrong to disobey you, no doubt, Sir Edward, but his wife is not what you think her. She is a lady, and a daughter to be proud of; and your grandson is a fine little fellow. You need be ashamed of neither. Surely, if you cannot forgive your son, as any other man would do, you will leave enough to keep him from starving. Let me add a codicil;" and I took up the pen again. Sir Edward Farradale had listened without emotion—without, indeed, any signs of interest—to what I had been saying. When I had finished he turned and struck the gong without any remark.

"Tell Burditt I want him immediately, and then remain yourself," were his orders to the man.

I made one last appeal, full of anger, but with a sinking heart.

"Sir Edward, I cannot think that you fully understand what you are about to do. Do you realize that by signing this will you will incur the everlasting disgrace of leaving your only son and grandchild dependent upon charity; if, indeed, they do not starve to death before charity intervenes? You cannot mean to sign this—this most disgraceful document. Let me add a codicil. Leave them but enough to keep them respectably out of these many thousands of yours, and I will say no more. We are not sentimental men, Sir Edward, but I may remind you that no time could be more suitable for a reconciliation with your son than now. To-morrow is Christmas Day, and—" I was interrupted by the opening of the door and the entrance of the butler and footman.

"Robert and Heggs, come here," said Sir Edward, in his clear, cold tones. "I require you to witness my signature to this document—my will;" and he dipped the pen in the ink.

I leaned over the table, and, for once in my life in a towering passion, tore into fragments the will which I had prepared.

"Never in my presence!" I exclaimed, scattering the fragments all over the floor. "I would not have my name associated with such an infamous document, Sir Edward Farradale, for the whole of your fortune! I wish you good evening;" and I caught up my hat and made for the door.

"Robert, show Mr. Armitage out," said Sir Edward, without the least sign of anger, "and then put on your coat at once. I shall have a note ready for you in a moment. Good evening, Mr. Armitage; I'm sorry to have troubled you."

I walked home full of burning indignation against Sir Edward Farradale. From what I had previously seen and heard of him, I had been prepared to find him a man of firm will and difficult to move; but that he could be so absolutely and heartlessly adamant I had never contemplated. It had seemed to me that his sense of justice would, at any rate, have led him to make some provision for his son, even if he refused to forgive him. But of that now there appeared to be no probability.

I slept badly that night, and cut my *Times* in the morning with less animation than usual. The first paragraph which caught my eye, however, gave me a violent shock.

"SUDDEN DEATH OF A CITY MILLIONAIRE.—We regret to announce that Sir Edward Farradale, well known in all financial circles as a large holder of railway and other stock, and chairman of several companies, died suddenly of heart disease early this morning at his town mansion, Dysart House, Kensington. Deceased was," etc.

I flung the paper into a corner, and, leaving my breakfast untasted, hurried out into the street and hailed a hansom. In a quarter of an hour I was at Dysart House, and was at once admitted. I asked for Robert, and questioned him breathlessly about the note which his master had told him to deliver.

"The moment you left sir," said Robert, "Sir Edward wrote a note to Mr. Parsons, the lawyer, and told me to take it to his house. I took a cab there, but Mr. Parsons had a dinner-party, and sent out word to me that he would call at Dysart House at nine o'clock this morning. Sir Edward seemed rather annoyed when I gave him this message, but said it would do then, he supposed. As I was leaving the room he called me back, and told me that we need none of us sit up, as he had some writing to do; so we all went to bed. But about two o' clock I came down to make sure about the lights, and he was sitting in his chair bolt upright like, with a glassy sort of look in his eyes which gave me quite a turn. I spoke to him, but he never answered, and then I went close up to him and touched his hand. It was cold as ice, and then it seemed to strike me that he must be dead," concluded Robert, in an awestruck tone. "I rang every one up, and sent for a doctor, but it was all no use, of course."

"Had he done any writing? Were there any papers about?" I queried.

Robert put a piece of paper silently in my hands. It was a sheet of plain foolscap, with these words written on it in Sir Edward Farradale's writing:—

"Last will and testament of Edward Farradale, Knight, December 24th, 188-. I, Edward Farradale, being in sound—"

And there the pen had slipped from his fingers and left a long scrawling mark down the paper. I shuddered. Sudden death is an awful thing.

A few hours later Philip Farradale stood by his dead father's body, and on the third day, chief mourner amongst an imposing assemblage, followed it to the grave. I never told him of that will which I had been bidden to prepare. *Cui bono*? And why should I, their most intimate friend, be the first to cast a cloud over their unsullied happiness, which surely they have richly deserved? For the days of their misery are forgotten, and, thanks to excellent constitutions, it has left no evil traces behind. A long cruise in the most luxurious of yachts brought the colour back to Mrs. Farradale's cheeks, and the southern breezes and restful life renewed in her the strength and youth which privation and misery had taken from her; whilst he came back to England broad-shouldered and sunburnt, with happy, careless laugh and animated manners, a different man from the Philip Farradale who, by his stolid expression of hopeless misery, had excited my sympathy in that Oxfordshire lane. And little Philip. Well, I have just read in *The Times* that he is looked upon as the most promising, although the youngest, batsman in The Harrow eleven. So it may reasonably be inferred that he too has suffered little from early privations.

One word as to our genial little manager, Mr. Andrews. They would have done anything for him, and I myself could have helped him in many ways, but he would have none of it.

"I'm a confirmed Bohemian," he laughed, when we first delicately hinted at some little assistance. "I delight in being hard up. I delight in having to walk now and then because I haven't enough money to pay my railway fare. Surfeit would trouble me more than privation. When I want your help I shall not forget that I have good friends."

And so we had to let him have his own way. I often see him, though, for walking tours are still my hobby; and if I can plan one so as to fall in with a shabby little company of strolling players in some out-of-the-way town-village, why, then I am always heartily welcomed, and Dick Andrews, as merry and beaming as ever, will take up his quarters with me until the three days or a week are up, and tents are struck and the show moves on.

# THE HIDDEN ARMY

A dozen men were seated around a table in the stuffy, stale-odoured room—and a spokesman on whom all their eyes were bent.

"It is for that, my brothers, that you are summoned here to-night," he was saying in a low yet distinct tone. "It is to bid you prepare. We have sure advices. The wrath of the Fatherland is kindled. Even now, our great and invincible army is being mobilized. Soon you shall rule in the country where you have served!"

There was a little murmur of guttural approval. The faces of the men turned towards the speaker were of various types enough, but their dress was uniform—the grease-stained, shapeless livery of the waiter fresh from his night's toil.

The man at the head of the table twirled his fair moustache fiercely.

"Ah!" he cried, "my children, think what it means! They force a landing, our brave German soldiers, and what do they find? An opposing army of the cowards who ran from the Boers! Perhaps—but what else! An army of brave men, many thousands strong, trained, armed, sprung from who knows where—as eager to strike for the Fatherland and crush these fat stiff-necked English, as their brothers who come fresh from the barracks. Think what a joyful surprise—what a certainty of victory, what glory for all of us who have secretly planned and organized the army of hidden men! Brothers! The Fatherland!—and victory!"

They grunted and drank and grunted again. The chairman took up his hat.

"I ask you," he said, "to drink one more toast—success to my mission! I cannot tell you what it is. One man only, save myself, knows it. But I can tell you this: If I am successful your rifles will be on your shoulders before many days are past, and you will see these English, as you march through the streets, scurry to their holes like rabbits. I go to make the war!"

They drank, and set down their empty tankards. Their voices were scarcely raised above a whisper, for this was a business meeting of the Waiters' Trade Union Association.

"Success to Max! To the war!"

A neatly dressed young man, fair, with waxed moustache, and a bearing which seemed to indicate some sort of military training, stepped out from a small pony-cart in front of the Grand Hotel, Settlingham-by-the-Sea, and promptly commenced a spirited argument with the driver as to the fare. Having ascertained the exact legal amount, he paid it in a shilling and some carefully counted coppers. Then, carrying his own bag, he marched into the hotel.

"Is the manager, Mr. Rice, in, Miss?" he asked the young lady at the office.

She glanced behind her. The manager stepped forward. The young man took off his hat.

"My name," he said, "is Spielman. I received your wire, and I have come by the earliest possible train."

The manager was disposed to be affable and held out his hand.

"Glad to see you, Mr. Spielman," he said. "The hall-boy here will show you your room, and you had better change as soon as possible. Will you step inside and have something first?"

"I should enjoy," the young man answered, "a glass of beer. It is a warm afternoon!"

He entered the little bar behind the office and bowed to the young ladies, who received his greeting with a mixture of condescension and reserve. A head-waiter was a person who had been known to presume upon his position.

"I trust," Mr. Spielman said, "that business is fairly good, sir?"

"We are very nearly full up," the manager answered. "You will find plenty to do."

"I like work," the young man said simply. "Is there any one to whom you wish me to show special attention?"

"Certainly," the manager answered—"I am glad you mentioned it. I will give you the names of the others to-morrow, but our most important visitor just now is Lord Brentmore."

The head-waiter bowed. It was one of his professional habits always to bow at the mention of a lord's name.

"A very rich gentleman?" he inquired deferentially.

"Not only rich," the manager answered, "but he is a Cabinet Minister—Secretary of State for Foreign Affairs. He has come down here, with all his family, for a rest and a month's golf. Not that he gets much rest, poor fellow, with all these Continental troubles getting worse every day. By the by, Mr. Spielman, are you a German?"

"I am a Swiss," lied Mr. Spielman.

"Can't say I'm sorry," the manager admitted. "Mr. Spielman. I don't want to hurry you, but—"

Mr. Spielman finished his beer at once.

"In one quarter of an hour," he announced, "I shall be in the dining-room."

The new arrival was shown to his room on the fifth floor, and with expressionless face made a rapid toilet. On his way to the dining-room he met, in the hall, a young man who was lounging against a table, with a paper in his hand, and who surveyed him curiously through an eyeglass. Mr. Spielman bowed and passed on to his duties, but a slight frown had gathered upon his forehead.

"I was an ass!" he murmured softly.

The young man, who was called the Honourable Philip Usher, and was Lord Brentmore's private secretary, strolled towards the door and met his lordship, who was just coming in from golf.

"Good match, sir?"

Lord Brentmore's face was beaming.

"Excellent," he answered. "We played a fourball—the Colonel and I against Holland and Dick. The Colonel was off the game, only came in once, but we won two up. I did five threes."

Usher nodded sympathetically. "There is one despatch, sir," he said. "I have decoded it. Shall I come upstairs with you now?"

Lord Brentmore led the way to a private sitting room on the first floor and listened to the message. His face clouded over a little.

"A bit stiff, eh?" he remarked.

Usher nodded.

"It may be your fancy, sir," he said, "but it really seems to me that they want to force a quarrel."

"We won't have it," Brentmore answered. "We can't afford it. If war must come it must, but not now. Another couple of years, and we can snap our fingers at them."

"I am afraid," Usher remarked, "that our friends realize that."

"I wouldn't mind so much," Lord Brentmore continued, "if I could get the chief and Morland to realize the position. Practically, you know, Usher," he added, glancing round the room and lowering his voice a little, "I am the only man in the Cabinet who is hot for peace."

"I know it, sir," Usher answered, "and I know that you are right. That is why I am glad that you are so much better just now. If you were laid up, I believe that we should be at war in a week."

Lord Brentmore nodded.

"Fortunately," he said, "I never felt better in my life. This place suits me exactly. I shall build a house here some day."

"I wish that you had one now, sir," Usher answered. "When so much depends upon you. I am not sure that it is wise to stay in a hotel."

Lord Brentmore shrugged his shoulders.

"Nothing could happen to me here," he remarked, "to which I should not be liable in my own house. Besides, as you know, we could not get a house. Now then, Usher, if you are ready, I'll give you down a reply. I'm going to try the gentle answer."

The new head-waiter was apparently a great success. He was prompt, courteous, and possessed of obvious administrative gifts. No one in the room could complain of being neglected, but his chief attention was not unnaturally bestowed upon Lord Brentmore's party, which consisted of his Lordship himself, his wife, one daughter, Lady Eva, and Usher. He frequently brought them dishes with his own hands, and they found every want anticipated. Usher eyed him more than once curiously.

"I'm inclined to be a democrat," he remarked, when their new attendant was out of the room for a moment, "but I can't help thinking that fellow had rather a cheek to come down from town first class."

Lord Brentmore looked up amused. "Are you sure that he did?" he asked.

"Absolutely," Usher answered; "we were in the same carriage for some distance, until I changed into an empty one at Ipswich. Saw you coming down, didn't I?" he remarked, as Spielman reappeared.

"I believe so, sir," the head-waiter answered quietly. "A friend of mine gave me a pass."

"That's a lie," Usher muttered, as Spielman hurried off to another table. "I saw him give up his ticket."

Lord Brentmore smiled.

"After all, why not?" he remarked. "We all have one pet extravagance. His may be travelling first class. Mine, if I could afford to indulge in it, would be to put down a new ball on every tee."

"I don't see why he wanted to lie about it, anyhow," Usher remarked.

They left the room soon afterwards. Usher sought out the manager in his room.

"Mr. Rice," he said, "I hope you won't think me a nuisance, but can you tell me anything about your new head-waiter?"

"Certainly, sir," the manager answered. "I trust that he has given satisfaction?"

"Absolutely," Usher answered. "It isn't that. There are just a few things I should like to know. Is he a German?"

"No, sir, a Swiss."

"H'm!" Usher remarked. "He doesn't look like one. Now, can you tell me this? Lord Brentmore first wrote you about coming here in July didn't he?"

"Yes, sir."

"Did you engage this fellow before or after then?"

"Afterwards, sir. In fact, I did not engage him at all. Hausman was coming, the dark German from the Imperial, who was here last year—you may remember him, sir; but it seems he was taken ill, and Spielman has come on to take his place for a month."

"At Hausman's recommendation?"

"Yes, sir. I had other references, though."

"Does it pay these fellows to come down here?" Usher asked.

The manager smiled.

"Wonderfully well, sir," he answered. "I know for a fact that Hausman made more in his three months here last year than he could make in a twelvemonth at the Imperial. I shouldn't have engaged him again on the same terms, but he begged so hard, and the visitors here liked him so much."

Usher nodded.

"He wouldn't be likely to give up the job of his own accord, then?" he remarked. "Sham being ill, or anything of that sort?"

"Is it likely, sir," the manager asked. "Besides, I saw him in London only last week, and he was most eager about it."

Usher nodded and turned away.

"I trust that there isn't anything about the new man that you disapprove of, sir?" Mr. Rice asked with concern.

"Nothing at all," Usher answered. "He seems a most capable fellow. Please don't let him think that I've been complaining. He seems to know his business thoroughly."

"But," Usher added to himself as he went upstairs, "I am not quite sure what his business is."

Lady Eva waited below for her escort in their usual after-dinner stroll for a long time. Usher, having first locked the door, spent nearly an hour in the sitting-room where Lord Brentmore and he usually worked. He first of all re-set all the combination locks of the despatch-boxes and sealed them up with a signet-ring, which he carefully replaced upon his finger. Then he took out the code-book and disposed of it in a secret place about his own person. Finally, he destroyed the blotting paper and burnt all the fragments of destroyed letters which he could find in the waste-paper basket. Lord Brentmore came in just as he had finished.

"What on earth are you up to, Usher?" he asked.

"Taking precautions, sir," the young man answered.

"Against what?"

"I'm not sure. Espionage, I suppose."

Lord Brentmore's eyes twinkled. For a statesman, he was distinctively an unimaginative person.

"Do you suspect any one in particular?" he asked.

Usher nodded. "The new head-waiter," he answered briefly.

"Because he came first class?"

"That and many other reasons," Usher answered.

Lord Brentmore lit a cigar.

"Go ahead!" he said.

"Right!" Usher answered. "To begin with, he came first class because he wished to escape observation, and he was busy all the time sorting papers. I took him for some one's private secretary. Then, he came as substitute for another man, who is supposed to be ill, but who served me with my luncheon yesterday morning at the Imperial. The change was made since it was announced that you were coming here. Further, he calls himself a Swiss, when I'm perfectly certain he's a full-fledged German."

Lord Brentmore was unconvinced.

"Supposing he is a spy," he said, "what good can he do himself here? We are not likely to talk secrets before him, or to leave despatches about."

Usher shrugged his shoulders.

"I am sure of one thing only," he said, "he wants watching."

The next morning Lord Brentmore was late for breakfast. When, at last, he appeared, Usher regarded him anxiously. The healthy colour of the night before had gone. He was pale, almost sallow, his eyes were clouded, and the flesh under them was baggy. He had all the appearance of a man suffering from a bad bilious attack.

"Good morning," he said curtly, sinking into his chair. "Tea and dry toast only for me, waiter."

"Seedy?" Usher inquired laconically.

"Liver!" Lord Brentmore answered irritably. "That brutal sweet champagne, I suppose."

"Hard luck," Usher answered. "You'll have to take it easy to-day."

"I'm down here to play golf, and I shall play golf," Lord Brentmore growled. "The Colonel will knock my head off, I suppose, though. What's this?"

"Some fresh tea, sir," the head-waiter answered. "The other has been standing some little time."

Lord Brentmore drank two cups, and ate a little toast. Then he went out on the links, and returned to the hotel at lunch-time a little better. He ate a sole specially prepared, drank one whisky-and-soda, and went back to golf. About four o'clock, however, he returned, looking worse than ever.

"I shall have to lie down," he announced shortly. "Any despatches?"

"Two," Usher announced. "They are important. I will read them to you upstairs."

Lord Brentmore listened to the messages with darkening face.

"Upon my word," he said fiercely, "it makes one feel that the Chief and Morland are right. It's no use humbugging about with these fellows. I've a good mind to give them what they're asking for!"

Usher looked at his chief anxiously.

"Isn't that just what they are aiming at, sir?" he remarked. "They have been trying all the time to goad us into a belligerent frame of mind."

"And, egad, they'll succeed soon!" Lord Brentmore answered. "Here, take down."

It took Usher nearly an hour's persuasion before he got the message into reasonable terms. When he returned from sending it off he brought back with him the Settlingham doctor. Lord Brentmore was obviously annoyed, but submitted himself to the usual examination. The doctor was thoughtful for a moment or two afterwards. He sat with his note-book in his hand, as though about to write a prescription, but instead he asked a few more and apparently irrelevant questions.

"Liver, I suppose?" Lord Brentmore asked, when at last the physician's pencil began to move.

"Yes," the doctor answered. "You should be quite yourself in a couple of days."

He gave some instructions as to diet, and handed over his

prescription. Usher left the room with him.

"Rather sudden attack, isn't it?" he remarked.

"Very, I should say," was the answer. "The symptoms are a little puzzling, but they do not point to anything serious."

Usher drew a little closer to the doctor's side and took his arm as they descended the staircase.

"No trace at all of—poison, I suppose?" he inquired.

The doctor started. The suggestion was somewhat startling.

"No," he answered. "I can't say that. His Lordship must have taken something to disagree with him rather violently. Beyond that, there is nothing to be said. I think he will be better to-morrow."

Usher went back to his chief.

"If I were you, sir," he said, "I should leave this place."

"What do you mean?" Lord Brentmore asked testily.

"Frankly," Usher answered, "I believe that head-waiter has been interfering with your food."

"Then you're an ass!" Lord Brentmore declared. "I haven't patience to listen to such rubbish!" Usher went out and sent a telegram to Scotland Yard. He went also to the manager, and the next day there was a new assistant in the kitchen. Luncheon-time passed without incident. Lord Brentmore was very irritable, ate nothing, and looked worse than ever. He had abandoned any attempt to play golf, and sat studying some recent despatches with an ominous frown. He came in late to dinner, and gave an order to the head-waiter, who attended him obsequiously to his chair. Five minutes afterwards the trouble came.

Usher heard the clatter of falling dishes and the sound of raised voices, and springing from his chair hastened to the screened-off passage from the kitchen. The head-waiter, immaculate no longer, but with stained shirt-front and eyes almost starting from his head, was held by the throat by the new cook's assistant, and on the floor, by the side of a broken dish, was what seemed to be a small silver phial, with holes perforated at the top. The detective touched it with his foot.

"Pick up that, sir," he said, recognizing Usher. "I caught him shaking it over the sole he was taking to Lord Brentmore."

Usher stooped down and put it in his pocket. The waiters were beginning to gather round.

"Bring him this way," Usher directed. A minute later they were in an unoccupied room at the rear of the building. The detective let go his prisoner, who stood for a few minutes breathing heavily.

"Are you both mad," he asked, with a show at least of indignation. "What have I done to be treated like this?"

"I fancy," Usher answered coolly, "that we can answer your question better when we have had the contents of this little phial analysed. In the meantime the police had better take care of you!"

The man shrugged his shoulders.

"As you will," he answered contemptuously. "I am curious to know, however, what I shall be charged with."

The detective smiled.

"Perhaps I shall be able to tell you better, Mr. Max Meyell," he said, "when we have searched the premises of the Waiters' Trades Union. I've had a hint about you before."

There was a blinding flash—a loud report, and the detective staggered backwards. The room was full of smoke—Usher sprang to the door, but he was too late. He wrenched it open. At the end of the passage the head-waiter was coming calmly towards him.

"I am ready for your arrest, sir," he said, bowing and holding out his hands, as though for the handcuffs. "I trust that the gentleman inside is not hurt, but I was forced to send a message before I could comfortably make the acquaintance of your English prison. For Milord Brentmore you need have no anxiety; he will very soon be well."

The detective came out with his left arm hanging helpless.

"He done us, sir," he said gloomily. "There are forty-six German waiters here, and Heaven knows which one— Ah!"

He rushed for the telephone. The wire was cut and the instrument smashed. Outside a little German waiter, with his coat-tails flying behind him, was bending over a bicycle on his way to the post office.

"Quite a genius," Usher remarked. "Take his revolver away."

The head-waiter stepped back and bowed professionally. Then, without a moment's hesitation, he pressed the muzzle to his forehead and blew out his brains.

"The Fatherland!" he muttered, as he fell in a crumpled heap across the threshold.

"Quite *au Japonais*," Lord Brentmore remarked when they told him about it.

Lord Brentmore was playing golf again in two days, and once more the war clouds lightened. The premises of the Waiters' Union were duly raided, and it was a very harmless lot of documents which fell into the hands of the police, and a much injured society who shouted of their wrongs. But another reigns in Max Meyell, alias Spielman's place, and many a garret bedroom in Soho or thereabouts is still adorned with the waiting rifle.

# SIR GEOFFREY'S GUEST

Sir Geoffrey Powers Halledean, Bart., stood on the hearth-rug of his study, with an open letter in his hand and a perplexed frown on his brow. Twice he read the offending epistle through—it was not a long one—and then he rang the bell and summoned his housekeeper. A moment or two later there was a soft tap at the door, a rustling of stiff black silk, an apologetic cough, and that most discreet of matrons glided into the room.

"Good morning, Mrs. Burditt," said the baronet, glancing up from his letter.

"Good morning, Sir Geoffrey," returned the housekeeper respectfully, and added, after a short pause, "I understand from Burditt that you wished to speak to me."

Sir Geoffrey nodded.

"Yes, I wanted a few words with you about this letter," and he tapped it impatiently with his forefinger. "An old friend of mine, a Mr. Comlin, has been in India for twenty years and only returned yesterday. The moment he reached London he found a cablegram which necessitates his immediate return to Ceylon. He doesn't go into details, but says that he has some tea-gardens there, and something is wrong with the manager whom he left in charge. It seems that he brought his little girl over with him, and dare not take her back so soon, as she cannot stand the sea voyage. He has lost sight of all his English friends, so of course he doesn't know what to do with her, and—rather unreasonably, I must say—writes imploring me to have her down here until he can get back again, probably in six months' time. He appears almost to take my acceptance for granted, for he has secured his berth in a steamer which starts this afternoon, and says that he cannot go unless I wire him acquiescence. It's uncommonly awkward. What on earth shall we do with a child down here?" Sir Geoffrey inquired disconsolately. "And yet I can't refuse."

Perhaps Mrs. Burditt thought that the presence of a little girl might in some measure enliven the gloom of Halledean Court, and lighten a little its solitude. Anyhow, she seemed in no way inclined to raise difficulties.

"You can't refuse, Sir Geoffrey," she said decidedly, "and I don't see that it will put us about much. There's a large nursery right away in the south wing, never been opened for years. She'll be quite out of the way there, and won't disturb you a bit. How old did you say she was, sir?"

Sir Geoffrey referred again to the letter.

"I don't know that he mentions her—oh, yes, here it is. Nine next birthday. Isn't she almost old enough to send to school?"

"Dear me, no, Sir Geoffrey," replied Mrs. Burditt. "She'll want a nurse, though, and if she stops long, a governess. I'd better engage a nurse for her, sir."

"I suppose so," he assented dubiously; "and make any other necessary arrangements, Mrs. Burditt. I'll leave the entire matter in your hands, and I shall rely upon you to keep her to the south wing of the house as much as possible. That is all, I think. Be so good as to tell Thomas to saddle a horse at once. I shall want him to ride over to Harborough with a telegram."

The telegram was duly sent, and in a few hours' time came the reply:—

"A thousand thanks. Carry will arrive Harborough station 5.30. Going out this afternoon by the *Atalanta*. Will write first mail."

Sir Geoffrey Powers Halledean, of Halledean Court, Leicestershire, and the St. James' Club, Pall Mall, was a bachelor and a recluse. Perhaps recluse is scarcely a strong enough word, for the life he led was almost the life of a hermit. He was the despair of the county, for owning one of the richest estates, and being one of the finest horsemen and best-looking men in the neighbourhood, he neither hunted nor visited, but simply buried himself in his books and writing, and took not the slightest interest in the sports and pursuits of those who lived around him. To men this was tantalizing, but to women it was worse. It was simply torture to think that within a few miles of them lived so desirable a neighbour, who was utterly indifferent to their gracious regard and numberless invitations, and who preferred burying himself amongst his books and pamphlets to taking his proper place in the society of the county, and yielding himself up for a prize to the best-looking or most fortunate of the young ladies of the shire. Year followed year, however, and found all their efforts to draw him from his seclusion fruitless, and at last they gave it up. The men—some of them—read his articles in the fortnightly and other reviews, and pronounced them uncommonly clever, which, of course, increased the vain attempts of their wives to secure him on their visiting list and as their guest. He never sat on the bench, and the affairs of his estate were altogether in the hands of his steward. He never attended a meet, although he gave a hundred guineas yearly to the hunt; his keepers shot over his covers at their own sweet will, save on those very rare occasions when he had some learned friends down from London who could shoot, and Halledean Court, once the most hospitable house in the county, was, notwithstanding its owner's large rent-roll, partly closed up.

Of course there were plenty of stories about, malicious and otherwise, which professed to account for this extraordinary seclusion on the part of Sir Geoffrey Halladean, and perhaps it would be as well to at once declare that they were every one false. The facts were these: Sir Geoffrey had been educated for the bar, and had come into the title and estates quite unexpectedly when he was twenty-six years old. He was an orphan, and lived much alone, was of studious tastes and quiet habits, and he heard of his good fortune with something akin to indifference. His principal satisfaction was that now he could relinquish his profession, of which he had never been particularly fond, and devote his whole attention to branches of study which were more congenial to him. He began to read deeply, and if only he had commenced his career as a student under a suitable mentor the energy and intellect which he readily commanded would have carried him forward without doubt into the foremost ranks of the thinkers of the day. But he was versatile in his tastes, impressionable by nature, and a trifle morbid and pessimistic in his ideas of his fellows, which begat in him a slight censoriousness. His appetite for study was insatiable, but not altogether healthy. He had flitted from school to school of ancient and latter-day philosophy, reckoning himself at various times amongst the disciples of the most untenable, until he suddenly discovered the flaw in their doctrine and abruptly shifted his quarters. He read everything that came near him, reading, therefore, a little that was wholesome and a good deal that was not, until at thirty-five years of age it had commenced to dawn upon him that he had wasted some of the best years of his life in mastering doctrines and tenets which he had afterwards as religiously overthrown in grappling with monsters of his own rearing; and, in short, that his multifarious stock of learning had won him nothing but the reputation of a pedant, and the most decided consciousness that he was still an extremely ignorant and unsatisfied man.

But what was he to do? Avoidance of society becomes a habit more difficult to break through than any other, and his many years of rigid solitude had developed this habit strongly. He was shy and ill at ease if he came near one of the opposite sex; nor could he talk even with men upon everyday subjects without embarrassment. He had acquired all the *mauvaise honte* of the bookworm, and he knew that it would be a medicine too nauseous for him to seek relief for his disappointments in society. So he burnt all his notes on twenty different schools of irrational philosophy, took long walks or rides during the mornings, and settled down to study science the rest of the day. In person he was tall and finely built, and though constant study had stooped his shoulders somewhat, the stoop was not ungraceful. He was dark, with dark moustache and unkempt beard, for he never troubled to shave; of somewhat pallid complexion and high cheek bones, owing no doubt to his many years of intellectual toil; but his features were regular and well cut, and his eyes particularly keen and brilliant; in dress he was decidedly a sloven; as, indeed, he was in all matters of personal appearance. He was thirty-five years of age, and respectively as he was riding or writing looked ten years younger or older. Such was Sir Geoffrey Powers Halledean, Bart.

The matter of the reception of Mr. Comlin's little girl having been transferred to Mrs. Burditt's shoulders, and finding her unexpectedly amiable about it, Sir Geoffrey troubled himself no more about the affair. He returned from his morning's ride about two o'clock, gave orders for a carriage to meet the 5.30 train at Harborough station, but had directed that his little guest should have tea in the housekeeper's room on her arrival. Then he settled himself down to write an article for his favourite review. He heard the carriage return from the station, but, being immersed in his subject, did not deem it necessary to go out himself to welcome the little stranger. Suddenly his door was burst open without any one having knocked—a thing which he never recollected to have happened before—and on glancing up with a reproving frown, he beheld to his utter astonishment a stylishly-dressed and extremely pretty young lady crossing the floor towards him with outstretched hand and bewitching smile.

"How do you do, Sir Geoffrey Halledean?" she exclaimed brightly. "I am Carry Comlin."

Sir Geoffrey rose to his feet, and stared at the young lady, literally open-mouthed.

"Miss Comlin," he repeated vacantly while he mechanically shook hands.

"Papa had your telegram this morning," she continued, sweeping his carefully-written sheets from an arm-chair on to the floor, and coolly seating herself. "How awfully good it is of you to have me! You expected me by this train, didn't you? I fancied you looked rather surprised when I came in."

"I thought—there is some little mistake," he faltered. "I understood from Mr. Comlin's letter"—and he commenced a frantic search for it in each of his pockets. "You're more than nine years old, aren't you?" he burst out desperately.

"More than nine years old! Oh, Sir Geoffrey, of course I am! How ridiculous! I'm nineteen next birthday."

Sir Geoffrey had at last extracted Mr. Comlin's letter from his pocket, and was studying it.

"So it is, nineteen," he groaned; "I'm sure I thought it was nine. You see, Comlin never let me know when he was married, or I don't remember if he did. And you're his little daughter. Good heavens! what are we to do?"

"Do? It doesn't matter much, does it?" said the young lady, who was calmly unbuttoning her gloves.

"Matter?" groaned Sir Geoffrey; "why, I live here quite by myself; and—and there's a nursery for you up in the north wing, and a nurse coming to-night; and Mrs. Burditt's been looking out dolls, and Noah's arks, and things for you all this afternoon. And they've laid tea for you in the housekeeper's room, and—"

He broke off suddenly. She had been listening to him with an amused twinkle in her eyes, and was now leaning back in her chair, giving way to peal after peal of the merriest and most musical laughter he had ever heard in his life. He gazed at her for a moment bewildered, and then, despite a strong inclination to ring for Mrs. Burditt, or to make his escape somehow, he was suddenly, to his own great astonishment, constrained to resume his seat, and join heartily in the laugh, a thing he had not done for years. At last she stopped and wiped her eyes—very blue eyes they were—with a tiny lace handkerchief. He stopped too, and looked at her, and then—there was no resisting it—they both laughed again.

"Oh, dear! I feel quite exhausted," she said at length, smiling feebly up at him from the depths of the easy chair in which she had collapsed. "It's too ridiculous, isn't it? A nursery and a Noah's ark! How papa will laugh when I tell him!"

He was beginning to feel frightfully ill at ease again. "Wouldn't you—a—like to take your things off?" he suggested, with something very much like a blush.

"I suppose I must," she said, rising. "Mrs. Burditt will show me my room: I suppose that is your old housekeeper's name, isn't it? And can Celeste—Celeste is my maid—have one somewhere near me?"

"Certainly, of course," he assented hurriedly. "Mrs. Burditt will make any arrangements you like. You can choose your own room after to-day."

"Thank you so much, Sir Geoffrey. Good-bye. I shan't be long—"; and with a smile and nod, to which he had just presence of mind enough to respond with a stiff bow, she vanished.

Sir Geoffrey closed the door after her, and returned to his seat feeling very much like a man in a dream. It was years—many years—since he had exchanged half a dozen words with a lady, young or old; and now, without the least warning, there was a fashionable young lady quartered in the house, utterly ignorant of the character of her host, and who would no doubt expect to be talked to and amused. It was an awful situation for him. Who was to entertain her, and how was he to escape? Should he be taken ill and confined to his room—something with an ugly name, and catching, or— but at this point his cogitations were interrupted by the appearance of Mrs. Burditt on the scene.

"Oh, it's you, is it?" he exclaimed, after a nervous start. "This is very awkward, Mrs. Burditt."

Mrs. Burditt pursed her lips, and looked somewhat glum.

"It is very awkward, indeed, Sir Geoffrey," she assented.

"It all arises from Comlin's execrable writing," he continued, pulling out the letter. "I'm sure it looks like nine, doesn't it?"

Mrs. Burditt took out her spectacles, and acknowledged that the latter part of the word was indistinct.

"Well, what are we to do with her?" he asked helplessly.

Mrs. Burditt reflected.

"The nurse may as well go back again at once," she remarked. "Miss Comlin has brought her own maid."

"But she can't stop here, can she?" queried Sir Geoffrey.

"I don't know much about these sort of things," he continued nervously; "but it wouldn't be considered exactly proper, would it?"

"Decidedly not, sir."

"Well, then, what are we to do?" he reiterated impatiently.

Mrs. Burditt considered for a while.

"A companion," she suggested doubtfully, "would—"

"By no means," interrupted Sir Geoffrey hurriedly. "Another like her? No, thank you," vigorously.

"Well, then, there's your aunt, Sir Geoffrey— Mrs. Prim. Perhaps she would come and stop for awhile, if you wrote and asked her."

Mrs. Prim was a maiden lady of limited means, so the suggestion was reasonable.

"I'll write her at once," declared Sir Geoffrey, seizing a pen. "No, I won't, I'll telegraph. Tell Thomas to saddle a horse at once, and—er—Mrs. Burditt, don't you think it would be better if she dined alone, and something was sent in here to me? Couldn't you say that I was busy, or something— anything," he broke off anxiously.

Mrs. Burditt shook her head. "It would be scarcely kind, sir—the first evening, too," she said deprecatingly.

Sir Geoffrey groaned. "Well, I'll send that telegram, anyhow," he said, writing it out. "Don't forget to tell Thomas, Mrs. Burditt."

He had scarcely despatched it when the door opened and Miss Comlin entered.

"Do you know that the dinner bell has rung, Sir Geoffrey, and you're not dressed yet? Well, I shan't let you go now; I'm too desperately hungry to wait," she continued, laughing. "No one seemed to have the least idea what to do with me when I came downstairs. The drawing-room's closed up, they said, so I came in here. We'll go in to dinner now, if you're ready, please—"; and she laid a tiny white hand upon the sleeve of his shabby brown shooting-coat.

They moved across the magnificent hall, and into the small dining-room, a cosy little octagonal chamber really only a recess of the most imposing apartment, and separated from it by folding doors. A bright fire was burning in the marble grate, and dinner was laid for two on a round table in the centre of the room. Miss Comlin glanced around at the massive pictures, the wainscoted walls, the antique black oak furniture, and at the table sparkling with plate and glass, and gave a sigh of satisfaction as she sank into the high-backed chair, which a tall footman gravely held for her.

"What a charming room, Sir Geoffrey!" she exclaimed approvingly; "and what a dear little round table this is! I suppose you always dine here when you're alone? I just peeped in at the proper dining-room, and it made me feel quite shivery. It's so big. Do you really live in this enormous place all by yourself? It must be dull."

"Yes, I live here by myself," he replied. "But I expect my aunt, Mrs. Prim, here to-morrow," he hastened to assure her. "I've telegraphed for her."

"On my account, I suppose. I'm so sorry. I think it much nicer as it is, and I hate old women. I'm afraid I shall be a dreadful nuisance, though," she added with a smile that seemed to invite contradiction.

"I don't think you will," he said hesitatingly. "You see, I have a good deal of writing to do every day; but I'm quite sure that you'll find it very dull indeed. Mrs. Prim is very nice, though," he added consolingly, "if she wasn't so deaf."

"Oh, no, I shan't, I'm never dull," she declared confidently. "Sir Geoffrey, will you do me a favour?" she whispered, leaning over towards him.

"Certainly."

"Then do send that ridiculously solemn footman away. I declare it quite takes my appetite away to look at him. We can wait on ourselves."

"Oh, yes, by all means. Gravas, leave the room," said Sir Geoffrey.

"I beg your pardon, sir," said Gravas, turning round, astounded, from his occupation of cutting bread at the sideboard.

"You needn't wait. We don't want you. We're going to wait upon ourselves," exclaimed Sir Geoffrey with a desperate cheerfulness. He was woefully ill at ease, and envied beyond measure his guest's perfect composure.

Gravas retreated in a dignified manner, with his nose in the air, and leaving the bread uncut. His master watched him depart, and envied him.

"I'm so glad he's gone," remarked the young lady confidently. "I like Indian servants best, I must say. They are so graceful, and full of tact; altogether different from that pompous old fright. Have you ever been in India?"

Sir Geoffrey had travelled very little, and told her so.

"No? Well, I like England ten times better than India. I was brought up here, you know, and went to school at Brighton until two years ago, when papa sent for me to go out to Ceylon. The school was broken up directly I left, or I dare say I should have been there now. India didn't suit me a bit; I'm so glad to be in England again."

There was a short silence, and Sir Geoffrey racked his brains in vain for something to say to her.

"Wasn't it awful for poor papa to rush back to Ceylon before we'd been in England twenty-four hours? I was so sorry for him."

"It was most unfortunate," her host assented fervently; and then he ventured a question about the tea-gardens, which she immediately began to describe in a most graphic manner. He was interested, and for a while forgot his nervousness. On the whole, he got through dinner much better than he anticipated. It certainly was a decided novelty, after years of solitary banquets, with the silent Gravas and his thoughts for sole companions, to have a lively intelligent, and dazzlingly beautiful young lady seated scarcely a yard away from him, and keeping him engaged in conversation during the whole of the meal. It had not been quite so unpleasant, however, as he feared; indeed since the departure of Gravas he had been gradually recovering his self-possession to a most astonishing extent. When the time came for the removal of the sweets, however, he felt that a difficulty was at hand.

"I really don't quite know what room there is for you to go to," he remarked awkwardly. "Tomorrow the drawing-room or a smaller sitting-room shall be got ready, but at present there are only this one and my study in habitable condition."

"Oh, pray don't apologize," begged Miss Comlin, leaning back in her chair and leisurely sipping her moselle. "I shall like stopping with you, if I may. I don't mind smoking; there is nothing I like better than the smell of a cigar."

"I have a little writing "he commenced timidly.

"Ah, you want to go into the study," she interrupted. "Very well. I may come too, mayn't I? Celeste can unpack my fancy-work, and I'll promise to be as quiet as a mouse."

This was not exactly his idea.

"I'm afraid that it will be very dull for you," he said. "Wouldn't you rather go into Mrs. Burditt's room for an hour? She is an extremely respectable woman."

Miss Comlin shrugged a pair of the whitest shoulders in the world.

"Are the dolls and the Noah's ark there?" she inquired mischievously. "If you had rather I went there, I will, but I should prefer the study."

Of course, after that, what could he do but give her his arm again and take her there? and, having placed an easy chair for her near the fire, poked the embers into a blaze, and rung the bell for her maid to bring her fancy-work, he retreated to his writing table at the other end of the room. He took up his pen, and looked through his papers. Yes, he had left off in the middle of a very interesting sentence. He read it through again carefully.

"However highly qualified may be the inquirer into this portentous subject, alike by experience and intellect, he may yet fail through having imperfectly digested the—"

That was where he had left off, and now he dipped his pen in the ink, and prepared to dash off the remainder of the sentence. What was it that the inquirer ran a risk of imperfectly digesting? He hesitated. It had been as clear as day to him when he had commenced the paragraph, but somehow, now the whole subject seemed mixed up, in a most incongruous fashion, with blue eyes, a dainty figure, and a rippling laugh, and his eyes stole away from the paper to where the possessor of these charms was seated, and remained watching a little white hand, flashing with diamonds, dexterously passing a needle backwards and forwards, through a piece of black satin, and studying the graceful outlines of her lithesome figure, as she leaned back in the easy chair, with a pair of very shapely little black satin shoes resting upon the fender. Presently she laid her work down, and half closed her eyes. No doubt she was dull. Ought he not, after all, he thought uneasily, to make some effort to entertain her, as it was her first evening? Well, he would v just finish this sentence and try.

"He may yet fail through having imperfectly digested,"—digested what? Bah! it was no good, he was not in a writing mood; he must sacrifice this evening; anyhow, he could make it up to-morrow.

"You are tired, Miss Comlin."

She started, and opened her eyes, to see Sir Geoffrey standing on the hearth-rug beside her, with his elbow on the mantelpiece. How long had he been there? she wondered.

"A very little. Have you finished your writing?"

He laughed uneasily.

"Well, I haven't done a lot," he acknowledged with perfect truth. "I am scarcely in a working humour."

A knock at the door, and Gravas enters with the tea-tray. Generally a single cup was brought in for Sir Geoffrey, but to-night the tea-pot and whole equipage appeared, and were deposited on a small table by Miss Comlin's side. A minute later Sir Geoffrey was explaining that he took neither sugar nor cream, and was accepting with nervous fingers the delicate gold and white cup from a lady's hand the first time for many years.

"I wonder if there is a piano anywhere?" inquired Miss Comlin as she stirred her tea.

"There are two or three somewhere," he answered carelessly. "There is a grand in the drawing-room, which I don't believe has ever been played on, and a very fair one in the small dining-room. There's one here, too," and he pointed to the corner behind her.

"May I try it?" and, receiving his ready assent, she put down her cup, and seating herself before the instrument struck a few chords.

"It sounds like a good one, although it's a little out of tune," she pronounced. "What shall I play?"

"Anything—or something of Mendelssohn's," he added vaguely. To tell the truth, Mendelssohn was the only one of the masters whose name, on the spur of the moment, he could remember, although once he had been very fond of music.

She paused for a moment to think, and then her fingers glided softly over the keys in the musical prelude to one of the inimitable *Lieder ohne Worte*. She played well, and Sir Geoffrey listened eagerly. Many years had passed since he had listened to such music, and he was conscious of the revival of a pleasure which had been lost to him as he listened to the smoothly-flowing melody. When she had finished, she wheeled round abruptly and received more than thanks from the gratified smile by which he was listening.

"Shall I play again?" she asked; and taking his silence (for he was in a day-dream) for consent, she played on and on, gliding from Mendelssohn to Beethoven, from Beethoven to Schubert, and from Schubert back again to Mendelssohn. Then she closed the piano and rose.

He had taken her chair, and was contemplating with curiosity the piece of fancy-work gingerly poised in his hand.

"Are you going to finish my crewel-work for me?" she asked, laughing.

He blushed—actually blushed—as he sprang up and relinquished his seat.

"I was wondering what it was?" he said, laying it carelessly down. "Crewel-work, is it?"

"Yes, don't you see it's a table-cloth?" she explained. "I do believe it's just large enough for this little table. So it is! I'll finish it tomorrow. What do you generally do with yourself all day, Sir Geoffrey?

Ride, fish, shoot, or what? The meets have not commenced yet, have they?"

"Not yet, I think. I lead a somewhat peculiar life, Miss Comlin, and I—"

She interrupted him.

"Will you do me a favour?" she asked, looking up at him with a winning smile.

He bent his head in silence.

"Well, call me Carry, not Miss Comlin, do! If you won't, I shall call you Sir Geoffrey Powers Halledean every time I speak to you, and perhaps you have some other names which I could include. You wouldn't like that, would you?"

"Certainly not," he replied promptly. "I will call you whatever you please. I was going to explain to you that I was afraid you'll find it very dull here. I generally go for a very long walk or ride in the morning, and work all the rest of the day. I don't know any of the people round here, and have no visitors. You won't be able to help being dull, unless you're very fond of reading," he added disconsolately.

"I do wish you wouldn't bother about me, Sir Geoffrey," she answered cheerfully. "I think it's awfully kind of you to have me here at all; and really, I shan't expect you to put yourself out of the way one bit to amuse me. I'll go for a walk in the morning, if I may," she added. "You needn't be afraid that I can't walk, because I can, and I've got some boots upstairs as thick as yours. If you'll take me with you sometimes in the morning, I'm sure I can get through the rest of the day."

Of course he murmured a ready assent, but he was really most dismayed at the prospect. When on earth should he be able to digest his reading if his solitary walks and rides were done away with? and whatever would people think to see him, the bachelor recluse, walking all over the country with a young lady? Perhaps they would all call again. The bare idea made him shudder.

"I'm going to ring for Celeste now, if I may—oh, thanks," as he sprung up and hurried to the bell. "I'm so tired, and I'm sure you'll be glad to get rid of me."

"I assure you—" he began ruefully imagining that she was in earnest.

"Oh, you needn't deny it!" she said laughing. "Good night, Sir Geoffrey."

"Good night, Miss Comlin."

"Good night, who?" holding up her finger, and shaking her head playfully.

"Good night, Miss Carry." And he crossed the room and opened the door, bending his head as she passed out; for there was something in the clear, frank glance of those bewitching blue eyes, which made him continually deny himself the pleasure of gazing into them. He closed the door, and returned to his neglected article; but it did not progress much that night. It was scarcely to be wondered at, that so startling an innovation as Carry Comlin's presence in his bachelor home should interfere with his thoughts; and while to himself he regretted the serious interference to his work which it would occasion, he was nevertheless half-conscious of looking forward with, at any rate, curiosity, if not with actual pleasure, to her six months' visit.

The next morning, according to his invariable custom, the master of Halledean Court rose early and went for his three-mile walk. On his return he found Miss Comlin in the breakfast-room, reclining in his easy chair and reading *The Times*.

"Good morning, Sir Geoffrey; you're late," in a comical tone of reproof. "I've a good mind to give you your coffee cold. Do you know, I've been up three-quarters of an hour, and have been exploring all over the place. I believe your gardener thought that I was trespassing, but I explained matters to him, and he has given me a rose. Isn't it a beauty?" and she displayed the terra-cotta orange bud stuck coquettishly in the bosom of her well-fitting morning gown.

He bent down somewhat stiffly and admired it.

"I have been out, too," he said. "If I had known you were such an early riser, I should have waited for you."

"How kind of you! Do you know, Sir Geoffrey, I think that this is the most charming place I ever saw. I'm longing to get out of doors again. Such a splendid morning, too. You will take me for a very long walk, won't you?"

Of course he would. He persuaded himself that he should be wanting in courtesy to his guest if he refused, and that he was making a sacrifice of his inclination; but all the time he felt just a trifle hypocritical, for he was looking forward to the walk almost as much as she was.

Breakfast went on merrily, and, before its conclusion, he found himself (despite a previously formed intention of being just a trifle more dignified and patronizing, as became one so much her elder) laughing at her lively remarks, and even trying to cap them, to her unbounded amusement. The moment the meal was over she rushed away to put on her things; and Sir Geoffrey, as he lit a cheroot and unfolded his paper, decided that, so far as he could see at present, he could easily put up with this sort of thing for six months, and, indeed, it would not matter very much if Mr. Comlin stayed in Ceylon for a very considerable time.

Soon she reappeared, in a trim, short walking dress and black jacket, carrying an ebony walking stick, and evidently quite prepared for a long walk. He threw down his paper at once, and hurried off for his hat.

"I generally go to the stable first for the dogs," he said, when he returned. "Do you care to come?"

"I should like to," she answered readily. "I love horses."

"There's only a very poor lot of cattle here now," he remarked, as he rang the yard bell for Burditt. "If you ride, we must get something for you."

"Of course I ride, but you mustn't do anything of the sort, Sir Geoffrey, please. What a dear little dachshund! Tory, is his name? and the collie is Rover? Down, Rover! Down, Tory! I declare they're getting fond of me already."

The tour of the stables was soon made, and Sir Geoffrey felt almost ashamed as they passed stall after stall empty, and he noticed the generally dismantled appearance of the whole place. There was a pair of very good carriage horses, somewhat overfed and under-exercised, but otherwise very fair cattle; a trio of very indifferent hacks; an old hunter pensioned off; and his own magnificent dark bay, Prince Charles. There was absolutely nothing for his guest to ride, and he felt quite angry as he caught her look of disappointment.

"Never mind, Miss Carry," he said, "I shall ride over to Leicester this afternoon, and see if I can pick up anything there that will carry you. Do you know if that man Horton has got anything decent to sell?" he asked, turning to Burditt.

"Muster 'Orton's allus got some decent cattle, sir," replied the head groom. "I seed one or two very decent-looking animals at his yard only the day before yesterday. It's a powerful bad time o' the year to buy, though, sir. He'll be wanting a rare price if he's got anything as is really good."

Sir Geoffrey thought of his long income, never yet quarter spent, and smiled.

"I shall ride over this afternoon," he decided. "We want a few fresh horses."

"What! and leave me all alone?" exclaimed Miss Comlin disconsolately.

He smiled at her look of utter dismay.

"Well, I'm afraid there isn't room for two on Prince Charles, is there?" he said; "and you wouldn't care about walking by the side, would you?"

"We might drive," she suggested.

It was an idea which had not occurred to him. He considered for a moment.

"Very well, then," he decided. "The landau at three, Burditt."

"Don't you ever drive yourself, Sir Geoffrey?" she asked.

He shrugged his shoulders.

"Don't care about it; and besides, I don't think there's anything to drive. We'll see, if you like," and they entered the coachhouses.

There was a mail phaeton, nearly new, with great red wheels, which took Miss Comlin's fancy at once.

"Oh, do drive me in that!" she begged; and Sir Geoffrey, who had not yet learnt to refuse her anything, gave the necessary orders.

Their walk that morning he never forgot. It was a strange experience to him, after years of solitary tramps, with Tory and Rover his sole companions, to find himself side by side with a well-dressed and charming young lady, who expected to be helped over stiles and to be told all about the country. No time now for metaphysical speculations, or for leaning against a gate and planning his week's work, while Tory, wild after rabbits, deserted him, and even the faithful Rover grew impatient. This was a very different sort of walk, and very much more appreciated by his canine companions. His solitude had been wrested from him, and to his surprise he found society—such society as he had—far from disagreeable. Indeed, as they got further out into the country, the keen, sharp air seemed to exhilarate him as it had never done before, and he found himself actually monopolizing the conversation, throwing sticks for Rover and jumping ditches with Tory, like an overgrown schoolboy, while Carry gave her laughing encouragement to everything. When they reached home, mud all over, and, as Miss Comlin expressed it, "absolutely famished," he was forced to admit that he had never returned from a more enjoyable walk. At luncheon they talked over the morning, and petted Tory for his rabbit-chasing exploits, and altogether found it a very pleasant meal. Sir Geoffrey's luncheon generally consisted of a soda and milk and a biscuit only; but to-day he shared his companion's famished condition, and for the first time since he could remember felt really hungry. When they withdrew from the table he felt himself thinking, with almost a shudder, of his study, in which he always spent the afternoon, and looking eagerly forward to his drive. Punctually at three o'clock the phaeton came round, and almost simultaneously Carry appeared, in short seal-skin jacket and piquant hat. As he watched her drawing on her tan gloves, Sir Geoffrey found himself thinking of his own appearance with something of dismay. His long driving-coat was not so very shabby, however; and, besides, what an idiot he was, he thought, with almost a blush—as if she would notice his appearance!

He helped her up to the box-seat, lit the cigar which she begged him to smoke, and sprang up beside her; and they bowled down the wide avenue, the horses arching their necks and keeping well together, though the work was new to them. He was a good whip, although he drove so seldom; and with his fair companion by his side chattering pleasantly, and his horses quite fresh, gnawing at the bit and answering to his slightest touch, he thoroughly enjoyed the drive, and kept up the conversation with spirit. Just outside Leicester they overtook a barouche, whose occupants leaned right out of the carriage, to gaze with astonishment at the bachelor recluse (who was popularly supposed to be a staunch misogynist) driving an extremely stylish young lady in an irreproachable phaeton. An exclamation from the barouche caused Carry to turn her head, and with a start of surprise she nodded and waved her hand to its smiling occupants.

"Why, Sir Geoffrey," she exclaimed, "you never told me that Lord Hanesborough's place was near here! That was Ida Hanesborough in the back seat, and her brother on the box. I suppose the old lady is their mother. How delightful! Do they live far away?"

Sir Geoffrey touched his horses, and they bounded forward, leaving the barouche considerably in the rear.

"We passed close to Hanesborough Hall," he said. "I would have told you if I had known that they were friends of yours. Hanesborough Park is the next estate to Halledean."

"How singular! They are scarcely friends of mine; but I was at school with Ida, and Jack used to come down and take us out sometimes. Very pleased we girls were to see him then."

Sir Geoffrey conceived an instant and inexplicable aversion to Captain Hanesborough.

"I suppose you'll want to call," he remarked, flicking his horses' ears.

"Well, no; that would be scarcely proper, you know. I expect they will call on me. And this is Leicester! What a nice clean town!"

Sir Geoffrey smiled.

"We are entering it from the best side," he remarked; "but it really is not so bad for a manufacturing town."

They drove through the streets in silence. Arrived at the stables, he pulled up, and lifted her from her seat, and they walked up the yard together. The horse-dealer, to whom Sir Geoffrey mentioned his requirements, did not know him, and was disposed to be somewhat curt. There was such a run after 'osses just now, that he was very near cleared out, and doubted whether he had anything to suit. However, they would see what he had, and two or three very indifferent-looking animals were trotted up the yard.

Sir Geoffrey turned away in contempt.

"If that's a sample of what you have to offer, we needn't detain you any longer, I think," he said, moving away.

Mr. Horton looked at his would-be customer. The long driving coat was shabby and old-fashioned, and his hat was old and battered, but there was the stamp and bearing of a gentleman about him, which the horse-dealer was not slow in detecting; and the girl was thoroughbred, anyhow.

"You see, sir, it's like this," he said apologetically. "I've got a couple of particularly fine animals, but I want to sell them in the neighbourhood, if I can, to hunt with Sir Bache's or the Quorn. They'll do me good, these animals, that's where it is. Now you don't belong to these parts, sir, I think."

"I am Sir Geoffrey Halledean, of Halledean Court," his customer answered shortly, "and if you have anything in your stables worth buying, I will give you your price for it. I don't want a miserable screw, like those animals we've just seen. I want something that looks well, can go, and will carry a lady."

Mr. Horton removed a straw from his mouth, and took off his hat.

"I beg your pardon, Sir Geoffrey Halledean, I'm sure, for showing you those brutes. Dick, bring out Janette!" he shouted to his assistant. "I've got a lovely animal there, Sir Geoffrey, but I didn't want to sell her out of the county; that's why I didn't show her you at first, not having the pleasure of knowing you."

Janette was led out, and proved to be a bright bay with dark points, nearly thoroughbred, with easy action and perfectly proportioned. Miss Comlin was in ecstasies, and even Burditt, who was sent for to give his opinion, had not a fault to find.

"Can she jump?" asked Sir Geoffrey.

Mr. Horton was very eloquent on that score.

"I should like to try her, if it isn't inconvenient. You have a range there, I see."

A saddle was quickly brought, and Sir Geoffrey divested himself of his long coat and mounted. Janette was disposed to be fractious for a moment, but her rider's firm hand and reassuring voice quieted her instantly. He trotted her up the yard and then put her at the hurdles, which she negotiated skilfully.

"These are not much use in the south Leicestershire country, you know," said Sir Geoffrey, turning in his saddle. "Haven't you something a trifle stiffer?"

A five-barred gate was fetched and easily cleared.

"'Tain't the first time he's been astride of a 'oss," remarked Mr. Horton admiringly to Miss Comlin. "Don't he hold her beautiful at the fences?"

"I think she'll do," decided Sir Geoffrey, as he trotted down and dismounted. "Do you like her, Miss Carry?"

"Of course I do," she answered vigorously. "I think she's perfect. But you're not going to buy her for me! You must not, you know, really."

He laughed.

"I'm going to buy her for myself," he said. "Now, Mr. Horton," he continued, moving a little on one side, "what's her price?"

"Two hundred guineas, Sir Geoffrey; not a penny less."

"I didn't offer you a penny less," was the somewhat contemptuous reply. "Give me a pen, and I'll write you a cheque. And I shall send for her the first thing to-morrow morning," were Sir Geoffrey's last words as he issued from the little office a minute later, drawing on his gloves. "Now, Carry, are you ready?" He was beginning to find it quite easy to call her Carry now.

"Is there anywhere else you want to call?" he asked as they regained the carriage.

"I should like the Queen and the Whitehall," she said.

They drove up to the station, and he bought every magazine he could find. Then they drove into the town again to call at the saddler's. As they passed along the Market Street she suddenly told him to stop. He pulled up, and looked at her inquiringly.

"Look in that shop window," she directed.

He did so. "It's full of hats," he said dubiously.

She looked up at him with a mischievous smile.

"You're to go in and buy one!"

He coloured and laughed.

"All right; come in and choose one for me, then."

The hat was soon chosen, and the old one discarded. Then between them they discovered other things which he wanted, all of which she gravely selected. When they left the shop, he laughing and declaring he was ruined, there was quite a large parcel to be stowed away in the phaeton.

"Any other commands?" he asked.

"Yes, you're to go to a tailor's now, and have some new clothes made," she insisted merrily.

And of course he went.

They drove home quickly, for their shopping had taken time, and it was getting chilly. As they turned in at the avenue they met a fly lumbering down. Sir Geoffrey looked aghast.

"By jove, I quite forgot! That venerable aunt of mine was to turn up to-day. She's evidently arrived."

They looked at each other blankly.

"I suppose she has," Carry said with a sigh. "It's rather a nuisance, isn't it?"

"It is," he assented vigorously, bringing his horses up with a jerk at the entrance.

"Sir Geoffrey," she said, as he helped her down, "may I pour out the coffee in the morning, please?"

He looked at her, and burst out laughing.

"Of course you may, if you like. You shall be housekeeper, and she shall be guest."

She hurried away with a bright nod, and Sir Geoffrey strolled in to meet his aunt, feeling rather like a guilty schoolboy. She was a quaint, motherly old lady, and though it was rather a shock to her to find a lively and very handsome young lady established in her nephew's house, she entertained far too great an awe of him to make any remark. As he had assured Carry, she was not very dreadful, and went to sleep directly after dinner for the rest of the evening.

The next morning, just as Sir Geoffrey and his guest were starting for another country ramble, there was a trampling of horses' hoofs in the avenue. Sir Geoffrey strode to the window and frowned.

"Some friends of yours," he remarked, turning to Carry; "Miss Hanesborough and her brother. I shall go on with my writing for a while."

"You will stay?" she pleaded. "Do!"

But his old dread of society was upon him, and with a firm negative he made his escape.

They stayed for a long time—all the morning in fact—and the sound of their merry conversation, which penetrated into his study, somehow spoilt his chance of doing much work. At last they came out into the hall, and he heard young Hanesborough's cordial "Good-bye," and then some conversation in a lower key; finally, they mounted their horses and rode away, and immediately afterwards the door of his study was thrown open and Carry unceremoniously entered.

"Too late for a walk before lunch, isn't it?" she said, walking to the window to watch her visitors disappear.

"Certainly. Your friends have gone, then?" he remarked, continuing his writing.

"Yes; and oh, Sir Geoffrey, I may go, mayn't I? Jack, I mean Captain Hanesborough, and Ida are going to call for me to-morrow morning, and take me to the opening meet of the season. I may ride Janette, mayn't I?" she pleaded.

Sir Geoffrey gulped down the strongest feeling of disappointment which he had experienced for a very long time. He had quite made up his mind to overcome his antipathy to mixing with his fellows and to have taken her himself, and now she wanted to go with some one else. What an ass he was!

"Of course you can do as you like," he answered quietly. "Janette is quite at your service, and any orders you give Mrs. Burditt will be transmitted to the stables."

"Oh, thanks! thanks! thanks! How delightful! And how kind you are, Sir Geoffrey! I'm so sorry that you don't hunt. I forgot to tell you that luncheon was ready."

Mrs. Prim and Carry had all the conversation to themselves at lunch-time, for Sir Geoffrey hurried through his in grim silence, and before the meal was half over abruptly arose.

"You will excuse me, Mrs. Prim," he said hurriedly; "I have some writing which I am anxious to get on with."

"Aren't we going for a walk this afternoon, Sir Geoffrey?" asked Carry quietly.

He hesitated and glanced at her. She was looking down at her plate, and he could not see her face; but surely she could not be very anxious about it, or she would have looked up at him eagerly, as she had done only a few minutes before, when she had asked to go to the meet. No, she didn't care much about going, he decided.

"Not this afternoon, I think," he answered a little coldly. "If you and Mrs. Prim care about driving, pray order the carriage," and he retreated into the library.

At dinner time he was disposed to be a little more amiable, but Carry had a headache. Later on, when he made his way into the drawing-room for some tea, she had gone to her room, and Mrs. Prim was half asleep. Sir Geoffrey forgot to ask for his tea, and went back to his study.

Her headache was quite gone in the morning, to judge by her beaming face as she entered the morning room in her trim, well-fitting riding habit. She chatted incessantly the whole of breakfast time, and was extremely charming.

"I do wish you were going, Sir Geoffrey," she said sweetly.

He opened his lips to say that he would go, but before he could get the words out there was a trampling of horse's feet in the avenue, and she had rushed away to meet her friends. He turned on his heel, and vanished into the study.

It was a magnificent field, and the sport was keen. Carry, with Captain Hanesborough and his sister, kept well to the front, but she soon found that she was by far the best mounted, and, by a leap which Janette made nothing of, placed several fields between herself and her friends, who had to wait their turn at the gap. She was getting excited, and never dreamt of stopping for them, for there were several scarlet coats and one or two ladies in the field in front, and the hounds were in full cry. There was a thick, but not very high hedge in front of her, and she was just settling down in her saddle for the jump, when an imperative voice behind shouted her to stop, and she heard a horse coming up at a thundering gallop. She could see nothing amiss, but tightened her hold on the reins and tried to pull up. Janette, however, was eager for the jump, and despite her efforts would have gone at it, but that her pursuer circled round and, pulling up with a jerk which smothered them both with mud, laid an iron hand on Janette's curb and threw her on her haunches.

"You should be more careful, Miss Comlin, when you know nothing of the country," said a stern voice. "That hedge is wired, and there is a wired railing the other side. Where are your friends?"

"Sir Geoffrey!" she gasped. "You here! How fortunate that you stopped me!" and she gave a little shiver as a more careful inspection showed her the warning notice and the obstruction on the other side. "I should have had a nasty cropper, shouldn't I? You might have told me that you were coming."

"You didn't ask me, you see; but here are your friends," he added hastily. "There is a gate in the left-hand corner. Turn Janette round, please," and before she had realized that he meant to leave her, he had cantered off in the opposite direction.

Carry and her friends had not the best of fortune during the rest of the run, and they were never close up. Just at last, however, a lucky detour gave them a splendid view of the finish. It had been a trying run over some nasty country at a killing pace, and only one huntsman besides Sir Bache and the whip showed up at the death.

"Whoever's the man in the faded pink?" asked one of the Hanesborough party. "Hang it! I thought I knew every man in the hunt, but he's a stranger to me."

"So he is to me," said Captain Hanesborough; "but whoever he is he can ride like blazes. I never saw a horse better handled. I've seen him before somewhere, I'm sure."

"They all turned homewards, and somehow Carry found herself a little behind the others with Captain Hanesborough. As they neared Halledean Court they drew rein to bid good-bye to one of their party, and while they were talking in a group a horseman in a faded scarlet coat and seedy looking tops, riding a magnificent dark bay horse, cantered by and raised his hat slightly.

"Who is he?" asked every one as soon as he was out of earshot, for they recognized him as the man who was leading the field at the death.

"That is Sir Geoffrey Halledean," said Carry, smiling.

A bombshell could not have created a greater sensation. That handsome, distinguished-looking man, who rode like a centaur, and whom Ida Hanesborough declared had the most glorious eyes she had ever seen; the man who had apparently retired from the world, and was neither more nor less than a hermit!

"Didn't you see him driving me yesterday?" asked Carry, somewhat surprised at the universal bewilderment; for it did not strike her for the moment that Ida had only just returned from boarding-school, and that Captain Jack was never at home for longer than a month together. Perhaps, too, she scarcely realized the utter seclusion in which Sir Geoffrey had lived.

"We saw that some one was driving you; but, for my part, I was so astonished to see you at all," exclaimed Captain Hanesborough, "that I couldn't take my eyes off you to look at any one else. Besides, you passed so quickly."

"I call it a regular downright shame!" declared his sister vigorously. "Do you know, Carry, he absolutely refuses to know us, though mamma has pestered him with invitations? He is absolutely unapproachable. How I envy you! I declare I've fallen in love with him."

Carry's lips curled a little as she pulled up at the lodge gate.

"I'm sure Sir Geoffrey would be extremely flattered," she said. "Shall I tell him?"

"I don't care if you do," replied Miss Hanesborough laughing. "We shall come for you tomorrow," she called out.

"But I don't think you'd better," said Carry, turning round on her saddle. "I shall—"

"Oh, nonsense!" declared Miss Hanesborough; "I couldn't keep Jack away if I wanted to; and, besides, I'm dying to see Sir Geoffrey again. We may drop across him, you know. *Au revoir*," and she cantered away waving her hand.

Several weeks of Miss Comlin's stay at Halledean Court passed away. The Hanesboroughs were indefatigable in calling for her, and in taking her with them for rides to the meet, and home to dinner at Hanesborough hall, on which occasions Mrs. Prim always accompanied her. Sir Geoffrey made no sign of annoyance at her constant absence, but had relapsed more rigidly than ever into his former self, and his misanthropical habits; and even when Carry and Mrs. Prim were at home he never entered the drawing-room. He had not appeared in the hunting-field again, nor did he show any signs of intending to follow up his splendid debut. Once she had summoned up courage to ask him to take her to a meet, and he had hesitated and changed colour.

"Are your friends not coming for you, then?" he had asked; and she had been obliged to tell him "Yes," wishing in her heart that they were not.

"Then there is no necessity for me to go," he had said coldly; and after a moment's awkward silence he had made his escape into his sanctum.

She had never asked him again. Once or twice, as they were returning from the meets, Sir Geoffrey had passed them on Prince Charles; and on each occasion, to her secret annoyance, she had been riding with Captain Hanesborough. His bow, though always polite, was stiff and ceremonious, and on those evenings he was gloomier than usual. One evening, about a month after her arrival, he was busy writing in his study, when there was a timid knock at the door; and in response to his impatient "Come in," Carry entered.

He rose with no very pleased face, and, with a lingering glance at his papers, placed a chair for her.

"Is there anything I can do for you, Miss Comlin?" he said shortly. He never called her Carry now.

"N—no, nothing particular," she said, toying with her rings and regarding them intently.

There was a short silence, during which he resumed his seat, and fidgeted nervously with his pen.

"Sir Geoffrey," falteringly.

"Miss Comlin."

"I have something to ask you."

He bowed his head and waited.

"I—I think I must have offended you," she went on, speaking hurriedly, with her eyes fixed on the floor. "The first two days I was here you were so nice, and everything was delightful, and now you don't take the—the slightest notice of me, and—and I don't like it, and I think I'd better go away, please."

Something suspiciously like a sob followed the termination of her little speech, and something very much like a tear dropped on to the carpet.

Sir Geoffrey pretended to notice neither, but his voice was lower than usual when he spoke.

"I did not think it made any difference to you,"—with eyes fixed upon his desk as he spoke. "Of course I was very pleased to do my best to entertain you while you were here alone. But you have friends now more of your own age and disposition. I'm not a very agreeable companion, you know. I've lived a solitary life so long that I've become stupid and dull. The Hanesboroughs are very nice friends for you, and I'm glad you get on so well with them. I should only be a kill-joy if I joined you."

"Shall I tell you something, Sir Geoffrey?" she asked gently. He did not answer, and she continued, "I enjoyed those first two days better than any since. There!"

Sir Geoffrey could scarcely believe his ears. He felt in a strange state altogether.

"You are very kind," he murmured.

"Supposing they, the Hanesboroughs, were not to come again," she went on hesitatingly, "would—would it be like that again?"

"I daresay it may be," he said quietly.

"Well, then, you are my guardian for the present, aren't you? so I feel that I ought to tell you. Captain Hanesborough—"

"Well," impatiently.

"Wants me to marry him, and—and—"

"Well," more impatiently still.

"And, of course, I refused."

"Why?" with the most ridiculous and evident affectation of carelessness.

"Because I don't care for him."

He threw down his arms and surrendered.

"Carry, do you care for any one else?"

She stole a glance at him. He was pale, and his hands were shaking nervously.

"I—I might do, if some one were to ask me," she said demurely.

And some one did ask her, for she is now Lady Halledean.

## A SPRIG OF HEATHER

That was a halcyon month for Fred and for me—the month we spent with Dick down at his bungalow on the Norfolk coast. Never was anything more opportune than Dick's invitation. We were in one of the tightest corners I ever remember. David had turned rusty; nothing that we could either of us turn out seemed in the least to satisfy those mysterious purchasers of his. He had put his foot down firmly. He would not look at another picture for a month! And there we were, owing three weeks' rent, and our credit pledged up to the hilt at every commercial establishment in the neighbourhood. Even Jones, the tobacconist—Jones, the long-suffering and good-natured—had grumbled at that last half-pound of flake we had sent for, and had enclosed in the box our joint account, with an expression of his peremptory desire for some manner of settlement. And with it all the thermometer was ninety degrees in the shade, and the air of Stile's Row was foetid. We sat in our shirt-sleeves before the open window and stewed. The sight of a cab passing by laden with seaside luggage, steamer chairs, and travelling easel, white umbrella and golf clubs, came like the last straw. Fred got up and kicked our one hassock to the other end of the room.

"Oh, d—n!" he exclaimed savagely. "I beg your pardon, old chap. It's so beastly stuffy."

I murmured a sympathetic assent. It was undeniably stuffy.

"Fancy," Fred continued softly, with his eyes fixed upon me, "fancy a strong fresh sea breeze, just a dash of brine in it, you know, and sunshine fresh from heaven—not focussed upon us through the fogs and evil odours of this Sodom of a city! Bah! isn't it enough to make a man sick with longing?"

"It is," I groaned. "Pass the tobacco and shut up."

I relit my pipe, and Fred followed suit. The blue cloud around us grew thicker, and our hearts grew heavier. Then came Dick bounding into the room with hot, eager face and a roar of greeting.

"Hurrah! you fellows," he exclaimed. "I've an idea. Where's my pipe?"

He went to the mantelpiece and selected his own cherished briar.

He still kept it in the old place, although sometimes we saw nothing of him for a month together.

"Hand over the baccy," he continued, after a preliminary and apparently satisfactory blow down the stem.

Fred passed the already half-empty box, with a dismal glance at its diminishing contents. Dick helped himself recklessly. His pipe had a large bowl, and he pressed the tobacco down with an iron forefinger. I began to foresee the climax of our miseries—a tobaccoless evening.

"How are things?" he inquired tersely.

"Bad," Fred growled.

"Disgustingly bad," I echoed.

"Ah, I thought they might be," Dick continued, with unabated cheerfulness. "Wrong time of the year to work. Wrong time of the year to try and sell pictures. Now, you chaps, attention!"

We composed ourselves to listen. Dick had evidently something to say. He waited until his pipe was well alight, and then commenced.

"You fellows, you know, haven't treated me exactly well since I came into my tin," he said slowly. "I haven't said much about it, but I'm going to give my little growl now. You won't come to see me because I live at Mayfair. You wouldn't even come to shoot with me last September because—"

I laid my hand upon his arm.

"Shut up, Dick!" I said firmly. "We've been through all this before. What's the good of it? You know why we don't come. Our ways are not Mayfair ways, neither are our clothes. It's good of you to want us, but it's no go. We shouldn't be comfortable, and you wouldn't."

"And as to shooting," Fred put in, "we haven't a gun between us, nor any of the rig-out. Owen's quite right. We're glad to see you here, Dick, and we're glad—jolly glad—that you don't forget us. I hope we'll always be pals—the three of us—and all that; but it's no use closing our eyes to facts, is it? You belong to a different world now. You didn't come here to kick against the pricks again, surely?"

Dick cheered up. A gleam of satisfaction shone in his blue eyes.

"No, I did not," he assented. "The fact is, I've got you this time on toast, both of you. I saw an advertisement in last week's *Field*—bungalow to let on the Norfolk coast, close to sea; bathing, fishing, golf, and all the rest of it. I went down the day before yesterday and took it straight away. Now listen to me seriously. This is not a request; it is not an invitation. I insist upon it. You two fellows have just got to pack up and go down with me to-morrow. Not one other soul is going to be there except the servants. We'll have a glorious time. You can make it pay, too! Lots of pretty bits among the cliffs, and such a sea! Fred, old boy, it's on, isn't it? Owen, old chap?"

Fred and I exchanged rapid glances.

"No other visitors, did you say, Dick? None of your own people even?" I inquired, with assumed carelessness.

"Not a soul except us three, I pledge you my word," Dick declared earnestly. "No pier, no dressing-up, or promenading, or any of that sort of thing. Just flannels and a good old comfortable time."

Fred went to our vaulting-bar and performed a fancy acrobatic feat of his own invention.

"Hurrah!" he exclaimed, coming down upon his head. "It's on! Good old Dick!"

And in a more dignified manner I signified our acceptance of Dick's invitation.

What a time that was—what a halcyon month! It stands for ever in the wilderness of our memories, marked with a great white stone. The bungalow was simply perfect. It stood on a little tableland of green lawn, between two mighty cliffs, with a forest of pines and firs behind, and the sea, the sea sparkling, stretched away in front. The first breath of the place as we drove from the station in the evening was like a strong, sweet tonic, and that night we were like children, walking backwards and forwards upon the cliffs, sniffing the breeze, and watching the lights far out at sea.

We breakfasted the next morning in a long, low room, whose open windows looked full upon the German Ocean—and such a breakfast it was! Dick was always famous at the commissariat! Stile's Row seemed very far away.

"I don't know whether you fellows care about swimming," Dick said, as we filled our pipes.

"There are steps right away down to the beach from the bottom of the garden there, and I've had a tent fixed up and some bathing togs sent in. What do you say?"

What did we say? Not much. But with the first plunge into the salt water the burden of years was gone, the poison of weariness and disappointment had glided from out our veins and faded away in thin air. We were boys again, animal creatures only, glorying in our strength and the power of cleaving those long blue waves, whose murmuring and gurgling in our ears was like the sweetest of all music. Stroke for stroke, shoulder to shoulder, through the cool, rushing waters we swam. I opened my arms to the sea, and the joy of it was like the joy of fine wine. Most glorious of all physical emotions is the delight of meeting and buffeting those rolling waves.

That was a halcyon time indeed. Dick had a little yacht there, and we sailed her up and down the coast, lounging on the deck, with the sunlight we had longed for all around us and the salt spray flying in our faces. At the end of a week or so we began to feel a healthy desire for work, and on one hot day we fetched out our easels and settled down upon the cliffs in a spot where only choice of subject was difficult. And on that first day commenced our episode.

Our episode, of course, was feminine. She came up behind us with Dick and her father, just as we had got fairly to work. She had brown hair, which rippled and waved as a woman's should, a curiously childlike face, and large soft eyes. She was wearing a brown holland gown with a bunch of heather stuck in her bosom. She was fresh, and sweet, and well bred. That is all I know about her. Fred could have gone on describing her for an hour, but this is not Fred's story.

General Chesham, her father, lived in the white house we could see through the trees, and he was Dick's nearest neighbour. He was an Anglo-Indian, genial, hearty, and good-humoured. They stayed for some time, and the girl talked all the while to Fred, preferring, as I could see, his dashing style and easy manipulation of colour to my own slower and, in a sense, more laborious work. I never knew what they talked about then or on those other days; but they certainly did talk a good deal, and to some purpose. Morning after morning she came gliding down to us, flitting in and out of the pine trees in her father's grounds, a soft white figure in the glancing sunlight, and blithely crossing the cliffs towards our chosen spot, with a man-servant behind bearing her easel. She, too, painted not at all badly, and she was never weary of talking about art, and the beauty of devoting one's life to it. To amuse her, Fred would tell her stories of our life in London, dwelling only on the bright side of it, treating our impecuniosity as a joke, and blurring over our hardships. She sat and listened as though entranced. She was by no means an ordinary girl, and sometimes as I watched her face upturned to Fred's I became conscious of a dim feeling of uneasiness. I wished that her father would interfere. She certainly had more liberty than was good for her. But, after all, it seemed to be no business of mine. It was the first holiday I had had for years, and it might be the last for many more. I put away all thoughts of trouble. I would have none of them. The days were golden with June sunshine, and sweet with the perfume of fragrant winds. I read poetry among the cliffs, and now and then I began to dream again. Not altogether happy dreams are those when youth—or, at any rate, youth's most buoyant season—has gone, and a bushel of bright hopes has changed into a handful of dry sticks. Yet I was thankful enough to find that the capacity still lingered. To be past the age of dreams is to stand upon the threshold of death—the death of mediocre content, or mortally wounded sensibility. So I was glad to plant my foot once more—even though with difficulty—upon the borderland of the world of strange fancies, that glittering world of dreams. For while I dreamed of dead things Fred was drifting into a living trouble. I was walking homewards one evening through the heather, when I came suddenly upon two figures. Their easels were side by side; a field of waving scarlet poppies and yellowing corn ran down the sloping cliff to the sea before them. But they were not painting. She was standing, bending over him, her hands upon his shoulders; he was leaning forward, with his head bent low; and the light upon their faces was that light which comes but once in a lifetime, and which no man can mistake.

I dropped my easel with a crash, and they both started round.

"How you frightened us, Mr. Wrathall!" the girl cried, looking at me with flushed face and not too friendly aspect.

"Not so much as you frightened me," I answered gravely. "We shall have to hurry, shan't we, Fred?" I added.

The colour had mounted to his sunburnt brow, but he met my steady gaze fearlessly. I had done wrong to doubt Fred for a moment. Poor old chap! I passed my arm through his when the girl had gone. He commenced at once. His voice shook several times. Poor old chap!

"It isn't my fault, Owen," he said; "at least, I think not. I have never said a single word to her which her father might not have heard. I see, though, that it was not well for us to have been together so much. I thought that I was the only one who could suffer. I used to be fond of girls, you know—that sort of girl; and lately—well, the kind of feminine society we can command isn't exactly edifying, is it?" he broke off, with a hard little laugh. "Well, it's over."

I pressed his arm.

"Brace up, old chap!" I murmured. "We've had a glorious time. Nine-thirty's the morning train, I think. You can manage that?"

He nodded, and we went in to dinner. I felt a brute, but what else was there to do?

Stile's Row had never seemed more cheerless than when we slowly trudged up those interminable flights of stairs and unlocked our door. Yet I, at any rate, was a better man. We were both sunburnt—as brown as berries—and we were bringing back work which we should have no need to hawk about. We could pay our debts, and start with a bit in hand. We talked this over, smoking a late pipe, and Fred did his best to be cheerful. When we parted we smiled quite bravely.

"Don't you bother about me, Owen," he said, as we clasped hands the last thing—an old habit of ours. "I'm hit, but not mortally. And—and I wouldn't be without the memory of that month—not for worlds."

His voice shook a little, and we both looked out of the window at the entrancing vision of grey roofs stretching away in a dreary wilderness to the smoke-begrimed horizon. Then we went to our hard little beds and made mild jokes at our short lapse into luxury. But when I woke up in the middle of the night, Fred was sitting on the window-sill, half dressed, and smoking. I let him be. A fellow with grit in him gets over those things better without sympathy. I too had spent nights like that. Memory is a sweet torturer; yet who would not sometimes be a victim?

We sold our pictures well, and we went to work in grim earnest. A month passed. Then, one night, there was a timid knock at the door, and she walked in.

I sprang to my feet and stood between them. Fred was off his guard with a sudden joy, and had I not been there she would have been in his arms.

"Miss Chesham!" I exclaimed breathlessly. "Are you alone?"

She set down a dressing-bag which she had been carrying, and for a moment her eyes met mine defiantly.

"Yes, I am. I have run away. I am going to be an artist. I was miserable at home."

She held out her hands to Fred. He took them gravely; but he kept her at arm's length.

"Do they know where you have come?" I asked sternly.

She shook her head, impatient at my questioning.

"No. I shall write and tell them presently. Mr. Montavon—Fred—you are not angry? You don't seem at all pleased to see me!"

I suppose she knew that he cared, and she had hoped to find him alone. But I stood between them.

"You ought not to have come here," I said. "It is not a fit place for you."

Her lips trembled. She stamped her foot. She was half crying, half furiously angry with me. For all her child's face, she was bewitchingly pretty.

"I did not come here to see you," she exclaimed. "You have no right to interfere. You are very horrid. Fred, say that you are glad to see me!"

"I cannot," he answered hoarsely. "Wrathall is right; it sounds cruel, but it is right! This is not a fit place for you! You must go away!"

"I cannot," she answered doggedly. "I do not know a soul in London. I have some money, plenty of money, and I am going to take a studio here, and paint. You talk to me as though I were a child. I am not a child. I am a woman, and women do those things, I know. You treat me as though I were a girl who had run away from school. Don't be cruel, please! Let me stay here! I shall be no trouble, and I want to take that empty studio you told me about. I do not mind roughing it—not a little bit, Fred!"

He shook his head bravely. He could not trust himself to speak. She sat down on an empty box—our last chair had given way—and sobbed. Fred and I looked at one another. We had neither of us contemplated anything like this. I went up to him.

"Will you leave it to me, Fred?" I asked, laying my hand upon his shoulder.

He nodded.

"Yes. Take her away, old chap—quickly."

I snatched up my hat, and, hastily slipping oft my smock, put on my most decent coat.

"Miss Chesham," I said firmly, "will you come with me, please?"

She stood up, wiping her eyes.

"No, I won't!" she answered. "I hate you! Fred!"

He shook his head and kept away from her.

"You don't seem to understand," he said quietly. "Look around you. This is where and how we live. How—"

"It's all right, only it wants a good cleaning," she interposed. "Those cabinets are dreadful. Your landlady ought to be ashamed of herself."

"I daresay," Fred continued, "she thinks the same of us. We are nearly always behind with our rent. We earn just enough to keep body and soul together—and only just enough. There is not a woman in the whole building. It is not a fit place for women."

"You do not care for me!" she cried, with feminine irrelevance. "You have forgotten those days!"

"I shall never forget them," he answered; "but you must go away. Go with Wrathall, please. Do as he tells you. It is best."

She held out her hand to him, and he raised it gently to his lips. Then she let me lead her gently down the stairs. Her own eyes were blinded with tears. Outside we found a hansom, and I handed her in.

"Eighteen, Hereford Gardens," I told the driver. She pulled down her veil, and we spoke never a word all the way. I knew that she hated me. Yet she did everything as I told her.

A man-servant opened the door. To my great relief, his mistress was at home. She came to me in a moment or two—a stern-faced, grey-haired old lady, yet kindly enough, as I knew well. When she saw me, she stopped short.

"What, Owen," she cried.

"Yes, aunt," I answered. "I have come to ask you a favour. This young lady is the daughter of General Chesham, of Norfolk, and, owing to an unfortunate accident, she finds herself in London alone. Will you receive her as your guest until her father can take her away?"

She held out her hand to the girl, and I breathed freely.

"I had hoped, Owen," she said, with a shade of reproach in her tone, "that the first favour you have thought fit to ask me would have been for yourself. However, I shall be exceedingly glad to receive Miss Chesham. I know her father quite well."

I left them together, and walked back with a sense of huge relief. Fred was striding up and down the studio waiting for me.

"I have left her at my aunt's in Hereford Gardens," I said. "She will be all right there."

"You are a brick!" he declared. He knew that it had cost me something to ask that favour.

"And now we must telegraph to her father," I reminded him. "What shall we say?"

But there was no need to write that telegram. There was a sharp knock at our door, and the General himself appeared upon the threshold. He was white with fury. Fred was standing by his easel, and he marched straight up to him.

"Where is my daughter?" he thundered. "What have you done with her, you blackguard?"

I stepped between them.

"Your daughter, General Chesham, is quite safe," I told him. "She is with my aunt, Lady Wrathall, at Eighteen, Hereford Gardens."

He drew a long breath and looked at me from underneath his bushy eyebrows.

"Are you telling me the truth, sir?" he asked sternly.

"We are neither of us," I answered, "in the habit of telling untruths; nor are we accustomed to be addressed in such a fashion. Your daughter called here about an hour ago. We gathered that she had left home unknown to you, and we persuaded her to go to my aunt's. I have just returned from escorting her there."

He held out his hand. "Sir, I thank you," he said. "I apologize. Mr. Montavon, pray forgive my use of so unwarrantable an epithet. I was excited and nervous. Pray accept my apology."

Fred shook hands with him silently. Then he turned to me again.

"Eighteen, Hereford Gardens, I think you said? I will go there at once."

"It would be as well," I answered. "Allow me to light you downstairs."

When I returned Fred was groping upon the floor. He got up with a little sprig of heather in his hand. I pretended not to see him slip it into his pocket.

"What mad creatures girls are!" I remarked, lighting my pipe, with my back to him.

"Very," he answered absently.

The girl's name was Dorothy.

# LADY PRICE'S COMPANION

Lady Beatrice Price had reached that stage of a woman's existence when a husband becomes merely a possibility, although a very desirable possibility; and the idea had commenced to suggest itself to her that she ran a very fair chance of ending her days an old maid.

It was not her fault, poor girl! Through seven long seasons (she had missed one or two) had she answered to the roll-call of society, and had unflinchingly gone through the prescribed course of *matinées*, drives in the Park, lounges through picture galleries, garden-parties, receptions, dinners, and dances. Never had she been unduly coy when an eligible took her in to supper, or failed to accord an attentive ear and gracious smile when he leaned over her chair. She was not ill-looking; for although now the wear and tear of season after season had given to her fair features a somewhat *passée* appearance, she had, nevertheless, during her first year or two been considered somewhat of a beauty; and only a combination of the most fortuitous circumstances had prevented her from securing a prize.

The Duke of —— was reported to have been dead gone on her, and certain it was he followed her about with great assiduity, when his mother's death suddenly called him to Scotland. And, alas! when they met again the flame had died away, and she failed to rekindle it. There is no need, however, to go into these matters and explain how circumstances had gone against Lady Beatrice. Suffice it to say, that at thirty years of age (she only owned to twenty-five) Lady Beatrice Price was still unmarried, and it was not of her own choosing that this was so. She was an orphan, and her brother and two sisters were all married. Therefore she had a companion—a Miss Laura Dorse.

Now, why Lady Beatrice should have chosen this young lady for a companion is a matter for some surprise, for ladies who are gliding through their youth on oiled wheels do not generally care for a companion ten years their junior, and very much their superior in looks. Nevertheless, Miss Laura Dorse was certainly a remarkably nice-looking girl, a brunette with laughing eyes and piquant chin, and altogether charming. It is a wonder that Lady Beatrice should have chosen such a companion; but she did, and they appeared to get on very well together.

It was towards the end of July, and London was empty. Lady Beatrice was sick of London, of society, and almost of life.

"You are not looking well, my lady," remarked Miss Dorse one morning, with much anxiety in her tone, and very little in her heart. "Your ladyship looks absolutely seedy."

Lady Beatrice stretched herself and yawned. "I am *ennuyée*," she declared, "bored to death. We will go down to Pennedis—"; and to Pennedis they went.

Pennedis was an insignificant Cornish fishing village, where Lady Beatrice had a small property. The house was a large rambling building, fairly well kept up, for its mistress was not an infrequent visitor. It suited her, sometimes even in the middle of the season, to rush down here for a week, and, having imbibed a fresh supply of health and brightness from the pure air and invigorating breezes, to hurry back to town, and lose it all again in the whirl and bustle of the routine of society.

Miss Dorse liked these visits, brief though they were, for she was a healthy little thing, and preferred the country to the town; besides, in the latter, Lady Beatrice had continually her presence, and seldom let her out of her sight; but at Pennedis it was otherwise. She liked long walks, and Lady Beatrice, though she could not walk herself, could scarcely be so exacting as to deprive her companion of so innocent and simple an amusement.

Well, down to Pennedis they went, Miss Dorse exultant, Lady Beatrice worn-out and depressed. It was beginning to dawn upon her that she could not stand many more seasons in town, and that it was almost time for her to abandon her vain quest after a husband—for that was what it really meant—and settle down at Pennedis to her doom of spinsterhood. Perhaps her disappointments made her just a trifle ill-tempered and irritable. Certain it is that Miss Dorse hailed with delight the prospect of a little more liberty, and a little less supervision from her far from immaculate mistress.

Pennedis was glad to see them; in fact, Pennedis received them with open arms; but as all its inhabitants were tradespeople, who might be expected to profit by their coming, its welcome did not count for much. Neither Lady Beatrice nor her companion were much impressed thereby.

The day after their arrival Miss Dorse went for one of her long walks; when she returned her cheeks were much flushed, and she looked quite bewitchingly pretty. She had had such an adventure! had lost her way, and had been put right, and, indeed, escorted, by the curate in charge of the parish. Such a nice man he was! He would have called that afternoon, only he was afraid that they would scarcely be settled yet, but he did hope to see them at church on the morrow.

Lady Beatrice shrugged her shoulders and went on with her novel, very little interested. It was probable that a curate at Pennedis would be a short man with red hair and freckles, and champagne bottle shoulders. She was rather a connoisseur in men's looks, and her experience of country curates was not promising; so she merely nodded tranquilly, and made no remark.

The next day was Sunday, and, as was her invariable custom when in the country, Lady Beatrice, accompanied by Miss Dorse, went to church. When she had swept up the aisle, preceded by the obsequious pew-opener, into her cushioned seat, and, having arranged her rustling draperies, glanced carelessly around, she was at once conscious of a great surprise. The curate, whose probable appearance she had mentally derided, was a tall, powerfully built, and extremely handsome man, having far more the appearance of an officer in the Dragoons than a country curate. Lady Beatrice was at once conscious of a much-increased interest in the service, and detected herself secretly regretting that she had not taken a little more pains with her *toilette*, although such regret was altogether unnecessary, for she appeared then, as she always appeared, a stylishly dressed, somewhat *blasée* woman of the world. The Rev. George Westaby went through the service and read the lessons in a rich, melodious voice, and during the sermon, by no means a long one, his dark eyes rested continually upon her ladyship's pew. If it had not been too ridiculous, though, Lady Beatrice could almost have declared that they rested oftenest upon her companion's demure visage; anyhow, she felt it her duty to administer a few short words of reproof on their way home, with regard to that little episode of yesterday, which reproof Miss Dorse felt quite sure would not have been administered had the curate turned out to be, as Lady Beatrice had imagined him, red-haired, freckled, and champagne bottle-shouldered.

On the following afternoon Lady Beatrice donned one of her most becoming gowns, and appeared in the drawing-room with a book of somewhat more sombre appearance and contents than it was her wont to read. Miss Dorse felt that there was a purpose in this, and, pleading a headache, remained at home too, instead of taking her usual long ramble. At precisely four o'clock, just as they had laid down their books to welcome the afternoon tea-tray, a caller was announced, and the Rev. George Westaby was shown in.

He was, beyond question, an extremely handsome man, and he took tea with the ladies, and entertained them with most voluble and interesting conversation.

Lady Beatrice was charmed, and noticed with great satisfaction that he seemed almost to ignore her companion, and talked exclusively to herself. He accepted an invitation to stay and dine with them readily, and made himself especially agreeable. There was absolutely not one household in his parish, he assured Lady Beatrice, to visit whom was a pleasure, and he seemed as delighted as a schoolboy at the prospect of his evening's entertainment.

The entertainment was reciprocal, for he talked amusingly and with intelligence on every subject that was started. Lady Beatrice was in raptures with her guest, and Miss Dorse silently appreciative. When he joined them on the balcony after dinner (they permitted him to smoke a cigar there), the conversation grew more personal, and Lady Beatrice wondered that he was relegated to such an out-of-the-way hole as Pennedis.

"I can assure you," she murmured, in her most silvery accents, "that we expected to find some grey-haired septuagenarian or raw stripling here, who would bore us beyond measure by his visits, and want us to start clothing clubs, and attend mothers' meetings, or something of that sort." And she shuddered prettily. "You can't tell how relieved we are, aren't we, Laura? But you must feel buried alive here, Mr. Westaby."

Mr. Westaby sighed and looked moody.

Yes, he had found existence in Pennedis insufferably dull, and, he was obliged to confess, his duties were tedious.

But it was his misfortune to be quite without friends, and to be able to command no influence whatever; so he had had to go to the wall, while more fortunate and, he hinted, less efficient men had been pushed forward. The Church was, like all other professions, he explained, woefully overcrowded, and unless a man had influence, or family, or something to help him on, he might stagnate in such a place as this during the best years of his life. But perhaps he should find it a little less dull now. Was Lady Price contemplating a very long stay?

Yes, her ladyship had made up her mind to stay here for a couple of months at least, she assured him graciously. The ordinary watering-places were crowded and the Continent overrun; besides which, she found the absolute quiet of Pennedis so grateful after the noise and bustle of London. The Rev. Westaby would be welcome whenever he chose to call. She hoped that they should see much of him.

He bowed his thanks, and, perhaps unconsciously, his eyes rested for a moment on Miss Dorse's piquant face. She blushed the very slightest blush in the world, and dropped her eyes. Her ladyship noticed it, and frowned.

That night Lady Beatrice spent a considerable time before the looking-glass and in silent meditation in her easy chair. The upshot of her meditations was, that she decided to marry the Rev. George Westaby.

In accordance with this resolution, he was encouraged to become a frequent visitor at Pennedis Grange, and, as was only natural, Lady Beatrice received him with her sweetest smiles and in her most becoming gowns. Really he was a very distinguished-looking man, and would be a husband to be proud of.

She soon ascertained, by a little judicious pumping, that though he was not particularly well born, there was nothing ignoble in his parentage; and perhaps it was just as well that he had no relations likely to trouble him. Alone he would probably all his life remain a poor curate; as her husband it was her firm intention that he should end his days a bishop; for she had sense enough to see that his extempore sermons were above the average, and his delivery, a most important point in Lady Beatrice's estimation of a Churchman, was perfect.

Several weeks passed, and Lady Beatrice was perfectly satisfied with the course of events. The Rev. George Westaby was almost a daily caller, and his manner was all that a woman could desire who was endeavouring to effect a conquest. Indeed, so easy appeared to be the task of bringing this village curate to her feet, that she would have been almost inclined to call it tame, had not his splendid physique and distinguished bearing generated within her some vague emotion, which, no doubt, in a woman of the world is the substitute for love.

But there came a cloud, although only a passing one. One afternoon

Lady Beatrice was standing on the balcony of Pennedis Grange, idly gazing through a telescope which was fixed there, when she spied two figures on the sands. One was the Rev. George Westaby, and the other her companion, Miss Dorse. She watched them pacing to and fro, evidently talking very earnestly, watched them approach towards the house, and separate with a feeling at her heart very like jealousy. If she had made up her mind to stoop to marry this country curate, at any rate, she would brook no rivals. On that score she was very decided.

That night there were words between Lady Beatrice and her companion; in vulgar parlance there was a row. Lady Beatrice was sarcastic and spiteful, Miss Dorse was sullen and at last impertinent. The end was one which Lady Beatrice did not regret. The next morning's train bore Miss Dorse away to London, with six months' salary in her pocket, in lieu of notice.

The Rev. George Westaby took the matter very quietly, and, to Lady Beatrice's great satisfaction, did not exhibit any feeling beyond a mild surprise at Miss Dorse's sudden departure. This Lady Beatrice felt to be wholly satisfactory, and began to think that perhaps she had been unnecessarily severe with her companion. Still, she was better out of the way, and Lady Beatrice determined that her next companion should be one of a very different sort. The bishop-in-future spent quite as much of his time as formerly at the Grange; but Lady Beatrice felt that matters required a fillip. No doubt he felt considerable diffidence about declaring himself to a lady so much above him in rank and position. It was very natural, and, indeed, creditable, that he should. He must be encouraged; and he was encouraged, not only by speaking glances, but also by insinuations and innuendoes, which were at last successful; and one evening the Rev. Westaby left Pennedis Grange the accepted suitor of Lady Beatrice Price.

Perhaps it would be as well not inquire too closely into the exact manner in which this culmination was brought about. It might have been Leap Year; and there is a good deal of excuse for Lady Beatrice if, considering their relative positions, she did give him even a little more than encouragement. Suffice it to say that one proposed, and the other accepted.

Their courtship was not a particularly ardent one, but Lady Beatrice found it perfectly satisfactory. One day she unfolded to him her plans for the future, of which he quite approved.

"It would be very much nicer," she remarked *en passant*, "if the living could be arranged for before our marriage, wouldn't it, George? You would feel more independent then."

He agreed with her, as he did in everything, and the conversation dropped.

Two or three days later, however, he resumed it. He had heard of a living for sale in a very nice part of Derbyshire, which he thought eminently suitable, and he detailed with some enthusiasm its many advantages. Lady Beatrice listened with interest; and during the evening it was decided that her lover should journey up to London immediately, and make a few more inquiries.

He went up on the morrow, and very soon a letter came from him. Everything that he could hear of the living was more than satisfactory, and the price (£5,500) was moderate. He thought that Beatrice could not do better than arrange for it, and he would remain in town in case she cared for him to settle the matter; or, no doubt, it could be done by her lawyer.

By the return of post he received a most affectionate letter from his *fiancée*, and a cheque for £5,600. He immediately acknowledged receipt of these by a post-card. He was going to run down to Derbyshire, he said, and would write on the morrow; and then the next day, and the remainder of the week passed, and Lady Beatrice heard nothing of her lover. She began to be alarmed, for this silence was incomprehensible. Something had happened to him, she feared—perhaps he had been taken ill—and at last, unable to bear the suspense any longer, she packed a portmanteau, and, accompanied by her maid, journeyed up to London. She drove first of all to her bankers, and ascertained that her cheque had been cashed three days ago by a gentleman, who had taken a large amount of gold. Then she drove to the hotel where he had stopped, and, trembling with an indefinable fear, made her inquiries. Yes, the Rev. G. Westaby had stopped there, but he had left three days ago. If she was Lady Price, there was a letter for her.

Perplexed, she took it into a sitting-room, and tore it open. Directly she had read it she swooned.

"LANGHAM HOTEL,
"*August 20th*.

"MY DEAR LADY BEATRICE,—

"After a good deal of meditation I have come to the regrettable but unalterable decision that I cannot accept the flattering proposition which you were so kind as to make to me a short time since. I fear that I should not be able to make you happy, nor should I myself be satisfied and contented in the career which you purposed for me. The fact is, I have always had a great and increasing dislike for the profession which I was compelled by circumstances, which I will not here dilate upon, to adopt. Therefore I have come to the conclusion to absent myself for a while, and to seek in another country, and in another vocation, that happiness which I am confident that I should fail to attain here.

"With my prayers for your forgiveness,

"I remain, yours regretfully,

"GEORGE WESTABY.

"P.S.—I have taken the liberty of retaining the proceeds of the cheque which you were so kind as to send me, and if at any time I shall be able to repay it (a contingency which I do not, however, contemplate as very possible), I shall find pleasure in doing so."

The worst of the whole matter was, that the only point on which the manager of the hotel could give Lady Price any information was, that the gentleman in question had left the hotel in company with a young lady, who, from her description, could be none other than her ladyship's late companion.

Lady Beatrice is still a spinster.

# THE TRAGEDY OF A NIGHT

A man, stripped to the shirt, bruised and disfigured in many places with blood and dirt, lay prostrate upon a sandy hillock, his bloodshot eyes turned steadily westwards. He was in dire straits—starving, half mad with thirst, and exhausted with fruitless fighting. For every barrel of his empty, still smoking revolver, a dead or dying man lay upon the little plateau around him. He had fought as a man fights who sees his own life forfeited by reason of overmastering odds, yet girds himself to meet death as becomes one of a great race and a great country. The number of his assailants had been such as had made fighting a pantomime, and his desperate resistance a farce, as far as any chance of escape was concerned. A hundred savage soldiery, whose language was a mystery to him, and whose arms and whole appearance a revelation, had come upon him in his sleep a short hour ago. Away over the stony steppes and across the mountains his false guides were flying in mortal terror of their lives.

For this was an unknown country of horrors, at whose portals whole generations of explorers had perished, whose great city was still the home of mystery, the despair and the desire of travellers of all nations. Alone on the face of the earth the people had resisted the march of civilization, had held firm and unshaken the great barriers which Nature and their own savagery had reared about the sacred capital. Yonder it lay in the cold grey light across the plain, its great walls, monuments of marvellous masonry, encompassing it like an iron band, behind a heterogeneous multitude of minarets and strange square columns, flat-roofed houses, and curious watch towers. Even in those moments of his agony the man forgot his sufferings and his approaching doom in the mingled exultation and despair of the explorer. He, first of all Englishmen, first indeed of all Europeans, was looking, though from afar off and in grievous plight, upon the sacred city of Thibet. Even though he paid for his daring with his life, as seemed indeed certain, this was at least some measure of consolation. Yet it was consolation fraught with dismay and anger. To die so near the goal was maddening. A fit of ineffective rage seized him. Who were these wretched, half-starved savages to stand between him and the desire of his life? He measured them against himself, and the thought of their brute power over him made him almost hysterical in those first hours of his pain. He was a man of note in his country, rich, noble, young. If only he could make them understand. He cursed the grim barrier of non-comprehension which his little knowledge of Asiatic and their hideous dialect had reared between them. All his signs they had treated with contempt. He had pointed towards the city and had shown them papers—papers to which many seals had been affixed, and which proved him to be an Englishman of note, entitled to the respect and consideration of all foreign powers. He had pointed backwards across the hills whence he had come, a long and wearisome journey, which from days had grown into weeks, and from weeks to months.

Nothing had availed him. He had no presents with which to bribe them. Such few pieces of gold which he had possessed had been snatched from him by the first comers, their yellow Mongolian faces and narrow eyes on fire with cupidity. They had stripped him of his few possessions, with a ruthlessness peculiar to their race, and afterwards they had set upon him to destroy him. He had a horrible fear that even now they were hesitating to kill him only because, furious at his stout resistance, they were planning a more terrible thing. He had heard many stories of the tortures which these people inflicted upon chance travellers, drawn towards their city as a moth to the candle by its solemn and impenetrable mystery. He recalled them now with sickening distinctness. What they had done to others they would surely do to him. And presently it appeared that he was right.

A dozen of them came, dragging a pine trunk stripped of its branches up the side of a wooded ravine a hundred yards away. Others began to drill a hole in the rising ground close to where he lay. Backwards and forwards they passed, casting every now and then upon him glances of fierce and sickly hatred, shouting menaces at him in a heathen gibberish, throwing every now and then a stone at his uncovered head. The man realized then, more fully perhaps than ever before, the hideous, unconquerable hate of this people for all aliens, under which heading he, the European, most surely came. It was written in their sallow faces, it flashed in their black, narrow slit eyes, their gestures, and the vindictive torrent of abuse which flowed from their lips, proclaimed it.

Their dead comrades they kicked aside with indifference. It was no desire to avenge them which had kindled their rage, which had made death too slight a punishment to be meted out to him, which had put torture into their minds—for it was going to be torture. The man saw it in their faces, read it in every grin and leer which chilled his blood. He groaned aloud. It was an evil end for him, Geoffrey Felbrigge, Earl of Lechfort, Lord Lieutenant of his county and Master of Hounds.

An hour afterwards they left him. He was trussed and tied to the post which they had improvised, his hands and legs aching with the cords which cut into his flesh, his face turned with relentless irony to the city of his desires. They had trooped away, whither exactly he could not tell, with strange mocking cries, and with flourishing gestures which seemed like an invocation to the elements to rain their tortures upon him. He was alone, with no one save his thoughts to bear him company—a strange, lone figure in the rocky solitude.

A fierce sun beat upon him all day. For ten hours he had neither eaten nor drunk, and the roof of his mouth was like blistered leather. His eyes were bloodshot and his tongue swollen. He had tugged at his cords until his arms were bruised, and the blood had forced its way through his tightened skin. Then a partial but merciless unconsciousness came to him. The sandy desert faded away before his eyes, the sun gleaming minarets of the city mocked him no longer, the fierce heat ceased to torture his numbed flesh. He was back in London, back in the long drawing room, with its delicate perfumes and gently softened shade, face to face with the woman whose invincible pride and his own stubbornness had driven him forth a reckless wanderer, had kindled in him the old, wild spirit—the passion for new countries, which, before he had met her, had been the joy of his life. Tall and fair and slim, in her white evening gown, he could see her standing before him with eyes which bade him stay, which said things to him which her tongue had been too proud to utter. He could see the jewel which flashed upon her heaving bosom, the tears which welled slowly into her eyes. It was his fault, his fault. The thought of her—his wife—the woman, and the only woman he had ever loved, soothed him for one moment only to madden him the next. She would be waiting for him, and he would never return. He would never be able to take her hands, to look into her eyes, to smooth her hair and kiss away those tears, as he had longed to many a time since he had left London in a sudden fit of blind, unreasoning fury. She had been right. He had been brutal and unreasonable. After all, the difference between them had been so pitifully trivial. He was a brave man, and he had looked death in the face before, death as hideous as this if quicker. Yet he broke down now. It was the thought of Helen, not to see her—to let her know . . . .

Then sun went down, and the cooler air was rent with the sound of a man's sobs.

In another hemisphere, London was doing its best to amuse itself. Westwards the pavements were thronged with saunterers, the streets were blocked with hansoms, the night was warm, and the women's dresses were like the wings of summer butterflies. The playhouses were flaring with light, everywhere there was colour and movement and languorous content. Further westwards, from the great dwelling houses and the mansions of the squares, drugget crossed the pavement, there was the murmur of floating music and soft voices from the holland-shrouded balconies above. The whole city seemed steeped with pleasure this soft spring evening. Every one was entertaining or being entertained.

On the balcony of one of the great mansions in Cadogan Square a woman was standing alone. She had escaped for a moment unseen from the brilliantly lit ballroom behind; her face was turned eastwards, and her eyes were soft with unshed tears. It was a moment rendered necessary by a sudden rush of memories which had brought a lump into her throat and a strange sadness into her heart. The last time she had been a guest in this house he had been her companion. She remembered distinctly how he had arranged her cloak in the carriage, had thrown away his freshly-lit cigarette because she had coughed, had been, as it chanced, upon that evening more than ordinarily attentive to her in such little ways as woman sets store by. She remembered too, how he had seemed to her that night, in comparison with the other men who had thronged the rooms, more than ordinarily handsome; he had danced with her three times, and out here on the balcony he had leant over her with a little laugh, and had kissed her—his own wife. Oh, how mad, how foolish she had been to let him go, when a single word from her would have stopped him. Never a day had passed but she had repented the stupid, stubborn pride which had kept sealed her lips. Where was he now? Lost to her, perhaps, for ever. She gazed wistfully and tearfully eastwards. Many thousand miles away, a man was being tortured, and he too was thinking of that night.

"At last I have found you then, Helen. Do you know that I have been looking for you everywhere?"

She turned round slowly and unwillingly. A tall, soldierly man was standing by her side, a man who looked at her as a man looks only at the woman he loves. She saw and shrank from it, as she had done many a time before. She wanted no man's love save his who was gone.

"I came out for a breath of fresh air, Morton," she answered. "The rooms here are always too hot. I think that they must be badly ventilated. I was just going in. Will you give me your arm?"

"I wonder," he said, "would you do me a favour, Helen. I want to talk to you for five minutes before you meet with any of your friends inside, May I?"

She moved her head gravely, but her manner explained a certain unwillingness.

"If it is necessary," she answered, "I am quite ready to listen to you."

He drew a short breath and hesitated. So much depended upon the next few minutes. There were grey hairs in his head, he was approaching middle age, and all his life he had loved but one woman. For a time she had been lost to him. This was his chance of winning her again. It was for life or death. No wonder that he hesitated.

"Helen," he said at last, "there is some news which I wish you to hear first from me. The evidence of poor Geoffrey's death has been accepted unanimously and without question by the court. I believe that since mid-day I have had the right to call myself the Earl of Lechfort."

Once more she turned eastwards. Her cheeks were very pale, but her eyes were dry. She spoke distinctly enough, though her tone was hard and emotionless.

"I thought," she said, "that it would take a week for them to give a decision."

"The evidence," he answered, gently, "was too conclusive to leave room for a shadow of doubt. No one regrets poor Geoffrey's death more than I do, Helen; but as to doubting it—it is impossible."

"Very well, Morton," she said, "I do not complain. You must let me know about your other arrangements, and I will move into the Dower House, at Huncote, whenever you please. That, however, must not imply that I consider myself a widow."

He interrupted her—a frown upon his forehead, a note of passion in his tone.

"Give me credit at least, Helen," he cried, "for being ordinarily decent. You shall choose either Lechfort or Massingham, and it will be yours for life. Besides, I could not afford to live in them myself. I am forced to take the title and the estates; but, as you know, the income from them is not large, and all Geoffrey's money was, of course, left to you."

"I will agree to anything," she said listlessly, "which you and my solicitors advise."

He drew a little nearer to her, and the danger light flashed once more in his eyes.

"Helen," he said, "I want you to agree to something else, which has nothing to do with Mr. Cunliffe, which has nothing to do with anybody except yourself."

"Well?"

The attempt at discouragement was obvious. He chose to ignore it.

"Geoffrey has been dead now for three years—"

She stopped him.

"He has disappeared for three years," she corrected. "Do you mind leaving it like that?"

"He is dead. The proofs are absolute. We have his clothes and his belongings, the testimony of his guides, the word of those who saw him dead. God knows that I am not one who ever hankered after dead men's shoes. I would bring him to life if I could, but it is impossible. Helen, you must learn to realize this."

She looked him steadily in the eyes.

"The proofs," she said slowly, "may seem convincing. I do not blame the courts for admitting them, or you for taking the title; yet, for myself, I am a woman, and I must have something to live for. I am going on hoping. What else can I do?"

"You can make others happy," he cried, his voice thick with emotion. "Happiness for yourself lies—that way. It is useless to nurse a dead sorrow. Geoffrey is dead, poor chap, and believe me, Helen, I am sorry. But there is the future."

"I shall live on—and hope," she murmured.

"Helen, when you say that," he answered, "you rob me of the one great hope of my life. You know very well what I mean. You know that I love you. No, don't shrink from me. I am not a poisonous thing. There is nothing criminal in loving you. If there is, I have been a criminal all my life, for I have never cared for any other woman. I don't ask for anything now; no, not even for hope. It is too soon. You have not realized as yet that Geoffrey has gone. I am going to wait very quietly and very patiently. I ask for nothing, but I want you to know."

She drew her skirts coldly away from contact with him.

"Morton," she said, "perhaps it is as well that you have spoken. I can tell you my mind now plainly. If you wish to remain my friend, you will never breathe a word of this again. To you Geoffrey may seem dead; to me he is alive. I am a woman, you know, and I am hard to convince. Facts count for little with me against consciousness. I feel that Geoffrey is alive; I refuse to believe him dead. He may never come back to me, but I shall wait for him—and hope."

"What hope can you have?" he protested bitterly. "You read the letter from Colonel Denny?"

"Other Englishmen were travelling that way."

"His clothes? They were his. His tailor has proved it."

"He may have lent them, or they may have been stolen."

"His silence?"

"He is in a country as silent as the grave."

"It is ridiculous," he cried passionately. "You will not listen to reason. It is madness. You are offering up the best years of your life a fruitless sacrifice—to what? God knows. You mean that you will never listen to me, that you will cling to this miserable folly throughout your life and mine. You will wreck them both for a whim—a superstition."

"I am Geoffrey's wife," she said. "So I shall always feel myself until—"

"Until what?"

"Until I know that he is dead."

"Until you know that he is dead," the man repeated slowly. "That is certain enough already. Yet tell me this—what further proof will satisfy you?"

"The sight of his body, or speech with one who has actually seen it," she answered slowly. "Nothing else."

The man ground his heel upon the stone floor, and his face was set and white.

"Listen, Helen," he said. "I am an idle man. I will humour your fancy. You will not listen to me unless you have speech with some one who has seen Geoffrey's body, or can bring you certain word of his death. Very well. Where he went I will go. I will follow in his footsteps until I come to the end. He is dead. I know it. Never mind,

I will bring you the proof. And then?"

"You mean it!" she cried. "You will go?"

"Yes, I will go. And then?"

She shook her head sadly.

"I cannot make any bargain," she said. "If is too hideous. Besides, you know my belief. You will find Geoffrey alive. I am sure of it. You will bring him home to me. If you do that—oh, if you do that!"

The light upon her face was a brilliant revelation of her surpassing beauty. But the man who saw it was white to the lips. To him it was torture. If only she would ever care for him like that.

"I will take my chance," he said slowly; "but remember that before I start I warn you. I shall come back alone. That I am sure of before I start. Try and make up your mind to it, or you will only be courting a bitter disappointment."

She answered him with apparent irrelevance,

"When shall you start?"

"To-morrow."

There was a time when the man had clung to life, but that time had gone by. It was for death now that he prayed, for forgetfulness, for oblivion. Of time he had lost all count. There was no change in the days. The same pitiless sun burned and scorched his flesh from mid-day to sundown. Every evening he breathed the same little gasp of relief as the fiery red ball sank behind the low line of wild storm beaten rocks. Yet the nights brought no relief. As the darkness fell came the keen icy winds, the deathlike silence, the unutterable sense of desolation, which made him glad even to crane his neck and watch the dark forms of the savage warriors who guarded him gathered round a fire of logs outside their hut. At first he had treated the privations which he was made to endure, the leering gibes and hideous mockery of his yellow-skinned guards, with the full contempt of a strong, brave man. He had nerved himself to face death, and he had closed the door upon all that host of torturing thoughts which had made such an end so bitter. But the time had been too long. More than once already he had broken down, had felt a sudden burning at his eyeballs, and the rush of warm, unmanly tears. Beyond there seemed to be still more terrible things. Already he had experienced a hideous unloosing of all fixed thought, he had burst into violent and incoherent speech, which had sounded strangely even to his own ears. He had felt himself dimly to be on the threshold of that fearful world where the body lives and the mind is held by demons. Then he had looked about him with feverish and sick desire for a weapon with which to escape. Anything sooner than the horrible chains of madness—death a thousand times rather, if by any means he could compass his own self-destruction. But there was no weapon. The ill-clad, pitiless savages who guarded him took zealous care that the white-faced interloper, who had dared to journey to within sight of their holy city, should not escape them. By degrees he had learned a little of their language. One night he gathered easily from their signs and disjointed words that they were discussing his death. They were weary of their solitude, of their lonely guard upon the mountains. Better finish him off or swear that they had cut him down whilst endeavouring to escape. They die so slowly, these white-faced devils, and the time hung heavy upon their hands up here in the lonely pass. But there was always a majority who shook their heads solemnly and were firm. To end his tortures would mean death to every one of them. Their orders were to keep him alive. Their own heads would grin from the walls which bounded the slaughter-house of the city if they disobeyed. So those who were weary went out and kicked him savagely to relieve their feelings, and returned to the shelter of the hut.

Then there came a night when he awoke with a sharp cry and a rush of blood to his poor, numbed heart, from one of those long, agonizing dozes, which was as near as ever he could come to sleep.

The cry was stifled by a hot hand thrust upon his mouth, and a gentle exclamation of warning. A man had crept out from the shadow of the rocks, and was standing beside him. A man whose face was familiar, whose expression was one of horrified pity. He told himself that this must be a nightmare—he had had them before, and he dug at his eyeballs, and then opening them wider, stared and stared again. But the man's face did not fade away as those others had done. On the contrary he was drawing nearer, his trembling lips were parted, and a hoarse whisper came from them:—

"Geoffrey. Why, Geoffrey, this is horrible. What, in God's name, have they been doing to you?"

Then the sleeping mind of the man awoke, and his heart beat thick and strong. He had buried all hope long ago. This was like new life.

"Morton," he whispered faintly. "Speak to me again softly. Let me feel you. I want to be sure that you are flesh and blood. I have had so many fancies in the night time. Let me be sure that this is not another cursed dream."

The man drew nearer to him, and the glazed eyes of the captive lit up as though with fire. Whatever those others might have been this was a real and palpable presence.

"You know me, Geoffrey, old chap. I came out here to look for you. They said that these devils had done you to death. Thank God that I have found you. Have courage, Geoff."

"Thank God, indeed!" the man sobbed. "Be still for a moment, Morton; let me think."

There was a short, tense silence. His heart was thumping against his ribs, and his head swam. Yet with this sudden birth of hope something of his old coolness was back again. He was able to think, and to think clearly. Afar off there was a break in the night, the dawn was already brightening in the east. Soon they would be bringing his handful of dried peas and water. He looked anxiously towards the hut where all was still.

"You are not alone, Morton?" he whispered. "How many of you are there?"

"Only myself and one guide, an Afghan," the newcomer answered. "The others have all deserted. I started with twenty, and twenty carriers, but they have melted away. We have had to fight twice."

"There are twelve men guarding me," the prisoner whispered, motioning towards the hut. "Soon they will wake and bring me food. If you set me free now, we should not be able to get far enough away. Go and hide till night comes again. When it is dark enough I will call out as though with pain. They will take no notice. I have shrieked through a whole night, and they have not turned their heads. Come softly up to me then, and have a knife ready to cut these accursed ropes. How did you come—on foot?"

"I have horses; two spare ones—little mountain ponies. They climb the mountains like cats. Once away they will never catch us. Bear up, old chap, till to-night."

All through the long day the man, who seemed indeed to be enduring a perpetual crucifixion, appeared to be growing weaker and weaker. The soldiers who guarded him wagged their heads, came out to stare, and jabbered amongst themselves. He was nearing his end; that was certain. No one but a strong man could have held out so long. It was nearly all over now. They decided to send one of their number to the city with the news. Their instructions had been to keep him alive as long as possible. He was to remain there, alive or dead, an awful message from this people to the hated strangers who should seek to force their way on towards the sacred city. But when their backs were turned there was a change in the man. A new light was in his eyes, the fire of a new hope was burning once more in his veins. Yet that day was the longest he had ever known. Surely the sun had never moved so slowly, the darkness had never been so long delayed. Yet slowly though that fiery red ball sank into the west, his setting was none the less sure.

At last his rim touched the broken line of rocky hills, beyond which was home and freedom. Then, all quivering with impatience, the man waited whilst grey deepened into black, and the voices of his guards, seated together in the distance, grew drowsier and fainter. And the day too had been long, the longest of his life, to the man who lay behind a rock waiting only a few hundred yards away. Months ago, when first he had heard some vague rumours of an Englishman held in captivity and torture by this cruel and savage people, he had had only one thought—to push on at all hazards and at all risks. He had only half believed their story; even if there were truth in it, he had not expected to find in their captive the man to find some trace of whom was the avowed object of his expedition. During that long, horrible day he began to realize what the finding of Geoffrey must mean to him. It was the death-blow to his hopes. With this man's return to life must end the one great desire of his heart. It was like slow madness creeping into his brain. He had never doubted but that he would go home after many dangers and many privations to take her hand in his, to tell her that he had done all that a man could do, that failure was written in the book of death beforehand, and then, some day, to plead for his reward. He would not have hurried her; she was not a woman to be easily won, but in the end his persistence and his devotion must have triumphed. This was how he had thought of the future; his worst imaginings had never included such a possibility as this. He was to return shamefaced and corrected, to confess that she was right, to take her husband home to her, and leave them to their happiness. What was there left for him? Without Helen life in any form was barely endurable. The desire for her had been the one great desire of his life. He looked back over the bare, wild country across which he had come, across the iron-girt hills on which never a tree or a shrub could blossom, and up the great gorge where every footstep had been taken in peril, and every loose stone dislodged by their cautious progress had fallen a thousand feet. And as the day wore on, the man's passion grew, and voices whispered in his ear. Helen was so beautiful; she would so soon learn to love him. If he crept away now down into the little valley where the ponies were tethered and his worn-out guide was sleeping, in an hour he would be far away. The way back was easy. There would be no one to whisper of his treachery, rather he would be praised for his gallant journey into the heart of a dangerous country. What was Geoffrey to him? There had been no pretence of friendship between them; they were kin, and that was all.

And Helen. He closed his eyes and stood once more by her side upon the balcony. The perfume of her hair, the soft, silent music of her eyes—with a swift rush of memories these things became suddenly real to him in the deep silence of a brooding and unpeopled land.

When the sun set he was ten miles away, riding with white, hard face and loose hands, breathing sharply, and with a glare in his eyes which was like the glare of a madman. For he was pursued by ghosts, they were on every side of him, in front, their voices whispered to him through the gathering darkness. Was it he, Morton Felbrigge, soldier and gentleman, a man of honour and of good conscience, who was riding into the night with ashen cheeks? Never daring to look behind, trembling at every shadow and starting at every breath of wind which moaned through the few lone trees. He thought of his last campaign, of that terrible battle from whence he had come drenched with blood, with the body of his comrade upon his shoulders and the thunderous applause of his wildly excited regiment in his ears. He thought of the small iron cross which the Queen had pinned to his breast, and which, it had seemed to him, must for ever keep the man against whose heart it beat from even the passing thought of meanness or dishonour. He thought of the woman who trusted him, with whom his life, if indeed he ever dared to claim her, must be one long living lie. Of the grim secret which, as the years went on, would work in his veins like poison, until the hour of inevitable confession came, and the eyes, which had learned to look upon him kindly, blazed out the scorn of a wronged and deceived woman. He thought of these things until his head was full of horror, and he hated himself and what he was doing with a deadly, sickening hatred. Yet he rode on still into the night.

And behind, across the steppes and up the gorge, a man was waiting for him with breathless and passionate eagerness. The sun had set and the darkness had come. With pain and difficulty he moved his head a little and looked around. Where was Morton, his deliverer? Why did he not come? Every moment now was a golden moment wasted.

The night was dark, his guards were asleep. Many times his cry, strained at first, but pitifully now in earnest, had wailed out upon the thick darkness. Sometimes his guards had cursed, sometimes an animal from the distant belt of woods had yelped back an answer, but Morton never came, and of all the nights of torture which the man had passed that was the cruelest. When morning came he was very near to death, when the mid-day sun beat upon his head he was raving. When night came again, he was in a torpor, and death hovered around. He was still unconscious when a knife cut his bonds and the arm of a strong man lifted him, a poor helpless wreck, from the ground. The motion of a pony revived him for a moment, at the sound of a shot he opened his eyes. He was in a strange place, and, as he staggered back to consciousness, he saw such a sight as few have looked upon. He saw Morton, with blood streaming from his face, and eyes flashing like a man possessed of devils. With a two edged sword, which gleamed in his hand like whirling silver, he had cut down three of his assailants. In his left hand his revolver was flashing out the fires of death. The desire of life seized hold of the half-conscious man. He slipped from his pony, and snatching a sword from the dead hand of a prostrate man, joined in the fray. It was a battle against hideous odds, but when it was over Geoffrey was unhurt, and his deliverer, with the stump of an arm hanging useless by his side and the lust of blood in his red eyes, was looking about for more men to kill—and there were none.

It was years before Geoffrey knew the whole truth, but he and Helen heard it together one Christmas morning, when a great guest honoured them by coming straight to Elton Towers on his return from a campaign which had made his name a household one, and himself the idol of an enthusiastic country. Outside, the way across the park to church was lined with people who were waiting to see him pass out, who had come from far and near on the chance of seeing him. He took them both into the great library and bade them listen to him.

With slow bitter words and bent head he told them the story of that night and day. He told them of his flight and of the agony of his repentance, how he had ridden back through the soft, grey dawnlight and the burning heat as though the fires of hell were at his back. But they never let him finish. Geoffrey had seized his hands, and with a deep sob had begged him to stop. But the woman bent over and closed his white lips with hers. When they passed out across the park and between the lines of people who had been waiting with uncovered heads in deep respectful silence for a glimpse of him, he bowed to them with a smile which for many years no man had seen. Those who knew him from his photographs wondered. Later, in the clubs, men congratulated him upon his altered looks and obvious happiness. He laughed at them always and passed on. He alone knew how slight the joy which his fame and success had brought, how immeasurably sweet the dropping of that grim burden of self-hatred, which at the touch of her lips and the clasp of Geoffrey's hands had fallen away from him for ever. The tragedy of that night has still a dark corner in his mind—but the key has been turned upon it and the fires are extinct.

# MR. ASHLEY'S FAILURE

A somewhat short, precise-looking young man stood on the steps of a mansion in Hyde Park Gardens, deliberately scraping his boots; for the weather was showery, and he had walked from the Foreign Office. Having concluded that operation, he turned to the opened door, and instantly perceived, from the disturbed expression of the usually most impassive of doorkeepers, that something was wrong.

"Is anything the matter, Burditt?" he asked condescendingly, as he stepped into the hall. "Mrs. Tregarron and Miss Alice are quite well, I hope?"

The man first carefully secured the door, then turned round and bowed.

"The ladies are quite well, my lord," he said gravely; "but we are all a good deal upset this afternoon. Mrs. Tregarron will see you at once in the morning-room, if your Lordship will be so good as to come this way," and he ushered the visitor down the hall into a small room on the left-hand side.

Curiosity was not one of Lord Maclenie's failings, neither was impatience; so he did not question the man further, merely desiring him to at once inform Mrs. Tregarron of his arrival.

In less than a minute his prospective mother-in-law—a tall, aristocratic-looking woman, wearing a widow's cap and looking about fifty years old—swept into the room.

"My dear Robert," she exclaimed, holding out her hand, "how good of you to come so soon! Of course you have had my note?"

His Lordship shook his head. "I have had no note from you today," he answered. "Alice is—"

"But I wrote you to Cadogan Place nearly two hours ago," interrupted Mrs. Tregarron.

"Which note I have not yet had the pleasure of receiving," he returned. "We are busy at the Foreign Office, and I have not been home to lunch. Alice is—"

"Then you don't know anything about it?" broke in Mrs. Tregarron. "Dear me! I—"

"If you were to tell me—" he ventured to suggest.

Mrs. Tregarron became all impressiveness.

"You remember that diamond necklace you gave Alice yesterday morning?"

Of course he remembered it. Had he not spent nearly the whole of the previous afternoon at Filmoy and Morton's, undecided whether a less magnificent present would not be deemed a more suitable offering to a portionless *fiancée*? and had he not, after finally deciding upon its acquisition, then and there written out a cheque for fifteen hundred guineas, and left the shop with the little morocco case in his breast-pocket? Certainly he remembered that diamond necklace.

"Well, what about it?" he inquired almost impatiently. He was proud of his self-control, this rising young diplomatist, but Mrs. Tregarron's manner was irritating.

"It has been stolen," she said impressively, and then leaned back in her chair, waiting anxiously to see what effect her communication would have upon him.

It was instantaneous. Lord Maclenie was self-controlled, but parsimonious; and fifteen hundred guineas is a good deal of money.

"Stolen!" he exclaimed, starting from his seat. "Stolen!"

"Yes, stolen," repeated Mrs. Tregarron, gently pressing a little lace handkerchief to her eyes, and watching all the time with deep anxiety his disturbed expression. "Sit still, and I will tell you all about it. You have no idea how upset we have all been."

"Upset! I should think so!" exclaimed his Lordship vigorously. "Have you any idea what that necklace was worth, I wonder?"

Mrs. Tregarron knew quite well her future son-in-law had taken care that she should not remain in ignorance, but she shook her head.

"Don't tell me, please," she pleaded. "I really cannot bear it just now. Let me tell you how it happened."

"Just what I want to get at," he exclaimed impatiently. "Do you suspect anyone?"

"At present, no one; but I think, when you hear the circumstances, you will agree with me that the theft must have been carried out by someone resident in the house; and, if so, they can have had no opportunity of disposing of it, for I have allowed no one to go out on any pretext whatever. I look upon it as somewhat a suspicious circumstance that Ann (Alice's maid) has twice asked for leave to absent herself this afternoon. Of course I refused it."

"Of course. But please tell me exactly how it happened," entreated

Lord Maclenie.

Mrs. Tregarron cleared her throat and proceeded in her recital of the affair. Told in her own way and in her own words it took some time; but, briefly, the facts—very simple facts they were—appeared to be as follows:—

Directly after breakfast that morning, Alice (Mrs. Tregarron's only daughter and Lord Maclenie's betrothed) had left the room, and, a few minutes later, had summoned her mother into the apartment in which they now were to look at the diamonds by daylight. After admiring them for some time, Mrs. Tregarron was called away for her morning's interview with the cook, and about half an hour later Alice had come to her and announced her intention of visiting old Lady Somerville, her godmother. She did not return for luncheon—she very seldom did when she went to visit Lady Somerville—but got back early in the afternoon. She met her mother in the hall, and explained that she had hurried away immediately after lunch as it had suddenly occurred to her during that meal that she had left her necklace on the mantelpiece of the morning-room. Mrs. Tregarron and her daughter then entered the morning-room together and found that the necklace had disappeared. They searched everywhere, high and low, and then questioned the servants, who one and all denied having even entered that particular room during the whole morning.

"You can imagine what a state Alice and I were in then," concluded Mrs. Tregarron. "Poor girl! It made her quite ill, and she has gone to lie down for a while. Of course, I forbade any of the servants to leave the house, and sent round to you, and also a note to Scotland Yard. Did I do right?"

"I don't see that anything else could have been done," replied Lord Maclenie thoughtfully. "It seems a strange affair altogether. Could the room be entered from outside, I wonder?" and he crossed the room and looked out.

"Easily; but the window does not appear to have been tampered with, and you must remember it was in the middle of the day. Anyone getting through the window would certainly have been seen."

Once more the interior of the room was carefully examined. Nothing was to be discovered. All was in order. Neither could the sagacious officer from Scotland Yard, who arrived a quarter of an hour later, find anything at all suspicious in the entrance to or general appearance of the room. The servants one by one were had in and examined, and the trunks of all of them, from the newly installed scullery-maid to the gray-haired butler, thoroughly ransacked, but nothing affording the faintest shadow of a clue was discovered.

"Would you like to see my daughter herself?" inquired Mrs. Tregarron of the astute-looking detective, who stood sucking his pencil and looking thoroughly bewildered.

"Quite unnecessary," he declared. "I should be sorry to have her disturbed. There is really nothing to ask her beyond what you have told me. It's not a pleasant thing to say, ma'am," he continued, "but the thief must be one of your servants. I should like the name and address of each of them, and also, if you can oblige me with it, particulars of their last place; and I must ask you to let me know at once if one of them leaves your service or give notice."

"I suppose a reward had better be offered?" remarked Lord Maclenie.

The officer assented.

"Decidedly it would be better that there should be a reward."

"Then you can make it £250."

"Very good, your Lordship." And, after making a few more notes, the detective departed, with the usual promise that, should he discover a clue, etc.

A fortnight elapsed and nothing was heard from him. At the end of that time Lord Madenie had a conversation at the club with an acquaintance concerning the mysterious robbery.

"In the hands of Scotland Yard, is it?" remarked the latter. "Well, I don't want to revile any of our institutions, but I really do think that, so far as our established detective force is concerned, we are a long way behind the other countries of Europe. Scotland Yard very seldom discovers anything more than clues nowadays. Now, look here, Maclenie," he continued in a lower tone, "I could introduce you to a man—he's not regularly in the profession, but he'd do anything for me—who would find out all about this little affair for you, if anyone could. He's a regular sharp fellow, is Ashley; and only say the word, and I'll tell him to call and see you."

Lord Maclenie shook his head doubtfully.

"I don't believe in amateur detectives much," he remarked disparagingly. "I'm afraid if Scotland Yard can't make anything of it, that it would be waste of time and money trying anyone else. Of course, if he likes to take it up on the chance of the reward—I've offered £250 reward, you know—well, then I don't mind helping him with any information. If he likes to come down to Hyde Park Gardens tonight, I shall be there."

"Well, I'll tell him," replied his friend. "Detective business of any sort is his hobby, and I dare say he'll come."

The surmise was a correct one. About nine o'clock of the same evening a respectable-looking, middle-aged man, who gave his name as Mr. Ashley, called at Mrs. Tregarron's house in Hyde Park Gardens and asked for Lord Maclenie, who was spending the evening with his betrothed. His Lordship immediately explained the circumstances to Mrs. Tregarron, and begged leave to have the man shown in.

"You really must excuse me, then," pleaded Miss Tregarron, rising from her chair with a languid gesture and a slight frown of annoyance. "I'm perfectly sick of the whole matter, and shall go to my room until the man's gone."

"As you please," and Lord Maclenie rose and opened the door.

"Ask Mr. Ashley to step this way," he said to the servant, who had remained in the room. And, accordingly, Mr. Ashley was shown in.

The simple story of the theft was repeated to him in a few words. He listened attentively and grew thoughtful.

"I should rather like to see Miss Tregarron," he remarked, after a long pause, "if not inconvenient."

Mrs. Tregarron looked rather doubtful.

"Is it necessary?" she inquired, with her hand on the bell.

Mr. Ashley bowed in a deprecating manner.

"If she is engaged, pray don't disturb her," he said suavely. "Any time will do; but I should like to see her."

Mrs. Tregarron rang the ball, and, through the servant, conveyed Mr. Ashley's request to her daughter. In a minute or two he returned. Miss Tregarron was suffering from headache and had retired. She was sorry that she could not see Mr. Ashley.

The detective did not seem in the least disappointed; in fact, his eyes brightened as he received this message.

"It is of no consequence," he declared. "No doubt I have all the information available. I should like just a word with the coachman, though. May I step down stairs and speak to him?"

Mrs. Tregarron would have had him summoned, but the detective seemed bent on descending to the lower quarters, and, accordingly, he was ushered into the servants' hall, and the coachman brought to him; but when he arrived, Mr. Ashley seemed to have lost interest in him, and merely asked him carelessly a desultory question or two.

"Miss Tregarron kept you a good time waiting at Lady Somerville's?" he remarked.

"We didn't wait for her, sir; we had orders to come back and fetch her again in an hour and a half's time, which we did."

The detective seemed mildly surprised.

"I should have thought," he said reflectively, "that it would have been scarcely worth while for you to have come back again. It must have taken you all your time."

"It did that, sir, and no mistake," assented the coachman; "but young ladies never think of the 'osses. Anyways, them were her orders, and, of course, I was bound to obey them."

"Just so; and then she kept you a good time waiting, I expect, when you got back?"

"Not so very long, sir—not more than a quarter of an hour."

"Ah! well, good evening," said Mr. Ashley, turning away. "I am much obliged to you. Sorry to have disturbed you, though. I ought to have remembered that you were away during the time that the jewels were stolen."

"Seems a very mysterious affair, madam," he admitted, on his return to the upper regions. "If anything occurs to me, however, I will, of course, let you know. Good-night, ma'am; good-night, my lord," and Mr. Ashley bowed himself out of the room.

"Clear as daylight," he murmured to himself, as he walked slowly homewards; "but a nasty job to tackle."

Nevertheless, the quiet smile on his lips did not denote any great distaste in his task.

Early on the following morning he took the 'bus up to Highgate, and alighted at the road at which Lady Somerville resided. There was a cab-stand near, and he entered the shelter and made a few inquiries, the result of which appeared to be perfectly satisfactory. Then he took down a name and address, after which a certain coin of the realm found its way into the dirty but eager palm of one of the Jehus.

He seemed to be getting on. He set off, after leaving the shelter, for a very different part of town, and entered a low, dirty-looking little shop, from behind the counter of which a somewhat dirty-looking Jew bowed to him obsequiously.

"A few words with you, Jacob," said the detective shortly; and, in obedience to a gesture, he followed the man into a little back room.

The few words lasted fully an hour, at the end of which time Mr. Ashley emerged from the shop with a confident smile upon his lips.

His morning's work was not yet finished, though. He made some more calls, but chiefly now upon his most distinguished patrons, including Lord Maclenie's friend, who had recommended him. As a rule, Society doings possessed no manner of interest for him, but today he was incessantly asking questions about different people, and at the end of the morning his satisfied smile had not decreased.

The next day he called again at Hyde Park Gardens. Mrs. Tregarron was out; but the announcement of her absence did not appear to be an overwhelming shock to him. In fact, he had just watched her drive away. He would see Miss Tregarron.

The servant to whom he conveyed his request was not at all sanguine as to the young lady's willingness to see him, but he was shown into the morning-room and his message taken. In a very few minutes a tall, handsome girl swept into the room and confronted him. The detective rose and bowed.

"You wish to speak with me, Mr.—Mr. Ashley, I believe?" she said, slightly acknowledging his salutation. "Be as quick as you can, please, as I'm particularly engaged."

"I will not detain you a moment longer than is necessary, Miss Tregarron," he said quietly. "Permit me to offer you a chair."

She sat down and fixed her dark eyes upon him, full of impatient inquiry. Mr. Ashley hesitated. He had a delicate task before him, and he knew nothing of this young lady's disposition.

"Will you permit me," he said slowly, "to tell you a short story which has come under my notice lately? It will not detain you long, and you will, perhaps, find it interesting."

She arched her magnificent eyebrows, as if somewhat surprised at his presumption, but motioned him to proceed.

"We detectives come across some strange incidents sometimes," he began, "and unravel some curious tangles. Listen to this story, for instance, none the less interesting, perhaps, since it is strictly true. There was a young lady and young gentleman who fell in love with one another. Both were poor, both were in Society, and the young lady was everywhere expected to make a brilliant match, for she was beautiful and her mother ambitious. This young gentleman with whom she had unfortunately fallen in love, although of excellent family, was not only poor, but was also hopelessly in debt; and so, seeing the utter impossibility of ever being married to the man she loved, the young lady yields to her mother's solicitations and becomes engaged to a rich young nobleman.

"She has resolved to see no more of her unhappy lover, nor does she; but she hears of him often, for it happens that her maid and his manservant are brother and sister. She hears of his despair at the news of her engagement, of the terrible worry of his debts, and of his unsuccessful attempts to raise a certain sum of money to enable him to leave the country and start life afresh. Her pity for him is great, and she resolves anonymously to help him. At first, however, she is powerless, for she, too, is of a poor family, and the sum is an impossibility to her. Whilst she is striving hard to think of some means whereby to raise the money, her betrothed, a very rich but somewhat stingy young nobleman, makes her his first present—a diamond necklace of great value. An idea occurs to her. She cares nothing for the stones, and they are her own. Can she not secretly realize them, and thus obtain the money for her desperate lover? She resolves to do so, and lays her plans with considerable shrewdness. The necklace is believed by everyone to have been stolen; her lover receives the money in such a fashion that he imagines it to come from someone else from whom he has no hesitation in accepting it, and joyfully carries out his plans. Only two persons know the true facts of the cases—the young lady and myself."

"A very romantic story, Mr. Ashley," said the young lady quietly, with her eyes fixed upon the carpet. "I should like to know the end."

The detective smiled and cleared his throat.

"Well, the fact of—er—the second party becoming acquainted with this little story was most annoying to the young lady, as, of course, his disclosure of it would mean the breaking off of her marriage and social ruin. Fortunately, however, this second party was quite amenable to reason, and had not the slightest wish to ruin the young lady's prospects. He suggested to her, therefore, that she should promise him (on paper) to pay him twice the amount of the reward after her marriage and give him a small sum down to cover expenses. She, being a sensible girl, at once agreed to this."

Miss Tregarron rose and moved toward the door.

"You will excuse me for a moment?"

"Certainly," and during her brief absence Mr. Ashley occupied himself in drawing up a little document.

She was not gone long, and re-entered the room with a roll of notes in her hand.

"To continue your story, Mr. Ashley," she said, with a levity in her tones which scarcely harmonized with her pallor-stricken face, "the young lady handed over fifty pounds in notes—all she could spare before her marriage, for she was, as you observed, very poor—and signed the document which the second party had prepared for her," and, sitting down at the table, she signed with a firm hand the slip of paper which lay before her. "That ends the story, I think, Mr. Ashley," she added, rising.

"That ends the story, Miss Tregarron," the detective replied. "I wish you a very good-morning," and he bowed himself out of the room.

"Your detective didn't turn up trumps, after all," remarked Lord Madenie to his friend in the smoking-room of the club, about a fortnight after his return from his honeymoon. "A regular duffer, I thought him."

"I can't make it out," replied his friend thoughtfully. "Ashley doesn't often fail."

Perhaps Mr. Ashley, after all, does not reckon this little affair as amongst his failures.

## TWO GAMBLERS

When Sir Francis Cleydon, Bart., married the orphan daughter of a rich Australian planter, and suddenly exchanged the life of a man from town for the healthier but less exciting one of a country squire, society was very considerably astonished. The moral part of it expressed unbounded satisfaction and approval at the unexpected salvation of a man who had seemed to be going to the bad as fast as a man could go. The immoral faction sneered at his weakness in being led away from the lofty career of the pursuit of unlicensed pleasures by a girl's sweet face, and prophesied his speedy return to their ranks. They did not for a moment believe that his defection was a permanent one; their experience failed to recall to their minds a single case of a man who had gone as far on the road to ruin as their late *confrère* had done, and had yet been able to pull up short and abjure for ever the ways of unrighteousness. For six years Sir Francis had been the most reckless of turf plungers, and an almost nightly *habitué* of those clubs and private houses where the green tables form the principal part of the entertainment.

Other vices he had, but this latter one seemed to fascinate him the most, and for years men had spoken of him as a confirmed gamester. His losses had lately been as much the topic for gossip as on his debut his wealth had been, and already every one was prophesying the near approach of the end. He had spent a huge fortune, and his fine estates were heavily mortgaged. They could bear no more charges, and the final crash seemed just about to descend, when, without the least warning or notification of his intentions, the whole of his racing stud, his London house, carriages and horses, and sundry other possessions, were advertised for sale, and his marriage with Miss Golding and retirement to Cleydon Hall announced in all the society papers.

No one was more surprised than Sir Francis himself. He had lived so long amongst a school with whom it was considered *à la mode* to be *blasé* and used up, that he had almost forgotten that he possessed any feelings at all. It was quite a new sensation to him when he fell in love with Helen Golding; it speedily became a revelation. He felt himself suddenly galvanized into life from the dull lethargy into which a long course of palliating pleasures had plunged him.

At heart he was not a bad man, nor was he naturally vicious. His follies had been the not unnatural result of a slovenly guardianship on the part of a sporting uncle, and a careless, slipshod education. They had grown into habits, and he had yielded to them, never altogether without compunction; but the first breath of a good woman's influence, even though she was little more than a child, had awakened him into a keen and shameful realization of the miserable emptiness and folly of his grovelling life. He had wasted no time in irresolute regrets. He had confessed his whole life to Helen Golding, but he spoke of it as a thing of the past. He did not plead for her love as the price of his reformation, for that was a thing already assured; he only begged her to wait for a little while, and forget the Sir Francis of the past when the Sir Francis of the future should offer himself to her.

She felt that he was sincere, and did not attempt to conceal her love for him; and before he left her it had been decided that the period of probation might be dispensed with. It would be easier for him as a married man to break off at once all connection with his former life. And so in less than a month they were married; and, while London was still agape with the news, they were wandering through Italy, and Sir Francis was realizing for the first time what happiness really was.

Those sneering prophecies which Sir Francis's *quondam* associates had freely indulged in were not verified. The Leicestershire baronet never again formed one of their *coterie*, nor, indeed, did he ever feel the slightest inclination to do so. His reformation was sincere and complete, and his love for the woman whom he looked upon as his preserver was steadfast and unwavering. One only of his former tastes had survived the death-blow of his marriage, and with that one he had fought many desperate battles, and in all cases came off the victor. He had been reckoned a confirmed gambler, and, indeed, there had been in the old days no more ardent worshipper at the shrine of the green table than Sir Francis. It had become a passion with him, and several times since his marriage he had been horribly tempted. During his honeymoon he had shunned Monaco and other gambling centres, with the nervous dread inspired by his unwilling knowledge of the fascination which they still had over him; but subsequently his wife had unsuspectingly bidden him take her there, and he had been compelled to face a horrible temptation. He was nervous and ill at ease during the whole of their stay, scarcely venturing out of the hotel, and turning pale at the very mention of the gaming-tables.

At first Lady Cleydon had thought him ill; but suddenly the truth dawned upon her, and she had declared at once that she was bored to death and longing to be away. Her husband heard her with joy, and when they left Monaco the next day he left it with the feeling of a conqueror. Since then they had been careful to avoid such places without hinting to one another why, and as years passed by, and local interest grew stronger with him, Sir Francis began to congratulate himself that the battle at Monaco had been a final and decisive one. Lady Cleydon's fortune, although a large one, had been insufficient to totally free the Cleydon estates from all encumbrance. There had been a third mortgage which it had not been possible to redeem; but when, two years after their marriage, a little Francis was born, his father and mother at once determined that it must and should be paid off before the boy grew up. It was not an easy matter to save a little over thirty thousand pounds even out of such a rent-roll as the Cleydon estate showed, for times were bad and farmers were all expecting large abatements. It was done, however; and by the time the boy reached his tenth birthday the money was forthcoming, and in a week's time Sir Francis and his wife reflected with satisfaction that the mortgage would be no more.

One morning during that same week Sir Francis stood on the steps of the Cleydon Arms, smoking a cigar and lounging slightly against the side of the door. It was very seldom that he honoured the inn which bore his name (or the name of the estate) by his presence, still more seldom that he chose to advertise it by lingering about in the doorway; and the delighted proprietor, who remained discreetly in the rear rubbing his hands, and ready to rush forward at any moment if addressed, felt that every minute his distinguished guest remained there in that easy posture, in full view of the loiterers in the little town and right opposite the rival hostelry, was worth pounds to him. His sole regret was that Braggs the butcher, and Sneed the baker, and other frequenters of the Cleydon Arms were not present to witness this phenomenon; but even this regret was tempered by the reflection of how he would be able to embellish this unwonted occurrence, and astonish his little company with it at their evening meeting.

Sir Francis himself was quite unaware that his presence was creating such a commotion in the mind of his obsequious host, and was lingering there simply because, until the blacksmith had finished shoeing his horse, he had nothing better to do.

Presently it began to occur to him, however, that he was the object of a good deal of respectful curiosity on the part of the passers-by, and that his position was a trifle conspicuous. Accordingly he roused himself from some very pleasant meditations anent that scrip of legal parchment which he hoped soon to thrust on the fire, and decided upon a stroll down the street to the smithy. Before he had quitted his position, however, a figure approaching on the opposite side of the way attracted his notice, and he paused. Strangers were not common in Cleydon, and the man who was coming slowly towards him was not at all an ordinary stranger. He was tall, and of unmistakably well-bred appearance, with the slight stoop of a horseman, and attired in a riding suit and cover-coat of no provincial cut.

He favoured the loiterer on the steps with a bland, inoffensive stare as he passed him and entered the inn, but that his face invited no salutation, Sir Francis would have bidden him good morning promptly. When he had disappeared the baronet turned round and interviewed the landlord.

"Know that gentleman?" he inquired, indicating with the end of his cigar the stairs up which the stranger had passed.

"Certainly, Sir Francis. He's taken the whole of the first floor, and all my stabling for the hunting season. Honourable Bernard Granville's his name, Sir Francis. Got some very pretty animals, too, and looks like a straight goer."

Sir Francis was necessarily interested, for he was the master of the principal pack of hounds in the locality, and a very good master, too.

"Take my card up, Bowles," he told the landlord. "I should like to make Mr. Granville's acquaintance." And, delighted at the notice accorded to his guest, Bowles hurried obediently away.

Mr. Granville would be very pleased to see Sir Francis. And so the baronet was shown up into the sitting-room and announced with all pomp. The two men speedily fraternized. The most important consideration—who was Mr. Granville?—was satisfactorily explained in the first few minutes. The Granvilles of Somerset were a county family of undoubted respectability, members of whom, indeed, graced the pages of *Debrett's Peerage*, and to a younger branch of them Mr. Granville belonged.

This question settled, there was some desultory conversation about horses, dogs, cattle-breeding, and other agricultural matters, concerning all of which Mr. Granville seemed to know a good deal, and Sir Francis began to consider him a very decent sort of fellow. He explained that he had come down a fortnight before the opening of the regular season, meaning to spend the intervening period with an old friend, Colonel Ashton, but, unfortunately, Ashton was dangerously ill, and could receive no visitors, so he had been forced to occupy his hunting quarters earlier than he had intended. Sir Francis winced a little at the mention of Colonel Ashton's name, for he was notoriously a member of the fast set to which he himself had once belonged, but he did not on that account abate his favourable impressions of his new acquaintance. He had lived so long amongst rustics that the conversation of a well-bred and well-informed man was particularly pleasing—so pleasing, indeed, that, when he rose to go, he pressed Mr. Granville to return with him and spend at Cleydon Hall the period which he had intended to spend with Colonel Ashton. This Mr. Granville at first refused to do, but eventually he agreed to return with Sir Francis to dinner, and leave the matter of his further stay for subsequent discussion.

With Lady Cleydon Mr. Granville did not progress quite so well. She wondered what had brought the crow's feet and wrinkles into his otherwise young looking face, and she made a very shrewd guess as to their existence in conjunction with a pallid, almost sallow complexion. Still, she was, of course, civil to her husband's guest, and when she left them together to discuss, as she fondly imagined, the claret and the prospects of the approaching hunting season, she did so without any presentiment of evil. And yet, had she only known it, the Honourable Bernard Granville was the most dangerous man in England to leave alone with her husband.

For a while the two men chatted pretty well in the manner which she had anticipated; then Mr. Granville asked his host a fatal question.

"Do anything at *écarté*?" he inquired carelessly, toying with a dessert knife.

Sir Francis started quietly, and a shiver ran through his entire frame. The old passion was not yet dead.

"Not lately," he answered in a low tone. "I think we have no cards in the house."

Mr. Granville looked astonished. A country house which did not boast a single pack of cards was an anomaly such as he had rarely come across.

"Oh, as for that," he answered, "I have plenty in my portmanteau; but perhaps it's hardly worth the trouble of fetching them. Suppose we go in to Lady Cleydon instead," he suggested, drinking off his claret and rising.

Sir Francis was in the toils of a horrible temptation. Surely it was his duty to entertain his guest; a few hands could do no harm. Supposing he was unfortunate, he could afford to lose a hundred or two; and side by side with these plausible reflections was the old longing to handle once more the cards and experience the hopes and fears of the player. It was too strong for him.

"Lady Cleydon will scarcely expect us so soon," he remarked, hastily pouring out a glass of wine and drinking it off. "I should rather like just one game. Couldn't my man find the cards."

Mr. Granville shrugged his shoulders.

"Just as you please. I think there's a pack of cards in my great coat pocket. It hangs up in the hall."

Sir Francis rose to his feet.

"Well, fetch them, then," he said, with an excited sparkle in his eyes. "Come across into the library, Granville; we shall find it warmer there."

Mr. Granville rose, and having leisurely lighted another cigar followed his host across the hall into a smaller apartment. Sir Francis drew a small table up to the fire, and the two men seated themselves. At first the play seemed pretty even, but after a while the luck set steadily against Sir Francis. So far from causing him to desist, however, this seemed to render him more eager. He plunged, doubled the stakes, trebled them, but the result was always the same. Great beads of perspiration began to stand out on his forehead, and he dared not glance twice at the I.O.U.'s which he was constantly handing across to his adversary. At last the latter threw down the cards.

"I don't know whether you fully realize, Sir Francis," he said in a slow grave tone, rendered a little tremulous by the excitement which he was struggling to conceal, "that I have won an exceedingly large sum of money from you. I shall play no longer; the luck is all on my side."

"You will give me my revenge?" said Sir Francis eagerly. "Let us go on now."

"Certainly not," replied Mr. Granville, rising and collecting his I.O.U's; "don't you see that it is quite light? This evening, if you like, you shall try to relieve me of some of those," and he tapped the little bundle of papers which he held with his forefinger.

About an hour later Lady Cleydon was awakened by a slight noise in her room. At the foot of her bed stood her husband, with ghastly face, bloodshot eyes, and disordered attire. He stood there, in the full light of the early morning sun which was streaming in at the window, with folded arms looking at her.

"Francis," she cried, a dreadful fear settling down upon her, "what have you been doing?"

He laughed savagely.

"Gambling, Helen, gambling! A thousand curses upon the cards! I'll win it all back to-night, though! By God, I will! We'll pay off the mortgage yet! What a fool I was to double that last stake with the luck dead against me!"

She sprang up, her eyes ablaze with wrathful indignation.

"Francis, have you been gambling with that money?"

His eyes fell before hers, and he turned towards the door.

"Ay, and lost it!" he said sullenly. "I'll win it back, though; I'll win it back!"

She turned from him, her face full of loathing scorn. She uttered no words of reproach, no reminders of his broken vow. She spoke never another word, and he slunk away like a whipped dog.

That was a miserable day at Cleydon Hall. Sir Francis went for a long ride, and did not return until late in the afternoon. His guest lunched alone, and spent the afternoon strolling about the park, and Lady Cleydon did not leave her room until evening. When her husband returned, she followed him to his room.

"Francis," she pleaded, laying her hand upon his arm, "grant me a favour."

He listened without speaking.

"What is done cannot be undone," she continued softly. "Promise me not to play to-night, and we will forget everything else."

He shook his head. "Impossible, Helen. If I have to pay that man what I lost last night, I should never have another happy moment. I shall win it back."

Again she pleaded, but in vain. Then she left him; instinct told her that words would be wasted. Bernard Granville was lounging in an easy chair in the library, when the door opened, and admitted his beautiful hostess, for Lady Cleydon was a very beautiful woman still.

He rose at once, and offered her a chair. She declined it, and remained standing on the hearth-rug, nervously toying with a bracelet.

"Mr. Granville," she said abruptly, "you won a good deal of money from my husband last night."

He bowed. "Sir Francis was certainly most unfortunate," he remarked.

"I have come to ask you a favour," she went on hurriedly. "I want you to go away, and not play any more with him. You have won a fortune from him already. Isn't that enough?"

He looked at her steadily for a minute or two. With her large blue eyes, and simple, eager manner, she seemed almost like a child.

"I have promised to give Sir Francis his revenge," he said quietly, "and I am bound in honour to do so."

Her heart sank, but she did not lose courage.

"Will you come with me?" she said, moving towards the door. "I want to show you something."

He followed her in silence along many corridors and up many stairs. At last she paused, and opened the door of a large, lofty room.

"Francis, I have brought some one to see you," she said.

A fair-haired little boy, with his mother's large, blue eyes and his father's straight, well-cut features, bounded over towards them. Then, remembering his manners, he held out his hand to the visitor, and looked up shyly.

"How do you do, Mr. Granville? I know your name, you see, because we saw you in the park this afternoon, and nurse told me."

Mr. Granville nodded.

"It's a very beautiful park," he said, somewhat absently.

Little Francis agreed with him, and then turned to his mother. Presently she checked his flow of eager, childish conversation, and declared that they must go.

Mr. Granville shook hands with his little host, and silently followed her out of the room and down into the library. She closed the door, and moved close up to his side.

"Mr. Granville," she said earnestly, "I would not have taken you up there only that there is something in your face that I like. I am sure that you can be generous. I want you to put yourself in my place for one moment. I don't know whether you ever heard about my marriage; I should think not," she said, looking at his old-young face, guiltless of beard or moustache. "You cannot be very old, and it was some years ago. Sir Francis had been a gambler, and he was heavily in debt; but he promised never to touch a card again. I trusted him, and until last night he has kept his promise faithfully. For years we have been saving and pinching to free the estate from debt for little Francis. Last night has undone it all. Of course, you only did what any one else would have done," she went on hastily. "You won, and you had a right to win. I am not blaming you in the least; but, oh, if you would only go away now! If you go on playing you will win. I am sure you will; and—and—my poor little Francis, Mr. Granville; I took you up to see him because I thought you must have been something like him once, and you might think of that time and have pity on him. Fancy what your mother would have felt like if some one had threatened to ruin her little boy! Oh, do go away, Mr. Granville! I will never grudge what you have won! I—I will always think kindly of you, and bless you if you will go. You will, won't you?"

He looked down at her with an odd look in his boyish face.

"You ask a difficult thing, Lady Cleydon," he said, "for I am what your husband was—a confirmed gambler."

"But you will go?" she pleaded breathlessly. He shook his head.

"I can't refuse to give him his revenge," he said; "but—"

"But what?"

"On one condition I will promise to win no more money from him."

"What condition?"

"Simply that you will come and sit with us while we play."

She shuddered; but her resolution was soon taken.

"I consent," she said. "Now take me in to dinner."

It was a strange meal, and no one was sorry when it was over. Sir Francis, indeed, was recklessly gay; but both his wife and his guest were strangely silent. When the time came for Lady Cleydon to retire she kept her seat. Her husband looked at her questioningly.

"You are determined to play to-night?" she said quietly.

"Certainly. I am going to relieve Granville of a few of his pieces of paper," Sir Francis said, with a nervous attempt at jocularity.

"Very well, then," she replied; "I shall remain too."

Sir Francis protested querulously, angrily; but in vain. When they went into the library, Lady Cleydon followed them, and established herself in an easy-chair before the fire.

The game commenced, and proceeded hour after hour with the same result. The tide of luck seemed to have turned in favour of Sir Francis. One by one his I.O.U.'s were handed back to him, and were flung into the fire; at last there remained but one. The cards were dealt. Granville led; and Sir Francis played the king, and won the piece of paper.

He rose to his feet, pale, trembling, but determined.

"Granville," he said huskily, "we are quits, I believe."

The other nodded.

Sir Francis seized the pack of cards in his hand, and dashed them into the grate.

"Thank God!" he exclaimed. "Helen, look up. You will forgive me? This has been a lesson to me, and I am cured at last. Never again shall a card pass through my fingers. Need I swear it?"

She looked up, with a great relief in her face, and then turned round full of gratitude to Mr. Granville. He was leaning forward against the table, with his head buried in his hands. Scarcely noticing her husband, she rose, and, gliding noiselessly to his side, touched his arm.

"Mr. Granville!"

He shrank from her and started to his feet.

"Lady Cleydon," he said hastily, in a tone so full of agony that it brought the tears into her eyes, "don't speak to me! Don't come near me! Keep away, and listen."

The hard look had gone from his face, and he looked almost like a boy. He had moved to the other side of the table, and was leaning over towards them.

"Lady Cleydon," he said hastily, "I have a confession to make. You think that I'm a gentleman. I ought to be; but I'm not. I'm a blackguard and a card-sharper!"

Sir Francis started; Lady Cleydon never moved, but her soft blue eyes remained fixed upon him, full of a gentle pity.

"I will tell you a little of my story," he went on. "If Sir Francis lived in town, he would have known it, and he would not have received me here. I haven't deceived you about my name. My name is still Granville, although my family have offered me money to change it more than once. I was a younger son, and never had a penny of fortune. For that reason, I suppose, my father sent me into the Guards, and expected me to live like a gentleman on my pay. I became fond of cards, became skillful, and soon began to depend upon them to keep me. It was all very well for a time; but by degrees men began to get shy of playing with me, and gradually whispers began to get about that I—I cheated. It was a foul lie," he went on passionately; "but people believed it. I was obliged to leave the regiment, and I sank lower and lower. My luck began to desert me, and I was at my wit's end. Then Colonel Ashton told me that you had once been a desperate gambler, and now lived quite away from the world. I came to Cleydon for the sole purpose of ruining you if I could. You brought me here, and last night for the first time in my life I played with marked cards. I was sorry for it; and, Lady Cleydon, it was you who made me feel that if I did not undo what I had done I should be miserable for life! If I had kept that money I should have gone to Australia, and tried to live a new life; but I'm glad I didn't keep it. You can turn me out of the house now if you like, Sir Francis," he said, with a bitter smile.

There was a long silence, then Lady Cleydon rose and moved to his side.

"Mr. Granville," she said, "no one will turn you out of this house. Will you shake hands with me?"

He looked at her wistfully, incredulously. Then suddenly his lower lip grew tremulous, and he burst into tears. He was but a boy after all.

That last mortgage was not paid off until the following year, for Sir Francis and his wife found another use for a small part of the money. It was not much that Bernard Granville would accept as a loan from his new friends, but it was enough to win him fortune and honour in the new world. And the letter which Lady Cleydon gave him to her uncle and *quondam* guardian, Mr. Golding, won him something far more precious—a true, loving wife. He had loved her first for her sister's sake, but very soon for her own; and when the steamship *Oceana* deposits her passengers at Liverpool next week there will be a long-looked-for family party at Cleydon Hall.

# LENORE

It was very fashionable and very dull. Captain Herbert Crawford was heartily sorry that he had come; yet now he was there he could not in decency leave for half an hour, so he screwed his eyeglass firmly into his right eye, folded his arms with an air of invincible martyrdom, and detaching himself as much as possible from the crush, took up his favourite position against the wall.

Mrs. Archibald's afternoons had nothing particular to recommend them, and yet they were always crowded. Nothing unusual was ever offered in the way of entertainment, nor were the Archibalds themselves remarkably high up in the social scale, yet somehow it had got to be the fashion to go to their afternoons. Herbert Crawford, glancing languidly through the rooms, noticed a good many very distinguished people, and wondered why they came.

Nothing could be more stupid than this confused babel of small talk, in which he himself had been compelled to take his share. There were none of the attractions offered by more eager hostesses, no new beauty or lion of any sort to stimulate interest or curiosity. The whole thing was profoundly and unutterably stupid, and one young man in particular was profoundly and unutterably bored.

From boredom to disgust is only a stage. Just as he was calculating the chances of a well-timed movement towards the door, a servant crossed the room and opened the grand piano by his side. There was going to be music, then. Herbert Crawford, who was a Philistine and hated the music of the future, repressed with difficulty an impatient frown, and resigned himself to a quarter of an hour's agony. There was a slight hush, and he looked up wearily, never doubting but that he should see a young man of the usual type—a long-haired, weak-legged, weak-voiced tenor, with a roll of music under his arm, and a sickly simper on his pale face. This was an "advanced" house, and he felt pretty sure that he knew the sort of thing they would go in for. As it happened, he was wrong.

In the first place it was not a young man at all. Herbert Crawford was very nearly guilty of the unpardonable rudeness of an audible "egad!" as the musician approached. Not only was she a woman, but she was young, strikingly pretty, and was steadily returning his fixed gaze out of the largest, brightest, and most innocent-looking eyes he had ever seen in his life. She was demurely dressed in a plain black gown, relieved only by a white collar; but her figure was perfect, and the gown fitted. Everything about her was scrupulously neat and plain; even her wavy hair showed some signs of having been brushed back; yet there was something peculiarly piquant about her appearance, something which irresistibly suggested a spice of coquetry.

Captain Crawford watched her withdraw her eyes and calmly sit down to play with a sudden interest. He was no longer bored, he was puzzled.

Every one listened, every one admired, every one applauded when the performance was over, every one except Herbert Crawford. He was still in his old position, watching the little singer with a curious gleam in his blue eyes. Once she rose for a moment, and their eyes met over the top of the piano. She had just finished singing a gay little French chanson, during which every feature in her face had been alight with piquant merriment, and every one was applauding heartily. She looked at Herbert Crawford, whose handsome, languid face had assumed a sudden sternness, and met his intent gaze. The change which passed over her face was magical. Like a flash the gaiety and light left her features, and a dull grey pallor took its place. A momentary shiver passed through her frame, and her eyes seemed for a moment distended with horror. Then, at the sound of Mrs. Archibald's voice over her shoulder, she was herself again, and turned quietly round to meet her patroness.

"You have done very well, Miss Lemaine," said Mrs. Archibald suavely. "General Reid is quite delighted with your singing, and I have given him your address. Call here to-morrow afternoon at about this time, if you have no engagement, and I think I can promise you a pupil."

Miss Lemaine murmured her thanks, with her eyes fixed upon the carpet.

"You are very kind," she said. "You will not want me again this afternoon? May I go?"

"Certainly. The man in the hall will fetch a cab for you, if you ask him. Ah, Lady Erdmont, I am so pleased to see you! How good of you to come!"

Mrs. Archibald turned away to speak to a late arrival, and, gathering up her music, Miss Lemaine moved away. Between her and the door Herbert Crawford was standing, and he was the only man in that part of the room. His duty was obvious, and he did it; he rose and opened the door for her gravely, and without the vestige of a smile. As she passed she looked up into his face with a sudden, mutely appealing glance, and he saw that there were tears in her bright eyes.

"I want to speak to you," she said, in a low tone. "Please come away now. I shall wait in the square."

He had no time to answer her, for she walked away without even looking behind. He turned back into the room, and hesitated. If he went, she would certainly make a fool of him. Like most of his sex, he could not bear to see a woman cry; and yet he must go—of course he must go.

"Well, Captain Crawford, and what do you think of my young *protegée*?" asked Mrs. Archibald, as he advanced to make his *adieux*.

"I think her singing excellent," he answered.

"I'm so glad!" his hostess answered. "Do you know, I was thinking of recommending her to Lord Crawford for your sisters? He asked me only the other day if I knew of a singing mistress who had a style of her own, and Miss Lemaine's references are exceptionable."

"Indeed!" he answered. "May I ask in what shape they are? Miss Lemaine is not English, is she?"

"I believe she's a Frenchwoman," Mrs. Archibald answered. "I had quite an enthusiastic letter from the Countess d'Armayne about her."

He was a little surprised, but he made no remark. In a few minutes he took his leave, and hurried out into the street.

It was a dreary March afternoon, and a cold damp wind was blowing a drizzling rain into his face. He turned up his coat collar and looked around. At first he thought that she was nowhere in sight, and, curiously enough, he was conscious of a distinct feeling of disappointment. Then, through the iron railings of the square, he caught sight of a little patch of black frock fluttering in the wind, and recognized it at once. He crossed the road, and in a few moments was by her side with uplifted hat.

The last vestige of anger had left him as he looked down at her thin shabby jacket, and saw what pains she had taken to appear neat in clothes which had certainly seen better days. Perhaps she surprised the unconscious pity in his eyes. It seemed so, for a sudden flush stole into her pale cheeks, and she drew herself up with a dignified gesture.

"I forget," she said, stopping in the middle of the pavement and turning round upon him. "You will not care to walk—to be seen in the streets with me! You had better not come. I will write to you."

"That is not quite kind of you, Miss Lemaine," he said quietly. "Have I given you any reason to think me a snob? If you will let me see you home, I shall be quite happy."

Miss Lemaine looked up at him, and the flush died out of her face. He had meant it, and she felt a little ashamed of herself.

"Thank you, Captain Crawford," she said simply, and they walked on side by side in the fast-gathering twilight. As they passed a lamp-post he stole a glance into her pale, wan little face, and his heart smote him for his suspicions. How forlorn she looked, and yet how brave!

"Tell me," she said presently, "do you think that I am an adventuress, an impostor? I suppose you do, you must do."

"But I don't," he answered promptly. "I only want to know."

"You shall know everything," she said. "You shall come home with me, if you will. I cannot tell you in the streets."

They walked on together, a strange-looking couple. He tall, distinctly an aristocrat, with his hands thrust deep down into the pockets of his loose overcoat, with a white gardenia in his buttonhole—a figure such as one might meet on the pavement of Pall Mall or St. James', but a little noticeable in the region they were entering upon. She was pale and anxious, with a sad gleam in her large dark eyes, and something foreign in her appearance, even her movements. Now and then people paused and looked after them, but they were quite unconscious of it. Once when they passed a busy thoroughfare, and looked down the broad lines of glittering lamps, and at the pavements thronged with hurrying men and women, she drew a little closer to him; and when they had left it behind, and the roar of traffic was no longer in their ears, she gave a little shudder.

"I am glad it is quiet again," she said slowly. "That sound makes me sadder than anything in the world. It is dreadful!"

He looked down at her compassionately.

"You are too young to talk like that," he said.

"I have forgotten what youth is," she answered bitterly. "I am nineteen, I think; but I feel an old woman. Ah, monsieur!" she added, in a more natural tone, and with more of the foreign accent, "to be in a great city like this, alone, friendless, poor, and see every one around struggling for themselves against the world—ah! it is enough to make one feel faint-hearted."

"Don't call yourself friendless," he said impulsively. "May I not count?"

"As a friend or enemy?" she asked. "Nay, I will, not ask that. You were a true friend to me once, and, though I was terrified to see you looking so stern at Mrs. Archibald's I don't think you meant to expose me, did you? It has been my first chance, and you could ruin me if you liked; but you will not?"

"No, I will not," he assured her; "I would sooner die. But, forgive my asking, you will tell—"

"Oh, yes; I will tell you everything," she interrupted, looking at him curiously. "Perhaps you know that Mrs. Archibald thought of recommending me to your father, Lord Crawford. Of course you want to be sure that I am a fit person to teach singing to your sisters. Well, I am respectable. Yes, I am, although you may not think it."

He was pained by her tone, and a little hurt, for it was surely unjust in her. But, before he could say anything, she had timidly laid her hand upon his arm and was looking up into his face, her dark eyes swimming with tears.

"Forgive me," she said softly. "I ought not to talk like that; I had forgotten about that night. It was good of you not to have told Mrs. Archibald."

"As if I should do such a thing!" he said hotly. "I am not a brute."

"I am sure you are not," she answered, smiling up at him with a flash of her old mirth. "Now do you know where you are?"

He looked around with an involuntary shudder.

It was a dreary neighbourhood, a neighbourhood of shabby genteel six-roomed houses, where the smoke had discoloured the bricks, and laid a depressing hand everywhere. There was a green-grocer's shop on one side, and a public house on the other. The refuse from the former had been thrown out into the street, and some of it lay in a black puddle at their feet. The smell from a neighbouring tan-yard helped to poison the air. Dirty children were playing in the gutters, half-clad and ill-shaped. The windows of the long row of smoke-defaced houses were blindless and curtainless. The tiny strip of waste land in front of each was desolate, save for broken crockery and tin-ware, mingled with a few oyster shells. It was a land where the utter extinction of everything pertaining to beauty seemed to have been aimed at and successfully accomplished. In its place was utter wretchedness, utter ugliness, utter desolation.

"Yes, I remember the place," he said.

"It was here I left you on that night. I was ashamed to show you where I lived then. Now I am going to take you to it. Come!"

She crossed the road, and he followed her; then, holding her head proudly, but with a curious trembling of the lips, she entered a wretched-looking greengrocer's shop, the whole stock of which seemed to consist of a few strings of onions, and a pile of half-rotten apples and potatoes in a common heap. A stout, red-faced woman was standing behind the counter shaking a few sickly-looking sweets out of a glass bottle into the outstretched hands of a small customer. At the entrance of her lodger with Herbert Crawford she suspended her operations and stared at them dumbfounded. Miss Lemaine crossed the floor of the shop without glancing towards her, and, opening a door at the further end, turned round and beckoned to her escort.

"Will you come this way, please?" she said, looking steadily at him.

He followed her, stooping low, and stumbling over a basket of onions which lay in the way. They were in a narrow passage, and through the open door of a room on the other side they could see a coarse, half-dressed young man lolling across two stools with a pipe in his mouth, and a cracked jug of beer by his side. He stared at Herbert Crawford in blank amazement, and when he commenced to ascend the rickety staircase after his guide, the young man burst out in a half-derisive, half-indignant exclamation. Miss Lemaine looked round quickly.

"Take no notice, please," she whispered pleadingly. "He is my landlady's son, and I am afraid that he has had too much to drink."

He nodded silently—he would have found speech rather difficult just then—and followed her on to the landing. She turned the handle of a door, and with a gesture bade him enter.

She left him standing just inside the room, while she walked swiftly to a sofa, which was drawn up to the miserable, struggling fire. He only gave one quick glance around, but it was enough. It was just such a room as might have been expected in such a neighbourhood, in such a house. The tattered remains of a carpet only half covered the floor; a cheap, unwholesome-looking paper hung down from the wall; the horse hair sofa, with a great gap in its side, creaked and groaned on its castors. There had been curtains, but they had gone;

pictures on the wall, but their place was empty. The table was of deal, only half covered by a soiled cloth; a cracked looking-glass and one cheap vase were the only ornaments of the chimney-piece. There was but one thing in its favour—the room was clean.

He had taken it all in at a glance; and then his eyes rested upon the pale figure stretched on the sofa. It scarcely seemed like a living face, so thin and delicately chiselled were the features, and marble-white their pallor. The dark steadfast eyes—sightless he knew them to be—were turned towards him, but a pair of wonderfully thin arms were thrown around Miss Lemaine's neck, and he saw at once a certain likeness between the two faces.

"Lenore, Lenore, you have come back at last, then," a faint voice was saying; "I have been so tired and restless. Tell me quickly. Did you succeed. Were they kind?"

"Yes, dear, very," was the quiet reply. "How cold you are, and how bad the fire is! Hasn't Mrs. Rogers been up?"

There was a slight weary movement of the little head.

"Not once; no one has been. Lenore, there is some one with you; who is it?"

Lenore rose to her feet, and, still holding the thin white hands, turned round to Captain Crawford.

"It is a gentleman who has brought me home, Emilie. Captain Crawford, this is my sister. She is, as you see, an invalid."

A great saddening pity rushed into his heart as he looked into the two pale faces turned towards him, so alike, yet so different in expression. In Lenore's half-eager half-appealing look there was something which seemed to beg him to speak kindly to the little invalid, and it touched him to the heart. He walked to the sofa, and, stooping down, took the frail little hands which Lenore yielded him so readily.

"Your sister was good enough to let me walk home with her," he said. "She thought that you would like to hear from some one who was there how much every one liked her singing, and how successful she was. She is going to teach my sisters."

A wonderfully sweet light flashed across the tiny white face.

"Oh, how good of you to come and tell me," she cried, in a low tremulous voice. "Lenore, are you not happy? Tell me quick, shall we be able to leave this dreadful place?"

"Yes, dear; we shall be able to leave very soon now. To-morrow, I hope."

A sudden passion of tears and sobs convulsed the little face, but it was over in a moment, and she was smiling up into his face with a tremulous joy.

"Don't think me very silly, please," she said pleadingly. "It is such happiness to think that we can get away from this place. You have a flower in your coat, haven't you? How delicious it smells! Please to come a little nearer."

He drew it from his coat, and placed it between her eager fingers.

"Do you like flowers? I will send you some," he said.

"Oh, thank you; will you really? Yes, I like flowers, and all sweet perfumes; and I love the sunlight and the sound of the sea, and the country and soft voices—like yours and Lenore's—and music. I cannot see any of these things, you know, but I can feel them. Once we were so happy! I used to sit out in a garden and feel the sun, and hear the sea far away murmuring so faintly. But still I could hear it, rising and falling, even when it was very calm, and no one else could; and then there was a breeze rustling in the trees, and birds and insects creeping out into the sunshine and talking to one another (for they do talk, you know, though we cannot understand them); and then there was the sweet faint perfume of the flowers, and Lenore would read to me, and I would sit and think until I got drowsy and fell asleep. I don't think I minded much about being blind then, but it is all so different now—so different!"

A little choking sob stopped her speech, and somehow Captain Crawford, Guardsman and man of the world, felt wonderfully inclined to echo it. He pressed the child's hand, and was silent for a moment. Then Lenore spoke:—

"Emilie, dear, would you mind leaving Captain Crawford and me alone for a minute or two? I have something to say to him." The child raised herself a little and picked up a crutch from the floor. For the first time Herbert Crawford saw how shrunken her form really was, and an infinite pity filled his heart. He had seen so little of this sort of thing, so little real suffering and pain.

"Will Mr. Crawford come and see me again?" the child asked, turning a fair wistful face towards him.

"Many times, I hope," he answered. "I shall come and see you as often as your sister will let me."

She turned away with a sigh of contentment.

"I am so glad," she said softly. "Thank you for the flower, Captain Crawford. Good-bye."

He raised the little hand, which he had been holding, to his lips, and let it go. Then she left the room on her sister's arm.

Lenore was back again almost immediately.

Holding the door open she called to the woman below. Then, as the stairs began to creak beneath the heavy ascending footsteps, she came into the room.

"Captain Crawford," she said quietly. "I am going to explain to you about that night."

"It is not necessary," he began eagerly. "I—"

She held out her hand in a dignified manner.

"If you do not feel it necessary, I do," she said. "Come in, Mrs. Rogers."

The woman, who had been waiting in the shop below, came in, and took up a position just inside the door. She was dirty, half-dressed, with coarse red face and aggressive manners. Herbert Crawford looked away from her to the sad little figure by his side with relief.

"Mrs. Rogers," Lenore said, "I have sent for you to ask you a favour. I want you to explain to this gentleman how it happened that I was at the Star Music Hall one night last month."

Mrs. Rogers moved her great arms from under her apron and stuck them akimbo.

"Who be 'ee, to want ter know about your doings?" she inquired bluntly.

"This gentleman is a friend of mine, and I wish you to tell him," was the quiet reply.

Mrs. Rogers tossed her head in a manner which she meant to be sarcastic.

"I don't know that I mind doing that," she said. "My dortor Sal— she's a singer, down at the Star— got a reg'lar engagement like, and she was bad, in bed. We sent down word that she couldn't come out, and they sent back that unless she cum and did her turn, or sent summun else that would, she was sacked. This young 'ooman 'ere's a singer, and she went instead one night. That's 'ow it was, I reckon."

"Mrs. Rogers has omitted to mention," Lenore said, turning to Herbert Crawford," that Sal has been kind to us, kinder than any one else in this place, and she was very anxious not to have her engagement cancelled; also that I owed Mrs. Rogers money, and she threatened that unless I consented that she would turn Emilie and me out into the street. I sang one song there and then came away. Directly I got outside I was annoyed, and you were passing by and rescued me. Now you understand?"

"Perfectly," he answered.

"May I arsk, miss, was that hall you wanted me for?" asked Mrs. Rogers.

Lenore turned a shade paler.

"That is all now, Mrs. Rogers," she said softly. "To-morrow morning I shall be able—"

"To-morrow morning be d—d for a tale," interrupted Mrs. Rogers angrily. "I've heard it hoften enough. I wants my money, and I'll hev it, or out on the streets—"

"Silence, woman!" thundered Captain Crawford.

She paused, with her mouth wide open for a torrent of abuse, and stared in a stupefied way at the pale boyish face and flashing blue eyes. She was the virago of the neighbourhood, and neither man nor woman had dared to speak thus to her before. Yet there was something quelling in the quiet disdain of that aristocratic supercilious face, which had recovered its calm almost immediately. She did not understand it at all, but she felt conquered.

He had moved to the door, and was holding it open.

"You will go downstairs and fetch Miss Lemaine's bill at once," he said quietly.

She looked at him, made one last effort to recover her lost power of speech, and submitted. Herbert Crawford closed the door after her, and looked round for Lenore. She was very pale, and was leaning against the table, with her head half-hidden between her hands.

"Miss Lemaine," he said, "I am going to ask you a great favour. I am going to claim the right we all have of assisting our fellow creatures now and then. It is only for a very short time, remember, for things will be very different with you soon. There is your sister, too. For her sake you must let me help you a little; you will, won't you?"

"How can I help it?" she said, looking up at him with dim eyes. "How good you are! I have struggled, and struggled, and from a stranger I would sooner have died than taken help. But from you—"

She held out her hands, and he took them in his with a strange thrill of pleasure. Neither of them spoke. He was fighting against a sudden maddening desire to take that sad little figure in his arms, and hold it there, and to whisper into her ear that the long and weary struggle was over, that—

Suddenly he released her hands with a burning sense of shame.

God help him from such thoughts as these! He had been of the world, and its taint was upon him. But to think of her like that! it was foul heresy. His whole better self leaped up to strengthen him; they should be his sisters, and he would be very good to them.

There was something strange about that silence between them, and they were glad to have it broken even by strange means. There was a sound like a kick at the door, and it burst open. The man whom they had seen drinking below walked into the room. His coarse brutal face was inflamed with drink and anger, and his breath exhaled the mingled odour of drink and foul tobacco from the short pipe between his teeth.

"I'll be d—d if we're a-goin' to stand this 'ere sort of goings on!" he exclaimed, walking threateningly up to the pair. "Our lodgers 'ere has got to keep themselves respectable or else they go on to the blessed streets. We ain't going to allow no gemmun visitors 'ere, so there, miss. Why for all your proud ways, ye are no better than—"

The conclusion of his speech never came. Without moving a muscle of his face, Captain Crawford had first struck the pipe from between the man's teeth and then knocked him down. For a moment he was too stunned and too astonished to rise, and during that moment Captain Crawford turned rapidly to Lenore.

"I beg your pardon for doing that," he said. "It was stupid to be angry with such an animal. You must leave this place at once now. Bring what luggage you can, and leave the rest. Don't be frightened. Your room is next to this, isn't it? Go in and fetch Emilie and your things. I will wait for you on the landing."

She obeyed him trembling, and they left the room together, passing the semi-recumbent figure of Sam Rogers. He looked up with an evil smile, and then, gathering himself up, staggered out after them. He found Herbert Crawford on the landing alone.

Rogers had no small reputation as a bruiser, and he saw nothing in the straight slim figure before him to fear—nothing save that absolute coolness and languid self-assurance which irritated him beyond measure. He took his coat off and spat upon his hands.

Captain Crawford watched him unmoved.

"Look here, young man," he said quietly, "if you'll take my advice, you'll be satisfied with what you've had and be off. Well, if you will have it—"

Now Crawford had been reckoned the most skillful boxer of his college, and had kept in practice in the regimental gymnasium, besides which he was a young Englishman of the genuinely athletic type, and his limbs, though slim, were hard and sinewy. The consequence was that when Lenore opened the door of her room in terror a moment or two afterwards, Mr. Samuel Rogers was lying on his face sobbing drunken tears. Captain Crawford was quietly drawing on his gloves, without a scratch on his handsome face.

"Have you hurt him," cried Lenore fearfully.

"Not so much as he deserves," he answered coolly. "We will leave at once if you are ready. Give me the box, please."

He lifted it from the ground—a small tin trunk—and, taking Emilie, carried her downstairs. Lenore came close behind. There they met Mrs. Rogers.

"What 'ah yer been doin' to my Sam'l?" she cried fiercely; "and three pun ten shillings I want from you, young 'ooman, or you don't quit my house."

Herbert Crawford counted four pounds into her hand, and took up the box again.

"You can give the change to your son to cure his broken head. Come along, Miss Lemaine."

They walked through the shop and out into the street. Then he put down the box, and they all looked at one another.

They were certainly a strange-looking group. Crawford, handsome and debonair in the fashionable garments of his class, looked every inch an earl's son. Under his arm was a bundle of old umbrellas and wraps. His foot was resting lightly on a small tin box, and Emilie's hand was through his other arm. Both the girls looked lamentably shabby, and Emilie's crutch was patched up in many places. They were both watching him anxiously, and both were immensely relieved when they saw a slight twitching of the lips deepen into a smile as he looked from one to the other. He had not one atom of false pride, and he was enjoying the situation immensely, notwithstanding its perplexities.

"A council of war," he exclaimed lightly, "and I vote myself into the chair. The first thing which the lodgings-hunter does is to get a cab. Isn't that so?"

Emilie clapped her hands.

"Of course it is. Oh, how clever you are, Captain Crawford! Are we going far away from here?"

"As far as possible," he answered. "Now let me see, what part shall we try?"

"Somewhere where they are quite cheap, please," Lenore said anxiously.

"I'll see to that," he answered confidently. "You shall hear me bargaining with the landlady."

"What fun," laughed Emilie. "I shall like that."

Captain Crawford considered for a moment. It had suddenly occurred to him that without references, or, worse still, with his reference and presence, it would be no easy matter for them to obtain respectable lodgings. Nobody is so censorious and suspicious as the London landlady, and to be accompanied by Captain Crawford of the Guards, son of the Earl of Crawford, would scarcely be a recommendation for a poor singer and her sister. Watching him closely, Lenore divined something of his thoughts, and a deep flush stole into her face.

"I think Captain Crawford had better not come with us," she said faintly.

"Think you're going to get rid of me, do you?" he laughed "Come along; it's all right. I've got a capital idea. We only want a cab now, and we shall be right."

He took up the box again and looked along the road. There was no vehicle in sight, except a small handsome brougham with a pair of dark bays, the footman and coachman of which were gazing curiously at the little group. As it approached the coachman pulled his horses up, and touching his hat, looked inquiringly at Captain Crawford.

"Egad! here's a piece of luck!" he exclaimed.

"Why, Gregson, what on earth are you doing out here?" he asked the man as he brought the carriage round with a little sweep and drew up by the kerbstone.

"To the mission room at St. Philip's with some parcels, my lord. The bays wanted exercising, so I put them in the brougham."

"This is capital, girls," Captain Crawford exclaimed, as the tall footman shouldered the trunk and held the door open. "Emilie, take my hand. That's right. Now, Miss Lemaine. I want to go to No. 18, Pitt Street, John Reynolds' house, you know. This is better than a growler, isn't it?" he said, as the carriage rolled on.

"Yes; ought we to be here?" asked Lenore, a little awed, for she had seen the earl's coronet on the panel.

He laughed.

"Considering the carriage is mine," he said, "I don't think we're taking a great liberty. The horses are my father's, but I use them whenever I like. Now let me tell you where we're going to."

"If you please," Lenore said.

"Well, it's not a grand place by any means; but I think you'll be comfortable. Ten years ago a coachman of my father's married one of the housemaids—romantic affair, wasn't it—and they took a nice little house at Pitt Street, and a lodger. I happen to know that the lodger left last week, and that they haven't got another one. I think it will do capitally for you, because it's nicely situated, and you won't have so far to go backward and forwards, Miss Lemaine, and here we are."

The carriage had pulled up in a quiet street before a row of solid, comfortable-looking houses. In five minutes everything was arranged. A few words from Captain Crawford, and Mrs. Reynolds was dropping curtsies to the two young ladies, and welcoming them heartily. No need of references or certificates of respectability. One of the family had brought them, and that was enough for Mrs. Reynolds. Besides, the fair sweet face of the little invalid, and Lenore's darker but more impressive beauty, only a little marred by suffering and anxiety, had already won her heart. From the first moment she was enthusiastic about them.

As for the girls themselves, the utter change in their surroundings seemed almost incredible. The sitting-room, in which they were soon ensconced in cosy easy chairs before a bright fire, was not only comfortable, it was really tastefully and well furnished. Mrs. Rogers and her drunken son seemed to belong to another world. Here everything was pleasant, and smiling, and friendly. Emilie leaned back in her chair, steeped in a sort of dreamy satisfaction; Lenore, who had borne all the strain of their long struggle with poverty, was nervous and a little hysterical.

They were alone quite ten minutes, and then Captain Crawford came in, hat in hand. He was fast becoming quite a master of tact, and commenced talking at once.

"I think Mrs. Reynolds will make you girls comfortable," he said cheerily. "Don't you attempt to talk business with her, Miss Lenore. I'll arrange all that for you. And I must go now, because I asked a man to dine with me, and it's getting late. My sisters will come and see you in a day or two."

"But you will come, too, won't you?" begged Emilie, holding one of his hands between hers.

"Rather; you'll find I shall be a regular nuisance," he laughed. "I'm coming to read to you, Emilie, and I won't forget the flowers. Goodbye. Goodbye, Miss Lenore."

And then, before they had quite realized it, he had gone, and their proceedings became purely feminine. Lenore sank on her knees by her sister's side, and Emilie's arms stole round her neck.

"Isn't he good?" sobbed the little invalid. "We shall never, never, never be able to repay him. Wasn't it grand, Lennie, the way he brought us away from that awful place. Oh, I do wish I could see him. I know that he is tall, and brave, and handsome."

"He is, dear," Lenore answered between her tears.

"I wonder why he has done it all," Emilie went on. "Do you know, Lennie, I think he must like you a little."

Lenore was pale no longer, but she turned her head away.

"Hush, Emilie," she said softly. "We must not think of him like that. He is a great nobleman's son, and we—"

"I don't care," Emilie continued; "nobody is good enough for you."

And that night Herbert Crawford walked down to Knightsbridge under the stars, feeling like a man who had taken the first step in a new world. For the first time he saw, and saw clearly, wherein lay all the sweetness and happiness of life. The old life, with its false ideals, its false philosophy, and, alas! its many weaknesses, lay behind him like an evil nightmare. The good which he had done that day was as nothing compared to the good which he had received.

The triumph of a great singer is as the triumph of a queen. A new star had burst upon the world, and London was raving about her. And on the morning after her great success Captain Crawford sat in her drawing-room, the most envied man in town, because he alone was always sure of a welcome from her. She came in to him very soon, a little pale after the last night's excitement, but with her piquant delicate beauty wonderfully enhanced by the success of the last twelve months. She held out her hand to him with a glad smile, and he did not immediately release it.

"I did not come round to you last night. I thought you would be too tired," he said. "You got my note?"

"Yes, and the flowers," she answered warmly. "It was kind of you. But you are always kind."

"Can one help being kind when one loves?" he answered, with sudden passion. "Lenore, Lenore, you are all the world to me. I have loved you always. Darling, will you be my wife?"

For the first time in his life he took her into his arms, and his lips touched her forehead. Then he drew away from her, and looked into her face. It was deadly pale, and half-hidden in her hands.

"Lenore," he cried hoarsely. "Tell me what is the matter? Is it that you cannot care for me?"

She looked up, and he was dumb before the agony in her white face.

"I cannot marry you," she said slowly. "I will not. No, listen. Who am I? A singer, and that is all. I have no name even, no father, or money. Everything I have I owe to you. I will not marry you. You must marry one of your own order— some rich and noble woman. No, I will not marry you."

"Lenore, that is all nothing," he said softly. "I love you. No other woman would make me happy, my darling!"

She kept him away from her.

"Tell me," she said, "would your father consent?"

To her he would not lie.

"Not now," he answered. "He would some day. What does it matter? I love you."

"Herbert," she said softly, "you have been the truest, the noblest friend a lonely woman ever had. I did not think that such men lived. Now, listen, I will not marry you; it would not be fitting; it would ruin your life. I will not marry you."

"There is some one else," he cried, with a sudden dread.

She shrank back as though he had struck her. Then she looked up at him with quivering lips.

"That is the first cruel thing you have ever said to me, and God knows that it is false," she said. "My life belongs to Emilie. I will marry no one else. At least, I promise you that. Will you please go away?"

Then, without a word, he took up his hat, and for the first time in his life he left her in anger.

Lord St. Maurice lay dying in his great castle in the north, and by his bedside, still enveloped in his travelling coat, Captain Crawford was standing. They were alone, though doctors and nurses were close at hand. Relations there were none, save his nephew, for Lord St. Maurice had lived in solitude for many years, a worn-out, hardened cynic. The lights were dim, and the old man's life was ebbing fast away. Captain Crawford had been only just in time.

"Herbert," he whispered hoarsely, "I have deceived you; deceived everybody. My boy, I have daughters alive. I have left them my money. It is only justice."

It was a great shock, but he bore it well. Over and over again had this old man, who hated his father and hated his elder brother, told him that, save the title and lands of the marquisate, all would be his. He had been brought up for it. Besides it he had nothing.

"Where are they—your daughters?" he asked.

"I do not know. If they are dead all will be yours. I married, twenty-two years ago, a lady of France. She died. I kept the secret of our marriage. We had two daughters. I placed them with a notary of high repute, with ample means, and I made him swear that he would keep the secret of their birth till I sent for them. I sent for them. The notary had absconded, bankrupt; my daughters have gone—no one knows where. Find them, Herbert. I have twenty thou—"

He was obliged to stop struggling for breath. Captain Crawford was trembling. He drew a locket from his neck and opened it.

"Do you know the face?" he asked.

The old man looked, and gave a great cry.

"It is my wife, Lenore!"

Captain Crawford shook his head.

"It is your daughter, Lenore."

Lord St. Maurice fell back upon the pillow, and gave a little gasp. He was dead.

Again he stood in her little drawing-room, in deep mourning, and with a very serious face. When she came in she was frightened.

"What has happened, Herbert?" she asked.

"Lenore, I have found your father," he said, gravely.

"Is he alive?"

"I have come from his death-bed."

She sat down trembling, and speechless.

"Lenore, your father is dead, and you must think well of him. He left you, as he thought, well provided for. His last thoughts were of you."

"Who was he?"

"My uncle, the Marquis of St. Maurice. We are cousins, Lenore."

"Your uncle! Your uncle! The one who was to leave you all his money?"

"Yes; only he has done better with it. You and Emilie are the greatest heiresses in England, and I am your guardian."

"Have you not always been that?" she sobbed. "We do not want the money. We will not have it."

"But you must," he answered gently. "He was your father."

"Herbert," she whispered.

"Yes."

"We will only have it on one condition."

"And that is?"

She looked up at him with a curious look in her face.

"Cannot you guess?"

He shook his head."

"Please, will you marry me?"

He took her into his arms, and she hid her face upon his shoulder.

"Are you sure, quite sure, that you care for me?" he asked rapturously.

"You silly, silly boy," she answered. "Could you not see that I loved you heart and soul from that first night? How blind men are!"

So Captain Crawford married an heiress, and the world lost a great singer. And Emilie was almost as happy as they.

# MY FIRST DIPLOMATIC MISSION

"Don't hurry, Charlie. I want you for a minute or two. The billiard match can wait."

Rather reluctantly I resumed my seat, and refilled my glass. *Tête-à-têtes* with my uncle after dinner were wont to be somewhat wearisome, and my saucy little cousin's challenge, as I had held the door open for her a moment before, was decidedly more tempting. Still, was not my uncle also my guardian and a Cabinet Minister, and was not I his paid secretary? And there being no alternative save compliance, I obeyed and waited in silence, mildly wondering whether anything had happened in the House that afternoon which he purposed to communicate to me, or whether I was doomed to an hour or two's somewhat prosy meanderings about things in general.

An unusually long silence rather stimulated my curiosity. Something must have happened, I concluded, noting my uncle's thoughtful countenance, and I hinted at my growing curiosity by a gentle cough.

My uncle rose to the hint. "Charlie," he said abruptly, "could you go abroad to-morrow—to Rome?"

I stared at him in amazement, with my glass suspended midway between the table and my lips. Go to Rome to-morrow, with the London season at its height! What could the old buffer mean?

"Rome!" I repeated feebly, setting my glass down, and inserting the wrong end of my cigar between my teeth. "Ugh. D—. I beg your pardon. Certainly I could, if it were necessary."

My uncle bit his lip, but, leaning over the table towards me, went on seriously, "Take another cigar, and listen to me. I have been with Dash this afternoon, and he agrees with me that some one must leave tomorrow for Rome with most important dispatches for Sir Henry Odell. I mentioned your name—recommended you, in fact. Dash had no objection, so long as I vouched for your discretion, which I ventured to do. But remember, Charlie, the matter is an extremely important one, and we do not care for even the barest rumour of your mission to get about. And there must not be a second's delay. You must travel night and day until you reach Rome. A good deal hangs upon your zeal and discretion in this matter, and, unimportant though your part in it may be, do it well, and it will be a start for you."

Needless to say I was delighted with the mission, and swore to myself and to my uncle that I would be as discreet as Disraeli, and as swift as steamboat and express trains would allow me. Another thought, too, filled me with pleasurable anticipations of my coming journey. For had not Sir Henry Odell, grizzled old baronet, carried away from me my first sweetheart, pretty Nellie Aveland, the rector's only daughter down at Whilton, my old home, and had I not often wished to see her again? Poor little Nellie! Could I even forget her, as in our last stolen interview she had flung her little white arms around my neck, and with her large, innocent blue eyes filled with tears, had sobbed out that, though her parents insisted upon her marriage with the old baronet, her heart was always mine? How delightful to think that I should see her again so soon!

At noon on the following morning I was on the platform at Charing Cross, with a small portmanteau in my hand, my sole luggage, and in due course I crossed the channel, journeyed through the mighty tunnel, and found myself careering down through Italy, within a few hours of my destination. At L—— there was a brief halt for refreshments, and carrying with me my portmanteau (I knew too much of railway travelling in Italy to leave it in the carriage), I formed one of the mob of hungry and thirsty travellers who besieged the refreshment rooms.

At the door of the room I had a great surprise. I caught sight of a figure which struck me at once as being familiar, and my heart gave a sudden leap, half of astonishment, half of pleasure, for when I reached the entrance I stood face to face with Nellie.

"Lady Odell!" I exclaimed, and, with a violent start, she turned round and recognized me.

"Charlie!" and the look in her eyes, as well as her tone, fulfilled my most sanguine expectations. I was not forgotten.

"You here?" she went on in astonishment; "and carrying your own luggage too, like a veritable Cook's tourist! Where on earth are you going to?"

"To Rome. And you?"

"Also to Rome." She had gone to L—— to see an old school-fellow off to England, and was alone, except for her maid. She was waiting for a parcel—a letter in fact—which she had promised to deliver for her friend in Rome, and could not leave till the next train. It was only an hour's delay, and it was a faster train. Of course I would wait for her?

I hesitated, and alas! yielded. An hour could make no difference, and, besides, it would be too late to see Sir Henry that night. Yes, I would wait, and, amid a shower of eager questions, I watched the train glide off to Rome without me.

We stood talking for about half an hour, and then she stopped a porter and asked a question. She appeared perplexed at his reply; he repeated it, and passed on, and she looked up at me with a gesture of annoyance. She had been misinformed. There was no other train to Rome until 6.30 in the morning. Whatever should we do? and she looked up half-piteously, half-comically.

My first impulse was one of decided anger, and a very British oath escaped through my teeth. But how could I be angry with her? And, after all, it could make no real difference. I had travelled all the way without an hour's real repose, and a night's sleep would do me no harm; and so I determined to make the best of it, and console my companion in misfortune, consolation which she needed very little, however, and indeed, somewhat to my surprise, she seemed inclined to regard the contretemps as a capital joke. There was but one decent hotel in the place, we learnt, and there I proposed leaving her and her maid, while I sought quarters elsewhere. But to this she strongly objected.

"You silly goose, Charlie," she laughed; "we are not in England, you know, and you forget I have Hannah here with me. There isn't the least necessity for you to run away, unless you want to."

Needless to say, I did not run away. We dined alone, and lingered long over the meal, and until late in the evening, full of reminiscences of our childhood and barely veiled allusions to that other period of our life, and even that parting in the old rectory garden. We lived the old days over again, and never in those times had I found Nellie Aveland so fascinating and bewitching as Lady Odell now was. She seemed scarcely changed at all, except that her figure was improved and her face just a trifle thinner and paler. But her tones had never been more tender or her manner more captivating, and I began to fear that unless I was very careful indeed I should make a fool of myself, for Lady Odell was fully as attractive to me now as had been Nellie Aveland in the not very distant past. After a while our conversation gradually drifted into things of the present, and with some little importance in my tone I told her of my mission to her husband. She laughed merrily, and clapped her hands.

"Fancy you, Charlie, a special envoy! Do let me look at your dispatches!"

I shook my head. "Quite impossible!" I declared, in an official tone as near as possible a counterpart of my worthy uncle's.

She fairly screamed with laughing.

"Why, Charlie, I don't believe you've got any!" she cried. "You're only hoaxing me. Why, you couldn't get a dispatch box in that little portmanteau!"

I undid the strap, and held out a long black ebony case with silver knobs at each end.

"What a funny box for dispatches, Charlie!"

"They're generally used at the F.O. now," I replied carelessly.

This was a most atrocious fib. The fact was, my dispatches consisting only of one short letter, I had not been provided with a dispatch-box. The long black case was the exact facsimile of one in which I generally kept my shaving implements, and which was now reposing at the bottom of my portmanteau. I had bought the pair at a shop in Bond Street only a week or two before meaning to present them to my cousin for glove-boxes, but for some reason or other never did so. The one came in so nicely for my shaving things, and the other had caught my eye when glancing around for something in which to keep my precious document, and, attracted by its official-looking appearance, I had utilized it for that purpose.

"I wonder whether there is anything important in that letter," she remarked meditatively, after a short pause. "Nothing to call us back to England, I hope, Charlie; I hate England!"

I expressed my total ignorance of the contents of the letter.

"You could not expect me to divulge them even to you, Nellie," I added somewhat reprovingly, but she was silent.

It was very late before we said good-night, but at last Nellie rang for her maid and left me.

"Shall Hannah see about your bag being sent up?" she asked carelessly, as she rose to go.

"No thanks. When will you remember, Nellie, that a special envoy never lets his dispatches out of his sight?" I added laughing.

"Well, just as you like," she said. "Good-night."

It was not long before I also retired; but not feeling in the least sleepy, and finding a very comfortable lounge in my room, I lit a cigar and sat up for a while. The hotel seemed quite quiet; apparently everybody else had long ago retired. I was rather startled, therefore, when all of a sudden I heard a light footstep pass along the corridor and halt outside my room. I listened for a moment, and then, without quitting my position, shouted out, "Who's there?" No answer, no sound of retreating footsteps. Very strange, I thought, and, moving across the room, opened my door and looked out. Not a soul was in sight. I shut my door and very soon dismissed the circumstance from my mind. Some one, no doubt, retiring late had lost his way, and had paused to read the number over my door, and as I was beginning to feel sleepy, I slowly undressed and got into bed, and very soon was fast asleep. Scarcely half an hour could have passed when I awoke with a slight start, and an indefinable sense of something being wrong. The moment I opened my eyes and looked around I saw to what I owed my awakening.

The door of the room stood wide open and a woman was standing just inside, with her back to me, holding a shaded lamp in her hand. My first impulse, and I very nearly yielded to it, was to jump out of bed; my next to lie quite still, and watch the figure through half-closed eyes. She was standing nearly in the middle of the room, looking eagerly around, and with a start, which very nearly betrayed me, I recognized Nellie, with a white, scared look on her face. I could scarcely believe that it was not a dream, but I held my breath and waited. Suddenly she seemed to discover the whereabouts of what she sought, and with a rapid, gliding movement, she drew near the dressing-table and caught up a long black case which lay there. She tried to open it, but it was locked. Then she secreted it in her dress, and turning rapidly round—so rapidly that I only just had time to close my eyes—she glided softly out of the room and shut the door.

I sat up in bed and held my head in a maze of bewilderment. Then the thing grew clear to me, and I smiled as I felt under my pillow and drew out my dispatch box with the precious letter inside. Of course, I could see how it was now. Nellie had always been an inveterate practical joker, and she had no doubt hit upon the idea of making off with my dispatches, and herself conveying them to her husband. But I shouted with laughing, until the old bed grew creaky, and the shaky mahogany poles rattled, as I reflected that she had made off with my razor-case, and as it was locked she would not, in all probability, discover the mistake until she presented it to Sir Henry. Sleep now was out of the question, so I arose, smoked another cigar, read for awhile in the grey dawn, and then made an elaborate *toilette*, minus the shave, and descended into the breakfast room. As I expected, "*madame*" had left by the early train, and there was a note for me. I tore it open.

"Dear Charlie,—

"I think, perhaps, that I had better not be seen travelling in Rome with you alone, at such an unearthly hour, so I am going on by the early train. How I envy you in the express; you will reach Rome only half an hour later. Shall see you this afternoon, I suppose.

"Yours,
"Nellie."

I smiled; nay, I laughed many times during the consumption of my matutinal meal to the great surprise of the waiter, who seemed astonished to see an *Anglais* milord indulge in such unseemly, and, apparently, causeless mirth. In due course I arrived in Rome, and drove straight to the Embassy. Business first, I thought, and presented my letter, rather surprised that Sir Henry did not greet me with a burst of merriment. He was very courteous, though, and affable; but as I watched him read, although he had never been a friend of mine, I was greatly grieved to see how bowed down and ill he looked, and an idea which had occurred to me, that this letter concerned his resignation, was confirmed. He read it through slowly, and then folded it up.

"Has Lady Odell returned?" I burst out.

To my astonishment, Sir Henry, drew himself up and flashed a haughty glance upon me.

"Sir?" he said, in a tone of stern interrogation.

I stammered, and then hastened to explain, but my tale seemed very little to amuse him.

"You have had a very narrow escape, sir," he said quietly. "Lady Odell left me a fortnight ago."

"Left you?" I repeated, in an idiotic manner.

"Yes," he went on, in a low tone and with averted head; "her conduct has repeatedly been a source of annoyance to me, and, recently, has been such as to make her the talk of Rome. A fortnight ago she left me. Rumour asserts that she is—is under the protection of a certain Signor Tubelli, the Secretary for Foreign Affairs here. I have taken the necessary steps to procure a divorce. You have had a very narrow escape, sir; Tubelli is a dangerous man, and would give much to learn the contents of this letter," and he touched it lightly with his forefinger. "Let us change the subject."

I left Rome the next day on very good terms with Sir Henry, but Nellie I did not meet again, I wonder whether Signor Tubelli uses my razors.

## SOMETHING IN A NAME

"I think her very charming indeed!" declared Major Cunningham, thoughtfully stroking his moustache. "So delightfully unsophisticated and girlish!"

"H'm! A season in town would improve her," replied his aunt; "she is rather gauche."

"A season in town, on the contrary, would probably spoil her. It is that very gaucherie, as you term it, that pleases me most. I admire Miss Hunt exceedingly." And the major strolled away to give his arm to the young lady in question, who had just risen from the piano.

She was only a girl, just escaped from the schoolroom—the daughter of a country squire, whose little circle of life had been bounded by a few calls paid and returned, one or two tennis-parties, a single dinner party, and this fortnight which she was spending at a country house.

No wonder that her hostess, Lady Mary Allthrop, a woman of the world, and a leader of society, observed in her guest what to her town-bred instincts appeared to be gaucherie, but which her nephew, Major Cunningham, looked upon with a far different and more indulgent aspect. He had told his aunt and hostess that he thought her charming, and she was charming.

She was not only beautiful, but her expression and manners were winning, and her large grey eyes almost perfect. True, her immature figure was the figure of a girl, and at times her shyness was easily apparent; but these were trifles which he readily pardoned. The latter, indeed, he found attractive. And if he admired her, what did she think of him? She was given to hero-worship, and he possessed all the qualities to inspire it. He had distinguished himself in a recent campaign. He was tall, with well-knit, stalwart frame, and handsome face, bronzed by exposure to the Eastern suns, for his had been no toy soldiering.

He had seen much life, had travelled far, was rich, and heir to a title; and, withal, it was whispered he was a woman-hater. Could there be stronger attributes to attract her fancy?

All that first evening of her visit to Roughton Manor she watched him with interest. She listened eagerly to his monosyllabic conversation at the dinner table, and she detected with a smile his air of relief when her hostess rose, and the ladies followed her out of the room.

Later on she watched him furtively in the drawing room, the last to appear, listening with forced interest and bored expression to the gushing conversation of one of the daughters of the house. Roughton Manor was a country house of a somewhat free-and-easy type, and with the additional licence of Christmas-time there was every opportunity for indulging in flirtations more or less pronounced. But Major Cunningham did not seem disposed to avail himself of his opportunities although more than one pair of bright eyes challenged him temptingly, and more than one pair of ruby lips seemed disposed to take the initiative. He was courteous, and even agreeable, but cold, and appeared to find more pleasure in talking to deaf old Professor Hutchinson than in bandying words with younger guests. Once she—May Hunt—caught his eye fixed upon her, and, despite her efforts, she blushed. She was fair and beautiful, with almost an ethereal beauty, and she had admirers in plenty. But she also was reserved and silent, and gave them no encouragement; so one by one they voted her shy, or stupid, or both, and left her alone, to her great satisfaction.

There was an impromptu dance later on in the evening, but she danced little, and he not at all. She was surprised, therefore, and unaccountably nervous when he suddenly left his seat, and, whispering to Lady Mary, crossed the room towards her with his aunt on his arm.

"My nephew, Major Cunningham—Miss Hunt." And, the formal words of introduction spoken, she left them together, and passed on to speak to others of the guests. He bowed gravely, and begged for the pleasure of a dance. Of course she assented, and, of course, she danced with him again, sat out dances with him, and spent the whole evening, and many succeeding ones, in a whirl of delicious excitement.

He was attracted by her shyness, which repelled others. He took pains to penetrate beneath the surface, and was no whit surprised to find her both charming and intelligent, although strangely naive and girlish, and he was amused and not a little flattered by her only half-concealed reverence for him.

The sequence was a natural one, and needs no explanation. He lost his heart, received another in exchange, and when the fortnight's visit was up they were engaged.

His had been a stern, joyless life, full of hardships in his early youth, the remembrance of which seemed to have embittered in some measure his later life. But in her love he seemed suddenly to find relief and happiness. With her his severity and gravity vanished, and none could have been more kind and tender; and, withal, the change made him appear, as every one remarked, ten years younger.

And how he loved her! Not with the passionate ardour of youth, but with the full, deep, unchangeable love of a man of strong will and principles. It was the first love of his life, for women before had never attracted him. He had looked upon them as something outside his life, playthings for younger men of more susceptible mould; and the idea that he himself would some day find consolation and happiness at a woman's hands he would have deemed ridiculous.

But so it was; and fervently he blessed the chance which had led him down to spend Christmas at Roughton Manor, for May's love had changed the whole tenor of his life, and made the world a different place for him.

His whole nature was softened, and by rapid degrees his manners changed from the hard sternness of a reserved and unhappy man to the genial pleasantness of a happy and contented disposition. He seemed to be commencing life anew, and his friends were never tired of congratulating him on his changed appearance and manners.

There were no difficulties in the way of their engagement, and he was eager that it should be a short one, and, indeed, that they should be married almost at once. But Mr. Hunt urged otherwise, pointing out his daughter's extreme youth.

"A year's waiting will do neither of you any harm, Hugh," he urged; "and besides, May will be stronger then. You can wait a year, surely?"

"But you don't consider her really delicate?" Major Cunningham asked anxiously.

"Not she," Mr. Hunt assured him encouragingly. "Outgrown herself a little, that's all. She'll be a different girl in a year's time."

And so it was arranged. Major Cunningham was to spend the rest of his time with the Hunts, and then return to his regiment for a month or two preparatory to sending in his papers and selling out, for Mr. Hunt insisted that he should do so before his marriage, and he himself had no wish to do otherwise.

Happily the days passed by for both of them, he revelling in his new-found happiness, and she none less happy in his love. And then came the first cloud. His leave was suddenly shortened, and his regiment ordered to Burmah.

It was a great trial; but he was a soldier first and a lover afterwards, and he never dreamt of evading the trouble by exchanging or selling out.

"My last campaign," he whispered to her on the night before his departure, "and soon over, I trust. And when I get back home again I shall expect to see you quite well and strong, darling," he added tenderly.

She smiled at his anxiety through her tears.

"I shall be all right, Hugh dear. But just fancy, if anything were to happen to you in that horrid Burmah "And she shuddered.

He laughed, and shook his head. Then he said, in a somewhat graver tone:—

"We can never tell what may happen, but I don't think there's much fear. Those beggars will have to knock under. I shouldn't wonder if the fighting wasn't all over by the time we get there."

No: he could not tell what was going to happen, or he would never have left England. As it was he went, and after a weary voyage landed with his regiment at Rangoon.

In the very first skirmish he was wounded in the arm by a Burmese spear, and his campaign was over. His arm was perfectly useless, so, after a weary time in the hospital, he was put on the invalided list and shipped off to England.

The change and the sea-breeze soon set him up again, and by the time the Mediterranean was reached his health was almost restored, although he was compelled to keep his arm in a sling.

He had received but few letters from England, as indeed there had been no time; but those which he had received from the Hunts had seemed to him to dwell strangely on May's increasing delicacy, and had even hinted at the possibility of having to remove her to a warmer climate.

But May in her letters had made light of her rumoured illness, and declared that she felt well and strong. Still, though he comforted himself with her assurances, he was nervously anxious to reach England, and see for himself whether there was any ground for her parents' fears.

In due course the long voyage came to an end, and, with scarcely an hour's delay in London, he travelled down to Calton Hall. Mr. Hunt was at the little station to meet him, and welcomed him heartily.

"And May, how is she?" was almost the first question Major Cunningham asked, as they walked down the narrow platform together.

Mr. Hunt looked very grave.

"We fear that she is getting no better," he said with a sigh; "but she persists in saying otherwise. Anyhow, I've made up my mind to have Jenner down and know the worst—though I hope that won't be very bad," he added, with an attempt at cheerfulness, as he saw the sudden pallor in the other's face, and caught a half-smothered ejaculation. "You are scarcely strong yourself yet, Cunningham," he said kindly, passing his arm through his companion's, and leading him out of the station. "Was it wise to hurry down like this, do you think?"

"I could not rest until I had seen her," was the reply, and then in silence they were driven through the country lanes to Calton Hall.

Mrs. Hunt was in the hall to welcome her future son-in-law; but he was too impatient to pay much attention to her voluble greetings.

"Where is she?" he asked.

"In the morning-room. She is expecting you."

And Mrs. Hunt threw open the door, and, closing it with a sigh, left them together.

She was reclining on a couch; but as he entered she half rose and stretched out her arms.

"Oh, Hugh! Thank God you have come!"

And in a moment he was by her side on his knees, and her arms were round his neck.

In those first few minutes of exquisite joy he forgot his fears; but after a while he drew back a little to survey her more closely, and a strange anxiety filled him as he watched her hollow cheeks, flushed with a delicate streak of colour, her large grey eyes unnaturally brilliant, and noticed, too, how thin she was and fragile-looking—far more so than when he had left her.

"My darling, you have been ill!" he exclaimed anxiously, striving hard to keep from his tones and his expression the nervous dread which was filling him as he realized her altered appearance.

She smiled—a faint, wintry smile, though.

"I have not been very ill, Hugh, but I shall soon be all right now that you are come back." And the little white hand, with its long thin fingers, stole softly into his, and, while he smoothed it gently between his own, and caught the pleading look in her eyes, he had hard work to bear himself like a man.

"I hope so," he murmured with passionate earnestness; and he bent close over the imprisoned hand that she might not see the glistening in his eyes. "I hope to God you will!" And then he forced himself to talk more cheerfully; but it was with a heavy heart that he left her.

The great physician from London came down and examined his patient; but he either would not or could not pronounce a decided opinion.

"Take her to the South of France at once, and keep her there," he said. "She will need the greatest care."

"But she will recover?" asked Mr. Hunt anxiously.

The great man hesitated. "There is danger," he admitted "and where there is danger one should always be prepared for the worst. Your daughter may die, and she may live; but she certainly will not live in this climate." And with this scanty consolation he pocketed the cheque, and was driven off to catch the express back to town.

To the South of France they went, all four—Mr. and Mrs. Hunt and their daughter and Major Cunningham. A skilled nurse was in attendance, but her labours and care were nothing to the major's. Night and day he passed by May's bedside, reading, talking cheerfully to her, or sitting by her side in a silence more eloquent than words, holding her hand in his, and trying hard to look smiling and happy, and to banish the misery and anxiety from his careworn face.

Mother and father, loving and tender though they were, could not do for her what he did. He never left her, save for a minute or two at a time to ransack the shops of the little French town for fruit, flowers, or anything which he thought would tempt the invalid's fancy; and, hurrying back to her side, he thought himself amply repaid by one sad, sweet smile from her wasted face.

Such devotion awed father and mother, and tacitly they seemed to recognize his right to watch over her, and keep the place by her side; and even in the midst of their own sorrow they trembled when they thought what would come to him when the time for inevitable separation arrived; for it was inevitable.

Not all the balmy breezes of the southern sea, nor the skilled physician who attended her, nor his devotion who watched over her, could do more than prolong for a little while the evil day; and it came at last.

It was Christmas-time; but at Nice there was little in the

surroundings to show it. Her couch had been drawn up by loving hands to the open window, and her eyes, tired with the monotony of the room, could rest upon the blue Mediterranean, stretching away in front, and the hosts of tiny white sails gently gliding over its placid surface, and here and there on the verge of the horizon the long, thin streak of black smoke which betokened a passing steamer.

Every now and then the laughter of joyous conversation of the crowds on the promenade below was borne to their ears by the soft breeze, in strange discord to the feelings of both of them, for there were tears in his eyes, and a pained look on her thin, white face.

"Don't, Hugh!" she whispered pleadingly, pressing his hand with a feeble pressure; and he forced a smile as he turned and bent over her, watching her with a tender, yearning look the while he rearranged the shawl and eased her pillows.

Soon after then the end came. A slight but sudden change in her face alarmed him, and hastily he dispatched the nurse for Mr. and Mrs. Hunt.

He was on his knees by her side, bending over her with awe-struck face, and, without moving his eyes towards them, held up his hand as the door opened.

"The doctor!" he muttered hoarsely; and the doctor, never far away, was speedily summoned. No one dared speak. Her mother took one hand, and the other he still retained; and her face was turned towards him. Suddenly she cried out:

"Hugh, Hugh! Lift me up! quick!" And, folding his arms around her, he lifted her to a sitting posture.

"Christmas Day!" she whispered softly. "Our first Christmas, Hugh, and our last!" she added sadly, after a short pause.

"Hold me tighter, Hugh!" And with a great lump in his throat, and his breath coming quickly, the tall soldier stooped down and drew her closer to him.

"Kiss me!" she whispered, turning half round.

And mother and father, weeping bitterly, in turn bent over and kissed her; but, though her head was turned towards them, she still clung to him.

"Now, Hugh," she whispered. And with a sob which shook his strong frame he, too, kissed her.

"Don't tremble so!" she murmured, with a faint attempt at a smile, and her eyes fixed lovingly upon him. "We shall meet again some time, some day. How good you have been to me, Hugh! Good-bye!"

And then, after a brief silence, a strange look flitted across her face, and with a groan he laid her reverently down, for in his arms her spirit had passed away.

None saw him again until the funeral; and then he came forth from his room like a ghost, and mechanically took part in the dismal ceremony.

Mother and father, sorrow-stricken though they were, felt their own grief eclipsed by the dull agony in that white, drawn face; but they scarcely dared to speak to him, and, pitying greatly, they left him alone, making no vain attempts at consolation. They travelled together as far as London, and there they parted.

"Try and bear up, Cunningham," said Mr. Hunt, as they stood together at Charing Cross station. "Come down home with us, and be quiet for a time. You need a rest." But he shook his head.

"I must go back to my regiment," he said. "Good-bye."

"You will come and see us when you return to England?" begged Mrs. Hunt, with tears in her eyes.

He shook his head again.

"You are very good, but I shall never return to England," he said sadly. And, looking at his shrunken form and hopeless bearing, they felt that his words were surely true; and so, in sorrow and with heavy hearts, they bade him *adieu*.

Christmas Day in a fine, old country mansion in the north of England, and such a Christmas Day! For to all the joys and pleasures of the holiday season was added another joy which was sufficient of itself to plunge every occupant of the Hall, and every inhabitant of the little village, into a very fever of excitement and anticipation.

They knew little about soldiering, these simple country folks, and had heard very little indeed about the war in "furrin parts"; but they knew that young Tom Carlyon, the squire's youngest son, was back from his first campaign just in time to spend Christmas Day at home, and man and boy, woman and child, they all turned out and cheered him lustily as the dogcart which brought him from the wayside station passed by their cottages and turned in at the Hall gates.

And why not, indeed? Had they not known him from earliest childhood—this tall, boyish-looking young officer? And was he not a universal favourite with them all, young and old?

"Hurrah for Mr. Tom!" And the sturdy villagers would have stopped his carriage and insisted upon a sturdy grip of the hand, which they knew would not be refused, but that their womenkind reminded them that there were those at the Hall, eagerly waiting, who had the first right to welcome him; and so they let him pass unhindered up the broad drive to the Hall, where loving voices choked with sobs bade him welcome, and loving arms encircled his neck.

And May Hildyard, she, too, was there, blushing and happy—as what girl would not have been?—to welcome home her soldier-lover, and to read in his ardent gaze that she was unforgotten.

Such a chorus of welcoming there was; but at last it died away, and things went on much as usual, except that no one was spoken to but Tom, and nothing talked about but Burmah. Then dinner-time came; and afterwards they all drew their chairs round the blazing fire, Tom, between his mother and Bessie, still decidedly the hero of the hour.

"Thank God that my boy is safe!" said Mrs. Carlyon, her hand seeking his for a moment. He was her favourite child, and his absence had been terrible to her.

He returned the gentle pressure, and the boyish face grew suddenly grave, and the reckless gaiety died out of his tones.

"Yes, mother," he said quietly, "I am home safe, you see, but I had a very narrow escape once, I never cared to mention it in my letters, but I should like to tell you all about it now."

A slight shudder ran through the little circle, for the sudden gravity was infectious; and then they pushed their chairs a little closer towards him, and leant eagerly forward to hear Tom's tale.

"It was twelve months ago to-day, mother," he went on, addressing himself chiefly to her, "and Frank Pomerill, Major Cunningham (you have heard me speak of him), and I had a day's leave for shooting up by the ruby-mines. We were only a few miles from the outposts, but somehow we managed to lose our way in a Burmese jungle—nasty sort of places, I can tell you—and when we did get out in the open again it was night, and we were in a bit of a fog as to the track.

"We didn't care about losing our way again—once was quite enough—and so, rather than run any risk, we picketed our horses, lit a fire, and prepared to spend the night. Pomerill was asleep in a minute; he was dead beat. But somehow I was restless—perhaps because it was Christmas night, and I was thinking a good deal of you all here—and after a while I got up and, going over to the remains of the fire, drew out your photograph, May, and had a good look at it.

"When I put it in my pocket again and turned round, I found, to my surprise, Major Cunningham was wide awake, and watching me. I never told you much about Cunningham, did I? Perhaps because none of us knew very much. He was one of our best officers, but very severe and reserved, and we youngsters were awfully afraid of him, I can tell you.

"And yet some of the men almost worshipped him, and told no end of tales about his kindness to them, and how he used to go and see one of the drummer boys who was down with fever, and nurse him himself, while every one else gave the tent as wide a berth as possible. There were plenty of tales like that about him, but he was so grim and reserved that we scarcely dared to speak to him even at lunch.

"They used to say that he had been engaged to a girl, and she died. If that was it, he must have been awfully fond of her, for he seldom smiled, and when in action exposed himself with the reckless daring of a man who was tired of his life, and sought to throw it away. Well, you can guess the sort of man he was; and when I caught him watching me devouring your photograph, May, I felt rather dropped upon, I can tell you; but I laughed it off as well as I could.

"'Christmas Day, you know, major,' I said, 'and one can't help thinking a little of the people at home.' To my surprise he smiled quite pleasantly, and began asking me questions about you all. I was only too glad to have some one to talk to, so I chatted away, and he listened, and seemed quite interested until I mentioned your name, May.

"Then his face clouded suddenly over, and I don't think he heard anything else. And then it struck me that I had heard somewhere that he had been engaged to a May some one or other. Well, I didn't venture to ask him any questions, of course; so I shut up, and turning round went off fast to sleep. I suppose it must have been quite an hour later when a slight sound aroused me, and I sprang up in a fright.

"Pomerill was snoring like a trooper, but Cunningham had evidently heard the sound, whatever it was, and was standing up peering into a semi-darkness. In less than a minute we heard it again, a rustling among the bamboos, and a subdued murmur of voices, and, turning sharply round, we could dimly see a mass of dark, crouching forms, scarcely eighty yards away, with their eyes glistening like beads as they stole on their hands and feet nearer to us every moment.

"I kicked Pomerill, and he was on his feet in a twinkling. 'To horse!' Cunningham shouted. 'Look alive, Carlyon; the dacoits are upon us!' And we made for the animals like a shot. We reached the spot where we had tethered them before the dacoits were clear of the jungle; and then my blood ran cold for a minute, I can tell you. I hadn't been very careful about tethering my mare, and she had made off—nothing but a broken bridle left. All up with me, I thought, as Pomerill vaulted into the saddle; and then I heard Cunningham's strong voice at my elbow.

"'Your mare hasn't gone far,' he said quickly. 'She's round the other side of the hillock grazing. Ride mine, and I'll soon catch her.' And he held the stirrup out for me and motioned me impatiently to mount.

"I was in the saddle like a shot; but then I hesitated and looked round.

"'I can't see my mare,' I said, perplexed.

"'Off you go, and never mind your mare!' he shouted in a voice of thunder. 'I'll see to her. Be off, sir!' he continued, as a spear from the foremost of the dacoits sank quivering into the ground only a few feet from us.

"'Remember May, and ride for your life! I'm coming round the other way.' And, without another word, I bent down in my saddle and galloped away for dear life. It was no use looking behind for Cunningham, for there were dozens of routes by which he might follow us, and without a doubt he would choose a different one to ours.

"We were nearer to the camp by a good five miles than we had reckoned on, and after half an hour's hard galloping we passed the outposts and pulled up. The first thing I saw was my mare, tethered by the side of our tent, and quietly feeding.

"'Has any one seen Cunningham?' I cried out, suddenly alarmed. But they all shook their heads.

"'How long has Brown Bess been here?' I asked Duncan, who had just hurried up. Duncan was my man then.

"'About three hours, sir,' he answered. 'Galloped in with a broken bridle and no saddle, as if for all the world she'd broken loose from tether. In a rare sweat she was, too,' he added.

"Then I saw it all; and, with a groan, I turned Cunningham's powerful chestnut round and galloped straight back again. I scarcely knew how to go on," he continued, and his voice faltered and his eyes grew dim. "I was back there in half an hour at the most; but it was all over.

"He was lying on his back at the foot of a giant tree, with his tunic off and his shirt literally soaked with blood. The dacoits were all gone—they must have heard me coming, for Pomerill had followed me with a skirmishing party—but they had done their deadly work. He was just breathing his last when I leapt off and bent over him.

"His right hand, stretched out, clenched his sword with such a grip that we never got it away, and it was buried with him; the other hand was inside his shirt clutching a photograph stained and soaked in his life's blood. His eyes opened as he felt my touch, and he tried to smile—a grim, ghastly attempt. He only faltered one word—a woman's name—May, and then he died without a gasp or struggle. Oh, God, it is awful to think of!"

And the young man rose and paced the room, while Mrs. Carlyon and May wept aloud.

"He must have fought like a lion," Tom went on, looking up for a moment and dashing a suspicious moisture from his eyes, "for around him were the bodies of three dacoits, all stone dead, and from the blood on their trail there must have been some wounded; but at the moment of his death his features relaxed into a quiet smile, as if he had died at peace with the world. I never saw him look so happy in life."

"God bless him!" murmured Mrs. Carlyon through her tears. "But for him I should never have had my boy back. God bless him!"

"Amen!" said Mr. Carlyon solemnly. "He was a hero."

Years passed on, but Hugh Cunningham was not forgotten. In that happy English home there is a golden-haired, prattling youngster named Hugh Cunningham Carlyon, who is never tired of telling his youthful and grown-up friends of the gallant officer whose name he bears, who gave his life to save his father's, who died a fearful death in order that his father might come home and marry mamma—and all because her name was May.

And so, though he sleeps in a soldier's grave in a far-off country, there is one household in England who hold his name in reverence and cherish his memory, and who fervently pray that in another world he has found that happiness which on earth was taken from him.

## THE END

# BLACKMAN'S WOOD
## E. Phillips Oppenheim

It was when they reached the end of the wood, which should provide the best sport of the day, that Heggs first showed signs of a curious, unbucolic disquietude. He still answered his master's remarks respectfully, but his eyes kept wandering to a long, sinister-looking belt of wood lying about a quarter of a mile away eastward. It was Ella Cartnell who first appreciated the half-mystic, half-terrified stare of those uneasy blue eyes.

"Why do you keep looking across at Blackman's Wood, Heggs?" she asked him.

He touched his hat mechanically. He was a short, cheery-faced man, in a worn velveteen coat, breeches and leggings—a man whom you would have hailed as a gamekeeper if you had met him on another planet. Sniffing restlessly about him were two good-looking Labradors. A rough-coated retriever sat by his side, wagging his tail persistently. The man was typical of his class in build, feature and speech. Yet the mystery of his eyes was the mystery of fear.

"Begging your pardon, my lady," he said, "I was just hoping that we'd keep the pheasants from flying that way. If I might make so bold, sir," he went on, turning to his master, who was standing by with half a dozen labelled sticks under his arm, "I'd like an extra gun here."

Richard Cartnell, a good-looking, large-framed young man, nodded.

"Perhaps you're right, Heggs," he acquiesced. "There's never any shooting the other side to speak of. I'll let Mr. Samson, who's walking on the left, keep well ahead and come into the ride. Then Sir John can move further down, and Mr. Johnson can come out on the meadow."

"If you'd take the corner yourself, sir," Heggs begged eagerly, "and have Mr. Morden between you and Sir John, I think that ought to stop 'em, sir, provided there ain't much wind blowing."

Cartnell handed over the sticks.

"You can place these yourself then, Heggs," he said. "Of course, I know why you want to keep the pheasants out of Blackman's Wood, but remember this can't go on for ever. We left it alone last year because it was poor old Middleton's beat, and we haven't been in this season, but if pheasants go there, have 'em out we must. There are always woodcock round the lower end, as you know."

Again there was that curious glint in the man's eyes.

"I'll never get the beaters in there, sir," he declared.

Cartnell frowned.

"What do you mean—not get them in?" he demanded. "They're the regular lot, aren't they—mostly our own men? Surely they'll go where they're told?"

"They'll go where they're told anywhere else, sir," Heggs assented. "For beaters they're as good a lot as ever I handled. But Blackman's Wood! There's a-many as wouldn't go within a half a mile of that, day-time or night-time."

They were all three at the corner of the ride and they turned and looked at the wood below. Even in the clear, frosty light of the December afternoon, there was something grim, almost repellent, in its broken outline. Every description of tree seemed to have been planted there—tall firs, standing out stark and stiff in the middle, a medley of larches, dwarfed oaks, spruces and hollies towards the further end. Even from where they stood they could realize that the undergrowth was almost like a jungle. In a small field, at the furthest extremity, was a cottage, with a row of pheasant coops stretching away from it, and a little fenced-in garden.

"What's the idea with these fellows?" Cartnell asked moodily.

Heggs took command of himself, but there was a shiver in his voice as he spoke.

"They do say, sir," he confided, "that after Barney Middleton had strangled his wife, he made his way into the wood and hanged himself. There's some in the village who do hold by that story—old man Fouldes for one, who'd been after a few sticks, and he do swear to this moment that he saw Barney's body dangling down from a tree."

"What damned rubbish!" Cartnell exclaimed. "Everyone knows Middleton got clear away from the place. The police tracked him to Southampton."

"So us have heard, sir," Heggs acknowledged; "and though a hot-tempered man he was, for sure, I've never believed that Barney Middleton was one who would lay hands on himself. Still, there's old man Fouldes as swears he's seen his body, and many others declare they've seen his ghost. I'm not one as believes in these things myself, sir," the gamekeeper went on, "but I'd rather forfeit a week's wages than take the beaters through Blackman's Wood, even if they was willing to go."

"What do you think about it, Ella?" Cartnell asked his wife.

She turned and looked at him, without a smile on her face. She was a blond, handsome woman, tall, and with a splendid figure.

There was something inscrutable about her expression as she answered her husband's question.

"What do you think about it yourself, Dick?" she rejoined.

"I don't happen to be superstitious," he answered shortly. "I was down at the cottage this morning, and if I'd had gaiters on I think I should have tried for a woodcock in the lower end. Wherever I could see it looked terribly thick, though."

"You don't want any trouble with the beaters," Ella said. "I should try and keep the pheasants from breaking that way, if I were you."

"Very well," Cartnell decided. "I'll do the best I can for you, Heggs. I'll come down this end myself with Mr. Morden and Mr. Johnson. I suppose we should be considered the three best shots, and I should think we ought to be able to stop them. On the other hand, if we make a mess of it, to Blackman's Wood we shall have to go. I'll talk to the beaters if you like, Heggs."

"Don't 'e say a word to them, sir, please," the man implored. "If they've any sort of a belief that they'll be asked to go through Blackman's Wood, there isn't one of them will turn up to-morrow. Don't 'e say nothing beforehand, sir, whatever 'e do."

"All right, I won't," Cartnell promised. "Anyhow, if we can keep the pheasants out, I'll forget about the woodcock and leave the wood alone this season."

Heggs touched his hat gratefully.

"It's for the sake of all concerned, sir," he said.

They strolled up the meadow to where Cartnell's two-seater car was waiting in the lane.

"It's all clear about to-morrow now, I think, Heggs," his master summarised. "We start with two partridge drives. You send your men out early, over Barrow's land, and bring in those two outlying fields of roots, and Josiah Brown's low meadows. Bring everything you can in to the rough grasses, and plan to have it done by ten o'clock. Then, unless there's a change in the wind, we'll bring them over towards Swallow Farm, and line the bottom hedge,"

"There's a rare lot of birds if I can get hold of them, sir," Heggs observed.

"The second drive you know all about, but of course we must see which way the birds break."

They paused for a minute at the gate to look back. Again there was something of that curious expression in Heggs's eyes. With his ash stick he pointed downwards to the pleasant little stretch of country which they had left.

"D'you mark that, my lady?" he asked, turning to Ella. "There's pigeons coming in over Salter's Wood, and in the home spinneys yonder, and Gregory's cover, and never a one anywhere near Blackman's Wood. Just you look, sir," he went on, with a note almost of excitement in his tone. "Pigeons everywhere, and not a single one over Blackman's, though there's many of the trees there they do reckon to be fond of. Them birds knows something, they does. Sometimes they knows more than human beings."

Cartnell climbed into the car, where his wife had already seated herself.

"You go home and have a good night's rest, Heggs," he advised; "and put Blackman's Wood out of your mind."

During the whole of the drive home, Ella Cartnell sat speechless, her eyes fixed on the country ahead. As they turned in at the avenue, her husband took his pipe from his mouth and broke the silence.

"You're not tired, Ella?"

"Not in the least," she answered.

"Feeling all right?"

"Perfectly."

He looked at her in rather helpless fashion. Something had come down between them, which for months he had battled against unsuccessfully. It was there now, visible in her air of detachment, her cold aloofness, as though she were unaware even of his presence.

"What were you thinking of?" he inquired.

She turned and looked at him.

"I was wondering," she confessed, "whether we should ever know who poor Betty Middleton's lover was—the man whom Barney Middleton found her with that afternoon?"

Cartnell almost grazed a white post, as he swung into the avenue.

"Why do you want to know?" he asked.

"It would ease my mind," she replied.

The remainder of the guests for the morrow's shoot had arrived during the absence of their host and hostess, and were being served with tea by Sybil Cartnell, Richard's young sister. Hugh Morden, a long, lean man, with the typical clean-shaven barrister's face, rather full lips, and eyes of a curious grey-green shade, was standing with his back to the fire, a cup of tea in his hand, listening to Cunningham's description of a public dinner on the night before.

Sir John Cunningham, as a brief-giving lawyer, was entitled to his attention, which was certainly all that he did receive, for Morden was evidently distrait. At the entrance of his host and hostess, however, his whole expression changed. He greeted Cartnell in the perfunctory manner of old friends who were constantly meeting, but his eyes glowed as he took Ella's hand and, bending down, whispered something in her ear. She turned away, with a little laugh.

"So sorry to be late, you people," she apologized. "I hope Sybil's been looking after you. We've been out marking the stands for to-morrow's shoot."

"Up against a superstitious gamekeeper, too," Cartnell observed. "You and I, Morden, and Johnson, too, have got to shoot our best to-morrow. Heggs tells me that if we can't keep the pheasants from going into Blackman's Wood, there'll be a riot amongst the beaters."

Freddie Samson, a pink-and-white athletic-looking young stockbroker, who had been whispering in Sybil's ear, glanced up.

"What's the trouble with Blackman's Wood?" he inquired.

"Haunted," Cartnell explained. "One old man in the village declares that he has seen Barney Middleton's body hanging there, and there are twenty or thirty who swear that they've seen his ghost on moonlight nights."

"I thought that sort of thing had died out, even in these remote districts," Morden remarked, a little satirically. "You're not going to humour the louts, I hope, Cartnell."

The latter shrugged his shoulders.

"I can't drive them in if they won't go," he pointed out. "As a matter of fact, though, unless we lose our pheasants from the big wood, and they find their way there, it won't be worth going through."

Conversation drifted into other channels. In the background of the little circle, Richard Cartnell, with a cup of tea in his hand, lounged against the corner of a table, apparently listening to a discussion upon a recent election, but in reality watching his wife and Morden. He was by nature an unsuspicious man. In their twelve years of married life, Ella had never once given him cause for serious uneasiness.

Her undoubted attraction had always brought her a train of admirers, with whom she had amused herself light-heartedly but discreetly. Morden, however, from the first, although silent in manner and secretive in his methods, had betrayed an infatuation which half surprised and half provoked his host. He watched them now gloomily. There was something about their confidential whispers, their reserves, the slightly forced smile with which Ella answered the remarks addressed to her by any of the others, which puzzled him.

They were all intimates. Jack Mason, an old friend of Ella's, a clubman who seemed to spend half his time in country houses, Sinclair Johnson, M.P. for the Division, and Jack Halloway, a nephew of the house, were all talking away of their mutual friends, and exchanging gossip as to their doings.

More and more, Ella and Morden remained outside the little circle. What the devil could the fellow be saying, Cartnell wondered, as he watched him lean closer and closer towards her. Finally, in a fit of restlessness he strolled off, with his hands in his pockets to the gun-room. He took down one of his Purdeys, to be sure that it was properly oiled, removed the lid from a fresh case of cartridges, tried to occupy himself in any way in order to regain a normal attitude of mind. When he returned to the lounge, Ella and Morden had disappeared.

"Where's Morden?" he inquired.

"Gone with Ella to the billiard-room," Sybil replied, bending forward to light a cigarette. "I say, Dick, what's the matter with Ella? She seems up in the clouds half the time. Is she having a flirtation with Hugh Morden?"

"Not that I'm aware of," her brother answered. "Perhaps," he added, with gloomy sarcasm, "even if they were, I might be just the one person whom they wouldn't take into their confidence."

"That's all very well," Sybil complained, "but I'd marked Hugh Morden down for my own. He never leaves Ella's side if he can help it. See to it, Dick, there's a dear! Separate them, and hint that there's another of the same family without a hulking husband in the way."

"Talking about Blackman's Wood," young Samson observed, throwing down an evening paper and joining them, "that gamekeeper of yours was never caught, was he, Cartnell? What was it all about, anyhow?"

"A simple, but alas! a common story," Cunningham recounted. "Middleton was supposed to have gone home towards the end of a day's shooting earlier than he was expected, and found his wife a little too pleasantly engaged with a caller. He adopted primitive measures, and strangled her."

"How sweet of him!" Sybil exclaimed. "So unlike the modern

husband!"

Some impulse prompted Cartnell to turn his head. Morden and Ella had apparently been crossing the hall, and were standing now, as though transfixed, upon the edge of the circle. To Cartnell there was something terrifying about the strained look in his wife's face, an expression almost of horror in the eyes that met his. By her side Morden stood, grave and expressionless, save that there was a faintly cynical turn at the corners of his lips.

"Please don't depress us any more by talking about that horrible affair," she insisted angrily. "You've all had a longish journey—why don't we change early and have more time for cocktails? Perhaps by then you'll all think of something more cheerful to talk about. This isn't a palace, as you know, and you've only two bathrooms to scramble for."

Everyone acquiesced, and there was a prompt exodus from the hall. Cartnell, after a few minutes' reflection, went sombrely to his room, knocked at the door of his wife's apartment, and entered.

"What is it?" she asked, startled.

"Need it be anything particular?" he rejoined quietly. "I just strolled in."

"Why—of course not," she answered. "Do you want the bathroom?"

"Presently."

He sank into an easy-chair, and pondered for a moment or two.

"Ella," he said, "I have never interfered with any of your harmless flirtations—in fact, I have sometimes encouraged them—but I cannot absolutely ignore the fact that this change in your manner, which I ventured to hint at the other afternoon, all dates from this summer, when Morden stayed down with us. Are you falling in love with him?"

She swung round, relentlessly beautiful notwithstanding the trouble which lurked in her eyes.

"If I am," she demanded, "do you complain?"

"Most vehemently," he replied, "if it is in any way the cause of your altered demeanour towards me. Furthermore, I don't mind telling you that I would rather you had chosen any other friend I have to amuse yourself with."

"And why?"

"Because," Cartnell answered deliberately, "Morden, who is a good fellow with us men, and whom we all like and admire because he is fiendishly clever, is not to be trusted with a woman."

"You say that!" she murmured.

"I do," he assented. "A good many men with attractive wives have found it out before, and have had to have him on the carpet. I am wondering whether that will happen to me."

She rose to her feet and moved slowly towards him. She was almost as tall as he was.

"Dick," she said, "I never believed that you were mean enough to say these things about a man who is a guest in your house. Why do you ask him to shoot? Why do you have him here at all?"

"Because, my dear," he replied, "I have always believed in the old saying—that there is honour amongst thieves. I know very well that Morden can't be trusted with a woman, but that isn't my business until it becomes my business. If ever it should," he added, rising to his feet, "I should know how to deal with him."

He passed back to his room. His wife, looked after him until the door was closed. Then she returned to her seat before the-looking-glass.

Late that night, Heggs, after he had knocked out his pipe and prepared for bed, slipped out from his cottage door, glanced up into the tops of the trees, listened, moistened his finger, and held it up in seafaring fashion.

"What are you after, John?" his wife called from the open door. "Be you thinking there's poachers about to-night?"

John Heggs shook his head.

"No fear of that," he answered. "The Sergeant's sending a couple of men round to give me a night's rest. It was just the wind."

It was a somewhat listlessly spent evening at Cawston Farms, as Cartnell's country house was called. For some reason or other, everyone was sleepy and anxious to go to bed early in view of the shoot on the following day. There was difficulty, even, in making up a rubber of bridge for Cunningham. Morden flatly refused to play, Ella also excused herself; so, eventually, Cartnell, an indifferent performer who loathed the game, was forced to cut in.

They played in the lounge, and Cartnell committed every sin known to the card tyro. He revoked, he neglected to attempt the simplest finesse, he led to no trumps as though it were a trump suit, he reduced his respective partners to tears and blasphemy. After the game was over, Cunningham walked to the sideboard and mixed himself a whisky-and-soda. For a Portland Club authority, he had kept his temper admirably.

"Dick," he advised, "get away to bed and have a long rest. No man could make such an utter idiot of himself with the cards if he hadn't something on his mind. Go and sleep it off before to-morrow."

Cartnell accepted the rebuke humbly,

"I'll just round the others up first," he observed. "I think everyone's for turning in early."

In the smoking-room he found only Jack Mason and Samson yarning, and Johnson fast asleep. He passed on to the billiard-room, opened the door, and stood for a moment upon the threshold. Morden and Ella were leaning over the billiard-table, Morden talking earnestly, his hand resting upon hers. With a swiftness which bespoke long practice, he drew his fingers away at the opening of the door. He was careful, however, not to change his position.

"Got a hiding, as I knew I should, Dick," he remarked. "No one can give Ella fifty."

Cartnell advanced further into the room. His wife turned and faced him. She was a little nervous, but his expression told her nothing.

"I think you had better go and look after your other guests, Ella," he suggested. "They are all thinking of going to bed."

He held the door open for her, and she passed out silently.

"Bed's not a bad idea. I think I'll be off, too," Morden announced with a yawn.

Cartnell, however, closed the door and stood with his back to it.

"Just one word with you, Hugh," he said. "You spoke just now of Ella having given you a hiding at billiards. Aren't you rather asking for one yourself?"

"Am I?" was the cool rejoinder. "I don't think so."

"A man's private life," Cartnell went on, "is usually disregarded by other men. I won't allude to yours, Hugh, except so far as to say that you will be a welcome guest here in the future only if you change your attitude towards my wife."

"My dear fellow!" Morden expostulated. "You don't imagine for a moment—"

"Of course I don't," Cartnell interrupted, "but that is all because I trust my wife, not you. However, wait one moment; that isn't all I have to say."

"With a man of your physique blocking the way," Morden drawled, "I hesitate to confess that I am dying for a whisky-and-soda."

"Someone," his host went on deliberately, "seems, ever since last summer, to have been poisoning my wife's mind against me. I don't know what I am supposed to have done—I can only make the vaguest guess—but I want you to understand this, Hugh. If I discover that anyone at any time has been lying to her about a particular incident concerning which I am free to admit that I have rather stifled inquiries, for certain reasons, it will not be a matter of a hiding. I shall take that man by the throat, and I shall let him go when his lips are black—you know what that means."

Hugh Morden, for a moment, had lost his equanimity.

"What incident?" he demanded. "What are you talking about?"

Cartnell opened the door.

"You know very well, Hugh," he concluded, "that I am referring to the incident of Barney Middleton's wife. Go and get your whisky-and-soda."

No more successful partridge drives had ever been organized on the Cawston shooting than the two which, on the following morning, formed the prelude to the serious business of the day. The wind had completely dropped, and, wild though a great many of the birds were, the intervening cover was so scanty that, although the drive was a long one, covey after covey dropped down in the great field of rough grass according to plan.

The seven guns lining the hedge saw the silent, flag-bearing procession of men and boys move down the hillside and slowly close in towards the boundaries of the field. There was a brief silence—then Heggs's whistle, followed by Cartnell's reply, and the beaters made their way through the hedges. A little thrill ran down the line. There was no uncertainty about this. Even the loaders—an impassive race of men as a rule—showed genuine interest in what was happening, and Cunningham, who shot but rarely, practised changing guns with his man. Then came the first warning whistle as a covey rose from just under the feet of one of the beaters, flew straight for the hedge, broke beautifully round some trees, and came over high and scattered.

The next twenty minutes was almost an epic in the history of the shoot. For once, birds, when they did swerve, left it too late, and flew high and fast down the line of the guns. Scarcely a covey went back, and just as the sport was thinning down, odd Frenchmen kept getting up one by one, flying like bullets to their melancholy but glorious end.

"Very nearly the best drive I ever had in my life," Freddie Samson declared, as he lit a cigarette and handed his gun over to his loader. "Very few runners, either. Dick, I never thought this little crowd could shoot so well. What do you think we got?"

"No idea," Cartnell replied. "I got twelve brace, and Morden was shooting beautifully. He must have got more. What did you do?"

"Ten brace and a half, and a couple of runners," Samson announced.

"Heggs has picked up one of the runners already, sir," his loader put in.

"What a day for driving!" Mason exclaimed, as he strolled up. "Never had such a ten minutes that I can remember. Not a breath of wind, and they came marvellously, I never saw the crowd shoot better, either. That was a peach of a right-and-left you got out of the second covey, Dick."

They all strolled away together across the stubble, everyone a little exhilarated. Only the host and Hugh Morden remained somewhat silent. The latter's long-drawn face seemed more than usually set. He smoked countless cigarettes, and kept on a line of his own, a few yards away from the others. His unsociability, however, gave rise to no comment, for everyone knew that he talked but seldom when shooting. As soon as the game had been collected and the cart loaded, Heggs hurried up to his master.

"I've sent half the beaters round to bring in Richards's stubbles, sir," he announced, "and I thought if so be you were willing to wait a bit, I'd sweep the left-hand beaters right round to the Orford boundary, fall in with the others, and all come on together from the Lone Farm. You'll line the thirty-acre meadow hedge, but I think you'll have to take it a little wide, sir."

"Quite sound, Heggs," Cartnell approved. "We shan't be able to see you until you're actually in the roots, so don't forget to whistle."

The man suddenly turned his head and sniffed.

"What's the matter?" his master asked.

"Nothing, sir. I just thought—I fancied there was a breeze coming up."

Cartnell glanced at the sky.

"Might get one later on—not much sign of it at present. . . . Guns this way! We've half a mile to walk. Anyone like a lift in the game-cart? There's John with the whiskies-and-sodas and cocktails somewhere about, too."

"It's exactly an hour too early," Cunningham declared, looking at his watch. "Only one hour, mind you. We'll keep John in sight!"

The next drive, though not quite so productive, was almost as exciting as the first. Then there were three spinneys to knock out—one of which produced an unexpected show of woodcock. When they sat down to lunch on the lawn in front of Heggs's cottage, everyone was a little exultant, and good-tempered. Cunningham, who was a man of figures, produced his note-book.

"We're ahead of last year on this beat, by seventeen and a half brace of partridges, thirty-one pheasants and seven woodcock. Hares—we only got twenty-seven, did we? We're three hares short. What a morning! Ella, you and I must have a cocktail together, and, if you don't mind, Dick, I'd like to take a double one to Heggs. With only one other man who knew anything at all about the job, he brought those birds to-day as cleverly as anything I've ever seen."

Heggs accepted congratulations with a modest grin, and drained the contents of the glass offered him. They lunched at a long table set out on trestles, after Sybil, from a hastily improvised bar, had served everyone with cocktails. Hugh Morden, as usual, found a place by Ella's side. Cartnell, at the other end of the table, was as far removed as possible. To all appearance, he never glanced either towards his wife or Morden. Nevertheless, both were at times uneasily conscious of his presence. No one else appeared to notice that there was a cloud upon what was otherwise certainly a wonderful party.

After lunch came the *pièce de résistance*—the shooting of the wood. From the moment when the places were taken for the first drive—usually an unimportant one—a change came over Heggs. The effect of the extra glass of beer he had drunk at luncheon time, with a view to drowning his apprehensions, had passed. He kept looking at the sky. Already the tops of the trees in the wood were rustling. He turned to his master almost despairingly.

"There's a west wind coming up for sure, sir," he groaned. "It will carry them pheasants right away to Blackman's Wood."

Cartnell, moody and depressed himself, was unsympathetic.

"Let 'em go there, then, if they can get past Mr. Morden and me," he said. "The woodcock are worth one beat, anyway."

For a moment Heggs stood quite motionless. Again that rare expression of mysterious terror brought out the lines in his weather-beaten face. It lurked there in his eyes as he glanced furtively down towards the hated spot.

"Come along, Heggs," his master enjoined sharply. "These two first beats aren't up to much, but we'd better get them over."

The shooting began—a trifle erratic after a somewhat gay luncheon party, but soon settling down. As was always the case, the result of the first two beats was simply to drive the birds into the lower end of the wood, where the undergrowth was much thicker. The twenty or thirty that came out were satisfactorily disposed of, and certainly not half a dozen reached the dreaded shelter of Blackman's Wood. For the final beat, Heggs himself came forward to superintend the placing of the guns. He brought Sinclair Johnson down to the extreme end of the ride, almost in the meadow, in line with Cartnell and Morden. The wind had freshened by now, and a couple of cocks, disturbed before their time, simply vol-planed down to Blackman's Wood. Heggs watched them with a groan.

"They'll come out this side, sir, whatever we do," he muttered, as he passed his master on the way back.

"Don't be a fool, Heggs," Cartnell enjoined irritably. "Keep your right well forward, and have the hedge knocked from outside."

Heggs's reply was respectful but gloomy.

"I'll do all that man can to keep they birds straight, sir," he promised.

He rejoined the beaters and blew his whistle. The familiar sound of the tapping of trees recommenced, and almost at once the pheasants began to come over. Ella had been in the ride with Mason and Samson, but as soon as the shooting started she came out into the meadow, and deliberately planted her stick a few paces behind Morden's loader. One or two pheasants broke early over Cartnell, and a woodcock, all of which he disposed of. Then, without the slightest warning, the tragedy of the day loomed up. The whistle blew continually, pheasants seemed to be rising from all parts of the wood, and practically the whole of them streamed over Morden's head, or between him and Johnson. That Morden should have missed the first one with both barrels, and have done no better with his second gun, was unusual, but comprehensible, because he had had very little shooting since luncheon, but what followed was simply amazing. Difficult or easy, high or low, overhead, to his left or to his right, Morden, the crack shot of the party, missed every bird he aimed at.

Everyone in sight looked at him in astonishment. Heggs came staggering out of the wood to see what had happened, and stood transfixed, as he watched the long line of pheasants streaming away to Blackman's Wood. Cartnell, abandoning all etiquette, moved up ten paces, and a little backwards, and continually shot the birds which sailed over Morden unscathed. Johnson, in response to a gesture from his host, did the same, but the situation was already lost. Nothing that they could do could atone altogether for the fact that Morden, in the one commanding position, seemed completely paralysed. Every vestige of colour had gone from his cheeks, and there was a savage gleam in his eyes. As one huge cock passed smoothly over his head untouched, he threw down upon the ground the gun which he had just discharged, and almost forgot to take the second which his loader was handing him.

"Anything wrong with you, Morden; are you ill?" Cartnell called out.

Morden just turned his head, and his expression was ghastly.

"I don't know," he muttered. "Change places with me, quickly."

Cartnell obeyed, bringing down a right-and-left of cock pheasants even as he took up Morden's vacated place. And then a stranger thing than ever happened. The pheasants which, with one accord, seemed to have made for Morden, made for him still, and the tragedy was once more repeated. Cartnell and Johnson missed nothing, but an odd bird now and then was all they got. Towards the end Morden suddenly threw down his gun again and held his head with both hands. Cartnell moved back behind him, and waved Johnson to come out into the field, but the mischief was done. There were a couple of hundred pheasants in Blackman's Wood, and Morden, with his hands still clasping the sides of his head, was swaying as though about to collapse. Ella leaned forward and touched him on the shoulder.

"Are you ill?" she whispered.

"I don't know," he gasped. "I don't know what's come over me. I think I'll go home—come with me."

Cartnell strolled up to him, and the two men looked one another in the eyes. Morden still seemed on the point of collapse.

"You can't go home, Hugh," Cartnell said brutally. "You put 'em into Blackman's wood, you let 'em go there—God knows why. You must shoot 'em when we fetch them out."

Morden made no reply. The refreshment cart, which Ella had sent for, came lumbering up. He stumbled towards it and helped himself to a strong brandy-and-soda. The effect was instantaneous. There was a more natural colour in his cheeks, and he regained some measure of his self-possession.

"All right," he agreed; "I'll do my best. I don't know what came over me—a liver attack, perhaps. I'm damnably sorry."

Very slowly, and like a man bent on a portentous errand, Heggs approached his master. The beaters were standing about in little groups, talking.

"Sorry Heggs, but we'll have to have those birds out of Blackman's Wood," Cartnell told him firmly. "Get it at the bottom end, and bring them this way. I'll send a couple of guns with you for the outsides. I'll place the others. We'll leave this side open. They aren't likely to come out against the wind. If they do, they'll be going home."

Heggs touched his hat. In his tone there was a note of desperation.

"I'm sorry, sir," he announced. "Them beaters, they won't go in Blackman's Wood."

"You mean that they refuse to obey orders?"

"Most on 'em, sir, and the rest ain't willing."

"And why not?" Cartnell demanded.

"It's no good beating about the bush, sir," Heggs replied, his coarse hands with the broken nails trembling as he leaned forward on his gnarled stick, "There's a dozen at least amongst 'em as can swear that they've seen Barney Middleton's ghost hanging round at the back end, just outside his cottage. They say he drownded heself somewhere, and keeps coming back to see the spot where he strangled his wife. I can't get 'em in no-how, sir."

"I'll talk to them myself," Cartnell announced.

He walked across and confronted them—a motley group, boys, youths and elderly men, in every variety of costume, but all of them wearing the leggings which had been Ella's Christmas gift.

"Look here, my men," Cartnell began, "what's this nonsense about not wanting to go into Blackman's Wood? You've seen for yourselves that the pheasants are there, and we know there are woodcock."

No one was willing to be spokesman. They shifted their feet and moved about nervously.

"Gosling, now—what about you?"

Gosling took off his hat and scratched his head.

"Mr. Cartnell, sir," he said, "I be a serious man as you know, and a man as has found religion. I don't hold with these stories of ghosts, but when there's half the village swears they've seen Barney Middleton's spirit wandering round in that there wood and round about the cottage, well, it does make one think, so to speak; and for the sake of the eight bob and beer we get for a day's beating, I'd just as soon keep out of trouble, sir. I never met a spirit yet, and I ain't anxious."

There was a little murmur of assent. One or two of the younger ones, however, laughed.

"I don't mind," a nephew of Middleton declared. "The old man wouldn't do me no harm."

"Same here," another lad joined in. "It ain't like as though it were night."

"Look here, then," Cartnell announced, "I'll give an extra five shillings to every beater who will come through Blackman's Wood. Now then, who's for the back of it?"

One by one, like sheep, they followed young Middleton. There were only five who refused, and they stood in a little group by themselves outside the wood. Heggs came up to his master with laggard footsteps. He seemed suddenly to be many years older.

"Is it your will, then, sir," he asked in a low tone, "that we go through the wood?"

"Of course it is, Heggs. Take your men along. Mr. Mason and Mr. Halloway will walk up with you. Knock the place out as well as you can, and don't forget the holly bushes."

They straggled off in a long, irregular line, and Cartnell busied himself in arranging the stands. Morden, after another brandy-and-soda, seemed to have recovered himself. He sat on his shooting-stick, his gun balanced across his knees, and his eyes fixed upon the forbidding little wood in front. The edge of it was bordered by a quantity of small black firs, but behind was a curious medley of trees of every description, and an undergrowth of bracken and rank grass, which appeared not to have been touched for years. A cock pheasant came flying out at a great height, almost before the beaters were in, and Morden brought it down with his first barrel, a crumpled mass of feathers, shot through the head.

"You're all right again now," Ella whispered. "Splendid!"

The whistle sounded continually, and pheasants began to come over. Everyone shot well, and Morden especially. The sound of the tapping of the trees grew nearer and nearer. Suddenly there was a silence. The whole line of beaters seemed to have stopped. The silence continued. Cartnell walked forward a yard or two.

"What's wrong, Heggs?" he called out.

Almost before the words were out of his mouth, there arose a chorus of wild yells, blasphemous, panic-stricken shrieks of unrestrained terror. Out from the wood, on both sides, tumbling through the hedges, running in frantic haste, came the beaters. Even when they were clear of the borders and in the meadow, they ran like madmen. Middleton's nephew, who had led the way in, fell head over heels and picked himself up, sobbing, to tear after the others.

"What the devil's the matter!" Cartnell shouted. "Heggs!"

A choked voice from somewhere in the wood:

"For the love of God stand clear, sir. Get the lady away! He's coming!"

"What's got the fellows?" Cartnell cried. "Have they all gone mad? Can anyone see anything?"

Almost at that moment the horror arrived. Crashing down the middle of the wood came some undistinguishable shape, too big for a fox, too big for a stray deer even—it was something which seemed to come in bounds, like a huge dog plunging straight ahead.

"Are you loaded, Hugh?" Cartnell asked him swiftly.

Morden made no answer. He was standing as though petrified, looking at something clear now of the trees, leaping through the bracken. It came over the low hedge and rails in its stride, and for that first moment there was not a person who saw it who was not paralysed with fear. It came like an orang-outang, six feet high, sometimes on all fours, then upright, a creature who had once been a man, with some fragments of filthy clothing and sacking still left, a great ragged beard, hair almost down his back, gaunt, deep-set horrible eyes, fingers black, patches of his body bleeding. Not for one instant did it hesitate. Clear of the wood, it went straight, like a savage animal who has marked its prey, towards Morden. It had come out on all fours, but as it approached it reared itself, and with a terrifying yell—a yell which no one ever forgot who heard it—and with great lopping springs, drew near to its cowering victim.

"Shoot!" Cartnell cried. "Shoot it, Hugh!"

Morden's gun, irresolutely lifted, wobbled in his hand. Suddenly his loader leaned past him, raised the second gun to his shoulder, and fired. For a single second the brute faltered. Then it came on again, its black, talon-like hands stretched out towards Morden, who stood there too terrified for flight, his gun, which had slipped through his nerveless fingers, lying upon the ground. At the last moment he turned and ran, ran blindly away, with a shriek of fear. His start was too late, however. He stumbled, and over he went, with his pursuer on the top of him. Cartnell had a horrible moment's view of those fingers clutching Morden's white throat, grinding their way into his windpipe, whilst Ella's shrieks filled the air.

Cartnell, who had sprung forward hurled himself upon the attacking beast. The loader seized him from behind, but their united strength was absolutely useless. They might as well have tried to move a mountain, until the last breath of life had sobbed itself away from Morden's lips. Then, and not till then, that grip relaxed, and the beast rolled over, the blood streaming from a wound in his chest where the loader had shot him.

"My God!" Cartnell faltered, "it's a man—it's Middleton!"

It was not until a fortnight after the inquest and funeral that Ella Cartnell, stretched upon a steamer-chair in mid-ocean on her way to Kenya, broke the silence which seemed to have been established by mutual consent upon a certain subject. She looked away from the sea, and turned her head towards her husband.

"Dick," she asked, "did you know that it was Hugh Morden who had been the lover of Barney Middleton's wife?"

"I guessed it," he acknowledged. "That's why I rather went out of my way to have the matter hushed up. He was always making some excuse to stroll down there, and the day the thing happened, I knew that the telephone call back to the house was faked."

"And yet you said nothing to me?"

"What could I say?"

"You must have guessed what he was trying to make me believe."

"Not until the day before the shooting party," Cartnell assured her. "You see, he'd been a kind of a pal once. I couldn't believe he'd do such a dirty trick. Before that day, until then, I simply thought—I feared that you'd taken a fancy to him."

"Yet you wouldn't tell me?"

"Don't see how I could exactly."

She shivered a little. Her left hand stole underneath the rug, her fingers felt for his and clutched them convulsively,

"Men are different," she murmured.

## THE END

# E. Phillips Oppenheim
## The Prince of Storytellers
"Prepare to be fascinated." –Boston Globe

**Secrets & Sovereigns: The Uncollected Stories** $19.95
"Oppenheim's uncanny storytelling instincts put the reader in the palm of his hand, and his mastery of structure and suspense remain unaffected by a century of changing fashions."
—Ellery Queen's Mystery Magazine

**The Amazing Judgment / Mr. Laxworthy's Adventures** $19.95
"A duel book of the mysteries of E. Phillips Oppenheim, providing a source of the most intriguing pulp mysteries of the early twentieth century."—The Midwest Book Review

**Ghosts & Gamblers: Further Uncollected Stories** $19.95
Includes the rare early novel, A Modern Prometheus. "...an interesting collection of stories with a wide range of settings and characters." —Andrew McDowell

**Ghosts of Society** $15.95
International intrigue involving a secret society, originally published under the author's 1920s pseudonym, Anthony Partridge.

"Readers of Mr. Oppenheim's novels may always count on a story of absorbing interest, turning on a complicated plot, worked out with dexterous craftsmanship." –Literary Digest, New York

*Each trade paperback includes a new introduction by Daniel Paul Morrison and a collector's bibliography.*

**Stark House Press, 1315 H Street, Eureka, CA 95501**
griffinskye3@sbcglobal.net / StarkHousePress.com
Available from your local bookstore, or order direct via our website.

www.ingramcontent.com/pod-product-compliance
Lightning Source LLC
LaVergne TN
LVHW021604300525
812595LV00001B/105